TRUTH
OR DARE

Also by Tania Carver

The Surrogate

The Creeper

Cage of Bones

Choked

The Doll's House

TRUTH
OR DARE

TANIA
CARVER

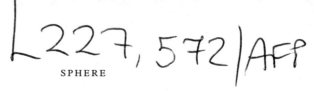

SPHERE

First published in Great Britain in 2014 by Sphere

A CIP catalogue record for this book
is available from the British Library.

ISBN 978-0-7515-5055-9

Typeset in Plantin by M Rules
Printed and bound in Great Britain by Clays Ltd, St Ives plc

Papers used by Sphere are from well-managed forests
and other responsible sources.

MIX
Paper from
responsible sources
FSC
www.fsc.org   FSC® C104740

Sphere
An imprint of
Little, Brown Book Group
100 Victoria Embankment
London EC4Y 0DY

An Hachette UK Company
www.hachette.co.uk

www.littlebrown.co.uk

TRUTH
OR DARE

PART ONE:

BREAKING THE LAW

1

Darren Richards opened his eyes. Closed them quickly as an intense light shone straight at him.

'Back with us again?' said a muffled voice. 'Good.'

He opened his eyes slowly once more, blinking all the while. The light was still as bright, like a film or TV arc lamp directed right at his retinas. Like he was the centre of attention. So bright it hurt. He closed his eyes again. Saw veins flash and throb on the inside of his eyelids, then the ghosts of veins. Then back to blackness once more. He chanced opening them again, for longer this time.

His head swam as his eyes took a while to focus. His head was heavy, his arms and legs tingling, his stomach nauseous, like he felt coming down from a massive skunk bender. He blinked away the brightness, tried to squint beyond it.

A figure moved about on the fringes of the light, creating sudden eclipses. Darren couldn't make much out beyond a black body and a grey/white face. No, not a face. A head. Eyes too big and round, mouth . . . what was that instead of a mouth? He blinked again. Was he still on that bender? No. He tried to peel back layers of memory. He hadn't been on one, hadn't had anything. Well, he'd had a can of lager or two on the walk to Wayne's crib but that was nothing. He frowned. Wayne's crib. What had happened at Wayne's crib? Had he actually arrived there? He thought some more, tried to ignore the pain in his head, the shining light, the moving figure. Tried to think. No. He hadn't.

'Ah, Darren . . . ' said the muffled voice.

Darren tried to rise from the chair, found that his arms and legs wouldn't move. He was held firm. He looked down. Heavy-duty silver duct tape was wrapped from his wrists to his elbows, his ankles to his knees, right round his torso. He was secured to the chair, near-mummified. He tried to move, stand.

'No, don't get up,' said the voice.

The chair wouldn't budge. Darren looked down. Bolted to the floor. Darren was getting really scared now. The fear focused his mind, cleared it. He could hear his own breathing, the blood pumping round his body. And something above that. Another muffled sound, like a trapped cat trying to meow, to call for help.

Darren found his voice. It was a small, insecure thing. 'What . . . what you doin'?'

The figure didn't answer, just moved slowly to the side of the light. In shadow, cocking its head on one side, it studied Darren.

'Whuh . . . what? What you doin'?' Darren tried to pull against his bindings. They didn't budge.

'Justice,' said the muffled voice.

Justice, thought Darren, or *just us*? What had he said? What did he mean?

'What you on about?' he asked.

'Justice,' the figure repeated. No mistaking the word this time, despite it being muffled. 'Payback. Fair play. Righting wrongs. Balancing things out. That's what I'm on about.'

Too many questions bombarded Darren's mind. He picked one at random. 'How did I get here?'

'I brought you here. Took you off the street.'

Darren tried to remember. The walk to Wayne's, then . . .

4

blackness. He looked around once more, tried to make out his surroundings. The place looked old, derelict. Felt cold. Something fluttered at the back wall. The night sky. How could that be? 'Where am I?'

The figure made another muffled sound. Darren thought it was choking. Then realised it must be laughing.

'You're developing an inquisitive mind,' the figure said. 'So many questions. But still not the right ones. Just the old boring, prosaic ones.'

'What ... what should I be askin', then?'

The figure moved slowly towards him. The mewling sound was still there, faint in the background. Darren could just hear it over the throbbing inside his head.

Approaching, Darren made out the figure's features. A bone-grey, close-fitting rubber gas mask made its head appear smooth and skull-like. It was dressed all in shapeless black, like a boiler suit. Big, strong boots. Gloves. He couldn't tell if it was a man or a woman but thought it might be a man. He remembered seeing a heavy-metal group who all wore masks and boiler suits. It looked like one of them. He thought they looked good at the time. Scary. The music was still shit, though.

'Ask your question, Darren.'

Darren thought. Hard. This was important. He had to get the right question. That way he might get the right answer.

It came to him. 'Why ... why am I here?'

The figure stopped advancing. Darren wasn't sure, but he imagined the person smiling behind the mask. 'Is the right question. Well done.'

Darren waited. 'So?' he said eventually.

'You know,' the figure said, turning and walking back to behind the light.

Darren thought once more. 'No,' he said, shaking his head, 'I don't.'

Movement from behind the light. Something being pulled along the floor. Positioned to the right place.

'You know,' said the muffled voice. 'It's what you did. What you got away with.'

'What?' said Darren. 'What did I get away with?'

'You killed two people, Darren. You were never punished for it.'

Darren screwed up his face in concentration. Killed two people? When? He wasn't a murderer. And then he remembered. 'Oh,' he said. 'That.'

'Yes,' said the masked figure, a note of controlled anger coming into its voice. 'That. You stole a car. With your mates. Remember?'

'Yeah, all right,' said Darren. 'That's it, is it? That's what this is all about? Fuck's sake, I can hardly remember it.'

'You stole a car,' continued the figure. 'Off your heads on whatever you could get. That's why you can't remember it, Darren. And when you were driving that car, full of skunk and alcohol and E and cocaine and God knows what else, you mounted the pavement and killed two pedestrians. Didn't you?'

Darren became defensive. He remembered now. Or at least he remembered the aftermath. The cell. The police station. Remand. The trial. Once he'd come round and been presented with what he had done he felt terrible about it. Not the deaths, although yeah, they were bad. But he knew he could go to prison for a long time for that. That had been terrifying. He'd done time for other stuff when he was coming up, but that was just small bits of things. Drugs, street robbery. Little stuff, here and there. Nothing much. Few months in a YOI then back on the street with bragging rights and a better rep. But this, he knew, had been serious.

'You should have gone to prison, shouldn't you?' said the figure. 'For a long time. A long, long time.'

'Yeah, but I didn't, did I?' said Darren. He felt once more the cockiness he had experienced in the courtroom that day. When his defence barrister had picked up on the mistake in the police procedure that made the arrest unlawful. The judge had been given no option but to reluctantly stop the trial. Darren had walked free.

'No,' said the figure. 'You didn't.'

The cockiness was still there within him. Carried over, even in his present situation. 'Nothing you can do about it, mate,' he said. 'Stood trial for it, got off. End of. Solicitor said it should never have gone to trial.' He looked down at his arms. 'So you can't touch me. Got to let me go.'

'Is that so?' said the figure.

'Yeah,' said Darren. 'I know my fuckin' rights.'

The figure didn't reply. Just went behind the light, threw a switch. Another light came on, next to the one shining on Darren. He looked at what it illuminated. And found the source of the mewling. His girlfriend Chloe and their daughter Shannon. Their baby daughter, not yet a year old. Chloe was taped to an identical, floor-bolted chair next to him. Shannon was taped to Chloe.

Chloe looked at him, her mouth gagged, her eyes filled with tears and terror.

'Wha' . . . wha' the fuck's goin' on?' said Darren.

'Justice,' said the figure. 'What I said. You killed a woman and her child. Innocent victims of yours. You didn't even know you'd done it.'

'But I didn't mean to, though, did I? It was an accident.'

'Nevertheless, you did it. And you need to pay for what you've done. You deprived the world of two people who should be living. And you think you got away with it. But you haven't. So what are we going to do about it?'

Darren looked at Chloe and Shannon. The baby girl was

terrified. Completely uncomprehending. Struggling to escape, held fast by the tape, unable even to cry. Her struggles making the tape pull tighter. She looked to her father, eyes wide, expecting him to reassure her, put things right. Darren just looked helplessly back at her.

'You've got a choice,' said the figure, moving something else into place beside the lights as it spoke. 'Someone has to pay for what you've done. For the lives you've taken. And it should really be you, shouldn't it?'

'Whuh . . . what?'

And then Darren saw what the figure had been moving. A crossbow. Tripod mounted, it pointed first at him, then at Chloe and Shannon.

'Your choice,' said the figure.

Panic rose within him. He caught sight of Chloe's imploring eyes, his daughter's uncomprehending ones. He tried to pull against the restraints once more.

'This is a joke,' he shouted, 'a fucking joke, right?'

'It's no joke, Darren. It's deadly serious. You deprived two people of their lives. And that wasn't all. There were ripples from your actions. You took away a wife. A mother to two boys. A daughter. You didn't just kill two people that day. You ended so many other lives. Devastated so many more.'

'Mental,' shouted Darren, 'you're fuckin' mental.'

'I'm deadly serious, Darren. I'm not joking. You either pay for what you've done with your own life or . . . ' The figure gestured towards Chloe and Shannon. 'Choice is yours. But you will pay.'

'You're goin' to kill us all anyway,' said Darren. 'Why mess about?'

'No, no, no . . . You're wrong. I'm not going to kill you all. That's what you do, not me.'

'What then?'

'I just dispense justice. If you choose to accept the consequences of your actions and take the shot, it'll kill you and you'll have paid for your crimes. Then Chloe and Shannon can just walk away.'

'Or?'

'Or they take the shot. And you walk away. But someone has to pay. There will be justice.'

Darren couldn't look at Chloe. He knew she was trying to get his attention, craning her neck against the tape restraints, shouting through her gag, trying to pull herself free. And the baby, sensing her mother's ramped-up discomfort, was trying to scream too.

No, he thought, don't look at them. It's easier if you don't look at them.

'You've made up your mind,' said the figure.

'Yeah,' said Darren. His pulse was racing. He was sweating. It was horrible, yes, but it would be over in a matter of seconds. And he couldn't do it, could he? What was the point of that? 'No brainer, innit? I mean, really.'

Chloe's muffled screams increased. Darren turned his head away from her.

'Just remember,' said the figure, getting behind the crossbow, 'this is what you wanted. This is your justice.'

'Just get on with it. Then I get to leave, yeah?'

Darren closed his eyes. He would miss them. But really, when he thought about it, it wasn't too bad. Yeah, he told himself, not too bad. Chloe had been getting on his nerves for a while now. Whining and whinging, on his back the whole fucking time. And she wasn't taking care of herself like she used to. Her arse was getting bigger and she didn't seem to care. And the kid . . . well, to be honest, she was a fucking accident. If Chloe hadn't messed up her pills and let herself get pregnant none of this would ever have happened. He'd been planning to ditch her anyway. Hayley had been giving him the glad eye. And he'd already given her something, too. And there was still Letisha to go back to if everything else went tits up. And besides, he wasn't cut out for fatherhood. Not really. Better as a free agent, a lone wolf. Yeah.

Next to him, Chloe was still trying to scream. Darren ignored her.

Yeah, he thought. Bit drastic but still.

The figure readied himself. Darren closed his eyes.

The crossbow fired.

Darren couldn't help himself. He opened his eyes, looked. Saw Chloe and Shannon.

And began to scream.

He didn't stop.

PART TWO:

THE SENTINEL

2

'Jesus Christ . . .' Detective Sergeant Ian Sperring bent down
and hunched forward, hands on knees, his breathing becoming
increasingly laboured as his bulk shifted, constricting the
airways. He stared at the scene before him, mouth curled in
distaste. He shook his head, closed his eyes. Stepped away.
Breathing all the while through his mouth to minimise the
smell. 'Well, boss,' he said, 'reckon your mate's a right nutter.'

'He's no mate of mine,' said Detective Inspector Phil Brennan. He was younger than his junior officer by at least ten years
and lighter than him by at least one hundred pounds. But
whatever differences the two men had, either physical or professional, were negated by the sight before them.

Arc lamps cut through the darkness, illuminated the warehouse with a sense of unreality as if it was a film set, they were
all actors and the scene before them only an elaborate piece of
FX prosthetics. But it was all real. Deadly real.

All around them, paper-suited SOCOs went about their
occult business, gathering clues in the dust, conjuring answers
up from nothing.

Phil, similarly suited, had been gazing around the dilapidated
warehouse, trying to get a sense of the place in connection with
what had occurred here, to work out a reason why this particular building had been chosen. This particular area. This
particular staging. And doing that, while absolutely necessary

13

deduction and groundwork, also stopped him from actually seeing the sight before him.

Phil turned, faced Sperring. No longer able to avoid looking at the bodies.

It was like a warped version of a Renaissance Madonna and child tableau. The artist not depicting transcendence or rapture as his or her predecessors had done, just demonstrating ... what? Phil scrutinised. Twisted rage? Madness?

The woman sat with her head back, flung into that final position by the shot, kept that way by the initial rigor, skin darkening. The baby taped to her lap now bloated from decomposition, an obese, purple cherub. Both faces retained lasting images of frozen horror. The woman's fingers contracted into claws, gripping the arm of the stationary chair, an ultimately futile gesture of escape.

Phil had seen some unpleasant scenes since he had joined the West Midlands Major Incident Squad. This undoubtedly ranked as one of the worst. A nightmare dragged into the living world.

'Definitely the work of a crossbow.'

Sperring and Phil turned. Esme Russell, the pathologist, joined them. Her blonde hair was pulled back into a ponytail, her normally indestructible upper-class demeanour – all champagne picnics and gymkhanas – had taken a severe blow.

'A crossbow?' said Sperring, horror creeping into his voice once more. 'A fucking crossbow?'

'You sure?' asked Phil. 'You've not examined the bodies yet.'

'Head start, I'm afraid,' said Esme. 'My brother used to take part in archery tournaments. Very good, actually, county level. Talk of the Olympics at one point. If it's got a string and an arrow, he once said, then I'll hit the target every time.' She smiled at the memory. 'Slightly arrogant, but he was right, usually.'

'What, and you think he did this?' said Sperring bluntly, trying to keep her on topic.

Esme reddened slightly. 'No. Sorry. I'm just saying that even without a preliminary examination I recognise the work of a crossbow when I see one.'

While Sperring was still shaking his head, Phil was studying the scene. The Scene Of Crime Officers had surveyed the area and allowed them limited access by the common approach path, elevated metal plates that minimised crime scene contamination. He looked from where the woman and child were sitting to the empty chair next to them. The tape had been cut and the young man they had found there taken to hospital. He hadn't regained consciousness yet.

Phil knelt down, carefully balancing on the metal plate, looked at the floor. They were in the Hockley area of Birmingham, fringed by the Jewellery Quarter and the gentrification of St Paul's, surrounded by old redbrick buildings, the legacy of Birmingham's reputation as a manufacturing powerhouse at the heart of the country a century ago. Now lying derelict and empty, waiting for someone to make imaginative use of them in a post-industrial twenty-first-century society. Waiting to turn them into desirable living spaces with overinflated price tags. Or a nightclub catering to the self-regarding cool and edgy crowd or a media start-up company, or a gallery.

But not this building. Phil had assumed it had once been a warehouse but it could have been a factory, storage facility, anything. Now it was just rotting away. It only existed on three sides. Demolition had started on the back and the buildings adjacent to it, leaving it open to the elements, rendering it down to a pile of bricks and rubble, wooden boards asking the general public to keep out.

The shell that remained had three floors. The bodies had been found on the middle one. A plastic traffic barrier stood at the open back along with a loosely hanging tarpaulin sheet. Neither looked like they would stand up to the scrutiny of health and safety. The floor was wooden, the boards pitted and gouged from years of work, coming to an abrupt, jagged edge. Rusted metal pillars supported the ceiling. The window frames held only broken – if any – glass. The walls were tired, crumbling brick.

Still kneeling, Phil put on his reading glasses, bent in close, scrutinising the wood.

'Mecca's the other way,' said Sperring, recovering enough to make a bad joke.

Phil ignored him. Studied the floor. Eventually he stood up, removed his glasses, looked at the other two.

'I think you're right, Esme,' he said. 'Look.' He pointed to the floor. 'See there, round the chairs? Very little dust. See over there? Directly facing the chairs? Very little dust. Signs of movement. See in between? Thicker dust.'

'Meaning . . . ?' said Sperring.

'Meaning someone stood there and . . . ' Phil crossed on the CAP, stood a couple of metres in front of the chair. He turned and faced the dead bodies. Pointed his finger at them. Pulled an imaginary trigger. First the woman then the child. 'This high,' he said, aiming. 'Stable. Must have been mounted.' He looked down at the floor once more. 'Couple of nicks in the wood. Like something's been moved. Into place, probably.'

Sperring frowned. 'What about the bloke in the other chair, then?'

Phil turned, still imagining he had a weapon in front of him. Took aim. Remaining standing he then studied the floor once more. 'Same thing here. Less dust, more movement where I'm standing. Then nothing between, then activity round the chair.'

'Trying to cut him out and get him to hospital,' said Sperring. 'Couldn't be helped.'

'Definitely not,' said Phil. The chair held not only cut tape but also the remains of bodily liquids and secretions. Its occupant had clearly been held there for some time. 'But look. Something was mounted here. Right between the two seats. It could have been swung to one . . . ' He turned, faced the empty chair. 'Or the other.' He turned to the two dead bodies. 'I hate jumping to conclusions, but I think you're right, Esme. Crossbow looks the most likely. Tripod mounted, probably.'

'So why not the bloke, then?' asked Sperring.

'Good question,' said Phil. 'How is he? D'you know?'

'Alive, last I heard,' said Sperring. 'Just. At the hospital. DC Oliver's with him, waiting for him to come round.'

'Good,' said Phil. 'If there's anything to be got out of him, Imani'll do it.'

Sperring said nothing. Phil was aware he didn't hold the DC in the same regard. He didn't want to make an issue of it. Just mark it down as something else they disagreed about.

'So I'll say it again,' said Sperring. 'The crossbow's mounted and pointing at both chairs. Can turn either way. But it's only the woman and kid that get killed. The bloke's left alive. Why? What's your mate trying to tell us?'

Phil sighed. 'He's not my mate.'

'Really?' said Sperring. 'Bet he thinks he is.'

'Then he's deluded.'

Sperring looked at the bodies once more, wincing as he did so. 'Deluded? I'd say that's the least of his troubles.'

17

3

The first of the calls came in the previous night on the non-emergency number to West Midlands Police.

Janice Chisholm, the call-centre operative, vividly remembered taking it. She had just started on her shift as usual, paper cup of expensive take-out coffee on her desk, a chocolate brownie – greasing up the paper bag – for when she became hungry later and needed a break. She had been doing the job for months, was thoroughly and comprehensively briefed and trained. She knew all the procedures. How to make the reticent talk, keep the ramblers on track, assure the timid, calm the aggressive. It was a real skill, more than a person could be given training for. She enjoyed doing it, talking to the public, helping them. She felt that she was performing a valuable service.

But occasionally there would be calls that she remembered. For one reason or another. The genuinely distressing. The abusive. The sad. The odd.

The downright scary.

'I want to talk to Philip Brennan. Detective Inspector Philip Brennan.' The voice was muffled, the words difficult to hear.

'Sorry?' said Janice. 'Could you speak up, please? It's a little difficult to hear you.'

More noise from the other end, what she took to be heavy breathing, but no more words. She began to think she had a nuisance call on her hands. She got them sometimes.

Timewasters, kids usually, making obscene remarks, asking her filthy things. Telling them that the call was being traced was usually enough to get them off the line. But this one seemed different. That was why she remembered it.

'I want to talk to Detective Inspector Philip Brennan.' Slower this time. No less muffled but enunciating more.

'I'm afraid that's not possible at the moment. I can't transfer you directly. Is it to do with an ongoing investigation?'

Silence. Just more breathing. Janice began to feel unnerved.

'If you'd like to tell me what it's concerning,' she said, 'then perhaps I can get a message to him?'

The line went dead. Janice tried to put it out of her mind, took more calls. Genuine ones this time.

The second call came in just over an hour later. It had been a relatively quiet night until then. Janice had put herself on a break, started on her chocolate brownie. She heard Ann, her colleague two cubicles away, mention a familiar name.

'I'm afraid that Detective Inspector Brennan isn't based at this office. Could you tell me what it's concerning and I could pass the message on?'

Janice immediately became interested. She gestured to Ann.

'Just a moment . . .' said Ann and transferred the call to Janice.

That wasn't what Janice had intended but she was left with no option but to take the call. She swallowed the mouthful of brownie as quickly as she could.

'Hello,' she said, 'I think we spoke earlier.'

That same heavy breathing. More frantic now, harder, rasping. 'Detective Inspector Brennan. I need to talk to him.'

'As my colleague just explained, he's not actually here. He doesn't work in this office. He's—'

'Put me through to him. Now.'

Janice sat back, silenced for a few seconds. She knew she was

often dealing with people who were desperate but she still didn't respond well to rudeness. 'Please don't take that tone with me. Or I'll discontinue this call.' She waited for a response. Heard only more breathing. She pressed the record button on her handset.

As she did so, the voice continued. 'I need to talk to Detective Inspector Brennan. There is a life at stake.'

'This is a non-emergency number,' said Janice. 'If it's urgent why don't you try 999? Would you like me to connect you?'

'No.' The voice sounded exasperated. 'Detective Inspector Philip Brennan. West Midlands Major Incident Squad. Him and him only.'

Janice paused. Procedure and protocol were there to be followed. It had been drummed into them she didn't know how many times. Under no circumstances were they allowed to directly connect callers with named police officers. Nine times out of ten they were fantasists or mentalists who had seen someone on TV and developed an unhealthy attachment to them.

Nine times out of ten.

'I'm going to put you on hold,' she said. 'Just wait there, please.'

Without waiting for a reply she placed the caller on hold. Dialled Steelhouse Lane station. The call was answered. She identified herself, told the desk sergeant who answered about the call.

'Sounds like some nutter,' he said.

'He does,' said Janice. 'But listen, I wouldn't be bothering you if I thought that was the case. We get more than our fair share here, believe me.'

'Just tell him you're tracing the call,' said the desk sergeant, not bothering to hide the boredom in his voice. 'Or tell him his mum's got his tea ready.'

'Normally I would,' said Janice, trying to ignore the dismissive,

20

patronising tone. 'I've done this job long enough to know when something's up. And there's something not right about this one. If he's telling the truth, I'd hate to be the one who didn't flag it up.'

Silence. Then a sigh. 'All right then . . . ' A shuffle of papers, the click of a mouse. 'Gone home. Shift's finished. Doesn't he want to talk to anyone else?'

'Has he got a mobile? Can you not connect him?'

Another sigh from the desk sergeant, as if he'd been asked to paint the Forth Bridge singlehandedly. 'All right then – but you owe me for this one.'

'What happened to the satisfaction of a job well done?'

A laugh. 'Maybe they do things differently where you work. Just a minute.'

Janice was then put on hold. She waited. Eventually another voice came on. Younger than the desk sergeant, from somewhere else in the country. London? Somewhere like that? Not Birmingham, that was for sure.'

'Phil Brennan,' said the voice.

Janice introduced herself. 'I wouldn't normally bother you, Detective Inspector, and I know it's not procedure but . . . ' She told him about the voice.

'Thanks, Janice,' he said. 'You never know. Put him through.'

She did so.

And that was the end of her involvement. Until she saw the news the next day. Saw Detective Inspector Phil Brennan being interviewed, talking about one of the most horrendous double murders he had ever seen and appealing for witnesses, for someone, anyone, who knew anything to come forward.

She watched the news the day after that. And the next day. And . . .

She thought of the voice she had spoken to on the phone.

And began to tremble.

4

A pair of uniforms had been dispatched immediately to the address the voice provided. A derelict building on Legge Lane, Hockley .

'Be quick,' the voice had told Phil, 'he doesn't have long. And he wanted to live. He chose to live. So we have to grant him his wish, don't we? What kind of a society would we be living in if we didn't?'

'Who are you?' Phil had asked. 'And what's all this about?'

'Yes, of course I'll tell you that. Don't worry, you'll find out. All in good time.'

'Who are we looking for?'

'You'll recognise him.'

A shudder ran through Phil at those words. He immediately thought it must be someone he knew. A friend, even. 'Who?' he had asked, quicker this time.

'Just go to the address. Look for yourself. Everything will make sense then. Everything will fall into place.'

'What will?'

'Justice. Fairness. That's what it's all about. And I hope we're on the same side when it comes to that. I really do.'

'You got a name?'

There was a pause and Phil expected either a flippant answer or no answer at all.

'Nemesis,' the voice said, unmistakably proud.

Phil tried asking more questions but was soon left holding a dead phone. He called the station, got through to the desk sergeant. Asked him if he'd heard any of that. He hadn't. Told him to dispatch two uniforms to the address given and that he was on his way. 'Get Sperring up. Tell him to meet me there.'

'I'm sure he'll thank you for that, boss,' said the desk sergeant, laughing.

'I'm sure he will.'

Phil hung up, checked the time. Nearly midnight. Checked the other side of the bed. Empty. He didn't like it when Marina wasn't there. Often woke up with her pillows hugged in close to him. He had never told her that. Didn't want to appear foolish. Besotted. But that was what he was. After all this time he was still in love with his wife. Still got butterflies when he saw her, still got hard when she moved her body next to his in bed. He had never admitted that to anyone but judging from what he'd heard some of his colleagues say on the subject what he felt was unnatural. He didn't care. He was glad of it. He knew what a mess he had been before she had come into his life. He didn't want to go back to that again.

He stood up, began to dress. A plaid western shirt with white pearl studs, selvedge jeans, Red Wing boots, his leather jacket. He deliberately didn't wear the dull, accountant-like suit that most of his peers were encouraged to dress in, seeing that as just another extension of a uniform. Neither was his hair parade-ground neat. He encouraged his team to do the same. Be expressive, he always said. It encourages you to think creatively. And thinking creatively solves crimes. They didn't all agree with him – some remained almost pathologically opposed to his ideas – but he was tolerated. As long as he got results.

He brushed his teeth, gulped down some water, got in the car and drove to the address he had been given.

All the while playing the conversation he had just had over and over again in his mind.

This wasn't going to be an easy one. He could feel it.

5

'So what else did your new best mate have to say?' asked Sperring, looking at the empty chair. 'Did he tell you who he is and why he's doing this? What he's up to? Make our job a hell of a lot simpler.'

'I think we can work out what he's up to,' said Detective Constable Nadish Khan, crossing to join them. He had on the same blue paper suit as everyone else but he still managed to put some swagger into his walk, like he was in a club rather than at a murder scene. 'He's a nut job. He's a killer.'

'Let's not jump to conclusions,' said Phil.

'What?' said Khan, looking aggrieved. 'You don't think he did this? Or you don't think he's a nutter?'

'First things first,' said Phil. 'Have we managed to find out who the victims are? Who the guy in the hospital is? And have we traced the call?'

'Just come from the station,' said Khan. 'Been checking some stuff out. Guy's name is Darren Richards. Ran his name. Got a bit of previous. Twoccing, street robbery, that sort of thing. From Lea Hall way. Your common or garden low-life.'

Phil pointed to the dead bodies. 'And the other two?'

Khan's face became pale. He looked anywhere but at where Phil indicated. Despite his seeming arrogance and swagger, Nadish Khan was famously squeamish. Phil had had to tell him to exit more than one murder scene for fear that he would vomit and contaminate it. Khan was starting to sway.

'Nadish . . . '

'I'm all right, boss. I'm fine.'

He looked anything but. However Phil didn't press the matter. 'Just remember,' he said.

'Locard's Exchange Principle. Yeah, yeah. I know. You tell me every time. Don't worry. I'm not going to—'

He ran for the exit.

Phil exchanged looks with Sperring, raised an eyebrow.

'He's a good lad,' said Sperring. 'He'll get used to it.'

Phil said nothing. Just waited for Khan to return. He did so, his face even paler, wiping his mouth with a tissue.

'You were saying?' said Phil.

'Yeah,' said Khan, trying to regain his composure, finding the space behind Phil's head fascinating. 'Darren Richards . . . '

'And the other two?'

'As much as we can tell,' said Khan, knowing he had to look at the bodies but trying not to at the same time, 'they're Darren Richards' girlfriend, Chloe Hannon, and their daughter, Shannon.'

'Shannon Hannon?' said Sperring with a snort. 'Bloody imbeciles. Never think, do they, this lot.'

'Let's hope Mr Richards planned on marrying her, then,' said Phil. 'Moot point now, though. Anything on her?'

Khan shook his head. 'Not much. Just an altercation outside a pub with another girl.' He pocketed the tissue, took out his notepad. 'Letisha Watson. Claimed she was trying to steal her boyfriend. Got cross about it. Apparently Darren Richards and Letisha Watson had a thing going. He left her when he got Chloe Hannon pregnant.'

'Don't need a detective, need Jeremy bloody Kyle to sort this one out,' said Sperring. 'Where d'you get all this from?'

25

'All on record,' said Khan. 'Seems Darren Richards was a popular man.'

'Someone thought so,' said Phil. 'But this looks ... not like the work of a jealous ex-partner. I may be jumping to conclusions but I think we can rule out Letisha Watson. I doubt she would go to all this trouble.'

'Dunno,' said Khan. 'I've been out with some right psychos.'

'I don't doubt it,' said Phil. 'But this is different. This is a whole different level of ... something. I don't know what.'

'Or why,' said Sperring. 'What else did your mate tell you?'

'Look,' said Phil, turning to face his junior officer, 'can we please stop calling this person my mate?'

Sperring looked away. 'Sorry, boss.' The apology had no weight behind it.

'All the voice gave me was an address. Here. Told me that someone wanted to live, that he had chosen to live and we had to grant him his wish.'

'*Chosen* to live?' said Khan, frowning.

'Chosen, yeah. Then he went on about justice. And fairness. And that he hoped we were on the same side.'

'Justice?' said Khan, frowning again. He consulted his notes once more. 'He said justice?'

'Yeah,' said Phil. 'Why? Ring a bell?'

'Dunno.' Khan leafed through his notes. 'Justice ...' He found what he wanted, read it to himself. Shook his head. 'Dunno if this is anything, maybe I'm grasping here, but – here. Darren Richards was in court not so long ago for stealing and driving away while under the influence. Dangerous driving, the lot. Apparently he took a car and killed two pedestrians ...' His voice tailed off.

'What?' asked Phil. 'What's wrong?'

Khan looked up. 'Killed two pedestrians. Ploughed into them. A mother and daughter.'

Phil felt a shudder run up his spine. He looked at the bodies once more. 'A mother and daughter?'

'Yeah,' said Khan, checking his notes. 'That's not all. He got off.'

'What?' said Sperring. 'Hate to have been the CIO on that one. Poor bastard.'

'Yeah,' said Khan. 'He got off. Some technicality, something wrong with the investigation. His brief found a hole and pulled it. Destroyed the case.'

'So now he's alive and another mother and daughter are dead,' said Phil. 'That's what the voice said. He wanted to be alive. He had chosen to live. *Chosen . . .*' He looked back at the bodies. Then at the place where they had been shot from. Then at the other chair. His hand absently stoked the side of his face, felt the faint traces of scars.

'Chosen to live . . .' He turned to the other two. 'Let's see if we can get that call traced. I think you're right. I think we do have a nutter on our hands.'

6

The needle dropped on the vinyl. A bump-in-the-road hiss of static, repeated, then a third time, then it began. A snare drum kicked in followed by vibes languidly spelling out the hook, followed by Jerry Butler's wounded, soulful but lyrical croon telling his woman that he would never give her up, no matter how badly she treated him.

He sat back in his armchair, closed his eyes. Letting the music wash over him, perform its magic. He immersed himself in it. A perfect song in so many ways. Not only for what it stated but for what could be read into it. Sixties soul. Never bettered. Craftsmanship and skill. Heart and soul. All together. A production line, yes. But one that spoke to dreams. The only music worth still listening to.

The sun was beginning its creep round the heavy velvet curtains, weak rays illuminating shafts of lazily dancing dust motes, bringing in its wake a tiny but gradual warmth to the room. He didn't notice. Just sat there, head back, smiling. Mind wandering.

They would be there by now, he thought. Phil Brennan and his team. All over the place. Measuring, bagging, calculating. Searching. They wouldn't find anything, though. He had been too meticulous, too clean. Too clever for them. They didn't know that. Yet. But they would realise soon enough.

If they were there now then Darren must be alive. Good. That was as it should be.

He had expected to see Darren's face on the news before now, his woman and child also. He had watched every bulletin, scanned every online news site for days. Barely sleeping, eating. Too excited, just wanting to see his handiwork acknowledged, the change begin. But there had been nothing. He thought of Darren, still strapped to the chair, unable to escape, to move. That wasn't right. He could die. So he had given them a little nudge in the right direction. A quick phone call to Phil Brennan and Darren would live. Everything was right again. The scales balanced.

Darren must live. It was the way things had to work. If Darren died then that exposed his word as a lie, his *work* as a lie. And that couldn't be allowed to happen. Justice not only had to be done but had to be seen to be done. Darren had made his choice. And it was down to him to honour that. If there was no honour, no fairness, *no justice,* then what was left? Nothing. He would be as bad as them. And then there would be no point. No lessons learned. That couldn't happen.

The song finished. The needle made a couple of crackling circuits then lifted. He sat still, waiting. The arm dropped. James Carr: 'The Dark End of the Street'. Even better than the last one. The adulterer's lament, he had heard it described. But he found much more than that in it. It wasn't about sex. Nothing as sordid, as disgustingly ephemeral, as that. It was about secrets, darkness. Lies. Everyday masks hiding real lives beneath. The spark of recognising kindred spirits in daylight but doing nothing until darkness falls and the masks come off. Then the truth of who they really were could be acknowledged. Much more exciting, more visceral, *more alive* than plain, old, boring sex.

He kept his eyes closed, thought again of Darren. The choice he had made. Saving himself at the expense of his woman and child. And the look on his face as he came to realise what that choice was actually going to cost him, the reality of his actions. He would have been lying if he didn't admit that it gave him a thrill to see that. He had expected it, of course; in fact, he had imagined it would be one of the more pleasant by-products of his decision to embark on this course of action in the first place. But he hadn't expected it to be so enjoyable. Not to mention the delicious trembling in his body as the woman and child had been fatally penetrated.

He replayed those few seconds in his mind again and again, feeding off them. Darren's expression, the torment as he struggled to reach his decision, then the emotions fighting for prominence on his features once he had done so. Self-loathing battling it out with self-preservation. Sorrow with stoicism. Horror with acceptance. Then, finally, disbelief giving way to dread acceptance. And harrowing, aching loss.

Beautiful.

Righteous vengeance. Perfect. Even more perfect than he had imagined.

The shiver that had run through him in that moment, the power he had felt as he delivered justice – a justice most believed to be beyond reach or impossible to resolve – was palpable. Thrillingly palpable. *And he had made it happen.*

Once Darren had made his decision his woman had stared at him, terrified beyond rational thought, unable to believe that her man could condemn her like that, how the world could be so wrong. He should have felt something for them as he watched that dumb show play out. Sorrow. Regret. Something like that. But he felt nothing. The woman had taken up with Darren. Had his child. Stuck with him. It was all her fault and she had to take the consequences of her actions. Just like Darren. He hadn't killed her. Darren had.

Darren had closed his eyes as the crossbow was fired. Then screamed and kept on, screaming and screaming and screaming, until he had no breath, no voice left.

After that it had been a simple matter of getting out as quickly as possible. Covering his tracks, removing his traces, and then off. He wasn't stupid. He knew they would hunt him down for what he had done. But he wouldn't make it easy for them. He would provide no clues, no help. And in the meantime, he would talk to them. Open up a dialogue with his pursuers so they could understand what he was doing. Empathise, even. After all, weren't they supposed to be on the same side when it came to justice?

The song finished, the needle spinning, jumping, spinning again. Stuck in a groove.

He crossed to the jukebox. It was a thing of beauty. A Rock-ola Princess 435. Perfect. He pressed the manual override; the arm returning the needle to its resting position, switching off. He scanned the song titles. So much stuff on there, so many of his favourites. But nothing more that he wanted to hear. Usually, music did the trick, got into his head, his heart, kept everything at bay. But for the last few days all he had thought of was Darren and his fate. It had consumed him.

He put on the TV, flicking to a twenty-four-hour news channel, checked the laptop next to it at the same time. Smiled. His handiwork was just beginning to appear. Vague stories, no details emerging. Just pictures of a white-plastic shrouded building that he knew very well, confused reporters standing in front of it. That gave him a thrill. He knew more than the news crews, than the general public. Than the police. He knew everything.

He crossed to the window, opened the curtains. Sunlight transformed the room. He looked around. With all the old furniture and antiques, not to mention the scale models on every

31

available shelf, it was like living in a museum. Or a mausoleum. But it was the way he liked it. He had his jukebox. And more importantly, his job.

No. More than a job. A calling.

Darren's face would appear on the news soon. Then they would work it out. What had happened. How justice had been served. And with that realisation the thrill, he thought sadly, would leave him.

He knew what he had to do. Smiled at the thought.

He was just getting started.

7

Marina Esposito stared at the young woman sitting opposite her. She tried not to make snap judgements, jump to hasty conclusions that would ultimately prejudice her findings. But it was difficult.

The woman seemed to be only physically present. The small eyes in her large, bovine face swept the room, searching for anything of interest, a small smile playing at the corners of her wet, fleshy lips. Her hair was greasy and tied back, her body lumpen and shapeless inside the regulation itchy grey jogging suit. Marina picked up her pen, made a note.

'Joanne,' she said. The woman slowly brought her face back down to earth, fixed her vacant smile on Marina. She continued. 'Joanne, do you know why you're here?'

Joanne shrugged.

Marina persisted, her voice low and steady. 'Joanne, I need you to tell me that you understand why you're here. Can you do that?'

Joanne's eyes washed in and out of focus, eventually settling on Marina. 'Because of the men,' she said slowly.

'That's part of it, yes,' she continued. 'The men. But that's not the whole reason why you're here, is it?'

'Because of the men,' Joanne insisted, her voice rising. 'Because they wanted me to stop seeing my men.'

Marina nodded. 'The men. Right. But the men weren't the

real problem, were they? No one wanted to stop you seeing the men. No one was telling you to stop that, were they?'

'They said I couldn't see my men again. That I couldn't meet them off the computer. That I couldn't go out any more. Then they brought me here.'

'And why couldn't you go out any more, Joanne? Why didn't they want you to meet your men?'

Joanne's eyes rolled backwards, her features darkened. Thinking. And not very pleasant thoughts, Marina reckoned.

'Oh,' Joanne said eventually. 'You mean the babies.'

'That's right,' said Marina. 'The babies.'

'You were the first person we thought of,' DC Anni Hepburn had said when Marina had arrived the previous night. 'To be honest, you were the only person we thought of.'

'I don't know whether to be flattered or not,' Marina had replied.

Anni had phoned her a couple of days previously. Marina had met her when they worked together as part of the unit headed up by Phil Brennan, Marina's husband, in Colchester, Essex. They had become close friends and had kept in touch when Marina and Phil moved to Birmingham, even working together on another case Marina had become involved in. Now Anni had returned the favour.

They had met in the Garden Café at the Minories Art Gallery in Colchester. Anni had arranged the location specially, knowing it was one of Marina's favourite places to eat in the town. Anni had to admit that she liked it too. Hidden behind high-brick, secret-garden walls and with its unexpected pieces of architecture jumping out at surprising intervals, it reminded her of a mini Portmeirion just off the high street.

'You trying to tempt me back by bringing me here?' Marina had asked.

Anni laughed. 'I should know better, shouldn't I?' Her smile faded as she passed over a folder. 'Her name's Joanne Marsh,' Anni said, 'and we need an assessment.'

Marina removed the documents, scanned them. 'I think I've heard of her.'

'I'm sure you have. She's not what you'd call low profile.'

Marina looked up. 'Where's she being kept presently?'

'Finnister. Just up the road.'

Marina nodded. Finnister was a secure hospital for the criminally insane just outside Norfolk. It specialised in rehabilitative and therapeutic treatment and housed almost exclusively female inmates. Marina only knew it by reputation. And what she had heard she had her doubts about.

'And that's where we're going?'

'First thing in the morning.' Anni smiled, a mischievous glint in her eye. 'So tonight is our own. No husbands, boyfriends or kids. Let's hit the town.'

'And doing that is supposed to make me want to come back here to live?'

Anni laughed. 'Kill or cure.'

'So, Joanne. Tell me about the babies.'

Joanne's earlier good humour had dissipated. She now sat sullen, staring at Marina.

'The babies.' Marina's voice was gentle but insistent. 'What did you do with the babies?'

Joanne gave an exaggerated, moody teenager's shrug. 'Just ... got rid of them.'

'Why, Joanne? Why did you get rid of them?'

'They were in the way. Stopping me doing what I wanted to do.'

'Meet men.'

Joanne nodded.

The case had been all over the media. Joanne Marsh had lived on a remote farm outside Clacton on the Essex coast with only her father for company. She had developed a passion for meeting men through internet sex contact sites, having random, unprotected sex with them. Sometimes in multiples. There was plenty of amateur video footage of her doing so.

She had been on the social services radar for quite some time, dating back to her childhood where there had been allegations of incest and abuse. Her father and other men, some family, some just friends, using the underage Joanne for sex. The allegations were never proven but Joanne had become a person of interest to them. When she had posted a message on a sex site saying, 'Got rid of the baby out tonit now whers my MEN?' they became interested.

Upon investigation, they discovered Joanne had been made pregnant as a result of one of her meetings. She hadn't let this deter her enjoyment, playing with various partners until she was full term. As far as they could gather, the baby had been delivered at home, probably by her father, and Joanne had then been out meeting men the same night.

Anni's Major Incident Squad had been called in and they had found the corpse of a newborn child buried in a shallow grave just outside the back door of the farmhouse. Suspicions aroused, they had dug up the rest of the land. A further seven tiny corpses had been found.

Now Joanne was in Finnister awaiting psychiatric assessment.

'So,' Marina continued, her voice low, her demeanour professional, 'how did you get rid of the babies? What did you do?'

Joanne looked around the room, bored once more. 'Dug a hole, put them in.'

'And that's it?'

'Closed it up again. Patted it down.'

36

'And then what?'

'What d'you mean?'

'What did you do then?'

Another shrug. 'Went out.'

Marina nodded. Swallowed down the revulsion she was feeling, tried, once again, to remain professional.

'Can I go now?'

'Go?' asked Marina. 'Where?'

'Home.'

Marina shook her head. 'Well, Joanne, I think it's fair to say that, one way or another, you won't be going home for quite some time.'

8

Phil stared up at the tower block. Even the bright morning sun and the clear blue sky failed to lift the clouds of despondency and gloom around it. Handsworth was an area of Birmingham notable for its deprivation, poverty and social exclusion. And out of that deprivation rode the usual horsemen: crime, violence, gangs, drugs. Life during wartime.

'Bet the fuckin' lift's out of order,' said Sperring, also looking up.

'Stop complaining,' said Phil. 'You need the exercise.'

Sperring affected not to hear him. 'Or if it is working, I bet they'll have used it as a toilet.'

Phil stared at him. Sperring, reluctantly, acknowledged the gaze. 'What?' he said, eyebrows rising in mock-effrontery. 'Don't start all that *Guardian*-reader holier-than-thou liberal bullshit. You know what this sort are like. We deal with them every day. We'd be out of a job if it wasn't for them. Spend our days helping old ladies across the road and getting cats out of trees. That'd be us.'

Phil kept staring at him.

Sperring flinched under the gaze. 'What? You know I'm right.'

'A bit of respect, that's all. Doesn't hurt.'

Sperring shrugged. That would be the only answer Phil would be getting.

'Come on,' said Phil, walking towards the entrance, Sperring, reluctantly, following. 'And besides,' said Phil once they had almost reached the door, 'helping old ladies across the road? You'd be dead from boredom within a month.'

Sperring didn't answer.

Letisha Watson lived on the ninth floor of Trescothick Tower. An inner-city Sixties tower block that, like all other inner-city Sixties tower blocks, had promised to be the future of housing. Cities in the sky. And like all other inner-city Sixties tower blocks soon became the exact opposite. The concrete and brick were crumbling, the wind ghosting through the widening cracks. Walkways were sided by wire mesh to stop children climbing off, being thrown off or, like those depressed just by having to live there, throwing themselves off. It had become a textbook sink estate; a dumping ground for the problem families and the socially undesirable, the unwelcome asylum seekers and immigrants. Like a rescue shelter for stray, mistreated and aggressive animals. But unlike the animal shelter, no one would come to release these people, give them a new start, a new life.

Phil had left the crime scene, giving orders as he did so. Khan was to head up the door-to-door, checking to see if anyone in the vicinity had seen or heard anything. Seeing how carefully the crime scene had been left he didn't expect much. But it was something that had to be done, a cosmetic exercise in hopeless hope.

Imani Oliver was still at the hospital with Darren Richards with instructions to call Phil as soon as he came round.

In the meantime, Phil and Sperring had decided to question Letisha Watson, Darren Richards' previous girlfriend. Phil didn't think she would come up with anything useful but it had to be done.

Hopeless hope.

They found the door they wanted. The flat looked semi-derelict; the windows filthy, the surrounds stained and mildewed.

The door itself, all dents, scratches, gouges and flaked paint, looked like a failed boxer who had come off second best throughout his fight career. Phil knocked. Waited.

'Bit early for her sort,' said Sperring.

Phil looked at him. 'What are you doing?'

Sperring held up his hands in the process of pulling on latex gloves. 'Can't be too careful, can you? Wouldn't want to put my hand down on some upturned needle. Or anything else, for that matter.'

Phil shook his head, knocked again.

Eventually the door was opened. Phil held up his warrant card. 'Letisha Watson?'

The woman who had opened the door looked to be still asleep. She was wearing an old T-shirt with a faded gold logo on the front proclaiming how fabulous she was. A pair of equally old pyjama bottoms covered her lower body. Her skin was naturally dark, mixed race, but pallid and unhealthy looking, and she was young but the tiredness and strain in her eyes aged her.

'Oh fuck,' she said and walked away down the hall, leaving the front door open.

Phil and Sperring exchanged glances and followed her in, Sperring carefully closing the door behind them.

They followed her into the living room. A fake-leather three-piece suite, worn and stained, cheap wooden furniture with an off-brand flatscreen TV in one corner. There was soiled clothing and other domestic debris scattered about. It looked like the owner had started out with good intentions where upkeep was concerned but found it all too much trouble.

'What d'you want?' Letisha Watson said, sitting down in an armchair and lighting up a Rothmans. Phil thought it would take more than a good night's sleep to displace the black rings round her eyes.

'Darren Richards,' said Phil, sitting down on the sofa. Sperring perched on the edge, like he was either frightened of catching something or wanted to make a run for it. Or both.

Letisha Watson sucked down a lungful of air, let it go. It hung in the living room like a miserable cloud, creating its own microclimate around her. 'What about him?'

'We believe you were his girlfriend.'

'I was. Till he got that slag pregnant.'

'That would be Chloe Hannon?'

'Yeah.' Letisha Watson looked between the two men. 'What's this about? What's he done now?'

'He's . . . well, we don't know, Letisha. We were hoping you might tell us.'

Her eyes narrowed. Suspicion in her features. 'Why?'

Sperring stood up. 'Can I use your loo?'

'Yeah,' she said, not even looking at him. Sperring left the room. 'What d'you want with me? Whatever it is, I didn't do it. Darren, though, I bet he did whatever it was.'

'When was the last time you saw Darren Richards, Letisha?'

She shrugged. 'Dunno. Weeks ago. Haven't spoken in ages.'

'And Chloe Hannon?'

Her features darkened. Anger danced behind her eyes. 'She keeps out of my way.'

'So it still hurts, losing Darren to her?'

Letisha Watson snorted. 'He can have the fucking bitch. Made for each other. Wouldn't take him back now, might catch something. Skank.'

Phil nodded, seemingly in thought. 'Letisha . . . how much would you say you disliked Chloe Hannon?'

'Hated her.'

Phil nodded, didn't speak. In the silence Letisha Watson became nervous. 'What's this about?'

Phil leaned forward. 'Letisha, Chloe Hannon is dead. She

was murdered.' He waited, scrutinising her features to see what her response would be.

Her eyes widened, suddenly fully awake. 'You think I did it?'

Phil kept his voice as calm and reasonable as possible. 'We're just talking to everyone who knew her and may have harboured a grudge against her. That's all.'

'And you think I did it?' Her voice raised, anger and fear intermingling.

'As I said, we're—'

She leaned forward, pointed with her lit cigarette. 'You come into my home making accusations like that. What proof have you got? What proof?'

'Can you tell us where you were Monday and Tuesday night this week, please, Letisha?'

She paused, conflicting emotions on her face. 'I was busy,' she said.

'You were here, weren't you?' said Sperring from the door-way. Phil and Letisha Watson turned. He continued. 'Or were you out working? How long you been on the game, then?'

Her face reddened. 'None of your fuckin' business.'

'Just had a look in your bedroom. Not much of a boudoir, is it? Bit bargain basement, if you ask me. You could at least put some covers on the mattress. Hide the stains if nothing else.' He stepped into the room. 'You always meet them here, do you? Or do you do house calls? I'd do house calls if I were you. Be hard enough getting a hard-on surrounded by all this bloody rubbish.'

She stood up, pointed to the door. 'Get out. Now. Both of you.'

Phil stood, irritated at his DS's behaviour, trying to salvage something from the situation. 'Look, Letisha, we just want to know—'

'I said out. And if you've got anything further to say to me, you do it through a solicitor.'

'Bet you're used to saying that,' said Sperring. 'We'll see ourselves out.'

Outside, walking along the landing, Phil was furious.

'What the hell was all that about? What were you doing? We only went to question her.'

'I know,' said Sperring, smiling. 'And I thought it was as pointless as you did. But there was something familiar about her. That's why I went for a look round.'

'Unprofessional,' said Phil. 'Just the kind of behaviour that could get a case kicked out of court. Or us in trouble.'

Sperring said nothing until they were descending the stairs.

'Aren't you going to ask me what I found?'

Phil sighed. 'What did you find, Ian?'

He gave a big grin. 'Plenty.'

9

'What d'you think?' asked Anni.

'Guilty. Definitely.'

'No doubt,' said Anni, 'but is she sane enough to stand trial?'

'Ah,' said Marina. 'That's the question.'

They were sitting in the staff canteen at Finnister House. All around them sat medical staff and care workers, taking time off, recharging, swapping gossipy work stories that professional etiquette wouldn't allow to travel further.

Marina leaned forward, looked Anni square in the face. 'Why did you bring me here?'

Anni looked slightly uncomfortable. 'To ... assess Joanne Marsh. See that she's sane enough to stand trial.' Her dark skin flushed.

'Anyone could have done that, Anni. You could have found someone local, East Anglia, anywhere round here. I know I'm good, but I'm not that good.'

Anni sighed. Before she could reply, another voice spoke.

'Fiona Welch.'

Marina turned. Detective Sergeant Mickey Phillips was standing behind her. Tall, shaven-headed and well-built, his eyes held an intelligence and compassion that belied his size. He was Anni Hepburn's partner both in and out of work.

Marina made to greet him with a hug but his words stopped her. 'Fiona Welch?'

He looked at Anni, then nodded at Marina. 'Yeah. Remember her?'

'Of course.' The previous head of Phil's team in Colchester had brought psychologist Fiona Welch in to advise on a case during Marina's absence. Phil hadn't taken to her on a personal level, which wouldn't have mattered had he not found her judgement on a professional level seriously flawed. She was eventually revealed to be manipulating the flow of intelligence behind a series of murders that had been committed at her instigation in order to prove her theories on human behaviour correct. She had been adjudged criminally insane but had fallen to her death before she could be taken into custody. 'Phil's still got the scars. Literally.' Marina looked between the two. 'But she's dead, so . . . ?' She let the question hang.

'Is she?' asked Anni.

'Isn't she?'

'That's what we thought,' said Mickey, sitting down to join them, 'but – well, Anni'll tell you.'

Anni leaned forward, across the table. 'About six months ago there was a murder in the Colchester area. A young guy, mid-twenties, killed his girlfriend. Just a domestic, we thought at first, nothing out of the ordinary, unfortunately.'

'Our team wasn't even called in,' said Mickey. 'Open and shut. The guy admitted he'd done it, no question. Didn't seem to have a reason for it, but that wasn't our problem.'

'But then,' said Anni, 'there was another one a month or so later. Identical. Same age, same everything. The girls even looked a bit similar.'

'How?' asked Marina.

Another look between Anni and Mickey.

'Tall. Dark hair.'

'Like you, really,' said Anni. 'Your looks, in fact. Dressed like you, too.'

Marina, shocked and now feeling more than a little uneasy, said nothing.

'And that's when we became involved,' said Mickey. 'Our department. Two too much to be a coincidence. We questioned the blokes again, asked them things the original teams hadn't. Asked about other women. And that's when the name came up.'

'Fiona Welch,' said Anni.

'Except she's dead,' said Marina.

'Exactly,' said Mickey. 'Considering we saw her die and watched her body being taken away. But these guys were adamant that they had met her, knew her. They'd had affairs with her. She'd told them to get rid of their girlfriends for her. She persuaded them to kill.'

'Manipulated them?' asked Marina.

They both nodded.

'But why didn't this come out at their trials? Why didn't they say so? They wouldn't have got off, but they might have lost some years on their sentences.'

'She told them not to,' said Anni.

'And they didn't.'

'Had quite a hold on them.'

'Anyway,' said Mickey, 'we tracked down this woman. She'd already chosen her next target. She was working on him to leave his girlfriend for her.'

'Permanently,' said Anni.

'But before that,' said Mickey, 'this Fiona Welch was getting these guys to change their girlfriends' looks. Hair darker, more curly, your dress sense . . . '

'You sure you're not just flattering me?'

Mickey and Anni said nothing.

46

'How did you find her?' asked Marina. 'This Fiona Welch?'

'Simple,' said Anni. 'She was a teaching post-grad at the university. Psychology. All the guys had been her students.'

'So she was arrested,' said Mickey. 'We questioned her, tried to break her down . . . nothing. She stuck to her story. She was Fiona Welch. The one who died was an imposter.'

'She knew everything,' said Anni, 'had her whole life story memorised. Told it like it had happened to her. She was so convincing that we began to think maybe she was right. Maybe the woman who died was an imposter and she was the real one.'

'We tried everything,' said Mickey. 'Everything. Got nowhere. She was Fiona Welch. And nothing we could say or do would shift that opinion from her mind.'

'So she admitted to making the two men kill their girlfriends? Working on the third one to do the same?'

Anni nodded. 'Completely. We didn't even have to prompt her. Like she was proud of the fact. Like she wanted to be caught.'

'So we could all see how brilliant she is,' said Marina. 'How clever, manipulative.'

'Showing off,' said Mickey. 'But it didn't get her very far. She still got found out. Still got caught.'

'That's true,' said Marina. She frowned, thinking. 'Strange, though. She goes to all that trouble to pretend to be Fiona Welch. Puts in all that effort. Why? Just to end up being caught?'

Mickey shrugged. 'We got wise to the original Fiona Welch,' he said. 'If she hadn't died we'd have put her away. And she wouldn't have been let out. Ever.'

'True,' said Marina. 'But the original Fiona Welch wanted that. Or would have accepted it. Because that way she would have been famous. That was what she wanted. Notoriety. She would have been listened to. Feared, even. She would be a famous

47

serial killer. She would have her writing published. She would be, she thought, taken seriously.'

'That's right,' said Anni. 'So?'

'So,' said Marina, 'what's this one playing at?'

'How d'you mean?' asked Mickey.

'Well, if what Anni said is true, it's as if she wanted to be caught.'

Mickey shrugged. 'So?'

'So she's manipulated you, too. She's in here because she wants to be.'

Mickey fell silent.

'But why?' asked Marina.

Anni stood up. 'Let's go and ask her, shall we?'

10

'She'd left her phone on the bed,' said Sperring once he and Phil were back in the Audi.

Phil had given a silent prayer that the Audi was where he had left it and intact. He pulled away, hoping that the brakes still worked. Even though they hadn't noticed anyone they would have been seen, made as police. He just hoped no one had had the time or inclination to tamper.

'So you had a look,' said Phil, leaning forward to turn down the Midlake CD that was playing. 'You know that's inadmissible.'

Sperring shrugged. 'Won't come to that. Anyway, I just had a look. She'd be none the wiser. Left no prints.' He started to remove his latex gloves.

Phil drove in silence for a while, surreptitiously testing his brakes. They seemed to work fine. He relaxed slightly. 'So,' he said eventually, 'you're dying to tell me. What did you find?'

'And you're dying to hear it. Don't try and kid me that you're not. Well,' he said, settling into the seat, making himself comfortable, 'I had a look at her calendar, see if she'd marked down any dates and that. Strangely, she wasn't the type to be that organised. So I had a look in her contacts.' Sperring smiled. 'Found a few names worth looking at.'

'Such as?' Phil kept his eyes on the road. He was still

relatively new to Birmingham and had to concentrate every time he drove. Not just because the roads were confusing but because the other drivers were so aggressive. He had thought London drivers were bad but they had nothing on these second-city citizens.

'Moses Heap.' Sperring smiled as he said it, pleased with himself.

The name meant nothing to Phil. 'Right. Good.'

'You don't know Moses Heap?' Sperring smirked. 'Must be before your time. There were two big gangs in this city.'

'Were?'

'Coming to that. There were two big gangs, been going for years. Back to the Handsworth riots in the mid-Eighties. The Handsworth Boys and the Chicken Shack Crew.'

'Right. Those names meant to mean anything?'

'Watson's Café in Handsworth was where one of them formed. They controlled virtually all of the drugs, women and door security for nightclubs across the city. We could barely get a hook in them. Then there were some arguments – drugs, women, whatever it is that sort argue over – and the Chicken Shack Crew were formed, running out of the Chicken Shack on Soho Road. The Handsworth Boys took Aston, Erdington and Lozells, the other lot Handsworth, Perry Barr and Ladywood. Crack cocaine, heroin, the lot.'

'Ironic that the Handsworth Boys shouldn't run Handsworth.'

'And a source of much anger, I gather. Long story short, they started to get out of control. Like the fucking wild west for shootings round there. School kids involved, the lot. Moses Heap ran the Handsworth Boys. Anyway, after the leader of the Chicken Shack Boys, Julian Wilson, was murdered – and no one was ever done for it – Moses Heap decided things had gotten out of hand so he tried to reach across to the new gang leader, Julian's brother Tiny. They sat down like it was fucking Northern Ireland and brokered some kind of peace treaty.'

'Good for them,' said Phil.

'Yeah. But not all of them got the memo. So it's shaky, still. Dangerous. But some of them, Moses Heap being a prime example, are claiming to have given up the dark path and reinventing themselves as community spokesmen, educators, a force for good, all that.'

'All very interesting,' said Phil, 'but how does that help us find Chloe and Shannon's killer?'

'Well, call me a cynic if you must, but I reckon that Moses's sudden conversion is a load of bollo. He's playing a game. Playing everyone. He always was a player. Bit of a pimp. He's got previous for that as well as the other stuff and if he's a friend of Letisha Watson, or if she's one of his ladies, maybe he's not above getting her a favour done in return for her doing him one?'

'Like killing her rival and child?'

Sperring shrugged. 'Worth looking into.'

Phil nodded. 'So where can we find Moses Heap?'

Sperring smiled. 'From what I hear, he's discovered the healing power of music.'

As soon as Phil opened the door his ears were assaulted by a barrage of sound. Hip hop beats punched up to ear-bleed level, an angry, violent rap fantasy of guns, gangs and hoes being spat over the top. At least Phil assumed it was a fantasy. Given the people he was visiting he wasn't so sure if they weren't just recording their day-to-day life.

The studio was in an old Victorian redbrick building in a rundown area of Aston, given over to the No Postcode Organisation, as it said on the front, a charity-funded community base. He and Sperring had shown their warrant cards on the way in, asked the young black man on the reception desk if Moses Heap was in the building. The young man had clearly had dealings with the police before and regarded them with suspicion if not downright hatred. He told them he would call through to the studio and see if Mr Heap was available.

'No need for that, son,' said Sperring. 'We'll go and see if he's there ourselves. Wouldn't want you spoiling the surprise.'

He walked off down a corridor, Phil following. Phil wanted to take issue with his subordinate's aggressive approach but he also wanted to see Moses Heap in his own surroundings. Gauge his responses from that.

They walked through the building, the original green ceramic tiled walls incongruous with newer plasterboard partitions and corridors, the walls covered with posters imploring the viewer to put down their knives and guns, with inspirational messages from figures such as Martin Luther King, Bob Marley and Tupac Shakur. They stopped before a plain wooden door with red and green lights above it. The green light was on.

'After you,' said Sperring.

All eyes turned as Phil and Sperring entered. Even given Phil's casual clothing they were immediately made as police. The room was full of black youths in their twenties and thirties relaxing on low sofas and chairs, and their expressions showed that their experience with the police had been negative. One of them stood up, stepped up to Phil. Eyeball to eyeball.

'I'm looking for Moses Heap,' said Phil, ensuring his voice was calm, his gaze level. Not matching aggression with aggression but careful not to back down.

'What you want him for?' said the man in front of him.

The room stank of sweat, skunk and alcohol.

'Just want a word,' said Phil. 'That's all.'

Another man stood up. He was better dressed than the

man who had stepped up to Phil, the same kind of street uniform but with better labels. ''S okay, Clinton,' he said. 'Stand down.'

The man reluctantly moved away but kept his eyes tight on Phil.

The other man crossed to Phil, took Clinton's place. 'I'm Moses Heap.' He swallowed down his ingrained distaste of police. Despite the anger Phil noticed a clear intelligence in his eyes. 'What can I do for you, gentlemen?'

'Can you turn the music down, please,' said Phil, 'or shall we step outside?'

Moses Heap gestured to a teenager sitting behind the mixing desk. The music disappeared. The silence that replaced it was deafening. Phil's ears were ringing.

'You can say what you got to say in front of my bredren. We got no secrets from Five-0 here.'

'Letisha Watson,' said Phil. 'She a friend of yours?'

Moses Heap frowned. 'Letisha Watson ... ' He shrugged. 'Don't recognise the name.'

'She's a working girl, lives on the Trescothick Estate,' said Sperring.

Moses Heap kept his face impassive, shrugged. 'So?'

'She knows you,' said Phil. 'Her ex-boyfriend's Darren Richards. Ring any bells?'

Moses Heap said nothing.

'And her ex-boyfriend's current girlfriend has met with a very untimely demise.'

Moses Heap kept his gaze focused on Phil, but Phil was sure he saw something flinch behind his eyes. 'My condolences to the family,' he said.

'Her baby daughter was killed too,' said Sperring. 'Murdered. Not an accident.'

Moses Heap acknowledged Sperring for the first time. 'Why

you telling me this? You think I did it? You think I murder children?'

'We're just asking anyone who knows either the deceased or anyone connected with the deceased,' said Phil. 'Routine. That's all. Your name came up. We came to see you.'

Moses Heap thought. Nodded. 'Yeah. Well, you've had a wasted journey. I can't help you. I don't know anything about Chloe Hannon's murder. Or her daughter.'

Phil did a double take. 'I didn't tell you her name.'

Fear flashed across Moses Heap's face, his composure crumbling for a few seconds before he regained it. 'Must have been on the news.'

'We haven't released the details. Or the names.'

Heap shrugged, tried for casual. Missed. 'Must have heard it somewhere.'

'Where?' asked Phil.

'Dunno.' His voice raised, anger dancing in his eyes. 'You want to arrest me for it? You wanna charge me? Go ahead. Charge me. My brief'll have me out in an hour. Have your jobs, too. I'm a businessman. A respected figure in the community. These here are my associates. And you come in and accuse me of murder in front of them? I don't think so, man. I don't think so at all.'

Phil looked around the room. It was tense to start with but the tension had palpably increased in the last few seconds. He knew there was nothing more to be done then and there.

'We'll be in touch, Mr Heap,' Phil said. He turned to go.

'Don't plan on leaving town,' said Sperring, following him out.

The music resumed before they had reached the door, louder this time, more aggressive. Once outside, Phil breathed a sigh of relief. 'Well, that went as well as expected,' he said.

'Dunno,' said Sperring. 'Saw quite a few familiar faces in

there. Not all from the same gang, neither. Must've been having a meeting or something.'

'Maybe they were settling their differences over a few beers, a bit of a smoke and some music.'

Sperring snorted. 'Carving up territory, probably. Hardly the bloody *Godfather*, is it?'

Before Phil could reply his phone rang. He answered it. Listened, spoke, turned to Sperring.

'That was Imani. Darren Richards has come round.'

11

The needle clicked, returned. Clicked, returned. Again. And again. Stuck after the fade-out, hissing and crackling, time looping on dead air.

'Come on, Philip, where are you?'

He stared at the TV screen, sound down, waiting. He was becoming impatient, his earlier euphoria wearing off, the thrill of seeing his handiwork, his mission, on TV becoming something of a let-down.

'Who are you talking to?'

He looked around, jumped a little. Christ, what a time for his sister to appear.

'No one. The TV. That's all.'

His sister looked at the TV also. 'Oh,' she said. 'That's just over the road.'

'It is, yes. That's why I'm watching it.'

'Oh.'

His sister stayed there. He wanted her to leave again, go back to where she had come from but she didn't move.

'D'you want anything? You here for anything?'

'What? No.'

'Then why don't you pop off for a while. I'll let you know if anything happens.'

'Okay then.'

And off she went. He waited until he knew she was gone then gave his attention back to the TV.

No one from the police had spoken directly to camera. No one. He had expected DI Brennan, considering their previous exchange, but no. Nothing.

He had played it over in his mind, what he was expecting, what he wanted. DI Brennan to be interviewed on TV, to stand in front of the camera, microphone thrust into his face, and tell him he knew what he was doing. He *understood*. Justice. Right. And he applauded his work.

And he would nod as he said this, listening, understanding what the detective was saying, feeling their bond. Knowing that his work was going to make him famous.

Famous. He felt immediately guilty at the thought. No. That wasn't right. Famous. That wasn't why he was doing this, not the reason behind it. No. Famous meant *X Factor. The Voice.* That jungle show. All those kinds of people. Katie Price. The Kardashians. He smirked. He had thought they were aliens off *Star Trek* when he first heard the name. Then after he saw them he was convinced that's what they were. No. That's what famous was. Being a celebrity because you couldn't do anything else. Being famous because you were famous. Vacuous non-entities, all of them. Not like him. Not like what he was doing. *Why* he was doing it.

His job. His calling. After waiting so long for acknowledgement from the police on the TV and in the downer of a mood he was currently in, he felt slightly ridiculous saying it. Calling. But that's what it was. He knew it. Like when religious types hear the voice of God and get called to be a priest. Or go and work as a missionary with Mexican street kids or something. Yes it was his work, but it was pure. Unsullied by financial transaction. Or by God. It was a service he had decided to provide but in return he didn't want payment. All he wanted was recognition for what he was doing. Fame didn't enter into it.

He shook his head once more, concentrated on the TV screen. It was brand new. A huge, smart flatscreen TV. Almost the size of a cinema screen. And surrounded by all the latest equipment for the enhanced home cinema experience, the brochure said. But he needed it. All of it. It was for work.

He watched as the news came on once more, back to the same scene. He held his breath.

'... at this time, but from what I can gather ...'

The reporter stood at the bottom of Legge Lane, young and ambitious, tie tight, hair perfect, eyes shining with the thrill that this could be the story that gets him out of the provinces. Behind him, the half-demolished building cordoned off with police tape, covered with white plastic sheeting. Shadows moved against it from inside and it ruffled in the breeze, making the building look like a becalmed sailing ship. .

'You'll find nothing there,' he said out loud, 'nothing. I promise you.'

'... two bodies have been carried out of the house. It's thought that one person was still alive when police arrived at the scene. This person was in a critical condition and has been taken to hospital. There's no news yet on the identity of the two dead individuals, nor who is responsible. But the police are treating these deaths as suspicious.'

He laughed. Was that as much as the reporter had managed to get out of the police? With everything that had gone on in there? Pitiful. No national jump for him. A life in the provinces beckoned.

The camera panned round the area then ended up back on the fluttering white plastic sheet. The reporter was talking over the top but the more he went on, the less he said. Eventually he was left standing in the street as the news returned to the anchor in the studio.

He sat back. His heart sank even further. Where was Brennan? Why wasn't he on there, talking to him, making an appeal? Why? Blood pumped quickly round his body. He became short of breath, slightly giddy. Yes, he had done it. That was true. All that planning and it had paid off, actually worked. Hooray for him. But they hadn't worked it out. Hadn't got it.

He closed his eyes. Perhaps he had been too oblique. Too obscure. Maybe they really were as thick as he had heard, maybe he was giving them too much credit. He had thought Brennan was clever. Or at least cleverer than the rest. That's what he had been led to believe, anyway. What his research had told him. Maybe he had been told wrong.

He opened his eyes, looked at the screen once more. The news had moved on and they were now talking about a traffic accident on the M6. The feeling of sudden, euphoric elation was just as suddenly disappearing. Yes, that was his work up there on the TV for everyone to see but . . . there was something missing. He thought, staring hard at the TV. Not seeing the images, only the thin, black frame. Something missing.

But what?

He kept staring. And it began to reveal itself to him.

No word from the police. No news yet. One person in a critical condition. Treating the deaths as suspicious.

He nodded. Yes. That was it. That's what was missing. What had he just seen on TV? What had he *really* just witnessed? Just a breathless, slightly incompetent reporter talking about a double murder. That's all.

And what was missing?

Everything.

The work. The explanation. What he was really doing. What had actually happened.

Justice.

Yes. A sense of justice.

He flicked off the TV, sat back. All around him were the carefully made structures of ages gone by. Craft. Pride. Old words now, he thought. Dirty words.

He heard, as if for the first time, the click and hiss of the old 45 as the needle caught the groove. Dropping back, never finishing.

The room began to feel dark and oppressive. He began to feel uncomfortable in it.

He closed his eyes once more, tried to think.

Justice. How could he let them know about his work, his quest?

He smiled. Quest. Yes. That was the right word. Quest. Something mythic, something epic. A great achievement. Quest. Good.

So. He had to explain. They had to understand. Only after they understood what he was doing could they realise that what he was saying was the truth. In fact, it was the only way until everyone learned from his example. And then he would be celebrated.

He laughed. Maybe he would be famous after all.

He thought some more. And smiled. A new thought occurred to him. Perhaps the police weren't so thick. Maybe they were clever. Maybe they were deliberately withholding things from the media, not telling them the full story, or indeed any part of the story.

So what to do next?

He opened his eyes. He knew. It was so obvious, so simple. He had their attention. Now he had to let them know he was serious.

He got up, crossed to the jukebox, set up another record. Garnet Mimms: 'Cry Baby'.

No need to cry, he thought. The future had never looked brighter.

12

'So has she been charged with anything?' Marina asked as she walked down the corridor in Finnister House, Anni and Mickey alongside her. A male nurse, tall and stocky, followed along behind them. 'This Fiona Welch looky-likey?'

'Well, that's the thing,' said Mickey. 'We're not sure what to charge her with.'

'We could have done her for accessory after the fact with regard to the murders or false impersonation, that kind of thing.' Anni shrugged. 'But I guess as soon as she announced herself as Fiona Welch alarm bells rang and we brought her in here.'

'And she came here of her own free will?' asked Marina.

'It was a compromise reached with her solicitor,' said Mickey. 'No prison, no remand. She can be studied and helped in here. She was all for it.'

'Didn't that make you suspicious?' said Marina.

'Yep,' said Anni. 'Which is why we brought you in.'

'Amongst other reasons,' said Marina.

Anni and Mickey said nothing.

They stopped walking. The corridor was bright and airy. It could have been an ordinary hospital were it not for the wire-reinforced glass in the windows, the heavy security locks on the doors. The constant monitoring presence of swivel-headed CCTV cameras in the top corners. They had even passed some inmates walking about unaccompanied. Marina knew that wouldn't have been the case. Unaccompanied perhaps. Alone and unwatched, never. That was the kind of place it was.

'Here we are,' said Anni.

The door in front of them looked like all the others on the corridor. Solid blond wood. A heavy metal security lock. The male nurse stepped forward, took a chained key from the leather pouch on his waist and unlocked the door. Before opening it he turned to the other three. 'You want me to come in?' he asked. 'Rules and that.'

'If you like,' said Mickey. 'But it'll be a bit crowded.'

'Suit yourself,' he said. 'I'll wait out here. But remember, no physical contact. Don't get too close. You've had the search, yeah? Left everything at the gate?'

'We have,' said Mickey.

'Can't be too careful.' He turned, opened the door. 'Hope you're decent, Fiona,' he shouted. 'You've got visitors.'

The door opened widely. Marina peered in. On the bed sat a woman. Young, late twenties, early thirties at the most. Her legs were drawn up beneath her and she was reading. She looked up. Scanned the faces of her visitors. Smiled.

'Come in,' she said. 'I don't often get guests.'

They stepped into the room, the door closing behind them. Marina sized up the woman calling herself Fiona Welch. Small. Compact. Dark-haired. Wearing the hospital standard issue of T-shirt and tracksuit bottoms. She slowly unfolded her legs from beneath her and got gracefully to her feet. The smile remained in place on her face, giving nothing away, letting nothing in.

'Please, sit down if you can find somewhere to sit,' she said.

Marina looked around the room. It had the spartan simplicity of a prison cell – bed, desk, toilet cubicle and washbasin – but there were signs it had been decorated. Toiletries lined the single shelf along with books and folders.

Marina found the desk chair and sat. Anni perched on the edge of the desk. Mickey remained standing.

'I'm afraid I can't offer you any tea,' Fiona Welch said. 'Or anything for that matter. We're not trusted with such things. Apparently they fear we can turn any household item into a weapon, an instrument of torture or an object for self-harm. It's like we're malevolent *Blue Peter* presenters.'

'I'm fine,' said Marina.

'Good,' said Fiona Welch, nodding. She resumed her seat on the bed. 'So to what do I owe this pleasure?' She paused and looked straight at Marina. 'Ms Esposito?'

'You know who I am?' asked Marina.

'Of course,' said Fiona Welch. 'I know your husband. We worked together.' Her expression changed, her eyes downcast. 'Alas no more. We . . . disagreed on too many things.'

'Disagreed.'

Fiona Welch smiled. 'I was very impulsive in those days. Very rash. You know how it is, first flush of youth and all that. One is sure one is right. All the time. I've mellowed considerably since then.'

'Have you now?'

'Absolutely. Oh, don't get me wrong, one can still hold the same views and convictions but one doesn't necessarily have to express them in so strident a fashion. In fact, one can often affect more change by employing more subtle methods. Don't you agree, Marina? May I call you Marina? After all, we have so much in common. I feel I know you.'

Despite the reassuring presence of Anni and Mickey, something about this woman was making Marina feel uncomfortable. Unsettled. 'What do we have in common, exactly?' she said, hoping her voice remained steady.

Another smile. 'How is your husband?' she asked. 'I genuinely did enjoy working with him. Despite the fact that he constantly belittled my theories. Theories which, I'm sure you're aware, have since been borne out to be true.'

'Which theories in particular?' asked Marina, her voice steady and neutral.

Fiona Welch sat back, enjoying the attention. 'Morality and manipulation,' she said. 'Especially where men are concerned. We like to fool ourselves constantly. Tell ourselves, as a community, a society, that we're moral. That we know the difference between right and wrong. And that, more importantly, we act on it. Always. Given the choice, that's what we do. What we would always do. We live our lives around those beliefs.' She shook her head. 'No. It's a lie. All of it. There's no such thing. No such differentiation. No right and wrong. No black and white. There aren't even any shades of grey.'

'What is there then?'

She continued talking, her voice patient as if she was a primary-school teacher explaining rudimentary mathematics to five-year-olds. 'An assumed set of values, of course. Relative ones, that can be dispensed with or bargained away depending on what one's needs are at any given time.'

'Is that right?' asked Marina.

'It is.' She moved forward, warming to her theme. 'For instance, you want to take care of your family. It's your primary concern. What lengths would you go to to do it? What kind of extreme behaviour could you justify to yourself in order to do that? Any, I would think. One can rationalise away anything if one has a good enough reason for doing so.'

'Yeah, yeah,' said Mickey. 'We've all seen *Breaking Bad*.'

A look of anger rippled across Fiona Welch's face. In that instant, Marina could imagine her raking her nails slowly and deeply down the side of her husband's face.

She managed to regain her composure, leaned forward once more, a small smile playing on her lips. 'Wouldn't you agree,

Marina? Wouldn't you say that you have done things to protect your family? Hmm? Things that could be considered morally dubious, if not outside the law?'

Marina stiffened. She was aware that both Anni and Mickey were watching her. She bit back her initial response, kept her voice low and calm. Professional sounding.

'So there's no such thing as morality,' said Marina. 'That's what you're saying. It's all relative.'

'Absolutely,' said Fiona Welch. She sounded disappointed that Marina hadn't risen to her words.

'So someone could commit a crime and they should get away with it providing they've got a good enough excuse, is that what you're saying?' said Mickey. 'That what you mean?'

She put back her head, closed her eyes. Smiled. 'The response I expected from a police officer. You've got a lot to learn,' she said quietly.

'So why are you here, then?' asked Marina. 'What are you doing in this place if your theories are true?'

Fiona Welch opened her eyes, leaned forward. 'I'll tell you.'

13

The man in the hospital bed looked exactly what he was, thought Phil: the only survivor of a great tragedy. He was pale, dehydrated. Skin sunken, mottled, discoloured to various unhealthy shades of sickness. He was awake – barely – but he appeared to be tired beyond sleep. His dead fish eyes were deep set, hollowed, staring at things no one else could see, open to a private world of horror. The rest of them round his bed were thankful they didn't share it.

'Darren Richards?' Phil asked.

At the mention of his name, Darren Richards seemed startled, fearful. If he had the energy to jump, thought Phil, he would have.

'Detective Inspector Brennan,' said Phil, holding up his warrant card.

Detective Constable Imani Oliver sat at the man's bedside. Darren Richards looked at her while Phil spoke, as if for guidance on how to respond.

Imani had been the first – and sometimes he thought, the only – one on his team to respond to his approach. Dress creatively, think creatively. She was dressed casually but practically in jeans, sweater and boots. Young and attractive, her dark skin contrasted with the white of her Aran sweater. Having worked with her, Phil knew how good she was and really valued her presence on the team in a way that Sperring often didn't.

Sperring was good at his job. And loyal and trustworthy. But he wasn't always a good judge of character, nor was he the most unprejudiced of people.

'It's all right, Darren,' said Imani, her voice soft, solicitous, 'you can talk to him. He's safe.'

Daren Richards didn't look convinced, seemed too traumatised even to speak.

Imani, sensing this, spoke again. 'Don't worry. He just wants to help. Help you. We all do.'

Phil found another chair, dragged it up to the bed. The nurse pulled the curtains round, giving them a semblance of privacy.

'Please don't stress or overtire him,' she said to Phil.

'I'll be as brief as I can,' he replied. 'Thank you.' He smiled.

The nurse returned it, quite shyly. 'You're welcome. I appreciate you've got your job to do.'

'And I'm aware that you do, too.'

Phil kept smiling at her. The nurse, reddening slightly, let herself out.

'Charmer,' said Imani quietly.

'Always be polite,' he said. 'I may have just bought us a bit of extra time because of that.' Then he turned to Darren Richards. The traumatised young man was surrounded by drips and monitors. It might have been the most attention he'd ever had, thought Phil, then amended his thought. Darren Richards had been before the judge. Several times. It was one of the reasons Sperring had given for not accompanying Phil to the hospital.

'You're better dealing with that sort than me,' he had said, not bothering to hide his distaste. 'I'll go back to the station. See if Nadish's come up with anything worth following through. Check a couple of leads from this morning.'

'Such as?' Phil had asked.

'Moses Heap, for one. Rings a bell for some reason. Not just 'cause of all the stuff in the papers, there's something else. Can't think what, though. But it's like an itch that needs scratching.'

'Lovely. I'll leave you to it.' And Phil had come to the hospital alone.

He moved his chair closer to the bedside. 'So, Darren,' he said, voice matching Imani's tones, 'what happened?'

Darren Richards' eyes widened, filled with shock. The fear subsided as his eyes emptied, became blank. Give nothing away in front of the law, thought Phil. Old habits dying hard.

'I dunno,' said Darren Richards.

'Oh, come on, Darren,' said Phil, 'you must have known what happened. You were there.'

Darren Richards closed up again. 'I don't remember.'

Maybe there was another reason he wasn't talking, thought Phil. A much more obvious one. 'I'm sure you don't want to remember,' he said. 'I'm sure it's very painful to remember. What you've been through is enough to horrify anyone.'

'So if you know what I've been through, why d'you want me to go through it again?'

'To find out who did it. Stop them doing it again.'

'I didn't do it,' said Darren Richards quickly. Too quickly: it was like the sudden exertion tired him out. He flopped back on the bed.

Phil kept on. 'No, I don't believe you did. But I'm sure you saw it. You saw the person who did it. And I need you to tell me all that you can about them.'

Darren, against his better judgement, was remembering. Phil could see it in his eyes. He had to get him to talk before he clammed up once more.

'Come on, Darren, please. Help me here.' Phil glanced at Imani, the cue for her to speak.

'We'll catch him, Darren,' she said. 'We'll bring Chloe and

Shannon's killer to justice. We'll do it for them, for their memory. But for us to do that you have to help us. I know it's difficult, I know it'll hurt but we need your help. Please.'

'Just tell us now,' said Phil. 'Get it out of the way and you can get on with forgetting.'

'Please,' said Imani.

'What did he look like?' said Phil, leaning forward. 'Can you remember? Did you get a good look at him? Was it a him?'

Darren began breathing heavily. His eyes spun, focusing in and out, fighting the urge to remember. Phil checked his heart monitor: the graph had started to speed up. They waited.

'Skull,' he said eventually, his voice cracked and broken, the word sounding like it was dragged from him.

Phil and Imani shared another glance. Puzzlement, this time. 'Skull?' repeated Phil. 'You mean he was thin? Like you could see his bones through his skin?'

Darren shook his head. 'No . . . skull . . . '

Imani leaned forward. 'Like make-up?'

He shook his head.

'A mask?' she said. 'Is that what you mean? A skull mask?'

Darren shook his head once more. 'No. A mask. Yes. Not a skull mask. Just looked like a skull mask.'

'What then?' asked Phil.

Darren frowned, concentrating. 'Gas . . . mask . . . '

Phil understood. 'Gas mask. He wore a gas mask.'

Darren nodded.

'And this gas mask,' said Phil, 'it had round eyes? Pale and close-fitting?'

Darren nodded.

'And it looked like a skull.'

Darren shuddered. Closed his eyes.

'Right,' said Phil. He could feel they were starting to get somewhere.

'So how did you get there, Darren? Into that building?'

'Dunno,' said Darren, his eyes remaining closed.

'No idea at all?'

Darren shook his head. 'Just woke up there. In that chair . . . '
He shuddered once more.

The shudder threatened to turn into a more prolonged
shake. Phil and Imani knew they had to get him to open up
more before they lost him.

'What's the last thing you remember?' asked Imani.

'Goin' to Wayne's,' said Darren, his voice reduced to a tired
tremble.

'Wayne,' said Phil. 'And were you drunk when you were off
to Wayne's?'

Darren shook his head.

'High?'

Darren shook his head. 'Nah, man.' Irritated now.

'Okay,' said Phil. 'You were on your way to Wayne's. Your
friend Wayne.' He made a mental note to check Darren
Richards' file for the name, follow it up. 'And the next thing you
knew you were in that building.'

Darren nodded.

'Taped to the chair.'

Darren nodded again, eyes tight shut.

'Who's Wayne?' asked Imani.

Darren shrugged. 'Mate.'

'Could he have done this? Been responsible for what happened to you?' Imani again.

Darren opened his eyes. 'Nah, man.' He sounded appalled.

Phil leaned forward once more. 'Do you have any idea who
could have done this? Who would have wanted to do this? Any
idea at all?'

Darren's sense of discomfort was growing. As the questioning became more and more insistent he began thrashing around

in his bed like he wanted to escape but lacked not only the strength but also the ability to issue the correct commands to his body.

'No idea at all, Darren?'

Darren shook his head, wilder this time.

'So what did he want, Darren?' Imani. 'Why did he do this?'

Darren began to shake. Any harder and he would vibrate his body into pieces. His mouth all the while twisting and contorting, like he wanted to speak but the words wouldn't birth.

Phil pressed on. 'Why, Darren? Why did he do it?'

Darren continued to shake, his mouth twisting. Phil and Imani stopped talking, waited to see what would happen next. Then the words came screaming out.

'Justice . . . justice . . . he wanted . . . he said he . . . I had to have . . . had to give, to give justice . . . '

Then a scream that became a sob that trailed away into the horrible, dying whimper of an animal that Phil had never encountered before.

The nurse pulled the curtain open and stepped in but Phil was already on his feet, issuing orders and walking to the exit.

Justice.

14

'Let's run through that again, shall we?' Glen Looker stared at his client, tried to keep the exasperation, not to mention sarcasm, out of his voice. 'Only this time you don't mention the trainers.'

'But they were my trainers.'

Glen Looker put his head in his hands and shook it slowly. Eventually he looked up. *Nope,* he thought. His problem hadn't gone away. He was still sitting there, larger than life and twice as stupid.

'Yes, Leon, I know they were your trainers. You know they were your trainers. And you know how the blood got on them.'

Leon smiled. ''Cause I kicked Milton in the side when he was bleeding.'

Glen sighed. 'Leon, if you mention that outside the confines of this room ...' He paused. *Confines* was probably too complex a word for his client. ' ... outside of this room – which I might remind you is a special room in that you can say what you like in it and it doesn't matter at all – if you tell anyone else that then they will put you in prison, Leon. Do you understand?'

Leon frowned.

No, thought Glen. He doesn't understand.

Glen sighed. 'Let's go through it from the top, shall we? You were out one night going to your favourite chicken take-away, is that right?'

Leon's face lit up. 'Yeah. Chicken Cottage. Love it. Do fries an' all.'

'Right. You were going to buy a meal for your family because you like to support your family and provide for them when you can.'

Leon frowned again. ''Snot right, Mr Looker. No.'

'What d'you mean it's not right? This is what we agreed on.'

Leon shook his head. 'No, Mr Looker. I went there 'cause I had beef with Milton. Went lookin' for Milton. He'd been dissin' me. Heard that. Can't have that. Was gonna shank him.' He smiled. 'Got him good, didn' I?'

Glen sighed, closed his eyes. This wasn't the way I thought my life would go, he thought. Why me? I thought I'd be in one of those swanky law firms with gorgeous secretaries and lines of coke for lunch. Instead, I end up representing the dregs. Why do I bother? I should just let him take the stand, spout his gibberish, get sent down. He nodded to himself. Yeah, he thought. Do that.

'So can I go now?' asked Leon.

'Where would you go, Leon? Back to your cell? Are you in a hurry to go back there?'

'Won't be for long, though, will it, Mr Looker? You'll do your magic. You always do. You'll find something. You'll get me out.'

Glen Looker sighed once more. 'Leon, let me explain. If you don't work with me here, if you don't see things the way I see them, if you don't think the way I'm telling you to think, do the things I'm telling you to do, then you won't be getting out. Do you understand?'

Leon looked hurt, as if he was about to cry.

'Let's try it again, Leon. You went to Chicken Cottage to get a meal for your family. On the way back someone ran into you. It was Milton. He was bleeding. You ran away from him. You didn't want to get involved with whatever had happened. People knew you and Milton didn't get on. You didn't want to be blamed for what had happened to him. You just wanted to get home and give your family the meal you had bought for them.'

'Don't get my mum nothin'. She's a skank.'

Glen sighed. Continued. 'And you slipped in the blood. And that's why your trainers ended up with Milton's blood on them. Right?'

Leon shook his head. 'Lot to remember.'

'Yes it is, Leon. Yes it is.'

He scrutinised the oversized child in front of him, sitting there in his prison-issue jogging suit. According to the local media, Leon was one of the city's most feared and dangerous gang members. Maybe I could plead diminished responsibility, Glen thought. As in he's too fucking thick to understand what he was doing. Trouble was, he wasn't too thick. Leon had been tested and found to be fully cognitive. Glen couldn't use that defence this time. He had tried.

'I don't know if I can do it, Mr Looker.'

'Practise, Leon. Practise. You can do it. Come on. Give it a go.'

Leon stared at him.

'Come on, Leon.'

'What, you mean now?'

Glen sat back, arms folded, stared at the ceiling. 'I wonder if it's not too late to be a fireman ... '

'What, Mr Looker? You leaving?'

He sat forward once more. 'No, Leon, I'm not. Come on. You've heard me say it, you try now.'

Leon screwed his eyes up in concentration. 'I went to Chicken Cottage to get a meal for my family.' He looked at Glen, beaming. 'I'm doing well, aren't I, Mr Looker?'

'Brilliant, Leon. Worthy of an Oscar. Now keep going.'

Leon screwed his eyes tight once more, reaching back in his mind for the words, trying to assemble them in the correct order. 'I like to provide for my family. Even my mother. 'Cause she doesn't. Skank.'

'You're going off the script now, Leon.'

'Sorry. Sorry.' He refocused. 'I like to provide for my family. Give them somethin' healthy an' nutritious.' He beamed once more. 'You like that, Mr Looker?'

'Brilliant, Leon. You're a marvel. Keep going.'

Pleased with himself, Leon kept talking. 'And then I saw Milton who I had a beef with.'

'No, Leon, don't say that.'

'Why not? I did. Everyone on my end knows I did.'

'Yes, but you have to persuade the jury that even though you and Milton didn't get on—'

'We had serious beef.'

'Indeed. But you have to forget that and persuade the jury that you had nothing to do with his death. Right? That it was all an accident. Right? You have to stick to the story that I just told you. That's the one you have to tell. The only one you can tell. Do you understand?'

Leon closed his eyes and frowned for such a long time that Glen thought he had drifted off to sleep.

'Yes, Mr Looker,' he said eventually, snapping open his eyes. 'It's like we're tellin' a story, innit? An' we have to make the story sound true so they believe us. Yeah?'

Glen smiled. 'That's exactly it, Leon.' He swallowed a yawn. 'Shall we give it one more try?'

Once outside Birmingham Prison, on the way to the car, and with Leon's woeful attempt at his testimony still ringing in his ears, Glen Looker checked his messages. What he heard on voicemail made him stop walking. He replayed it.

'Aw shit,' he said out loud, and headed for his car.

As if his day hadn't been bad enough already.

15

'I'm very happy here.' Fiona Welch sat back. Like she was reclining in her favourite seat at her favourite bar.

'Good,' said Marina. 'That's good. And is that why you're here? Because it makes you feel happy?'

A smile played across Fiona Welch's face. The kind that concealed secrets. Not altogether pleasant ones. 'Let's just say it suits my purposes at present.'

Marina waited for something more. Nothing came. 'That's it? That's why you wanted to come here?'

'I'm here of my own free will,' Fiona Welch said.

'While you're being investigated,' said Mickey. 'While your testimony is being checked out and we wait to charge you properly.'

Fiona Welch looked at Marina, her eyes mocking. 'How do you put up with him? Hmm? I mean not just him personally, but the whole police mindset? Especially the male police mindset. Intractable. Prosaic. Boring. Dull and predictable. Don't you think?'

Again, Marina didn't rise to it, although she was aware of Mickey's position stiffening. She hoped he would manage to rein in what he wanted to say too. Not give her the ammunition.

'This is the perfect place for me to continue my work,' said Fiona Welch.

'The perfect place?' said Marina. 'But you're a patient here.'

'Willingly,' she said. 'But it gives me ample opportunity to work. This place is alive with potential case studies. I have full, unfettered access to some of the most damaged, deviant psycho-pathologies in the country. And they're all female. The work that has been done in this area is sparse and, if I may say so, rather ill-informed. Ignorant. And I do know what I'm talking about. I've read it all. No. This is my opportunity, my chance, to contribute something truly groundbreaking to the body of work that exists about deviant female pathology. In fact, by the time I'm ready to leave, my work, I feel sure of this, will be hailed as the standard reference on the subject.'

'Right,' said Marina. 'I see.'

Fiona Welch's face darkened. Her eyes locked on Marina. 'Don't mock me.' Her voice was low, dangerous. 'Please don't make the mistake of doing that.'

Marina felt herself reddening. The sudden change in tone from the woman was unnerving. 'I wasn't mocking you. I just think it's a . . . lot to take in. That's all. Lot of work.'

'Which I am more than equal to, I assure you.' She stopped talking, stared at Marina. Head to one side, scrutinising her. 'You know,' she said eventually, 'I thought you'd be younger.'

Marina tried not to let her startled expression show. 'What d'you . . . what d'you mean?'

'Just that. Younger. I mean, knowing Phil as I do I thought the woman he married wouldn't be as . . . old as you. I thought he'd gone for someone younger, that's all.'

Marina regained her composure. 'Did you? Right. Well, what can I say? He didn't. He went for me.'

Fiona Welch nodded. 'He did. Yes. But . . . ' She shook her head. 'I'm sure sometimes when he looks at you, when he notices that your hair is no longer the natural colour it once was, even though it's a good match I'll admit, and your make-up has become slightly heavier, and you take longer in the gym, put in more effort for less results, I'm sure he must look at you and . . . well, not want someone else. That's not his style, is it? He's big on loyalty, Phil. No. But there must be flashes, don't you think? Just for a few seconds. Nothing more. Ripples of unease. When he thinks . . . she's old. She's getting older. And he'll still feel young inside himself, like he's staying still and you're not . . . and—'

'Is this leading anywhere?' said Marina, slightly louder and less controlled than she had intended.

Fiona Welch smiled. 'Just something to think about. That's all.'

Anni stood up. 'Was there anything else? If not, we should be on our way.'

Fiona Welch made a mock gesture of surrender. 'Don't let me hold you up.'

The other two made ready to leave. Fiona Welch got up, crossed to Marina. Took her hand. 'I'm glad I finally got the chance to meet you. Face to face.'

Marina said nothing.

'Please give my love to Phil, won't you?'

Marin took her hand away.

The three of them made for the door. Fiona Welch laughed. 'Yes, Marina, I'm sure we'll be seeing a lot more of each other soon.'

Marina turned, puzzled and, if she was honest, slightly unnerved. 'What d'you mean by that? How do you think we'll be seeing more of each other?'

'I think we will. Wait and see what happens. Then you will think the same too.' She made as if to turn away then turned back, struck by a sudden thought. 'How's your daughter? She must be . . . what, four now?'

Marina could feel herself shaking. 'That's none of your business.'

'Send her my love too. If you like.'

'Come on,' said Mickey. 'Let's go.'

The three of them reached the door.

'Oh, Marina,' said Fiona Welch, 'one last thing.'

Marina, despite herself, turned.

'Just tell Phil . . .' She paused, moved her mouth silently as if auditioning the right word. The perfect word. 'Tell Phil . . . Justice. It's all about justice.'

Marina frowned. 'What's all about justice?'

She turned away, looked out of the window. 'He'll know.'

They didn't speak until they were walking away from the hospital, out in the crisp autumn sunshine.

'Well, she wasn't creepy, was she?' said Mickey.

'I feel like I want a bath now,' said Anni. 'Jesus.'

Marina said nothing.

'What was all that about?' asked Anni. 'All that stuff aimed at you?'

'Oh, just crazy talk, I should think. The usual stuff that her kind of nutter spouts.' Marina was trying to brush it off, but there had been something in Fiona Welch's words that had unnerved her. Hit her. She knew that was the idea and she was cross with herself for letting her do that, but nevertheless, the feeling was there.

'I'm going home,' said Marina.

'Oh,' said Anni, unable to keep the disappointment out of her voice. 'We were hoping you'd come back to ours. Make a night of it.'

Marina looked around. Felt a chill in the air. Felt unseen eyes watching her.

'I'd better go home,' she said.

16

Bank restaurant in Brindleyplace, Birmingham. All glass and steel and fine dining, it looked out over the canal and a host of other chain restaurants and businesses. It had had a busy lunch-time. In fact, it was now well after lunch-time but some of the diners didn't seem to know when to stop, when to leave.

And, being one the worst offenders, that was just the way John Wright liked it. After all, what was the point of being in charge if you couldn't award yourself a few perks now and then?

Their meal was all but finished, the dessert plates cleared away. Coffees and liqueurs were now the order of the day. A supposed strategy meeting-cum-self-congratulatory lunch. He did it every time they were awarded bonuses. The staff looked forward to it and he always obliged. Liked to feel that he was still one of the workers. One of them. Up to a point, of course. Now their after-dinner drinks were being accompanied by them all trading war stories, the louder and cruder the better. Each one trying to outdo the previous one. Even lunch was competitive.

He looked around at the others in his party. He'd been in banking so long he could spot the types straight away. There were the young, eager sharks, the tyro princes who thought they were on the way to the top and didn't care who they sold out or what they sold to do it. Laughing raucously at all his jokes, angling with each other to be the one to sit nearest to him. He couldn't complain. He had been like them once.

Then there were the time servers, the loyal beta males and yes men, the court eunuchs. Just there to do their boss's bidding. Punch in, punch out. Usually older, they did their time, kept their heads down. He used to despise that sort until he moved higher up the ladder. Then he realised just how useful they were. Diary keepers. Gate keepers. Shit deflectors. Human shields. Worth their weight in – well, not gold exactly, they were too interchangeable, but something semi precious, perhaps.

And then there were the women. Always the women. A lot of his peers thought that banking was no place for a woman. The cut and thrust of such an intense, testosterone-driven environment, the sheer adrenalin rush, they thought it was all too much for them. Plus they were all too bloody fecund. That was the unspoken truth, of course, the one no one dare utter aloud for fear of a court case. But it was the truth, nonetheless. You couldn't trust them. Let them get into the organisation, start climbing the ladder, invest time and expend energy on them and then they ran off to start popping out babies. And you had to start again. But still, he didn't mind them. Especially when they were as attractive as Denise sitting opposite him. A shapely brunette, her figure-hugging skirt showed off not only her curves but also the outline of her suspenders and stockings. Just for him. He knew that.

He smiled at her over the general raucousness of the rest of them. She returned it. Put her glass provocatively to her lips, swallowed. He watched the liquid make its way down her throat. He knew she was doing it for him and felt himself getting hard at the sight.

God bless those little blue pills, he thought.

She replaced her glass on the table. The cue, he knew, for them to leave. He had been pacing himself all lunch-time. Not

81

overeating, keeping a fairly clear head. All for Denise. He didn't want the experience to be wasted.

He was sure the rest of them knew what was going on. He didn't care. He knew that most of the Young Turks would be jealous, seeing her as one of the perks of the job, a bonus they hadn't yet earned but would always aspire to. The others, the beta males, would just turn a blind eye. It was what they were best at. Banking needed a steady supply of those sorts.

John Wright stood up. 'Gentlemen . . . ' His voice cut through the latest anecdote, stopping the speaker in his tracks. Silence fell. 'As always, it's been a pleasure. Don will take care of the bill. Enjoy the rest of your afternoon.'

They all toasted him and, feeling like a king, he walked away from the table. Denise at his side.

They walked along by the canal.

'Same place as usual?' he said, knowing the answer.

'Of course.'

The Malmaison hotel was just opposite Harvey Nichols at the front of The Mailbox, an upmarket shopping centre that, John Wright thought, had never quite lived up to its potential. Denise threw covetous looks at the items in the Harvey Nicks window displays.

'Looks like you'd rather be shopping in there than spending the afternoon with me,' he said, smiling.

She grinned and grabbed his arm. 'Not at all.'

Liar, he thought, cheerfully.

'They have some beautiful things in there,' he said.

'Then perhaps I could spend my bonus there later.'

'Or perhaps you'd like me to treat you to something, hmm?'

She didn't reply immediately. He knew she wanted to say yes but she knew that perks like that had to be earned.

'You've already treated me to something,' she said eventually, almost whispering into his ear. 'I'm wearing it under my clothes.'

'Good girl,' he said.

He smiled. He loved it when they knew how to play the game.

She stood to one side while he went up to the reception desk and sorted out the room, then accompanied him up to the top floor in the lift. A suite all to themselves. The same suite they always had.

John Wright stepped into the room. The champagne was waiting, on ice, just as he had ordered.

'I'm just going to freshen up,' Denise said and disappeared into the bathroom.

He smiled again, anticipating the sensual, erotic sight that would emerge from the closed door. He opened the champagne, poured two glasses. Not waiting for Denise, he raised his to his lips, downing a little blue pill with it.

He sat on the bed, waiting for it to take effect, and began to remove his clothes. He always started with his socks. He hated the way so many people, especially Englishmen, kept their socks on during sex. Women he had been with on the continent and elsewhere had assured him of that. He now made damn sure it wasn't an accusation that could be levelled at him.

He neatly disrobed, hanging his suit up in the wardrobe. He crossed to the bed, ready to get in, caught sight of himself in the mirror. Saw not a flabby, overweight, middle-aged, balding jowly man. No. He saw a vital, energetic lover. A powerful man. An important man. He smiled. Got into bed.

And there was a knock at the door.

'Oh, for God's sake . . . '

He got up once more, pulled on the white towelling robe that was two sizes too small. They were always two sizes too small.

'Yes?' he said, letting the irritability show. 'We weren't to be disturbed.'

'I'm sorry, Mr Wright,' said a quavering, muffled voice from behind the door, 'and I realise that. But it's urgent. Your wife . . . '

He didn't need to hear any more. He flung open the door.

And stopped dead.

A figure was standing there, dressed from head to foot in black wearing a close-fitting, skull-like gas mask. He was carrying something in his hands.

John Wright was too surprised to call out, to move.

The figure stepped into the room. Sprayed him in the face.

Locked the door behind him.

17

'I'm not sayin' word one. Not word one. Till my brief gets here.'

Moses Heap sat behind the table in Number One Interrogation Room at Birmingham Central on Steelhouse Lane. He seemed angry enough to burst, as if his rage could spill out and illuminate the room with white heat.

Sperring and Khan sat down opposite him, Sperring with a manila folder in front of him and a smug smile in place. Khan was aping his mentor move for move.

'All in good time, Moses. We've sent for him. In the meantime, we just want a chat, that's all. Clear up a few things.'

'I'm not sayin' anythin'. You can try whatever copper tricks you like. I've seen them all. I'm sayin' nothin'.'

Sperring kept his smile in place. He'd dealt with this kind before. Loads of times. Built a whole career on it. The street lawyers. Prison smart-arses. Those that thought they could outsmart a detective, thought they were cleverer than the person doing the questioning. If that was the case, why were they always in and out of prison? Why was he, the stupid, thick copper, always the one to put them away? Some people, he thought.

'Whatever you say, Moses. We'll wait, DC Khan and I, we'll sit here patiently until your brief arrives. We don't mind. We've got nothing better to do. And then when he gets here we can charge you properly.'

Fear penetrated Moses Heap's mask of anger. 'Charge me? With what?'

Sperring shrugged, folded his arms. Leaned back in his uncomfortable chair. 'We'll wait till your brief gets here. Then you can say word one. And two and three, and all the rest, I shouldn't wonder.'

'What?' said Moses. 'What bullshit charge you got me on now, eh? You're stitchin' me up, an' you know it.'

Sperring shrugged. Khan, taking his cue, kept his features impassive.

'You got nothin' on me, 'cause I ain't done nothin'. An' you know it.'

'Whatever you say, Moses.' Sperring made a big show of checking his watch. 'Taking his time, isn't he?'

Moses's left leg began to vibrate. Up and down, faster and faster, like he couldn't keep it still, like it was readying itself to separate from his body. Sperring said nothing.

'So what's this charge, then? Eh? Come on, I've got a right to know.'

So easy to play, thought Sperring. All of them. All the hard men. Reel him in a little longer, though. Not quite yet. Make him beg first.

'All in good time.' Sperring leaned slowly forward. 'But if I were you, son, I wouldn't go making plans for Christmas. Not this year. Or for the next few, for that matter.'

Fear was ramping up behind Moses's eyes. He looked around the room, eyes darting to all corners, off the walls, the door. Like a captured wild animal thinking of making a desperate bid for freedom.

'You can't do this to me, man. You can't . . . Whatever it is, you got no evidence, nothin' . . . '

86

'We'll see.'

Moses sat silently for a few seconds. Tried to regain his breathing, steady himself. 'Just tell me, man. Tell me.'

'Thought you wanted to wait for your brief, Moses?' Sperring smiling once more as he spoke.

'Just tell me . . . tell me . . . ' His voice loud, desperate.

'Well, if you insist . . . ' Sperring sighed, as if it was costing him a great deal of effort, and opened the manila folder. He looked down at a piece of paper, read from it. 'It says here, Moses, that nearly two years ago you were arrested for threatening behaviour.'

Moses Heap frowned.

'Maybe you don't remember that particular incident,' said Sperring, 'maybe it was one of many back then. This one involved you confronting a rival gang member and threatening him with a crossbow.' He looked up, straight at him. 'That right?'

Moses Heap looked more confused than angry. 'That was years ago. When the gangs had beef. Nothin' more happened.'

'You got let off with a caution.'

'Right. An' the guy I did it with was with me today, chillin' at the studio.' He shrugged. Gave a stuttering laugh. 'So what? That all you got on me? You dragged me in for that?'

Sperring gave a patient smile. 'Not quite. Like I said to you earlier, I believe you're a friend of Letisha Watson.'

His manner changed, became suspicious. 'Used to know her. Not any more.'

'You used to be her pimp.' A statement, not a question.

'You can't make accusations like—'

'Don't fuck me about, Moses. You used to be her pimp. You know it, I know it.'

Moses shrugged, said nothing.

'Cast your mind back to earlier today when I paid you a visit.

Remember what I said? Letisha's ex-boyfriend, the one she had after she left your stable, when you got out of the game.' He made the sign of inverted commas with his fingers. 'He's in hospital now. His new girlfriend – the one he left Letisha for – is dead.'

'You told me that.'

'And their daughter.'

'You told me that, too.'

'Indeed I did, Moses.'

'An' I told you then and I'm tellin' you now. I had nothin' to do with it. An' I was never her pimp.'

Sperring sat back. Looked at Moses intently.

'You still got your crossbow, Moses?'

He looked between the two detectives, wondered what answer to give. Which would work best for him.

'Have you?'

'Why d'you want to know?'

'Just answer the question.' Khan's first contribution to the conversation.

Moses still didn't know which way to jump.

'I mean, we could find out,' said Sperring. 'Get a warrant, search your place, your crib, as your sort call it, and see what we find.' He leaned forward once more. 'But it's so much easier to ask a straight question and get an honest answer. Do you still have your crossbow?'

Moses sat back in the chair, hitting his back hard. Defeated. 'Yeah, yeah, I do.'

'There you go now, that was easy, wasn't it? And have you used it recently?'

'No.'

'Sure?'

'Yes. What's this got to do with Letisha Watson?'

Sperring smiled once more. Coming in for the kill. He

88

opened his mouth to speak but the words never emerged. The door to the interrogation room was flung open. In walked Glen Looker, seemingly as angry as Moses had previously been.

'Good afternoon, gentlemen. Trampling all over my client's rights once again, I see? Getting him to talk when you know it's against the law once he's asked for his solicitor to be present? What have you got to say for yourselves?'

Sperring felt anger rise within him. If there was one thing he hated more than the scum he had to question it was the professionals who made a living from representing them. He stood up.

'Your client's all yours.'

He slammed the door as he left the room, Khan barely making it out in time to avoid the blow.

18

John Wright opened his eyes. His head pounded from more than just the lunch-time alcohol and rich food. He tried to move. Couldn't. Looked around. He was still in his hotel room but he had been duct-taped to the room's upright wooden desk chair. He scanned the rest of the room: Denise was tied to the plush velvet chair, a gag over her mouth. Her eyes were wide, fear-filled. He recognised the expensive underwear he had bought for her that she was half undressed in, one stocking on, one rolled down. Despite his own rising fear, he noticed that he still had an erection.

Damn those little blue pills, he thought.

'Back with us?' said a muffled voice from behind the mask. 'Good.' The figure moved over to the window, drew the curtains. 'Don't want anyone looking in, do we? Not that they will. Not up here.' He turned back to the room. 'Now. Let's see . . .'

John Wright found his voice. 'If it's – if it's money you want . . .' A voice that was smaller and shakier than he had imagined.

'Money?' The masked figure laughed. 'Always money with you people, isn't it? Your sort. Think that money is the answer to everything. Isn't that right?'

'Well . . .' John Wright tried to shrug, as if the answer was obvious. 'What else is there? Why else would you do this?'

'Why else indeed? What else is there?'

'Quite.' John Wright felt hope rise within him. A small, hard glimmer of hope. He could bargain. He could deal. He had a chance of getting out of this now. 'What else?'

The masked figure leaned in close. 'Justice, Mr Wright. Justice.'

John Wright was confused now. 'Justice? For what?'

'What d'you think?'

Then John Wright understood. 'Oh, I see. Right. I see what you are. What you're doing. You're one of those Anonymous people, aren't you? I get it now. I'm the big bad banker and you're the . . . what? Masked hero? Is that what you think?'

'Yes, Mr Wright. That's exactly what I think.'

The figure turned away from John Wright and began to take out implements from his rucksack. He placed these implements on the desk. Denise's eyes widened when she saw what they were. She tried to scream. The gag stopped her.

John Wright, noticing her reaction and feeling that earlier fear return, tried to crane his neck, see what she was looking at. The figure blocked his view. That just made things worse.

The masked figure finished arranging things, turned back to John Wright. 'Mr Wright, you know what you've done, don't you?'

'I should imagine I've done all manner of evil things to someone like you.'

'Yes you have. Let's not deny it. You work for a bank that has not only laundered drug money but also engineered the crash of several years ago. And you did this . . . why? To make money, of course. For yourself.'

'So?' John Wright felt himself becoming defensive. 'Is it a crime to make money?'

'You work for a bank that short sold mortgage-backed

securities during the mortgage crisis. You knew what was happening and decided to bet on the collapse of sub-prime mortgages as well as shorting mortgage-related securities. You made your company four billion in the process.'

'So what? It's my job.'

'And you were handsomely rewarded. While the rest of the world, the rest of the people in this country, were forced into a life of hardship that even their grandparents hadn't had to endure. All because you wanted to make some money for yourself and your friends.'

John Wright had had enough. His earlier fear was giving way to anger now. 'It's the way the world works. And the sooner you and your naïve, idealist friends accept it the better. Now let me go and we'll say no more about it. Keep me here and I will make you very sorry for this. Very sorry.'

The masked figure walked round the room. 'Were any bankers punished for their actions? Did anyone go to jail? I mean, what you all did was criminal. But did you have to stand up in a court of law and answer for your crimes?'

'Of course not. As I said, that's the way the world works. Now don't be so bloody naïve and let me go.'

'The way the world works. Naïve. Right.' He took out of his bag a laptop, opened it. Showed John Wright the screen. 'Recognise this?'

John Wright stared. 'How did you—'

'Do you recognise this?'

He kept staring at the screen. 'It's . . . it's my account.'

'One of them. One of your off-shore accounts.' He flicked between screens. 'I've got several more here, too. More accounts. All full of your money. All of them.' He put the laptop down on the desk, turned back to John Wright. 'You're very rich, aren't you?'

'Yes. Yes, I am . . . ' He sounded like he was in shock.

'Very rich. And you became very rich by making other people very poor. Didn't you?'

John Wright didn't answer.

'Didn't you?'

'If you . . . if you say so.'

'So what are you going to do about it?'

'What . . . what d'you mean?'

'Well, as I said, no one stood trial for what they had done. You didn't stand trial. And you should have done. Your actions were criminal. And you never ever answered for them.' He leaned in close. 'Until now.'

He turned away from John Wright, picked up something heavy from the desktop. Examined it, hefted it in his hand, turned back to Wright.

'See this?'

He brandished what he was holding in John Wright's face. Wright flinched.

'This is . . . well, you can see what it is. A pair of bolt cutters. I was going to go for secateurs at first. But they would have been too messy. Not to mention too much like hard work. Something you're not used to, eh, John?'

Wright recoiled from the cutters. 'What . . . what are you going to do?'

'Well, as I said, you haven't answered for your crimes. And you should have. I think we're all agreed on that. So now, this is your chance. All you have to do is tell me what you value most. And I let you go.'

Wright waited. Not sure he had heard correctly. 'You . . .let me go?'

'Of course. This is justice, not vengeance. You have a choice. A genuine choice. I give you that choice, you pick one thing or the other. Depending on your answer, on what you pick, you get to go. Free. Now.'

'What's the catch?'

'No catch.'

The masked figure moved a drinks table in front of Wright, put the laptop on it so that Wright could see the screen. Next to the laptop he laid the bolt cutters.

'So here's the question.' The masked figure looked between Wright, Denise and the laptop. 'What do you value most?'

'What?' His voice was wary, sensing a trick.

'It's very simple,' said the masked figure, a note of irritation in his voice. 'What do you value most?'

'In ... this room? The world? What? What d'you mean?'

'In the world. I think we can rule out this woman here. I'm sure she's fine for a few hours of fun, if you can last that long, but she's just a distraction. So it's down to two things. You and your money.'

John Wright said nothing. The masked figure continued.

'You see, you were caught with your fingers in the till. Taking out other people's money and stuffing it into your own pockets. Or rather, your own accounts. And you got away with it. So I ask you again. What's more important? Your money or ... ' He picked up the bolt cutters. 'Your fingers?'

John Wright stared at the cutters. 'This is a joke. This is not real.'

'It's no joke.'

'It's ... it's some kind of prank. You're a ... a student. From some pressure group. You're filming this for YouTube or something.'

'That's a no. To either of those things. This is, as I said, for real. This is happening to you right now. So. What will it be? Fingers or money?'

Wright said nothing.

'This is boring, John. You need some incentive.' The masked figure leaned forward. Hit some keys. 'Watch the screen. See

94

there?' It was filled with rows and rows of numbers. 'That's your accounts. For every second that you take to decide, money is going out of your account. I've set up some random charities to be the beneficiaries. It'll be gone and it won't be coming back. And when it's gone, it's all gone. So come on, John, what'll it be?'

John Wright watched the screen, his eyes wide with horror. He saw everything he had worked for disappear in front of him. He thought hard, mind whirring. He could let the money go. Yes. Do that. He could always make some more. Yes. That's what he would do.

'Oh,' said the masked figure, as if reading his mind, 'I should say something else. I've set this program not only to empty your accounts but to cancel your credit cards too. And lose your personal credit rating. And lots of other lovely things. In short, I've set this up to personally ruin you. Once it's completed its run, there'll be nothing of you left. And it'll make you out to be too much of a financial liability to employ. Anywhere. So what'll it be?'

Wright saw the numbers disappear off the screen, the figure flex the bolt cutters.

'I'm not . . . not going to be intimidated by the likes of you.'

'The clock's ticking.'

The numbers seemed to be disappearing even quicker. Gone and never coming back. He felt his panic increase. If it kept going at the speed it was, he wouldn't be able to replace it. Not as much as would be lost. Not in this lifetime. The numbers speeded up even more.

'Fingers,' he called out. 'Take . . . take my fingers . . .'

He was sure that beneath the mask, the figure smiled. 'That's better.'

He moved over to where Denise was sitting, picked up something from the floor. A pair of her expensive silk and lace panties. Crossed back to Wright, stuffed them hard into his mouth.

'That should stop you screaming.' He picked up the cutters, positioned them round the little finger of Wright's right hand. 'One at a time, I think. Ready? Here we go.'

He brought the blades together.

19

'What the hell do you think you're doing? What are you playing at?'

Phil had just returned to the station and been informed of Sperring's actions. He wasn't happy. He found Sperring angrily entering the incident room and hauled him into his office, trying not to slam the door, not wanting to give the rest of the team any indication of what was happening, how angry he was.

Sperring turned to Phil, squared up to him, matched anger with anger. 'My job. What did you think I was doing?'

'You pull Moses Heap in without consulting me . . . on what? What charge, what suspicion? What have you got?'

'Nadish pulled it together. Heap's got previous. Threatening behaviour with a crossbow. Bit of a coincidence, don't you think?'

'And there's only one crossbow in Birmingham, is that what you're saying?'

'I'm saying,' said Sperring slowly, as if spelling it out for a retarded child, 'that it was too much of a coincidence to miss. We had to talk to him.'

'Yeah, I agree. We did have to talk to him. Maybe it is too much of a coincidence. But we didn't need to pull him into the station to do it, did we? Especially not someone who's had such a public road to Damascus conversion from gangster to good guy.'

Sperring snorted. 'If you believe all that bullshit.'

Phil said nothing, scrutinised his junior officer. 'That's what this is all about, isn't it?' he said, voice dangerously low. 'Once a villain, always a villain, right?'

Sperring shrugged. 'Statistically, yeah. That's right.'

'And you don't believe in the benefit of the doubt?'

'If he can go all Damascan road like you said, let's stick to biblical stuff and say I'm agnostic on that one.'

'And now you've got Glen Looker involved,' said Phil. 'Jesus Christ. Birmingham's biggest ambulance chaser. You know how many lawsuits he's brought against us?'

'Yeah, I do. And you know how many villains are walking around free because of him? Because he's got them out on some fucked-up bullshit technicality? Just shows. That's who Heap calls when he's in trouble. Stick together, that lot.'

Phil's door opened without a knock. Both men stopped talking, turned. DCI Alison Cotter, Phil's immediate superior, entered.

'What the hell is going on?' she said, once the door had slammed behind her. 'I've got a high-profile community leader talking about claims of police harassment and I've got his lawyer, that piece of shit scrote Looker, telling anyone who'll listen that he's going to raise a lawsuit against this department.' She looked between the two men. 'Would either of you care to explain what's going on?'

Neither spoke. Eventually Sperring, throwing razor-tipped glances at Phil, opened his mouth.

'Well—'

'He's got previous, ma'am,' said Phil, before Sperring could say any more. 'I know he's whiter than white now, especially to the media, but there are too many similarities in this case. Too many coincidences. Moses Heap seems to know or be associated with the victims and Darren Richards. And he also has a previous conviction for using a crossbow.'

Phil didn't actually know if it was a conviction or a caution but he had committed himself.

Cotter said nothing, looked once more between the pair of them.

'He didn't want to talk in front of his associates,' said Sperring, 'and we didn't think it a good idea if he did. So he gave us no choice but to bring him in for questioning.'

Cotter took a deep breath. Held it. Eventually she nodded, expelled the held air.

'And the harassment? The brutality?'

'What d'you think?' said Phil before Sperring could answer.

'I know exactly what I think,' Cotter said. 'And I think I know exactly what's happened.'

'He's got no case at all for harassment or brutality,' said Sperring. 'None whatsoever. And he knows it. He's just talking out of his arse.' Sperring stopped, stared at his superior. 'Ma'am.'

Cotter sighed. 'I suppose you're right. Okay. Leave it with me. I'll go and make penitent noises to Looker and let Heap go. And hope all this blows over.'

'Thank you, ma'am,' said Phil. 'It's appreciated.'

Cotter nodded. 'I don't suppose he confessed, did he?'

'Didn't get that far,' said Sperring.

'Pity. Would have made things a lot easier. Don't worry. We can spin this. A woman and her daughter have been murdered. If Heap wants to make this all about him and be seen as getting in the way of finding the real killer, then we can get very nasty with him. Very nasty.'

'Thank you,' said Phil.

Cotter left the room, closing the door behind her. Neither man spoke.

Eventually, Sperring broke the silence.

'Why'd you do that? Take a bullet for me?'

'What should I have done?' asked Phil. 'Thrown you under the proverbial bus?'

Sperring shrugged. 'What I expected.'

Phil's features were impassive as he spoke. 'We're a team, Ian. You, me, Nadish, Imani. And the rest. A team. And we back each other up. Even if we don't agree with what the other one says or does, we back them up. Right?'

Sperring took his time but eventually nodded. 'Thank you, boss.' He couldn't make eye contact with Phil but he held out his hand to shake.

Phil accepted it. Their hands dropped. They stood there in silence once more. Before either could speak, there was a knock at the door.

'What does she want this time?' said Sperring.

'Come in,' Phil said.

It was Elli, the team's resident tech expert. She was small, Asian and she took full advantage of the licence to dress down that Phil had instigated. In fact, she had been doing it before he arrived there and knew, in her shy but certain way, that she was too valuable to the team to be told off for it.

Today's T-shirt, worn with the usual jeans, boots and assortment of heavy-metal jewellery was a grid of primary-coloured TARDISes arranged in a faux-Andy Warhol style. At least Phil understood this one.

'Boss?' Her voice was hesitant, fearful of interrupting something, but her eyes spoke of urgency.

'Yes, Elli. What can I do for you?'

'He's . . . back.'

'Who?'

'The caller. The one from last night. He's on the line now.'

Phil and Sperring both ran from the room.

100

20

The Lawgiver. That was it. That felt right. The Lawgiver. Because that's what he was. What he did.

He had needed a name. Nemesis had been his first choice. He'd even said that on the phone to the police. But it wasn't right. Overly dramatic. And not quite representative of his calling.

And then he hit on it. As he had worked his way round to the middle finger of John Wright's left hand. When that arrogant banker, a person who thought nothing of bankrupting someone, or a whole company, putting families out on the street if there was profit to be made, was reduced to a screaming, sobbing, pleading, snivelling wretch. He knew what he was. Who he was.

The Lawgiver. That's who he would be from now on.

He had paused, looked down at his work. It was harder than he had expected, cutting off John Wright's fingers and thumbs. Even with the heavy-duty bolt cutter he had brought along. He had built up quite a sweat underneath his gas mask. The bone had proved to be surprisingly resilient.

But he had persevered. He had given Wright his word. Justice not only had to be done but had to be seen to be done. And despite the heat and the exertion, he had enjoyed it. No, more than enjoyed. Filled with an exultant joy, a righteous delight. He had felt all-powerful, a god among mortals. It had confirmed in his mind that this was the right thing to be doing. Making a stand. Fighting back. A champion of the oppressed, the underdog.

He grunted, bringing the bolt cutters together for one final assault.

The little finger snapped right off, fell to the floor.

The Lawgiver stood back, took a deep breath.

'Wow,' he said, looking at his work. 'Hungry now.'

The carpet around the chair was sticky and black with blood. Fingers and thumbs were scattered around like grisly ketchup and tomato relish-covered chips. Wright had long since passed out.

The Lawgiver took out a length of rope and tied it round Wright's wrist. It matched the one he had placed on the other wrist earlier.

'Don't want you bleeding to death now, do we? Fair's fair.'

The Lawgiver checked the laptop, hit a key. The numbers on the screen stopped moving. He peered in closer for a better look.

'Oh dear,' he said to the unconscious figure, 'you don't seem to have much left, I'm afraid. Harder than I thought it would be. Still, you can always start again, can't you? That's what your sort are always telling the rest of us. Get on your bike, and all that. Obviously not in your case. Not now, anyway.'

The Lawgiver began replacing his tools in his bag and saw the woman. Almost did a double take. He had been so involved, absorbed, in his work that he had forgotten she was there. She was curled up in the chair, moaning slightly, eyes tight shut as if she couldn't see him and what he was doing, he wouldn't be able to see her and get any more ideas.

He crossed to her, placed a blood-stained, gloved hand on her chin and turned her face towards him, almost tenderly.

'Hey,' he said, 'hey, I'm still here.'

Eyes remaining closed, she just whimpered.

In front of the half-naked, terrified woman he felt the stirrings of an erection. Power. Righteous, angry power. How sweet.

'Really,' he said, 'I should kill you too. Not because it would give me any pleasure, of course not. But . . . ' He sighed. 'You see, you're as guilty as him. You're complicit. In everything. In time, you might have even become as bad as him. And really, I would be doing the world a favour, getting rid of you. But . . . ' He shrugged. 'You weren't part of the deal. And I'm a man of my word.'

He let her face go, stood up. Stared down at her.

'Take this as a warning. See what happened to him? That'll be your fate if you don't mend your ways. You see? I'm here to help you.'

He turned away from her and surveyed the room once more.

'Oh yes,' he had said once he had finished, 'they're not going to be able to ignore me now.'

He took out his phone. Began dialling.

21

Dinner-time. Joanne Marsh loved dinner-time. Even here it was good. At home she would be eating whatever she wanted. She would buy some stuff and get some stuff off the farm and put it together and cook for her and her dad. And she was good at it, too. She thought so. Her dad never said anything about anything she made, either good or bad, but she liked to do it. Liked to have a man to cook for.

A man. A shiver ran through her. A sad little shiver. Man. She was never going to see her men again, the woman with the big hair had told her. Never. And she was never going to go home again either, that's what she had said. The shiver intensified and she felt herself starting to cry.

There was a noise at the door.

Joanne quickly wiped her eyes. She didn't want them to see her like this. She didn't know who it was going to be but she didn't want them to see her with her face all red and puffy and sad. The men never liked it when she got like that, they weren't interested in her then. And she thought it would be the same in here.

The door opened.

'Here you go, Joanne, dinner.'

She got up and sat at the little desk-cum-table. Looked up. It was the young one, the handsome one. Neat hair and a nice smile. Good body, too; she could see that under his uniform.

Oh yes, she'd been looking. She smiled at him. He returned it.

He likes me, she thought. And kept smiling.

He placed the tray on the table in front of her. Mashed potato, something green and a piece of brown meat with gravy on. A carton of yoghurt and a spoon next to it.

'Why do I have to eat on my own?' she asked.

'You know why, Joanne, they're the rules. Everyone has to eat on their own, in their rooms.'

'But why?'

He smiled again. She could smell his aftershave, he was so close.

'Rules are rules. Got to make sure all the cutlery comes back again, don't we? Don't worry. You'll be out again soon.'

'Right.' He had said that last time she had asked and she still didn't understand it.

He turned to go. 'Hey,' she said. He turned. 'Do you want to stay for a while?'

She started to pull her top down and push her titties together. She leaned forward while she did it, the way her men had told her they liked to see her.

'Come on, Joanne,' he said, still smiling, but his voice now softer, 'eat your dinner, eh?'

'You sure?' She was still pulling at her top.

'You're dancing at the wrong end of the ballroom for me, love.'

He left the room, closing and locking the door behind him.

Joanne left her top alone, felt sad once more. Men always liked her. Always wanted her. She felt good when she had her men, like she was sexy and attractive. And now he'd said something about ballrooms that she didn't understand but knew it wasn't good news. She would just have to get used to living without her men. Forever.

She felt the tears start to come again as she picked up her fork and ate.

Later, the dinner plates taken away and the cutlery accounted for, Joanne was allowed out of her room once more. Except she didn't want to go anywhere. She just sat there on her bed, staring straight ahead.

'Hey,' said a voice.

Joanne looked up. A woman was standing at the doorway to her room, looking in. Young with dark hair and glasses. She was smiling at Joanne.

'Can I come in?'

Joanne was startled. In the short time she had been in the hospital, no one had ever asked to enter her room before. Doctors and staff, the police and that woman with the big hair earlier had just come in. But this woman was asking. That was nice. That was polite.

Joanne nodded and the woman entered.

'What's your name?' asked Joanne.

'Fiona,' said the woman, looking round. There wasn't much to see. The walls and shelves were bare. Joanne had nothing. Fiona sat down on the bed.

'You fairly new here?' asked Fiona.

Joanne nodded once more. 'A few days.'

'Same with me. Not here long.'

'How long you staying? They said I might be here for ever.' Joanne's face fell as she spoke the words. She tried not to cry.

'Oh, I'll not be here long,' said Fiona. 'I'll be out soon.'

'That's good.' Joanne sighed. 'Wish I could come with you.'

Fiona looked at Joanne for what seemed like a long time, her gaze clear and level. 'I know about you,' she said eventually. 'I know why you're here.'

Joanne, fighting back tears, settled for sulking. 'They won't let me see my men.'

Fiona nodded. 'And that's a shame. A real shame.'

Joanne looked up. Frowned.

Fiona continued. 'Your men make you feel good, don't they? They make you feel young and pretty?'

Joanne was amazed. How did she know? She could barely answer. She managed a mumbled yes.

'And they make you feel loved. Most of all, they make you feel loved.'

Joanne, stunned, not trusting herself not to cry, said nothing.

'You give them your body and they make you feel like the most important woman in the world. Is that right?' She didn't wait for a reply, kept talking. 'And that's why you want to keep seeing them. Why you need to keep seeing them. It isn't just the sex, although that's important to you too, it's the way they make you feel. That really, lovely, gooey good feeling inside.'

She turned to Joanne, waited for a reply. Joanne started to cry.

'You . . . you're right . . . yes . . .' Joanna leaned into Fiona, sobbing on her chest.

'I know,' said Fiona, putting her arm round the other woman, 'I know . . .'

They sat like that for a while. Even amongst all the sadness she was feeling, Joanne was so happy to have found a friend.

Fiona spoke. Her voice was small, but strong. 'Joanna, you're never going to see them again. Ever.'

The crying started again. 'I know . . .'

'They're going to keep you in here and you're going to be alone for the rest of your life.'

More sobbing from Joanne, harder this time.

'You're never going to feel loved again.'

Joanne's heart broke. She sobbed and sobbed and sobbed.

Eventually, she didn't know how much time had passed, the tears burned themselves out. She sat there, curled into Fiona.

'How do you feel?' asked Fiona quietly.

'Like I wish I was dead.'

Fiona nodded as if she understood and drew from a pocket in her skirt a dinner knife. She handed it to Joanne. 'This'll do the trick,' she said.

Joanne stared at it. The light caught the blade. It had been sharpened much more than when they were given them to eat with.

'Joanne.' Fiona held both her hands, looked straight into her eyes. 'They're never going to let you out. You're never going to see your men again. This way, you'll find peace.' She smiled. 'Be brave. I know you can.'

Fiona stood up, left the room.

Joanne stared after her, watching her go.

Then turned her attention back to the knife.

22

The incident room was silent when Phil entered. The whole room concentrated, waiting to see what happened when Phil picked up the phone.

He did so.

'DI Brennan,' he said, voice as bland and non-committal as possible.

'You know who this is.' The voice was muffled, familiar.

'Right,' said Phil. 'What can I do for you?'

He noticed Elli go to her desk and begin punching keys. She was trying to trace the call. She looked over at Phil, nodded. *Keep him talking*, the gesture meant.

Something that Phil decided was a laugh came down the line. 'What can you do for me?' An edge of anger to the voice now. 'You can start by taking me seriously.'

'And why wouldn't we?' said Phil. 'Why wouldn't we take you seriously? You've already killed two people.'

'No,' said the voice. 'Not true. I didn't kill them. They allowed themselves to be killed.'

'How? How d'you mean? Didn't you kill them?'

An exasperated sigh. 'You're not listening, are you? You're hearing what I'm saying but you're not listening. They were responsible for their own deaths. The choices they made in their lives led to their deaths. I had nothing to do with it.'

'So that little baby, Shannon,' said Phil, 'she was responsible for her own death too?'

Only the rasping sound of laboured, heavy breathing down the line. Phil waited.

'Collateral damage,' the voice said. 'It was unfortunate but it would have happened to her sooner or later. And besides, it had to be her. It had to be her when he was given the choice. It had to mean something to him. It was useless if it didn't. He wouldn't learn.'

'Who wouldn't? Darren Richards?'

'Justice. That's what it's about. What it's all about. Justice.'

Phil glanced over to Elli. She made another 'keep him talking' gesture with her left hand, the other hand playing over the keyboard, eyes on the screen.

'So you gave Darren Richards a choice. Is that right? That what you're saying? What was his choice?'

The voice sighed. 'Come on, Phil, you're supposed to be an intelligent man. Work it out.'

'Justice. Is that what you mean?'

'He should have been punished for what he did. He killed a woman and her child.'

'Right.' Phil nodded. 'So you killed his girlfriend and daughter.'

'No, no, that's not right. He had to be punished. He had to choose. I just gave him the choice.'

'So . . . what? You gave him the choice of his girlfriend and daughter or his own life, is that it?'

'Now you're getting it.' The voice sounded proud. 'Justice. You see?'

Questions swirled round Phil's head. So much he wanted to know, to ask. Try to trip him up, reveal himself. Or even just keep him talking. Let him betray himself. He rejected several questions before deciding on the next one.

'Why Darren Richards, though?' he asked. 'Surely there are more important people than him.'

'Oh,' said the voice, 'so you think some people are more important than others? Is that right? That your idea of justice?'

'I didn't say that.' Phil kept his voice calm, tried not to lose him. 'I just asked you a question. What I meant was, there have been bigger crimes committed and gone unpunished. Why single out him?'

'As a calling card.' He could barely keep the pride out of his voice.

Phil felt dread within him. 'So you intend to keep going?'

'Oh yes. That was just the first.'

'Right.' Phil decided to change tack. 'Why me? Why did you want to talk to me in particular?'

The voice laughed. 'Lots of reasons. The main one being I know you.'

Phil's stomach flipped. 'Know me? From where?'

'Oh . . . around.' Then quickly: 'The TV mainly. Saw you on TV.'

'Right.' Phil wasn't so sure. Had he almost given himself away? 'So what do I call you, then? Have you got a name?'

There was a pause. For dramatic effect it seemed like, thought Phil.

'You can call me . . . The Lawgiver.'

Phil was aware of Sperring shaking his head and muttering, a wry smile on his face.

'The Lawgiver. Right. Okay. But—'

Phil didn't get a chance to finish. The voice interrupted. 'Oh, but look at me. I've been on the phone for ages nattering away and I haven't even got round to telling you why I called.'

'Why did you call?'

'Well, pleasant though it has been to catch up, I just wanted to tell you that I've done some more justice dispensing.'

Phil felt the whole room make a collective intake of breath.

'Where?' asked Phil.

'Well, I suppose you're trying to trace this call. I mean, I would, if I were you. So I'll save you the trouble. Come to the Malmaison. Room 702. Bring the paramedics. You'll need them.'

He rang off.

The room exploded into action.

23

Letisha Watson stared at the wall. She had put on the TV, but couldn't look at it. Didn't have the energy, the urge. She didn't even have the energy to go the kitchen, make herself something to eat. Not that there was anything in there worth eating. Not that there was anything in there. She had no hunger, just an empty, twisting gnawing inside her guts. She sat in her armchair, ignoring the TV, watching the sky darken, the day give way to night.

It was always faster in the films and on TV. There'd be a shot of a building, like a tower block, like the one she was in now, and the sky would rush across, clouds speeding away over the horizon, changing colour as they went, turning red then grey then black. Then the black would start to change, give way to pinks and greys, then day once more. Over in a few seconds. At least that was the view from outside. From inside, sitting there watching, it was a completely different story. Time dragged. And the more she watched it, the slower it went. Like it was doing it deliberately, trying to spite her.

The visit from the police had shaken her. She didn't mind admitting it, at least to herself. Not because she was worried that they would think she'd done that skank in, not really. Although if they wanted to they could bend the facts to make it fit for her. Put her in the frame for it. She'd seen them do that plenty of times to her mates, knew what they were capable of.

No. It wasn't that. It was because of the way that older one had been with her. He'd gone into her bedroom. She knew it. And she saw what he'd been doing. Hadn't even tried to hide it. Left her phone on the bed, open at the screen he'd been looking at. Like a challenge, a taunt. One name illuminated: Moses Heap.

It was like they knew. *They knew.* He had said as much. Sperring, wasn't it? The old one. And she had to deal with that. Head it off before it spiralled out of control. Before it became too big for her to deal with on her own.

And then there was Darren. She had liked Darren, maybe even loved him. She didn't tell people that she loved them often. She had done that when she was younger and the boys she'd said it to just seemed to use it as an excuse to treat her like shit. Like they didn't have to try any more, they had her where they wanted her. That was why she had started turning tricks. Why not? At least she got paid for it. Well, that was one of the reasons. Not the only one.

But Darren. He had seemed a bit different, a bit ... special. Not like the others. But he was, in the end. He had shown it by getting that slag pregnant and leaving her for her. Doing the right thing, he had called it. Being responsible. And yes, she had got that bitch one night and tried to teach her a lesson. And look how that had ended up. So she had let him go. Goodbye, good riddance, and all that. And she told herself she was over him.

But that didn't mean she had wanted what had happened to Darren and his skank and kid to have happened. Jesus Christ, no.

And now this. The police round. Again.

She looked around the flat once more. The TV was pumping out something that she didn't recognise as life. Not real life, not hers. That programme set in olden days where the posh

114

people are really nice and a bit odd and their servants, the common people, had to bow and curtsey and make sure their bosses' lives ran smoothly. Like doing that was the most important thing in their own lives. Like their own lives were worth nothing.

Nothing.

Maybe these people weren't so different to her after all.

She sighed, lit up another cigarette. Tried to tell herself that she had to do something, anything, that would make things better. For herself. For—

A knock on the door.

Letisha jumped, knocking her ashtray from the arm of the chair onto the carpet.

'Shit.'

She looked down. From the state of the carpet it wasn't the first time she had done that.

Another knock. Harder this time, insistent, not wanting to be ignored.

Letisha sighed. Got slowly to her feet. She felt like her body wouldn't respond to the commands her brain gave it, or didn't want to. And even when the signal got through it seemed her joints wouldn't work properly. Like she was old and damaged.

Another knock; this time accompanied by a voice. Harsh, threatening.

A sudden shiver hit Letisha like she'd been struck by lightning. She knew who it was. And what it meant.

Slowly, she got to her feet. She glanced at the ashtray, thought of tidying it up, realised that she didn't have any time. She had to answer the door. She looked around the living room. Living room. That was a joke too. It was filthy, not fit for receiving guests. Or at least this guest.

She walked to the door.

'Yeah, I'm comin' ... '

She opened it.

There stood one of the most handsome, best-dressed, sweetest smelling men she had ever seen in her life. He made her, with her bad clothes, her fag breath and her lack of a shower for a couple of days, feel like nothing. He was so perfect he always made her feel like nothing. Her heart skipped a beat. Then, for good measure, another.

He spoke.

'We've got to talk.'

'Yes,' she said.

'Can I come in?'

'It's . . . a bit of a tip.'

He smiled. And the night was illuminated.

'That's okay.'

She stood to one side and allowed Moses Heap into her flat. She closed the door behind them.

24

'Jesus Christ . . . '

The door to room 702 was flung open by one of the receptionists with a keycard. Phil then physically restrained her so she couldn't step into the room.

'You don't want to go in there,' he said. 'Crime scene. We'll take it from here, thank you.'

The young woman was relieved not to go any further. What she had glimpsed was enough.

The paramedics were next in.

'This is a crime scene,' shouted Phil, 'please be careful, people . . . '

He wasn't ignored, but no one paid him any heed. They all knew it was a crime scene. But from the state of the two people in the room, saving lives took precedence.

Phil watched from the doorway. Then, when he'd seen enough, turned and looked up and down the corridor.

'He's been here,' he said to Sperring. 'He called from here. He might still be around. Get onto management. Check the CCTV. Look for him. Look for anyone coming out of this room. He's given himself away this time. He has to.'

Sperring hurried off down the corridor.

Phil had already given orders to Khan as they entered the building. 'Nadish, get entrances and exits blocked. Pull in as many uniforms as you can to help. No one goes in or out. He can't have gone far, we need to catch him.'

Nadish had stayed where he was, began coordinating.

Now, Phil risked another look inside the room.

The paramedics had wasted no time in cutting the seated man free from his chair and attaching tourniquets to his wrists. The floor around him attested to how much blood he had lost. The carpet was thick with it; the paramedics' booted feet squelching it out of the weave with every move and step they took. Won't get much evidence from that now, thought Phil.

Also on the floor were what Phil realised were the man's fingers and thumbs. One of the paramedics was calling for ice to store them in but Phil doubted they would be able to do anything with them.

The half-dressed woman on the seat next to him looked physically unharmed but seemed in deep shock. Her expression told that she had witnessed things no one should ever see.

Phil moved out of the way as the paramedics stretchered the man and rolled him out of the room.

'Any ID on him?' asked Phil as they pushed him past.

'Sorry, mate,' said one of them. 'We'll have to look later.'

They went past him and down the hall.

Phil surveyed the room once more. He couldn't imagine what pain the man had gone though, couldn't begin to contemplate why this person had done what he had done. Justice dispensing, he had called it. Looking at the carnage he had left, Phil wondered what kind of justice this was.

He turned away, walked down the corridor. As he went, he took his phone out, made a call to Marina. Got her voicemail. He left a message, telling her he wasn't going to be back home any time soon but that he still loved her.

25

'How you feeling?' DC Imani Oliver saw Darren Richards' eyes flutter open.

'Dunno,' he said, looking round, realising where he was once more. Trying to lift his hand, finding the tubes restraining him, quelling his rising panic by looking at Imani's calm features.

'You've been through a lot,' she said, 'just rest.'

'Do you . . . are you here to ask me more questions?'

'When you're feeling up to it. Not before. The more we know about what happened to you, the better our chances of catching the person who did it.'

Darren nodded. 'Yeah,' he said. He lay back on the bed, stared at the ceiling.

Imani waited.

'Have . . . have you heard anythin'?'

'Not yet,' said Imani. 'We're hoping to have some news soon, though.'

Darren nodded again. 'You're nice, you are.'

Imani smiled. 'Thank you.'

'Not like other coppers. Treat me like shit, they do.'

'Well, you're a victim here, Darren.' She leaned over, took his hand. 'If you can think of anything, anything more at all that'll help, please say it.'

'Yeah,' he said, then seemed to fall back into a state of pre-sleep. Imani kept hold of his hand. Suddenly his eyes jerked open.

'You okay?'

'Yeah. Remembered. He said it was justice, that's what it was. Justice. That's why he had me there. He wanted me to suffer for what I've done.' Tears crept into Darren's eyes.

'Suffer, is that what he said?'

'He said . . . I had a choice. Between me an' . . . an' . . . ' The tears started in earnest now.

Imani waited until he had cried himself out. 'So,' she said eventually, her voice soft, solicitous, 'he killed Chloe and Shannon to make you suffer? Is that it?'

Darren, his eyes averted from her and unreadable, nodded.

'That's terrible,' she said.

'Yeah,' said Darren.

'Why did he say you needed punishing, Darren? Did he tell you?'

''Cause of . . . of what I did. When I nicked that car.'

'You killed a mother and daughter.'

Darren nodded once more.

'So he killed Chloe and Shannon because you killed a mother and child? Is that it?'

Darren sighed, expelling air so hard it could break chains. 'Yeah.'

'But . . . you didn't do time for that, did you?'

A quick, fox smile flickered across Darren's face. 'Nah. Got off.'

'How?'

'My brief. Found somethin' wrong with the investigation, didn't he? Got me off. Good fella.'

'Right.' Imani still held his hand but it now felt slick and greasy. 'And when you got off, did you not think about what you'd done?' Genuinely interested.

Darren frowned. 'You know, like, when you play, like, *Grand Theft Auto*? Shit like that?' He nodded again, enthused. 'You

120

know when you, like, when you hit people an' they go flyin', an' shit? Yeah? Like that. Boom.' He nodded once more, eyes closed, pleased with himself, like his words would impress her.

'So they were nothing to you, is that what you mean? The people you ran down?'

'Well, yeah.' He shrugged. 'Obviously. Never met them nor nothin'.'

'Don't you feel anything for them? Any remorse for what you did?'

'Ah,' said Darren, his eyes narrowing, voice hardening. 'That was what my brief said I should do. Remorse, an' shit. You're soundin' like him now.'

Imani took a couple of breaths, calmed herself down. 'So he killed Chloe and Shannon to . . . what? Teach you a lesson?'

'Yeah.'

'Because you didn't do time? Or because you didn't show remorse?'

'Both, probably. Got me to make a choice.'

'Choice? What d'you mean?'

'Them or me, wasn't it? Lose them or he'd kill me.'

Imani's stomach turned over. 'So – he gave you the choice. He would either kill you or kill them, is that it?'

'Yeah.' He looked away from her once more. 'Said I had to pay.' His voice small, saying more than he'd intended.

Imani let his hand drop.

'What?' he said. 'I just did what everyone would do. You'd do the same, wouldn't you?'

Imani was saved from answering by her phone. She answered. Phil urging her to get to the Malmaison as quickly as possible.

She stood up. 'I've got to go, Darren.'

'What?' He looked suddenly sad, as if he'd just asked a girl out and been knocked back. 'Where you goin'?'

'Got work to do.' She started to walk away from the bed.

'What about me?'

She stopped, turned. 'What d'you mean, what about you?'

'I thought . . . aren't you supposed to stay with me, or some-thin'? Look after me?'

'I think you're more than capable of looking after yourself, Darren. You chose to live. Now choose to live with what you've done.'

She turned and left the hospital ward.

26

Uniforms had arrived at the Malmaison. Phil gave them orders.

'He's still in here. Got to be. Make this place watertight. He can't just disappear into thin air. Go to it.'

They did.

He took Nadish off door duty and set him to work co-ordinating door-to-doors as well as interviews with anyone else in the hotel, trying to find out what they had seen, if anything.

His phone rang. His first thought was that it was Marina but on checking the display he saw that it was Sperring.

'Come and look at this,' he said.

Phil found his DS in a room on the ground floor, checking video footage.

'What is it?' asked Phil, entering the cramped, sweaty room.

'This, boss,' said Sperring. He sat forward, pointed at the screen.

The man sitting with Sperring paused the footage, rolled it back. Sperring told him to press play.

'Here's our couple,' said Sperring. 'Coming down the hall.' The screen showed the man and woman from the room arm in arm. The man kept trying to fondle and manhandle the woman. The woman was smiling, but even on grainy CCTV Phil could tell that she wasn't enjoying it and only tolerating it. 'Getting a bit amorous here,' said Sperring.

'Well, one of them is,' said Phil.

'And here they are, going into the room.'

The screen showed the door closing, the man with his hand gripping the woman's behind.

'What now?' asked Phil.

'Keep watching,' said Sperring.

He did. Another figure approached the door. Phil's stomach turned over. He knew instinctively who it was. He scrutinised the screen, trying to take in everything about the figure, every detail.

He saw someone wearing what looked like overalls or work clothes and boots with a hoody over the top. Phil felt a thrill run through his body.

'Turn round . . . turn round . . . '

The figure, as if listening to Phil, did so. And Phil's elation dropped. The figure was wearing a gas mask.

'Shit,' said Phil.

As they watched, the masked figure looked up at the camera, gave an elaborate salute.

'Fucker. He knew we'd be watching.' Sperring could barely contain his anger and frustration.

The figure hefted his bag onto his shoulder, knocked on the door. The door was opened. In the figure went.

'Fast forward,' said Phil. 'He must come out.'

'He does,' said Sperring.

The other man fast-forwarded the footage until they watched the same figure step from the room, walk down the hall and away.

Phil sat back. Then, thinking of something, leaned

forward again. 'Stop. Go back,' he said. 'To where he comes out.'

The man obliged. They watched the masked figure leave the room once more.

'Stop,' said Phil. He put his reading glasses on, screwed his eyes up tight. 'Is this the best you can get with the screen?'

The other man said it was.

'Look,' said Phil, pointing. 'There. His feet.'

'What about them?' asked Sperring.

'Different shoes. Or boots. The carpet in that room was thick with blood. He would leave a bloody trail if he just walked out wearing the same boots. He must have taken them off and replaced them. In the room.'

'You think they'll still be there?'

'I doubt it, but it's worth a look. If not, he'll have them in that bag of his. Should make him easier to find, even if he's got out of his gear. Or maybe he's left some DNA behind. Something. Anything.'

'In a hotel room?' said Sperring. 'No shortage of that.'

'We have to try.' Phil sighed. 'Do we know what their names are, this couple?'

'Booked in as John Wright,' said Sperring. 'Don't know if that's his real name or not. No idea about the woman.'

'The hotel should be able to tell us. He'd have booked with a credit card.'

Phil took off his glasses, rubbed his eyes. Before he could speak again, his phone rang. He took it from his pocket, again expecting Marina, and checked the display. The station. He answered.

'Sorry to disturb you,' said Elli, 'but I thought you'd want to take this. It's him.'

Phil's stomach flipped again. 'Put him on.'

He put his hand over the mouthpiece, mouthed the words 'It's him' to Sperring, then heard several clicks as the call was transferred.

'Hello, Phil,' said the same muffled voice. 'You don't mind if I call you Phil, do you? I mean, as we're going to be working together it's only fair that we should call each other by our names, don't you think?'

'So what do I call you, then?'

'I told you. The Lawgiver.'

'Right. The Lawgiver. And . . . and what makes you think we'll be working together?'

'Well, I'm sure you've seen my latest judgement by now. John Wright. Banker. Caught with his hands in the till.' A laugh. 'Can't do that any more, can he?'

Phil was lost for words. He didn't know how to proceed. Whether to humour the caller or go up against him. He tried to keep calm, keep asking questions. Remember his training.

'I presume you're still in the hotel.'

'You presume wrong.'

'Why don't you show yourself, eh? Come and talk and we can get this all sorted out now before it goes any further.'

Another laugh. 'Does anyone ever do that, d'you think? Someone, like your good self, says that and the other person thinks, "Why yes. I'm going to stop what I was doing and hand myself in. Just for a chat, of course. That's all it'll be."' The voice hardened. 'Don't treat me like an idiot. You've seen what I'm capable of. You know what I'm doing. Why I'm doing it. I'm not going to stop. And you'd better be prepared to help me. Or you won't like the consequences.'

'What should—'

'Shut up. Just shut up. Listen. You're going on TV. You're going to tell everyone watching what I've done and why. And you're going to take me seriously.'

126

'And if I don't?'

'You really want to find out? Really? You're on the right side at the moment. The same side as me. But go up against me and you'll become my enemy. And you've seen what I do to my enemies.'

The phone went dead.

Phil just stared at it.

PART THREE:

SCREAMING FOR VENGEANCE

27

Marina hadn't been able to sleep the previous night. At first she thought it was because she was spending her second night in an unfamiliar bed away from home but that hadn't been it. She had missed Phil. She always did. His presence was a comfort, his six-foot frame reassuring for her to reach to, to touch while she slept. But it wasn't the absence of her husband. It was her dreams.

When she had closed her eyes, slipped away, Fiona Welch had been there. Sitting in her room, looking at Marina, smiling. Just as she had been the previous afternoon. Her thoughts dancing behind eyes that held secrets. Terrible, dark secrets. In her dream, Fiona's hair had been different. Darker, curlier. More like her own. And her clothes had been different, too. Less like she had been wearing, more like Marina's own. She didn't say anything in the dream, or nothing that Marina could remember. But she had communicated something. Almost telepathically. Something about Phil wanting a younger woman. About Marina being too old for him, about how she, Fiona, was the one he wanted.

She had woken after that, unable to get back to sleep for ages.

That was when she phoned Phil. Marina felt a pang of guilt at waking him but it was important to speak to him. Having Phil in her life made her able to confront the day-to-day darkness she dealt with. And she knew she was the same to him. It was more than just a marriage. They had both looked into the abyss and had the abyss look into them. It was their mutual love that held the other back from stepping over the edge.

His voice was sleep-bleared when he answered. 'Hello . . .'

'Hey,' she said. 'Sorry about the time.'

She heard a shuffling from the other end of the phone as he checked what the time was. ''S okay.' She heard him rouse himself, sit up. 'Where are you?'

'On the way to Finnister. Something came up.'

'Yeah. I got your voicemail last night. Sorry, I was too tired to reply.'

Marina had phoned Phil to tell him she was staying over at Anni's, contrary to what she had told him earlier. She knew that Eileen, Phil's mother, would be looking after their daughter Josephina so that was one less thing to worry about.

'Sorry,' she said. 'I thought you'd be asleep. I just wanted to let you know what was happening. What you up to?'

'Was just about to get up. Had a late night. There's a . . . oh, you don't need to know.'

'Can I help?' She had desperately wanted to talk to him about her situation but knew his would be just as important too.

'Maybe later. Someone got away from us last night. I've got to get back on that horse. Catch him.'

'You will.'

'Wish I had your confidence.' Silence on the line. 'What's up?'

'Well . . .' Now that she was speaking to him it seemed slightly ridiculous to be bothering him. Then she thought of her dream, the last words of the woman calling herself Fiona Welch. Continued. 'There's a bit of a situation developed here.

You know how Anni and Mickey called me in to give a psychiatric assessment of this patient?'

'Yeah.'

'Well, it's more complicated than that.' She paused, took a deep breath. 'There's a woman here who thinks she's Fiona Welch.'

Phil was suddenly wide awake. 'What? Fiona Welch? You sure?'

'I mean, it's not her. Definitely not her.'

'Not unless she's come back from the dead. I saw her die. Watched her fall to her death.'

'I know. But she's . . . spooky. Uncanny. No one knows where she's from, who she really is. They've looked into her background, found nothing. All they know is that she's persuaded two young men to kill their girlfriends.'

'Jesus.'

Marina stopped talking. Phil sensed there was something more. 'And?'

Another deep breath. 'And the dead women all looked like me, apparently.'

'I . . . ' Phil was lost for words.

'I know. And she claimed to know you as well.'

'Impossible.'

'Yes, I know. And it all sounds so ridiculous when I say it out loud. But then I think about it, about her, and it's not. She gave me the creeps. Seriously.'

'Is that your professional opinion?'

'It's the only opinion I could have. And she said something else. To tell you one word. Justice.'

Silence on the line once more. The electronic static turned to ice.

'Phil?'

'Yeah, I'm here. Justice? That's all?'

'That's all.' Marina sighed. 'Phil . . . '

'What?'

'Am I too old for you?'

'What?'

'Do you want a younger woman?'

'What's – where's this come from?' He tried to laugh off her words.

'Fiona Welch. Sorry, the woman calling herself Fiona Welch. See how easy it is to believe it? She said it. Said you were . . . that I was too old for you.'

'Bullshit. She's just trying to mess with your head, whoever she is. Don't let her.'

Marina felt relieved. She knew it was a stupid thing to say, but the woman's words had upset, unnerved her. 'Thank you.'

'You don't need to thank me. You just need to find out who this woman is.'

'We're working on it. But there's also been a suicide last night. The woman Anni wanted me to profile. That's why I'm still here.'

'Oh, Jesus – doesn't rain but it pours.'

'Tell me about it. I'll get this sorted then come home.'

'Good. Look, don't worry about the Fiona Welch impersonator. She's stuck in Finnister. She can't do any more damage now.'

'I know.'

'But?'

'Yes there was a but. But she makes me feel . . . I don't know.'

'Don't worry about her. Mickey and Anni'll deal with her. They'll find out who she is.'

'I know.'

'Just come home soon. I miss you.'

Marina smiled, felt Phil smiling in return. 'Miss you too.'

'I'll see you later.'

They made their goodbyes and hung up.

Marina was glad she had phoned Phil. She felt better just talking to him. More secure. And yes, the woman who called herself Fiona Welch unnerved her. Scared her, if she was honest. But she had the strength to cope with her.

Or at least she now hoped she did.

She got ready, left for Finnister.

28

Morning had arrived but the sky hadn't got the memo. Dark, storm-rich clouds hung heavy over the East Anglian countryside, hastening day to premature evening, sucking whatever joy could usually be found from the hours, leaving depression in their stead. Imminent bursts threatening to turn the day to monochrome static.

Marina drove back towards Finnister House, not wanting to be stuck in the impending downpour, hoping the clouds wouldn't break until she got there. As she approached, it no longer seemed to be the place it had been the day before, a state-of-the-art secure hospital. It was now a brooding, Gothic pile, a bleak house with more than one madwoman in more than one attic.

Marina had been excused from her university work for a few days. They didn't mind as a rule – the department regarding it as quite prestigious that a member of their staff should be so in demand for consultancy work. A vindication that they had chosen the right person to teach the course.

She parked the Prius. Already the car park was host to police cars and tactical support units. She hurried to the entrance. Anni and Mickey were already there. She had followed them from Colchester. As soon as they saw her approach, they surreptitiously dropped their held hands. Back on duty.

Anni and Mickey were now officially an item. The short, mouthy black girl with the blonde spiky hair and the shaven-headed burly bloke with the warm, intelligent eyes. They had spent a long time dancing around each other, hesitantly trying to get together, each one waiting for the other to make the first move. They were worried it would jeopardise both their working relationship and their friendship but once the relationship had happened their friendship had only gone from strength to strength. They were also stronger colleagues as a result. Relationships between those working on the same team were still officially frowned upon but Mickey and Anni had successfully managed to compartmentalise their official and private lives to the extent that their work was never compromised, so a blind eye had been turned.

Marina couldn't have been happier for them; they were two of her dearest friends and favourite colleagues. But for now they all had work to do.

Anni turned to her as she joined them. 'Good job you changed your mind and stayed over.'

'Like I must have known,' said Marina.

'Spooky,' added Mickey. 'Like working with Derek Acorah.'

Marina looked up at the sky. The air had turned colder, sharper, rain now a loud, angry threat.

'Let's get inside,' she said.

Once they had passed through security they found a woman waiting to greet them. Small, dark hair tied back into a neat ponytail, clothes functional yet stylish. Her expression said that she was a capable woman doing a difficult and demanding job to the best of her abilities. But that today was severely testing her.

'Carol Blakemore,' she said, extending her hand and shaking each of theirs in turn. 'Director of Clinical Care. We didn't have a chance to talk yesterday.'

Marina introduced herself. 'I'm here in an advisory capacity only,' she said. 'I won't be part of the investigation.'

'At the moment,' said Anni, glancing at Marina, then back to Carol Blakemore. 'Are the local force here?'

'They are,' said Carol. 'Been here since first thing this morning. They're handling things well and in these instances it's their jurisdiction but obviously since you were here yesterday we thought you'd want to be informed.'

Anni nodded.

'Can you tell us what happened?' said Mickey.

Carol Blakemore puffed out her cheeks, expelled air as if she was slightly tired of repeating the same words.

'Please,' said Anni, 'I know it's difficult, but we've not heard it before. Just try to tell us as if it's the first time you've said it.'

Carol looked slightly shamefaced. 'Well, as I told the other officers, we unlocked Joanne's room this morning and found ... ' She paused, reliving the experience. 'We found her on the floor. Her wrists ... blood everywhere.'

Anni nodded. 'Can we look at the room yet?'

'Er, yes,' Carol said, as if waking from a particularly unpleasant dream. 'This way.'

She gestured them forwards down a corridor. They retraced the route they had taken the previous day. The hospital now had a wholly different atmosphere. The previous day it had been light, airy. The blond wood and white walls had reflected the sunlight coming in from the glass ceilings, the building busy and bustling with patients and staff. Now it seemed like a desolate, depressing place. The lighting seemed flat and depressing, conspiring with the oppressive overhead clouds to create long shadows, grey walls. The patients had been confined to their rooms, the staff all taken for questioning.

They reached Joanne Marsh's doorway. Access had been blocked by two-colour crime scene tape. On the other side of

138

the threshold, a team of paper-suited SOCOs were working diligently, trying to pick up any clues they could.

Mickey turned to Carol. 'So you unlocked Joanne's room this morning and found her body on the floor.'

'Right.' She was trying not to look in the room again, studying an abstract painting on the far wall. 'I should say, we did everything we could. Everything. Proper procedure was followed at every turn. It always is. I'm a stickler for it.'

'We're not doubting it,' said Anni. 'And it was definitely suicide?'

Carol frowned. 'What d'you mean?'

'Was she alone? Was anyone else with her? Did anyone else have access to her room during the night?'

'Well, the staff, obviously. But yes, she was alone. And when it was lights-out last night the room was checked. She was in there on her own. No one else.'

Anni nodded. 'What about the knife?'

'The knife?' said Carol. She nodded absently. 'Yes. She had a knife. A dinner knife. We don't know how she got it. We counted them all out last night, as usual, then we counted them all back again. As we do every night. The porter was adamant he took her cutlery from her last night after dinner. Adamant.'

'Okay,' said Anni. 'So you have no idea where she got the knife from?'

'No idea. None at all. We can't understand it. We're looking into it, obviously. Checking back.' She looked shamefaced once again. Her professional reputation on the line.

'Of course,' said Anni. 'Did no one check on her during the night? What would be the procedure there?'

'Just regular checks, nothing out of the ordinary. She wasn't on suicide watch, wasn't considered a particular risk for anything. We'd done a thorough risk assessment on her when she came here, as we would any other patient. She hadn't exhibited any signs. Nothing jumped out at us. Nothing . . . ' She tailed off, disbelieving.

Marina had been silent, listening. 'Carol,' she said, 'did Joanne have any visitors to her room last night? Before the doors were locked.'

'Visitors? I . . . don't know. She had some, probably. Everyone does. They can come and go freely. I've already been asked that. We'll be trying to find out for definite. We'll be cooperating fully.'

'Good. Can I just ask you . . . ?' said Marina again. 'Just an idea. One of her visitors wasn't Fiona Welch, by any chance, was it?' She was aware of Anni and Mickey looking at her.

'Fiona Welch?' Carol nodded. 'Yes, I think she may have been. She's certainly a name that's come up already.' Carol looked between the three of them, concern etched on her features. 'Are you suggesting . . . ?'

'I'm not suggesting anything,' said Marina, 'just asking.'

There was a crack of thunder. Marina jumped.

The storm had broken.

29

Moses opened his eyes. The daylight was grey and weak, filtered through curtains that were also grey and weak, making the morning doubly depressing.

He rolled over, the movement making him feel like he was on a small raft in a large sea. Christ, what had he drunk last night? Smoked, even? His mouth and throat felt like it had been pebble-dashed and sanded, his head like it was a kids' merry-go-round.

He put his arm out. Felt flesh. Warm, soft. Recoiled from the shock. And with the touch, he remembered.

Letisha Watson. Lying there, her back to him, naked, snoring softly.

He lay on his back, coaxed his memory to return. He had gone to see her after his brief had got him released from the law. *His brief. The law.* The words sent his mind off at a tangent.

He had hated himself for the way he had behaved, both in the studio and in the police station. Like some angry street gangsta. But that was how they made him feel. As soon as the police questioned him he became aggressive, antagonistic. Like the years of education and cultural achievement just fell away and his diction, his attitude regressed to what he used to be. It shamed him to behave that way but he couldn't help it. It was a conditioned reaction, his background kicking in once more, turning him into that frightened little kid with a problem with authority. He knew that no matter how far he went from the street, the street would always be in him. A part of him would always be held down, held back. And that was a painful admission for him to make.

He tried to clear his mind of those thoughts, concentrate instead on why he was where he was.

He had needed to talk to Letisha. And they had. Talked. But it hadn't been about what he had intended it to be about. It had been talk that had led them to the bedroom. To here. Now.

He moved his head, slowly this time, looked at the woman. He loved her skin. Had always loved her skin. The soft, smooth, delicate feel of it beneath his fingers as he had stroked and caressed her. And he knew she liked him doing that. Had said so. *You're not just some wham-bam merchant, are you?* she had said once when they were in another room, another time. *Nah, I ain't,* he had replied. *Got to take it slow with beauty. Treat beauty right an' beauty will reward you.* He'd used that line before. But it hadn't been a line with her. He had meant it. At the time. She had laughed then. *Oh, you think so, do you?* But she had rewarded him. And then some.

And now this. Again. Last night. Her skin not quite as soft as it used to be. A little rough in places, hard edged. A little too soft in others. But it was still her. And he was still him. Maybe not the person he used to be, maybe not any more. Maybe just a version of himself. But one she still recognised.

But she still had beauty. Inside and out. When the pain and the strain dropped away from her he had seen it. And he had responded to it. Over and over again. A need in her meeting a need in him. They knew there would be consequences but they both had enough alcohol and weed in their systems to ensure they didn't care about them then. And wouldn't till later. Much later.

Like now. Moses looked around the room. He had missed

the squalor the night before in his rush to get with Letisha. But now he took it in. A small mountain range of soiled laundry on the floor. The bed sheets filthy and stained. Dust almost the thickness of the carpet pile. The naked bulb overhead, like an interrogation room or a prison cell. And the token curtains at the window. Too thin to hold anything in or keep anything out.

He looked again at her skin. Saw now that it didn't hold the usual sweet, coffee tones that he loved. It had been muted by the room's dead light to a zombie grey.

He shook his head. Slowly. What rooms like this – lives like this – did to beauty. That old familiar burning sensation welled up inside him: depression and anger, but no longer in equal measures.

He threw back the onion-skin-thin sheet and tried to rise to his feet. The room became volatile and liquid and he felt nauseous once more. He lay back down again.

He had to leave. Before Letisha woke up. The postponed shame of the night's action was beginning to get a grip on him. And there was something else along with it, something equally familiar: fear. He had to leave.

He tried once again to get up, managed it this time. He stood on his feet, naked, finding his balance, and looked down at Letisha. She really was beautiful. The scars her life had left couldn't hide that. Not completely. He hoped they never would. But he was a realist. He knew better. He'd seen it happen too many times before. It was what happened. It was life.

She stirred, looked up at him. Smiled. And that smile belonged to a totally different room, a different girl in a different life.

He knew she was taking in his body. Knew she liked what she saw. His body was his diary, the map of his life. Every fight he had ever been in, every mark, every scar, every knife wound, it was all there. The patchwork man.

He used to be proud of his body when he was younger, when he was gangsta. It was his calling card. Showed his street value. But when he turned away from all that he grew ashamed of it. Now, he had tried to make peace with it. It was what it was. And he had to live with it.

But Letisha was the only woman who had ever looked at him and loved him for it. Not because it made him seem street-hard, there had been plenty who got their kicks from that. No. Because she understood pain. She understood healing. And he had never felt more naked with her, more vulnerable.

More alive.

'Morning, handsome,' she said.

Her voice was low, smoke-husky. He liked it.

'Morning, gorgeous,' he said in reply and almost instantly regretted it.

Their old greetings. Call and response from a gig that had long since finished.

She giggled. Happy to hear the words.

Letisha lay on her back, exposing her body to him. 'You getting back into bed?'

He was tempted. So very tempted. He had never been able to resist her. Even now, even here. Even after everything that had happened. But he had to. *Had to.*

'Nah, I got . . . got to go. Things to do.'

Disappointment crept into her eyes. And hurt.

'Sorry, babe,' he said. 'Got to.' His voice sounded small, the words weak and unconvincing.

She sat up. Her small, perfect breasts drawing his eyes. He felt himself getting an erection, began searching for his clothes.

'Stay,' she said. 'Please.'

'Can't, babe,' he said, making a point of not looking at her. He located one sock, another. Began putting them on. 'Got to go. Busy day.'

She got up, stood in front of him. Completely uninhibited about her naked body. She placed her hand on his chest. Fingers tracing scars. 'Come on, baby,' she said, 'don't be like that. You came to see me last night. And it was . . . ' She shook her head, smiling at the memory. 'Brilliant. Best night I've had in years.' Her hand began moving over his chest. 'Don't make it just a one-off. Please.'

He wrenched his body away from her, pulled on his T-shirt. Shook his head.

'Moses . . . '

His clothes were all there. He sped up, dressed as quick as he could, ignoring the nausea, the headache.

'Please, just . . . just wait. Spend the day with me. Just the day. Please.'

He was fully dressed now. He turned to her.

'I can't.'

'You can.'

'No. You know. We can't.' Fear was back in his eyes. He couldn't hide it from her. Had never been able to hide anything from her.

'Please . . . '

'We shouldn't.'

Letisha grabbed on to him, digging her fingers into his skin. 'Which one is it?'

'What d'you mean?'

'Which one? Can't or shouldn't?'

'There's no difference.'

'Moses, there's a huge difference. One means never, the other means . . . '

She couldn't finish.

'Means what?' He asked the question despite not wanting to hear the answer.

'Hope,' she said.

'I've got to go.' He sighed. 'It was a bad idea. I shouldn't have come around last night. It was ... more than just, just what happened. You know that.'

She smiled. It was tinged with his fear, her sadness. 'I'm glad you did.'

'Just ... ' He didn't know what to say. Just as there was a difference between can't and shouldn't, there was an even bigger difference between what he wanted to say and what he had to say.

'I'll see you. Remember what I said last night. Remember.'

He couldn't reach the door quick enough.

His head was upset, his stomach was upset, his heart was upset.

He didn't know which one hurt the most.

He was lying to himself. He did.

30

'Careful,' Anni said to Marina when Carol Blakemore was out of earshot, 'you don't want to put ideas into her head. And you don't want to look like you're a bit obsessed.'

'I'm not obsessed,' Marina replied, a little too snappily. 'It's just . . . an obvious question.' She looked between the pair of them. 'Isn't it? I mean, after yesterday, talking to her? And what she's in here for? Isn't it?'

'Suppose so,' said Mickey.

'But we have to explore all avenues,' said Anni with a glint in her eye. 'I was taught that. By the best.'

'Absolutely right,' said Marina, using a smile to break the tension.

Carol Blakemore returned to them. She had with her a small, compact, neatly dressed Asian man. He looked like he enjoyed the fastidiousness of detail. She turned to him. 'This is—'

'Hello, Deepak,' said Mickey.

Carol Blakemore looked slightly put out. 'You two know each other?'

'We've . . . worked together before,' said Mickey.

Deepak shook hands with Marina. 'Detective Sergeant Shah.'

'Marina Esposito. Criminal psychologist.'

Deepak's eyes narrowed. 'Marina . . . '

'Yes, it's her,' said Anni.

Deepak Shah had worked on in a case with Anni and Mickey a couple of years previously involving the kidnapping of Marina and Phil's daughter plus the murder of Phil's adoptive father.

'Right,' he said. 'Got back on the horse.'

'So it seems,' said Marina.

'What can you tell us?' asked Anni.

'Probably nothing more than you've already been told by Professor Blakemore, I should imagine,' Deepak said. He took out his notepad, referred to his immaculately written notes. 'Joanne Marsh was found dead in her room at approximately seven thirty this morning. There was no one else present and the wounds, to both wrists, look to be consistent with self-inflicted injuries. Foul play not suspected.' He snapped his notepad closed. 'Suicide, I'd say.'

'She was risk assessed and we had no indication,' said Carol Blakemore. 'None at all.'

'No,' said Marina. 'I didn't get that from her either when I questioned her yesterday.' She turned to Deepak. 'Is there a list of people who were inside her room last night?'

'It's being compiled. Obviously we're checking everything and questioning everyone. What are you thinking?'

'That if it wasn't in her room and it wasn't reported missing, someone must have given her the knife.'

'That's what we think too,' said Deepak. 'We're looking into it.'

'And . . . ' Marina looked between the rest of them, hesitating before speaking. 'I'm just throwing this out there, but maybe someone put the idea into her head?'

'She was very suggestive,' said Carol Blakemore, grasping at anything that could diminish the burden of her responsibility.

'Putting it mildly,' said Marina. 'What does everyone think?'

148

'You mean Fiona Welch,' said Anni.

Marina felt herself reddening. Saw her dream once more. Even talking to Phil couldn't entirely reassure her. 'The woman who calls herself Fiona Welch, let's not forget. It's a possibility. I mean, that's what she's here for. By her own admittance.'

Anni turned to Deepak. 'Would you like us to question her? We were here yesterday to see her too.'

Deepak shrugged. 'Don't see why not. There's clearly some overlap here. Be my guest. Just keep me in the loop.'

'No problem,' said Anni.

'You in charge of this, then?' asked Mickey.

'I am. Got promoted.'

'Congratulations,' said Mickey. He looked around. 'DS James not here?'

Deepak gave a small, sad smile. 'Sorry. I'm afraid Jessie, DS James, has left the force.'

'Oh. Shame,' said Mickey.

Marina could see him turning red. She could also see the filthy looks Anni was giving him.

'Retrained as a sports psychologist, I believe,' said Deepak.

'Well, good luck to her. Send her my regards. If, you know, you see her.'

'I will.'

Anni almost jumped in between the two men. 'Shall we get going? Work to do.'

'Sorry,' said Deepak, sensing the atmosphere and surmising what it was about, 'I'll let you get on. Good to see you both.' He turned to Marina. 'Glad to see you're safe and sound.'

'Thank you.' He turned, walked back down the corridor.

'You want to talk to Fiona Welch?' asked Carol Blakemore. 'Sorry. The woman who calls herself Fiona Welch. This way.'

She headed off in the other direction. Marina followed. Behind her, she could hear Mickey and Anni arguing.

'Send my regards.' said Anni, her voice low, the words twisted and unpleasant.

'I was just being polite,' said Mickey.

'Yeah, I know exactly what you were being. Just you wait. Just you wait till later . . . '

Marina smiled to herself. Kept walking.

31

'He calls himself the Lawgiver,' Phil said, eyes roving the incident room, hoping to catch the attention of all gathered there, focus them fully on the investigation. 'This much we know.'

The team had been called for a breakfast meeting, usual procedure when they were investigating a high-grade case. And this case had now been classified as such: the discovery of the fingerless banker had ensured it. The team were unkempt and red-eyed, as if rest and peace were concepts only other people ever enjoyed.

Phil himself had barely had any sleep and Marina's early-morning call hadn't helped. Not that he minded when she had told him what was troubling her. He wished he could be more help to her but at the moment, his own work took precedence.

Reluctantly, he put Marina to the back of his mind. Focused. He had his take-away cup of coffee on the desk next to him. He had bought it from outside, knowing from experience not to trust the stuff in the department. He gave another look round the room, wondered how many briefings had been conducted here. How many echoes the bare brick and wood panelled walls had heard, how many ghosts of cases they held. Couldn't think about that now. He had work to do.

'The victim's name is John Wright.' Phil looked at the murder wall behind them. It showed photos of victims and locations along with details of the case so far. Lines connected faces like a gruesome, grim game of snakes and ladders.

A photo of John Wright as he was had been stuck to the wall. Phil gestured at it, continued. 'A banker. With all that that entails.'

A few boos and profanities broke out.

'Nevertheless,' Phil went on, 'he didn't deserve what happened to him.'

'*Probably* didn't,' someone – Phil couldn't tell who – muttered. Someone else laughed. Phil ignored them.

'And we have to catch who did it. John Wright had apparently been addressing a business group then lunching with them at a restaurant in Brindleyplace. Then he went back to the Malmaison with,' Phil checked his notes, 'Denise Nettleworth. Not his wife. I think we can guess what he intended. But unfortunately for him, it didn't happen. The Lawgiver got there first. Because of Wright's dealings, the Lawgiver' – Phil still felt faintly ridiculous saying that – 'stupid name, decided he was a legitimate target for his crusade. It seems like he gave him a choice. Lose his money or his fingers. He chose his fingers.'

'Typical banker,' said Sperring, contempt mingling with dark mirth.

'Denise Nettleworth provided us with that information. She's in a bad state of shock, but we managed to get something out of her. Apparently, the Lawgiver,' Phil took a breath, 'set up a laptop with Wright's accounts on it. As he took off his fingers and thumbs the balances went down. It looks like he lost quite a bit of money. Maybe he found it harder work than he thought he would.'

'Or maybe he couldn't face letting him keep the money,' said Imani.

'Good point,' said Phil. 'Our villain is driven by anger. If Wright were to walk away financially intact, even if he had lost his fingers, then he felt like he wouldn't have gained anything. I'm surmising here, but it's an educated guess.'

'He gave the same choice to Darren Richards,' said Imani. 'Because a mother and child had been killed and he'd gone unpunished, he gave Richards the choice of dying himself or having his girlfriend and daughter die. He chose them.'

Gasps and profanities went round the room.

'And he's admitted this?' asked Phil.

'Yeah,' she said. 'Then wondered why I wasn't sympathetic.'

'Lovely,' said Phil. 'So. He picks his targets well. Researches them, plans what to do, finds a kind of justice that he thinks is appropriate or poetic or whatever. Then goes through with it. In his mind, he thinks he's a hero, the people's champion, something like that. We have to disabuse him of that notion.' He turned to DC Khan. 'Nadish, what you got?'

Khan checked his notes. 'Nothing much yet. I've been coordinating the door-to-doors on the first killing. The building was derelict, half demolished. Most of them up the street are in the same state. The area's been tarted up a bit but it hasn't reached that spot yet.'

'Probably why it was chosen,' said Phil.

'There's a Sikh temple nearby but there wasn't anyone about to talk to. I'll go back. There's a few little houses and small businesses around there. Some of the people in the houses weren't in so I'm going to check back at different times when they might be there. Long shot, but . . . ' He shrugged. 'You know.'

'That's what we do,' said Phil. 'Be thorough. Good work, though. So we know that he deliberately chose the first location because it's out of the way. No other reason that we can find. He must have checked the place out, recced it. He's thorough, he'll have done it more than once. He'll have checked entrances and exits. Someone must have seen him. At some time. How did he get the three of them there? He must have used a vehicle of some sort. Found a way on to the site. Keep checking, Nadish.'

Khan nodded solemnly.

'Also check with the company contracted to demolish the building. See if there's anyone on their staff who stands out. Any names or behaviour that rings any bells. Do a bit of cross-referencing with local criminals in the area who've come out of prison. Elli'll show you how if you need it.'

Khan looked slightly less pleased at that. He was only a young man but, as Phil had had cause to upbraid him on at times, his views and attitudes could have come from the 1970s. He knew he was Sperring's protégé. He thought it naïve to hope that he was only picking up the positive things.

'SOCOs are still going through both crime scenes,' said Phil. 'They haven't turned up anything from the first one. Clean as a whistle, Jo Howe said. Although personally I've always wondered how clean whistles actually are. All that saliva . . . Anyway. I digress.' He was aware of a few strange looks. A lot of the team still found him odd. Or at least at odds with the rest of them. But he got results. So they respected that. 'Right. The hotel. How's that going?'

'Early days,' said Sperring. 'Only a matter of hours so far. We've gone room to room, asking if anyone saw or heard anything. Nothing. The walls between rooms are quite thick and not all of them were occupied. We kept all the guests and staff on the premises all night. Which obviously everyone was thrilled about. Yardley and Chapman are still down there now, coordinating. But I have to say it doesn't look good. He seems to have just vanished into thin air.'

Thin air, thought Phil. Like a ghost. He looked around the room once more, thought of all the ghosts it held.

I'm not bothered about old ghosts, he thought. It's the current one I want to catch.

32

The woman calling herself Fiona Welch was sitting on her bed in almost the exact same place and the exact same posture as the previous day. She looked up as Anni and Marina entered, smiling. It was a knowing smile, thought Marina, as if she had expected them and was having a bet with herself as to how long they would take to arrive.

'I'm assuming you've been here, what? About an hour?' asked Fiona Welch.

'Something like that,' said Anni. 'Why is that important?'

The smile broke even further. 'I thought you'd have come to see me before now.'

It was Anni's turn to smile. When she spoke her voice was deliberately light, the words offhand and inconsequential. 'Do you think you're that important?'

The smile froze on Fiona Welch's face. Before she could speak, Anni continued. 'Someone is dead and we've got a lot of people to talk to, a lot of people to see. It takes time to get round everyone.'

Anni pulled up a chair and sat down. Marina stayed standing. She looked around the room once more. It was meticulously tidy, scrupulously clean. Marina scrutinised, trying to take in as much as she could from it. A small collection of books on the shelf. All psychology textbooks, kept in good condition. A file propped up next to them labelled 'Case Studies', the writing neat, contained. She kept scanning the room.

Fiona Welch noticed. 'Looking for something?'

Marina opened her mouth to answer her, thought better of it. 'Just looking,' she said. She gestured to the file. 'May I?'

Something passed over Fiona Welch's face. Marina couldn't tell whether it was fear, pride or a mixture of the two.

'Be my guest,' she said.

Marina took the file down, started to read. Anni continued the questioning.

'As I'm sure you're aware,' she said to Fiona Welch, 'Joanne Marsh was found dead this morning.'

'I heard,' she replied.

'Yes. And we're questioning everyone on the ward about their whereabouts last night.'

'And you want to talk to me.'

'We do.'

Fiona Welch smiled once more, as if pleased with the attention. 'What would you like to ask me?'

'Did you talk to Joanne last night?'

'Yes, I did.'

'Where did you talk to her?'

'In her room.'

'What did you talk about?'

She leaned backwards, sticking her arms out, arching her back, as if tired. She sighed. 'It's not important.'

'It might be.'

'I don't think so.' Her voice patronising, speaking to an inferior.

'Tell me. And I'll be the judge.'

'The judge?' Fiona Welch laughed. 'You are the law, after all. You may as well be the judge.'

Anni said nothing.

Fiona Welch finished stretching and leaned forward. 'And if the judge, you'll also become the jury on whatever answer I give.'

'If you say so.'

'And if I give an answer you don't want to hear, or you as the jury doesn't like, will you also be the executioner?'

Anni again didn't respond. Fiona Welch laughed.

'You haven't got that power, have you? You just collect information. Gather things up. That's all you are. A gatherer.'

'Yes,' said Anni, trying to choose her words carefully, 'that's what a detective does. Gathers information. Then when we've gathered that information we make a decision based on it. And if that decision goes the wrong way for the person we've gathered that information on, we charge them. And if the CPS agree, and then the jury agree, they go to prison. As you should know.'

'Oh, indeed I do. I know how the law works.' Her eyes twinkled, lit by a strange light. 'But don't you wish you could do more than just gather? Don't you wish that when you find someone you know is guilty, let's say, but can't actually prove it, don't you wish you could just skip the preliminaries and take decisive action?'

'Be an executioner, you mean?'

'Exactly what I mean.'

Anni sat back, smiling. 'I think we're getting off the subject in hand.'

'Really? I think this is the subject.'

Anni paused, regrouped her thoughts before speaking. Before she could say anything, Marina put down the file she had been reading and turned to Fiona Welch.

'These case studies,' she said, 'is that what you intended Joanne to be?'

'Yes,' said Fiona Welch. 'Exactly.'

'And,' said Marina, 'is that why you went to see her last night?'

'It is.'

'Then,' said Anni, 'why couldn't you say that earlier?'

'Because you never asked that particular question,' said Fiona Welch, her voice patronising once more.

'So she was a case study,' said Anni.

'Yes.'

'What kind? What were you studying her for?'

'I'm interested in deviant psychopathology. Especially sexually deviant psychopathology. She's a prime example to study.' She smiled. 'I'm sorry. Was.'

'And did she mention killing herself to you?'

'No. Why should she?'

'What did she say to you, then?'

Fiona Welch, seemingly bored by the question, didn't answer. Instead, she turned her attention towards Marina. 'What do you think?' she asked, her voice no longer patronising, now with pride. 'As one professional to another.'

'Very clever,' said Marina. 'Very good.'

Fiona Welch couldn't help but give out a beaming smile. 'Thank you. I'm glad you see merit in my work.'

'Oh, I didn't say that,' said Marina.

Fiona Welch frowned, wary now. 'What d'you mean?'

'I said your case notes are very clever. Very well done. But I don't believe a word of them.'

'What?' Her voice sharp, anger building.

Marina crossed the room until she was standing right in front of Fiona Welch. 'You've used all the correct jargon, definitely. I should think you got it from those textbooks there. They look barely read. But you've got just enough to give your work a sprinkling of verisimilitude. But just a sprinkling. Because the first and secondary sources in your arguments are weak, amounting to no more than guesswork and anecdotal evidence. When you have quoted other practitioners you seem to have gone out of your way to misinterpret them. And your conclusions are laughable.' She looked down at Fiona Welch. 'Would you like me to go on?'

Fiona Welch just stared at her.

Marina gestured round the room. 'This room,' she said. 'There's nothing here. No evidence of personality. Of individuality. Nothing. Just like the case notes. It's all an act. A clever one at first, but that's as far as it goes.'

Marina stopped talking, waited.

Fiona Welch just stared ahead, her chest rising and falling rapidly, saying nothing. She sat like that for a long time, her eyes simultaneously blank and angry.

'I exist,' she said eventually. 'Existence is identity.'

Marina frowned. She had heard that line before but she couldn't place where.

She didn't have time to dwell on it, because Anni was speaking. 'So why were you in Joanne's room last night? What did you talk to her about?'

'Case. Study.' The words had to fight their way out, as if Fiona Welch was struggling to keep control of herself.

'Case study,' repeated Anni.

'Yes. Case study.'

Fiona Welch sat back and stopped talking.

33

Ghosts, thought Phil. No. The Lawgiver wasn't a ghost. Whatever he was, he was real. 'Which is, of course, impossible,' said Phil. 'So he can't have done. CCTV must have him. Without his mask.'

'We haven't found him yet.'

Hopefully when John Wright comes round he can give us a better description.'

'Denise Nettleworth already did,' said Sperring. 'But don't get your hopes up. It's the same as the last one. Some kind of boilersuit thing, boots, gloves and a gas mask. Could be anyone in there.'

Phil shook his head. 'Okay. But we keep looking. We keep going. CCTV must have him on there somewhere. Somehow. It's just a matter of finding him. He must have disguised himself in some way. He'll have been carrying a bag with his gear in. Look for that.'

'We have been,' said Sperring, the strain showing in his voice, 'but it's a hotel. Everyone's got a bag. And some people aren't too happy about us raking through them without a—'

'Without a warrant, right,' said Phil. 'Too many TV cop shows to blame for that. And of course by the time you've argued with them . . .'

'It's tiring,' said Sperring. 'But we're still doing it.'

'Good. Something should turn up. Somehow.'

Before he could say anything more, DCI Cotter jumped in. 'Phil, I just want to stop you there,' she said.

Phil stopped.

She stood up, took the floor before the team.

'As you're all probably aware, the Lawgiver . . . ' She paused, shook her head. 'Bloody ridiculous name. Just tells you the level of person we're dealing with here.' She continued, the name repeated with heavy sarcasm. 'The Lawgiver has developed something of a connection with DI Brennan. We don't know why. Phil himself doesn't know why. But he has so we have to work with it. He's called here, asking to speak to DI Brennan personally. Built a rapport and become personally involved. It's clear that he's a very disturbed, possibly deranged, individual so we have to tread carefully. If the calls are to continue then obviously a psychologist could be of help to us in this instance, helping us to guide the conversation. I believe that DI Brennan's first choice of psychologist,' she glanced at Phil, a small smile curling the sides of her mouth, 'is unavailable at present. So we'll hang fire on that one.'

'I think we have a fair idea of the personality we're dealing with here,' said Phil.

'Indeed,' said Cotter. 'Deranged and narcissistic. And that's just for starters. As you know, he has asked DI Brennan to appear on TV to make a direct address to him.'

'That's narcissism for you,' said Sperring.

'Quite,' said Cotter. 'Now, usually I wouldn't allow that kind of behaviour. That kind of pandering. But given what he's already perpetrated and the fact that we seem to be no nearer to catching him, this would seem to be an extreme situation.'

She turned to Phil. 'You media trained, Phil?'

He seemed surprised by the question. 'Bit rusty, if I'm honest. I try not to do it if I can help it.'

161

Cotter nodded. Took in his attire. 'And you'll have to smarten yourself up for it.'

Phil inwardly groaned.

She turned back to the room. 'DI Brennan and I already spoke about this before the meeting. He's agreed to talk to the media. And hopefully, directly to the Lawgiver. But obviously everything that he says will be agreed in advance.'

'And can I just say,' said Phil, 'that since this person seems to have developed, or tried to develop, some kind of attachment to me I'm going to be reviewing all my previous arrests to see if anyone might fit the bill for what's happening here.'

'Good,' said Cotter. She scanned the room once more. 'Anything else?'

'Yeah,' said Sperring, sitting forward. 'Moses Heap. I know we got off to a bad start with him but I think he's connected to all this in some way. Want me to keep looking into it?'

Cotter stared at him. Phil knew what his own answer would have been but he didn't have the floor at that moment. Cotter seemed to be mulling over the proposition.

'Discreetly, if you can, Ian. I don't want a repeat of yesterday. If you think he's involved then we have to have cast-iron proof before confronting him. He's a media figure. And he's got that heinous lawyer in tow.'

'Thank you, ma'am.' Sperring smiled to himself.

'Anything else?'

No one spoke.

'Good. I'll hand you back to DI Brennan.'

Cotter resumed her seat. Phil stood up from the corner of the desk he had been perching on. He glanced at his coffee. Cold. He would need another one. He looked at the team. Knew he had to find something to say that would energise them. Concentrate them, motivate them.

'You've all seen how this Lawgiver operates by now. You

162

know what we're dealing with. Someone driven, someone unstable. A self-righteous narcissist who thinks he's on some kind of crusade. But, crucially, one who for all of that is very clever. We can't underestimate him, just dismiss him as some kind of nutter. He's cunning and clever. He hasn't left any DNA or forensic evidence at the crime scenes, or at least none that we've found yet. We don't know what we're dealing with. We don't know who he's going to target next. What we do know is that there will be another target. He's not going to stop. He's just getting started.'

He scanned the faces once more. The team were listening.

'Go through the files. Old cases. Cold cases. Anything. See if anyone or anything sticks out. Cross-reference criminal names with political agitators. He can't have come from nowhere. He must have built up to this. He must be known to us in some way, somehow.'

A final scan of the room.

'Let's find him. Before he claims another victim.'

34

'Well, you must be able to do somethin', man. I mean, they're violatin' me human rights, if nothin' else ...'

Glen Looker stared at his client, face impassive. Jesus, he thought. Never gets any easier. Darren Richards lay in his hospital bed, propped up on pillows, drips still going into his body. The hospital had insisted that he was strong enough to leave but Looker had argued that yes, they may want the bed, and in fact have someone who desperately needs it, but his client had been through a traumatic experience, one so profoundly horrific that most people could only imagine in their most terrible nightmares and he prayed it never happened to them, God forbid, so he needed to be somewhere safe and tranquil where he could rest a while. He wouldn't want to be discharged too soon and have a relapse, would he? And he was sure the hospital didn't want that. A lawsuit could be very costly. The hospital staff had, grudgingly, ceded to his demands.

But now, looking at Darren Richards lying there agitated and angry, expecting everyone to do everything for him, Looker was wondering why he had even bothered arguing.

If you're strong enough to argue, he thought, you're strong enough to leave.

'Violating your human rights. Well, we don't want that, do we?'

'Fuckin' right we don't. I mean, she was sittin' there, right where you are, the black one—'

'Whoa, whoa,' said Glen Looker. 'No racial discrimination. It'll rebound on you.'

'What did I say?'

'Black. You defined her by the colour of her skin.'

'But she is black,' Darren said, incomprehension etched on his features. 'What else am I supposed to call her?'

'DC Oliver. It's her name. You've got to remember these things.'

'Whatever. She's Five-0, ain't she? They're all the same. Anyway, she was talkin' to me, all nice like, an' then I tell her what happened in the warehouse. With Chloe an' Shannon, an' that. And then she starts on me. Walks away eventually, like I'm filth, or somethin'.'

'Darren, you shouldn't have spoken to her without me being here. You should know that by now.'

'Yeah, I know. But I thought this was different, you know. Me bein' the victim this time, an' that.' He sighed, his mouth turned downwards in an almost cartoon parody of a sulk. 'Turns out it's no different. Still treat me like shit, whatever.'

'So let me get this straight,' said Looker. 'You told them that this hooded character offered you a choice.'

'Wasn't hooded. Masked.'

'Right. Masked. Whatever. This person had a crossbow pointed at you and gave you a choice. And you chose to live.'

'Yeah. Right. Did what anyone would've done if they'd been me, didn't I?'

Glen Looker didn't have an answer for that. Not an honest one, anyway. 'Right. So now you think . . . what?' He shrugged.

'They're gonna do me, ain't they?'

'Do you?'

'Manslaughter, an' that. Cos I let them die.'

'But they're not going to charge you with that. How can they?'

'You weren't there, were you?' His voice rose, his arms flung about, almost ripping out the drips. 'You didn't see her face … I'm tellin' you, man, they're gonna do me. An' you gotta stop them.'

Glen Looker nodded. 'Fine. I'll have a word. But take it from me, they won't do anything. After the exposure this has had, they wouldn't dare.'

Darren Richards stared sullenly ahead. 'Still not convinced.'

'Leave it with me.'

Darren gave a reluctant nod.

They sat in silence for a minute. Eventually, Glen spoke.

'You still grieving, then?'

'What?' Darren frowned, like he hadn't understood the words.

'Grieving. Are you still grieving?'

Darren still frowned. 'What d'you mean? Grievin'?'

'For Chloe. And Shannon.'

'Oh.' His eyebrows lifted as he understood. 'Right. Yeah. Gotcha. Grievin'. Yeah.' He shrugged. 'Yeah.' His features were blank, almost non-committal.

'You sure?'

'Yeah, you know.' He shrugged. 'Miss them, an' that.'

Glen Looker nodded.

'So when you gonna talk to the cops for me, then?' Darren's face was animated once more. 'Today?'

Glen Looker stood up. 'Leave it with me.'

'Better be fuckin' today. Better be.'

'I'm glad you're feeling better.'

Glen Looker turned, walked from the ward.

As he approached his car, the opening bars of Robin Thicke's 'Blurred Lines' blared out from his suit pocket. Two

166

nurses walking past stopped to look at him and smile. He returned the smile thinking they must be impressed by his taste in tunes, but the expressions on their faces told a different story. He hurriedly took out his mobile before any more of the song could play, checked the display. MOSES HEAP.

He suppressed a groan, answered it.

'Yes, Moses, what can I do for you?'

'Listen, man, just wanted to say thanks for steppin' up for me yesterday. Five-0's on to me like a fucking rash.'

'Yes, well, that's what they do.' He tried opening his car door as he spoke. 'You know that by now.'

'Yeah, man, but I've not done anything this time. Not any more. You know me.'

'Yeah, Moses, I know you.'

'Yeah. Well, I'm just saying. New man, an' that. But they're not giving up on me just yet. Don't think of going anywhere in the next few days 'cause I just might need you again, you get me?'

'Don't you worry, Moses, I have no plans to go anywhere.'

'Cool, man. Take care, yeah? Speak soon.'

He hung up.

Glen got into the car, let out a heavy sigh. He looked down at the passenger seat, saw the holiday brochures piled up there. Some old, dog-eared and well-thumbed, some new, just picked up off the travel agent's shelves a day ago. He collected them. Stared at the photos of far-away places: white sand, blue sky and perfect tranquillity. Proving money bought you happiness. Knowing the price of where he wanted to go, where he could find peace, was far beyond what he earned.

'Not thinking of going anywhere,' he said out loud. 'God, I wish.'

He pulled away, Daft Punk cranked up as loud as possible so he didn't have to think while he drove.

35

'Case study.' Marina repeated the words back to Fiona Welch. 'Case study.'

Fiona Welch remained silent.

'And what kind of things were you studying? Hmm? What aspect of Joanne's psychological make-up interested you in particular?'

Fiona Welch's nostrils flared as she inhaled and exhaled, but she still didn't speak.

Marina felt her hands shaking. She kept her voice steady. 'I'd really like to know.'

Fiona Welch turned to her. Spoke slowly and deliberately. 'I'm sure you would.' She smiled. 'You're getting old, Marina. Old. It must be hard to try to keep up with the latest theory and practice, I would think. You must get set in your ways. Each generation comes up with better, more dynamic theories than the previous one. Discrediting everything that's gone before. It must be very difficult for you.'

Marina's voice began to rise. 'You haven't a clue what you're talking about.'

Fiona Welch went on. 'It must also be hard trying to maintain a man's interest when you're ageing. When there is a younger generation coming along. Better. More dynamic. It must be very difficult for you.'

Before Marina could speak, Anni stood up. 'This is getting

us nowhere.' She turned to Fiona Welch. 'I get the point. You're a fake but clearly quite a decent one. I don't know why you want to be Fiona Welch, why you picked on that particular low-life, and quite frankly, I don't care. I don't know who you really are. But do you know what I think? What I really think? Just between us three girls, of course.'

Fiona Welch affected boredom but Marina could see that she was genuinely interested to know. And also, if her expression was anything to go by, a little scared. She shrugged.

'I just want to know if you were responsible for Joanne Marsh's death. That's all. Like you said, that's all I do. I'm not interested in anything else. How clever you think you are. What you're doing this for. Not interested in the slightest. In fact, if anything I find the whole charade boring. So stop playing games and tell me. Did you have anything to do with Joanne Marsh's death?'

'Yes. She did.'

They all turned. Mickey had entered the room. Stood quietly at the door, listening. He moved forward to join them.

'She is responsible for Joanne Marsh's death. Definitely.'

The fear was ramping up in Fiona Welch's eyes. She began to bluster. 'What d'you mean? You don't know what you're talking about.'

'I do,' he said. 'Mind if I sit?' He pulled out a chair, looked at it. 'Actually, no, I think I'll stay standing. You're responsible for her death. You were careless. You were stupid. You left a witness.'

Fiona Welch said nothing, her eyes blazing.

He continued. 'Yes, a witness.'

Fiona Welch found her voice. 'No I didn't. I couldn't have because I didn't do it.'

'All right then.' He folded his arms. 'Does this sound familiar? Do it and you'll be at peace. They'll never let you out.

169

You're never going to see your men again. You'll be at peace.'
He unfolded his arms, looked directly at her. 'Ring any bells?'

Fiona Welch began to tremble.

'I've been talking to the other patients,' said Mickey.
'Including Eloise Brownley. She was in Joanne's room last night
after you'd been in. She told me what you'd said to Joanne, how
you told her to kill herself. And that Joanne was upset about it
but was going to do it. Eloise Brownley's not all there but she's
credible. And a jury would find her so if it came to that.'

She stood, stepped up close to him.

'You're good,' said Mickey. 'But we're better.'

Her breathing deepened, her teeth were bared. 'You bastard.'

And she was on him. Clawing at his face, screaming. Trying
to pull his hair out, rip his clothes from his body.

Anni jumped up, leapt on her back, began twisting her arms,
pulling her away from Mickey who regained his balance and
joined his partner in restraining her. Marina could do nothing
but watch.

Fiona Welch kicked and screamed. Tried to punch and bite
the two of them, screaming all the while, her ferocity huge.
Eventually they managed to hold her face down on the floor
and pull her hands behind her back. Mickey, sitting on her,
took out his cuffs, fastened them over her wrists.

'There, gotcha ...' he managed to gasp.

Once he had finished fastening the cuffs he stood up. Fiona
Welch tried to stand, to crawl, anything to get away. 'Call a
nurse,' said Anni to Marina. 'See if they've got any more
restraints on the ward. Place like this, they're bound to have.'

'No ...' said Fiona Welch, her movements lessening. 'No –
I'm ... I'm all right ...'

'Pleased to hear it,' said Anni. Then to Marina, 'Get the
restraints.'

'No,' Fiona Welch said again, louder, more shrill this time.

'I'm ... I'm calm. I'm calm. I'll ... I'll not give you any more trouble. I promise.'

Mickey and Anni stood back, wary. Ready to pounce once more if needed.

But it was unnecessary. Fiona Welch had regained control of herself. She lay still on the floor. Mickey and Anni shared a glance.

'Shall you do the honours or shall I?' he said.

Anni smiled, gave an elaborate hand gesture, bowing as she did. 'Be my guest.'

Mickey pulled Fiona Welch to her feet, placed her in the chair he had almost sat in. Looked straight into her eyes. 'Your little holiday here is over,' he said. 'Fiona Welch, or whoever you really are, you have the right to remain silent ... '

She stared straight back at him. The feral quality of a few moments earlier had completely disappeared. Now her face was calm, almost relaxed. As he talked, she smiled.

And that, thought Marina, was the most frightening thing the woman calling herself Fiona Welch had yet done.

36

Phil firmly closed his office door, shut the blinds and sat down behind his desk. He didn't want anyone watching what he was about to do next.

He took out his phone, called Marina.

Her earlier call had been preying on his mind. He had managed to concentrate on his work but her words kept bleeding into his mind. Fiona Welch. Justice. Phil couldn't get a grip on it. He knew he was being irrational, but he was worried about her. Not because of the words she had said but the way she had said them. He had heard something behind them. And it wasn't like her. He didn't really expect her to answer, thought she would be too busy, but had to try. He was surprised when he heard her voice.

'Hey,' she said.

He picked up the strain in her voice immediately.

'Hey yourself,' he said. 'How are things?'

'Oh, you know . . . ' A sigh. 'Looks like our mutual friend has struck again.'

Phil felt a chill run through him at his wife's words. 'Tell me about it.'

'My patient? Joanne Marsh? Seems like Fiona Welch—'

'The woman calling herself Fiona Welch,' Phil corrected.

'Right. But it's easier to call her that.'

'And just what she wants. Sorry. Go on.'

'Okay. Well, she seems to have used her silver tongue to persuade Joanna to commit suicide.'

'Oh, Jesus.'

'Exactly. She's going to be charged, cuffed, taken back to the station. Hopefully we'll find out a bit more about her there.'

'Good,' said Phil. 'Even better place for her. Do you know whether Franks and the team want me to come over at some point?'

'That's in the future for now. We'll see what Anni and Mickey can get out of her.'

'Probably just as well. I'm snowed under here. All kicked off when you left.'

'In what way?'

He hesitated. 'I've got to do a press conference.'

Marina laughed. It seemed to go some way to relieving the tension in her voice. 'Just imagine them naked or sitting on the loo, or something.'

'Thanks, but it's a bit more than that. I know you've got your hands full but we've had a bit of a situation here since you've been away. And it seems to be escalating quite quickly.'

Sensing the seriousness of his tone, her voice became all about business once more, focused on his words. 'Fill me in.'

'We've got a vigilante. Targeting people he thinks have got away with something. He gives them the choice: pay for their crimes, accept responsibility, or lose something they love.'

'Jesus.'

'Yeah. And for some reason he's taken a bit of a shine to me.'

'In what way?'

'Phone calls, that kind of thing. That's why I'm doing this press conference. He wants me to send him a message or he'll keep going.'

'What kind of a message?'

'Something to demonstrate that I'm on his side.'

'Oh great. So it's damned if you do, damned if you don't.'

'Exactly. Any ideas?'

Marina gave a hoarse laugh. 'Me?'

'More your area than mine. I just find the evidence and lock them up.'

Marina was silent for a few seconds. 'Second time I've heard that today. But you're not that kind of copper, Phil. You know that.'

'Yeah, but . . . ' He sighed. 'I think I'm out of my depth with this one. Press conference, coded messages, all of that. So what would you suggest?'

Just the hum of static and distance on the line. Marina was thinking. 'You need to play for time. Say something that feels like it's reinforcing his sense of self-worth but is also non-committal. Appeal to his narcissism. Flatter him. But skirt around the fact that you agree with him. Don't come out and say it.'

'I know. Public accountability, and all that. Wouldn't want a solicitor saying I was entrapping their client.' He got a mental image of Glen Looker and felt his stomach lurch. 'Any words I could use?'

'Loads. But they'll all make you sound like you've been coached. You'll think of the right ones. I've got faith in you.'

Phil smiled. Felt something warm inside at her words.

'Try to draw him out a bit,' Marina said. 'Ask him to arrange a meet, even, see what kind of response that gets. Is that helpful?'

Phil sighed. 'Yeah. Thanks.'

When Marina spoke next he could sense the smile in her voice once more. 'You could have come to all those conclusions. In fact, you probably have. Just admit it. You called me because you miss me.'

Phil smiled too. 'I do. Guilty as charged. And I wanted to know how you were getting on with your own maniac.'

She laughed. 'His and hers maniacs. Sums up our life, really.' Her laughter faded. 'And I miss you. How's Josephina?'

'Still with Eileen. They're both fine. I phoned.'

'Good.' Another sigh. 'Can't wait to see you. I'll be back later to—'

There was a commotion in the background and he could tell Marina was distracted by it. 'Look, I've got to go. Good luck.'

'Give my best to Anni and Mickey.'

'And I'm sure they'll return it.'

They said their goodbyes, spoke briefly of their love for each other and hung up.

Phil sat back in his office chair. Stared straight ahead. He still hadn't decorated his office. Not even a photo of Marina or Josephina. He carried plenty of them on his phone, could look at them any time he wanted to. He didn't even know whether he was staying or returning to Colchester. The job still felt temporary. He still sensed a slight feeling of unease. Of not fitting in fully with the team. Like they weren't truly his and he was just in charge of them until their real boss came along.

He pocketed his phone, shook his head.

Maybe Marina was right. Maybe he had only called to hear her voice.

He stood up, tried to concentrate on the job in hand. He had a press conference to address.

But first, he had to get changed.

He wasn't sure which he was dreading most.

37

Letisha Watson was sitting in her armchair, twirling her cigarette in her fingers, watching it burn down to ash. Focused on that and nothing else. The world, and everything in it, was beyond her cigarette. Watching it burn was all that mattered to her. It was her world.

She sighed. Knew there was something beyond the cigarette. Just didn't want to look.

There was a knock on the door.

She jumped up, knocking the long line of ash onto the carpet, her heart skipping a beat. Moses, she thought. He's come back . . .

Quickly, she looked around for her ashtray, stubbed out the butt. She pulled her dressing gown around her, not yet dressed from saying goodbye to him earlier in the morning. One hand went to her hair, primped, hoped it looked okay. She had fag breath and needed a shower but that could all be taken care of once he was in. She made her way to the door, flung it open, smile ready.

It froze on her face.

'Happy to see me? Or were you expecting someone else?'

Her facial muscles quickly regrouped, formed themselves into the stone features she used for talking to the police.

'What d'you want?'

DS Sperring smiled, put his arm against her doorframe as if

he was an old friend, chatting about nothing. She noticed he was wearing latex gloves. It made her feel unclean.

'Let's not stand here chatting, eh, Letisha? Aren't you going to ask me inside?'

She didn't answer, just walked away from the door, knowing he would follow her. She didn't care if he closed it or not.

He did. Followed her to the living room. Stood there looking round, taking it in. He turned to her. Smiled. It wasn't pleasant.

'Home sweet home,' he said.

'What d'you want? Got nothin' more to say to you. I said it all yesterday.'

'Did you now?'

He walked round the room, picking up ornaments, examining them as if he were a fine art expect. Or thought they might be stolen.

'Put them down. You've got no right to touch them.'

He replaced the china figurine he had been holding, turned back to her. 'I don't think you did tell me everything yesterday, did you, Letisha?'

She swallowed. Her throat felt full of stones. 'What . . . what d'you mean?'

'You held out on me, didn't you?' He walked over to her, stood right beside her, face to face.

She felt scared. She had always felt scared in front of the police. Even when she hadn't done anything wrong. She knew the way they threw their authority around. Hid behind their jobs. 'I— I didn't . . . '

'Oh yes you did, Letisha.'

'Get out of my flat. Now.' Her words sounded weak, even in her own ears.

Sperring just laughed. 'Don't mess me around. You tried that yesterday. And look where it got you. A return visit. Now

177

if you don't want me to come round again, you'll talk to me.'

She said nothing. Just wished him gone.

'I know you were Darren Richards' girlfriend. And we know what happened to him.'

'I didn't care about Darren Richards. That slag was welcome to him.'

'Not what I heard. The fight?'

She shrugged. 'Made a mistake.'

'Oh you did, Letisha. Because there was someone else more important that you didn't tell me about.'

She tried to swallow again. Couldn't. 'Who?' Her voice arid.

'Moses Heap.'

She hoped her face wasn't reflecting what she was feeling. She hoped she hadn't shown it, not even in her eyes.

'What ... what about him?'

'Big-time villain like that? Got previous, got a temper – might he have wanted to do you a favour?'

Letisha felt close to tears now. 'Get ... get out ... '

Sperring didn't move. 'Answer the question.'

'No. He's ... he's a friend, that's all. A friend. We go way back, him and me.'

Sperring nodded. 'I see. We had Mr Heap down at the station yesterday. He hid behind his solicitor.'

'Suh ... so?'

'I think he's lying. I think he's hiding something. I want to know what.'

He stepped in close, towered over her. She could see all the open pores, all the broken veins, in his nose. Letisha tried not to, but she couldn't help herself. She flinched.

'What's he hiding, Letisha?'

She hated him. Right at that moment she doubted she had hated anyone more. And within that hatred she found strength.

178

Drew on it, nurtured it, let it grow. She looked up at Sperring, fire back in her eyes.

'Get out of my flat, you fucking bastard. Or I'll be the one calling a solicitor. And doin' you for harassment.'

'No need to be like that.'

'Get out!' she screamed at him. Looking round she saw the figurine he had been playing with earlier, picked it up and started hitting him in the chest with it.

'Get out . . . get out.'

'All right, all right . . . '

She managed to beat him back down the hallway to the front door, screaming at him all the time. He fumbled open the lock, fell out onto the walkway. She stood over him, ready to bring the figurine down on him.

'All right – I'm off . . . '

She pulled back, watched him get slowly to his feet. He stood on the walkway about to say something to her but she pulled back her hand, ready to let the figurine fly. Instead, Sperring turned and walked away.

'And stay away, you fuckin' bastard!' she shouted at his retreating back.

She went back inside her flat, slammed the door behind her, stood up against it.

And burst into tears.

38

Phil felt that his tie was trying to strangle him. He pulled at it, tried to stick his finger down his collar, pull the stiff fabric away from his neck. Failed. It just sprang back into place.

He hated wearing a suit. Hated wearing a collar and tie. In fact, he only owned one suit, one dress shirt and one tie. It was the ensemble he wore for giving evidence in court. And possibly funerals if he couldn't get away with something else. And weddings if they were particularly formal. It was a good suit, he had to say that. If you liked that kind of thing, which he didn't. Marina had been with him when he bought it. Had guided him to something he wouldn't have gone for if he had been alone. Something expensive, well-tailored. It flattered and suited him. Marina really liked him in it, thought he should wear it more often. But on the few occasions he had worn it he couldn't wait to get it off afterwards. Get back into something more comfortable. Something he could think and work in.

'You ready?' DCI Cotter looked at him, brushed something from his shoulder.

'Yep,' he said. He glanced down at his notes. 'Got these. I'll try not to look like I'm reading from them, though.'

'Yes, remember to look up at all times. You'll be on camera. No one wants to see—'

'The top of my head. Yes, I know. I remember my media training.'

Cotter smiled. 'Good.' She stepped back, admiring him. 'You scrub up well. I should let you do more of these things.'

'No thanks,' he said.

She checked her watch. 'Time to go.'

He nodded. Stood still for a moment, trying to quell his nerves, running over what he had to say and more importantly what he couldn't say, in his mind.

'Don't worry, I'll be right beside you.'

He nodded. Took a deep breath, another, and walked on to the small stage.

Immediately he felt cameras turn to face him. Felt flashlights pop. He hoped he didn't blink. Or not too much. Blinking and recoiling from the light made a detective appear untrustworthy, so he and every other officer who had attended the same training course had been told. He sat down behind the table, a glass jug of water and tumbler at his right, like he was on a chat show. Which in a sense he was.

Cotter sat down next to him, seemingly as relaxed as if she was sitting on her sofa after work, just about to sip a large glass of merlot.

He looked out at the people gathered before him. Recognised a few of the faces from the local papers and TV news. But there were plenty he didn't recognise. The nationals were in town. They would be for a case like this.

He cleared his throat, put his papers down on the table before him. Leaned into the microphone. 'I'm ... Detective Inspector ...' His throat felt arid. He paused, cleared it. 'Detective Inspector Phil Brennan. This,' he gestured to Cotter, 'is Detective Chief Inspector Cotter.' Cotter nodded. 'I'm ... running the, in charge of the team looking into the murders of Chloe Hannon and her daughter Shannon. And also the ...' He didn't want to say the word mutilation but he didn't know what else to say. '... case of John Wright who was found injured in a city-centre hotel last night. We believe the two cases are linked.'

Hands were raised straight away.

'If you could . . . if you could just wait until I've finished talking . . . ' Finished talking? Christ, he sounded like a teacher. 'Then I'll answer any questions you might have, that I'm, I'm able to.'

He sat back, felt sweat running down his body. This was awful. He had been in life or death situations with criminals that were more pleasant than this.

He started to talk, outlining the details surrounding the discovery of the bodies of Chloe and Shannon. He also informed them that there was another male at the scene, Darren Richards, who was currently in a stable condition in hospital. He then went on to talk about the banker John Wright who had been discovered after an anonymous tip-off. He had been taken straight to hospital where it was hoped he would make a good recovery from his injuries. His condition was currently critical but stable.

He sat back once more, breathed out a sigh of relief. Then hoped that no one had captured that on camera. Considering who was in the room, he knew it was a forlorn hope.

'If . . . if anyone has any questions?'

Please don't, he thought.

But they did. Plenty of them. This was a high-profile case. The press, from what their sources had told them, knew that something was going on, that the police weren't telling them everything. Usually it would be Cotter in charge of the press conference, managing to deflect difficult questions with practised ease. Ensure that the information that entered into the public domain was only that which the police wanted to be there.

But Phil wasn't as good as her. He realised that now. Still, he knew why he was there. What he had to say. He just hoped that she would step in when needed.

'What makes you think the two cases are linked?'

He didn't know who had asked that. Someone from one of the nationals, he thought.

'There are . . . similarities in, in both cases.'

'Such as?'

'Well . . . there are—'

Cotter leaned forward into her microphone. 'I'm afraid we can't discuss that at this time.' She looked grave. 'If too much information, too many details, got into the public domain at this stage it could jeopardise our ability to catch whoever is doing this.'

'Do you have any idea at all who it is? Who's doing this?'

Phil looked at Cotter. She nodded. 'We do, yes,' he said. 'We have a number of leads, some promising. One in particular very promising. Yes. Unfortunately I can't say more about it at this time. But you'll know as soon as we do.'

And on it went. Questions from the floor answered professionally by Cotter and, Phil thought, ineptly by himself. Those asking the questions were trained reporters. Any hesitation on Phil's part, any chink in the armour, was swiftly dealt with. They were on him in seconds, following up with other questions, probing, fishing, making suppositions that were he to answer one way or another would be seen as an admission of something he hadn't actually intended. Cotter sensed when he was out of his depth, jumped in whenever needed. Eventually Cotter told them that it was time to wrap up and there would be no further questions, but that Detective Inspector Brennan had something to say.

Phil cleared his throat once more. This was why he was there. The part they had planned, the lines he had rehearsed. He looked straight ahead, resisting the urge to find a camera and stare down it. He knew that they would all find him.

'If . . . if you're watching this, and I'm sure you are,' he said, 'then know this. What you're doing is wrong. You might think it's right. You might think you have the right to do what you're doing. Or that you speak for people. Ordinary people who you think share your views. Well, perhaps they do. Perhaps we all do. But there's a difference between thinking something and acting on it the way you've been doing.' He leaned back, keeping his features blank, trying to appear in control. Hoping cameras weren't picking up his shaking hands. 'Talk to me. I know you want to. And you know I want to talk to you. Or come and meet me. Then we'll talk.' He said nothing. Stared straight ahead. Let those words sink in. 'You know how to contact me. Do it.'

Phil and Cotter stood up at that point. The room went into immediate uproar as reporters all shouted questions at the two of them. Phil's words had blindsided them all. None of them had been expecting that and they all wanted – demanded – to know more.

They walked through a door out of the media suite. Phil stood up against a wall, started loosening his tie. Exhaling loudly.

'Well,' said Cotter, 'I thought that went rather well.'

'We'll see,' said Phil. 'Depends what he does next.'

As they stood there, Phil gasping for air and Cotter waiting patiently for him, a figure began to approach. They both looked in the figure's direction.

'Detective Inspector Brennan, Detective Chief Inspector Cotter . . . '

'Oh Christ,' said Phil. 'As if that wasn't bad enough . . . '

It was Glen Looker.

39

The Lawgiver was not happy. Really, really not happy. He paced the floor, up and down, across, around. Clenching and unclenching his fists. Grinding his teeth. Breathing laboured, ragged. Unaware of what he was doing, where he was going. Pacing and snarling like a caged animal.

'Bastard . . . bastard . . . '

What you're doing is wrong . . .

How dare he? How fucking *dare* he . . . ? After everything he had said, the conversations they had already had. How he thought he had found an ally in Detective Inspector Phil Brennan, been led to believe that he would be amenable to what he was trying to achieve. Well, he wasn't. The Lawgiver had been lied to. Brennan was just like all the rest. Things are black and white. The Lawgiver knew that. No doubt. It was at the core of what he believed in. Why he did what he did.

To think or not to think. That was always the question. He had chosen to think. To question. He had chosen to confront those who wilfully made a mockery of society – the whim-worshippers and hedonists, the sub-humans – and do something about it. He stuck to his code of ethics. Had to. Had no choice. It was the only way he could live his life, the only way he knew how. But his actions, his glorious actions, made others see the correct way to live. Or should do.

And he thought Brennan would help him to achieve his aims.

How wrong he was. He should have known.

He stopped pacing, tried to get his breathing under control once more. He played back the whole of the press conference in his mind.

The first thing he had noticed was that Brennan looked different to when he had seen him last, how he had imagined him to be. A free thinker. Someone different. He didn't look different. He looked like all the rest of them now. An ordinary man in a cheap-looking suit. Another dull, boring copper. Had he known that, he might not have approached him in the first place.

What had Brennan said? *Talk to me. I know you want to.* Really? Really? They had talked. And look where it had got him. Nowhere. Lied to again.

Lied to again. Sometimes he thought there was no one left in the world that he could trust, believe in. His father had told him the truth. *Never be dependent on someone else. Never ask anyone to be dependent on you. Never live for another. Or ask him to live for you. Or to help you.* His father's mantra. The words that he had literally lived by. And that he had tried to do also. He should have known. Should have known.

His father had found strength through his philosophy of Objectivism. Live your life to make yourself happy. That was the only thing that mattered. Freedom through work, strength through work. A man works, a man sells. There is no such thing as society. He had stuck rigidly to that all his life.

And that's what this work as the Lawgiver was supposed to be. A life's work. A life's philosophy.

He crossed to the jukebox, scanned the lists, trying desperately to find something to play, something that would soothe him, take him out of himself, take him to a better place. He flicked the entries over and over until he reached the end. Then he began to go backwards. Eventually he turned away from the machine.

Nothing. Absolutely nothing.

'You okay?'

He felt fingers stroke along his shoulder. He shuddered at the touch, turned, smelling that familiar perfume. His sister was back again. 'Yeah, I'm fine. I didn't hear you. Didn't know you were back.'

'I've just arrived. You seem cross. Can I help? Let's talk.'

He sighed. 'It's ... maybe. Maybe you can. But not at the moment. Later, perhaps.'

'Would you rather I left you on your own?'

'Please. I need to think this through. I'll talk to you later.'

'Okay. I'll see you later.'

Her fingers lifted slowly from him as she left the room. Her perfume hung in the air then was gone. He was alone once more.

He tried to sit down. Tried not to think about Brennan.

No good. The suited bastard kept popping up in his mind's eye. Looking directly at him, his eyes honest and sincere.

It was enough to make him throw up.

He stood up once more. Inaction wouldn't solve anything. He didn't want to resume pacing so he stood still in the middle of the room. Closed his eyes. He had to think. Plan. Turn this negative into a positive. This setback into a leap forward.

Think. Think logically. He almost laughed. Logically. What other way was there to think? Objectively logical. *Think.*

He had accomplished a lot. Two successful missions. Perfect results. He couldn't have hoped for better outcomes. The second one had been the most exciting. Especially the phone call and what followed. The escape. That had been the kind of thing that they would remember. All of them. It would contribute to his legend in years to come. Keep it alive, let it grow. And best of all, they would never work out how he had done it. *Never*.

He had been meticulous, scrupulous. There was none of his DNA left at the scenes. Nothing that anyone could use to trace it back to him. He had covered his tracks well. Obsessively well.

But now this, now Brennan's betrayal . . .

He had to do something. He thought. He crossed to a locked antique desk, took a key from around his neck, opened the first drawer and took out a folder. No computers. Too dangerous. Too risky. Any online searches he had done had been made on different machines, none of them owned by him, in different locations around the city.

He placed the folder on the desk. Looked at it. This was it. The work. The missions, the calling. All in here. He opened it up. Riffled the pages, checking for the next one. That's what he had to do. Step it up, get it moving. He had their attention. Now he had to make sure he kept their attention. It could be risky, they would be looking out for him, the city on alert. But that didn't worry him, not really. Because he knew how to make himself invisible to them. How to move amongst them undetected. Oh yes. Just walk right past them and not be spotted. Brilliant. All he needed was to choose the next victim . . .

And there it was. Staring up at him. Perfect, he thought. Perfect.

And then the doorbell rang.

40

'Here to see Darren Richards.'

Sperring leaned over the counter at the nurses' station on the ward, flashed his warrant card. The nurse on duty was reading an instructional magazine informing her of the weight losses and gains of bikini-clad celebrities. Sperring glanced at the photos. There was no one there he recognised or was interested in so he promptly dismissed them.

Double-checking, that was all he was doing. Following up the correct procedure, seeing if the horrible little scrote – he mentally corrected himself – the poor victim had had any more thoughts.

He was glad that Phil was otherwise engaged. He had mellowed in his opinion of his new immediate boss – and he still thought of him as new – but they still rubbed each other up the wrong way. And the mellowing was only up to a point. Fair enough, his visit to Letisha Watson hadn't gone as well as he had wanted it to. But that was fine, live and learn. This time, the interview would be handled the way he wanted it to be. The way he thought it should be. And Phil wasn't around to say otherwise.

'Down there, third bed on the left,' said the nurse, irritated to be drawn away from her magazine.

He thanked her but she had already dismissed him quicker than he had her bikini-clad celebs.

Darren Richards was lying in his bed, iPhone buds in his

ears. His thumbs were moving over the glass screen. Sperring approached him.

'They let you use phones in the hospital now, Darren?'

Darren Richards looked up. His face initially registered shock at being disturbed, but a distrustful cunning entered his eyes when he realised who it was.

Never met me before, thought Sperring, but he's already made me as a copper. Not surprising. Sperring smiled, sat on the edge of the bed.

'How you feeling, Darren?' Sperring's smile was as big and false as a clown's red nose.

Darren Richards reluctantly removed his earbuds. 'Whah?'

'I said how are you feeling? Are they treating you well? Looking after you?'

Richards became suspicious. 'Yeah ... Why d'you want to know?'

'Just wondering, Darren, just checking.' Sperring, still smiling. 'It's what we do with victims of crime. Try to look after them, be concerned for their welfare.' The smile dropped. 'Course, you wouldn't know that, being as you're usually the one responsible for the crime in the first place.'

Darren Richards stared at him, trying to look defiant, not sure whether his fear was showing. 'I've ... If you've come to harass me, I've already spoken to my solicitor. He'll, he'll have ... he'll have you.'

Sperring gave an elaborate shrug. 'Harass you, Darren? Now why would I want to do that? You're a victim of crime, and as such entitled to all the help the police force can give. Including trying to catch the person who killed your girlfriend and daughter.'

Richards looked suspicious, eyes darting about. 'What d'you mean? What you tryin' to say?'

'I'm not trying to say anything. I am saying it. Now cast your mind back. What can you tell us about that night? You remembered anything more that might help us?'

'No.'

'Take your time, Darren. Think about it.'

Darren Richards gave a short, barking laugh. 'I know what you're doin'. You don't fool me.'

'Don't I?' Sperring fought to keep the amusement from his voice. 'Am I trying to?'

'Yeah. You're tryin' to get me to confess, that's what you're doing.'

'Confess to what? Did you do it? Did you pull the trigger?'

'No . . .'

Sperring made a show of slapping his head. 'Oh, I get you. You think that because you let him kill your girlfriend and daughter, because you said the word, told him to, you think that we're holding you responsible, is that it?'

'Well, that's what you're doin', isn't it? That's why you're here. Make me confess to it, make me an accessory, or somethin'.'

'Why, Darren, do you think you are responsible? Do you think it is your fault?'

Darren Richards sat further up in bed, his earphone cable tangling with the drips and monitor lines. 'No, none of it's my fault. None of it. I had nothin' to do with it. It was him.'

'Nothing?'

'Yeah, nothin'.'

'Well, that's one way of lookin' at it, I suppose. Of course, if you hadn't killed that woman and her child, none of this would have happened, would it?'

'So you're sayin' it is my fault?'

'I'm saying what I'm saying. If you hadn't killed that woman and her child, this killer, whoever he is, wouldn't have given you the choice of living or letting your girlfriend and kid die.'

191

Darren Richards looked away, shaking his head.

'I'm innocent. And this is harassment. I'm phoning my brief.'

'Do what you like. Another question. Letisha Watson. Moses Heap. What's the story there?'

Richards' eyes clouded over. 'What d'you mean?'

'Exactly that. What's going on between them? How do they know each other? How come you're involved? That kind of thing.'

His face became stone. 'I don't know. I know nothin' about them.'

'Bullshit, Darren. Tell me. What's the connection?'

'Nothin' as far as I know.'

Darren Richards swallowed hard. It looked like he had a rock in his throat, thought Sperring. A rock in his throat and fear in his eyes.

'I think you do.'

He shook his head, too quickly. 'I don't ... I don't ... now leave me alone. I'm ... I'm callin' my brief.'

Sperring stood up. 'Do what you feel you have to do, Darren. But there's something going on with Moses Heap and Letisha Watson. And you're involved.'

More head shaking, more fear in his eyes. 'I'm not. I'm not.'

'Suit yourself. But I'll be back. And if I find out you've been lying to me, then I'll be very cross. Very, very cross. And I'll let you know it. Victim of crime or no victim of crime.'

Darren Richards said nothing. Sperring could smell the sweat coming off him.

Sperring was about to leave, but paused, looked at Richards again, scrutinising him. 'Darren.'

'I told you I don't know nothin'.'

'Yeah, you said that. But I want to know something. You sat

there and let your girlfriend and daughter die. Right in front of you. What did you feel when that happened?'

Another short, barked laugh. 'Like I'm goin' to tell you.'

'No, Darren, do tell me. I want to know. What thoughts went through your head when you saw that happen? How did you feel?'

Darren Richards gave a sigh so heavy it was of Atlas-like proportions. 'It was, like, it was horrible. Horrible. I couldn't stop screaming. I just . . . couldn't stop screaming. Horrible.'

Sperring nodded. 'Right. That was how Graham Marshall felt.'

Richards frowned. 'Who?'

'The husband of the woman you killed. The father of the child you killed. Maybe this bloke's got a point after all, eh?'

Sperring walked away. A sound like an animal caught in a trap started to grow behind him.

Darren Richards was crying.

41

Nadish stepped back from the door, waited. He looked up and down Legge Lane. The derelict building was still cordoned off, uniforms and SOCO combing the floors, walls and surrounding debris for clues, patterns. He was back at his allotted task, going door to door, asking who, if anyone, had seen anything.

It was a fruitless task. Most of the buildings were on their way to being like the one Darren Richards and the bodies had been found in, waiting for time or an urban developer to either kill them or resurrect them. Once-solid brickwork now crumbling, rotting wooden window frames holding streaked and blackened windowpanes gently blowing in and out in the breeze, waiting for that one gust to shatter them on the pavement below.

Most of the buildings were like that, but not all. The one Khan was calling on was a much smarter affair. The brickwork had been looked after, the window frames replaced over the years and now barred too. The door looked like wood but on rapping his knuckles against it before he found the bell, he realised it was heavy metal. He didn't know what the story was, but it wasn't abandoned.

This was another part of the job he hated. Add that to the long list. It was all right when there was a few of them, then they would have a laugh, make it enjoyable. Race with each other to see how many doors they could do in an hour. Trade war stories about the state some people lived in, or the things they came out with. Have bets with each other over which phrases would be most overused. And best of all, give marks out of ten to the desperate housewives who wanted to go out of their way to help the strong, young policeman. Some of his mates even took phone numbers, went back round when they were off duty. Nadish hadn't done that.

At least not yet.

No. Doing the rounds on his own wasn't nearly as much fun.

He reached out again to try the bell one last time before moving on, when the door was jerked quickly open.

'Yes?' The voice was irritation bordering on anger.

Nadish was startled at the abruptness of the action but quickly regained his composure, his professionalism. He took the man in: white; late twenties or early thirties; medium height; slight build; mousy-brown hair cut neatly, unimaginatively and conservatively, parted on one side. Wearing a pair of dark cords, V-neck sweater and a plaid shirt underneath, he looked as non-descript, unremarkable and memorable as a lump of supermarket cheese.

But the eyes were different. They blazed with a fire at odds with his appearance, like they belonged to someone else, some-one more dynamic, more angry.

'Yes?' he said again, impatient this time.

Nadish held up his warrant card. 'Detective Constable Khan. Have you got time to answer a couple of questions? Won't take long.'

The eyes narrowed, became suspicious. 'What about?'

Nadish tried to keep his voice as matter-of-fact as possible. Doing the job he did, it was a well-practised skill. He turned, gestured to the building opposite. 'Just about what went on there the other night, if you saw anything. That kind of thing.'

The eyes were clouding over, becoming harder to read. 'I didn't. See anything.'

His abrupt, evasive responses were making Nadish become interested. 'Just a couple of questions, like I said. Won't take a minute.'

The man folded his arms. 'What d'you want to know?'

'Well, who I'm talking to for a start.'

'Hinchcliffe. Stuart Hinchcliffe.'

Something in the way he said his name – formal, studied – made Nadish think the man was older than he seemed. Or wanted to appear older.

'Thank you, Mr Hinchcliffe. Could I come inside a minute? Bit easier than doing this on the doorstep.'

Hinchcliffe thought it over then reluctantly stepped backwards, allowed Nadish to enter. 'Thank you, Mr Hinchcliffe. Sooner I ask my questions, sooner I'm gone.'

As the door closed behind him, Nadish Khan had a feeling that he was on to something.

42

'Yes, Mr Looker,' said Phil, ushering him into his office and closing the door behind him. 'How may I help you?'

Looker sat down without being asked, before Phil had even made his way round to the other side, and started talking. 'Harassment, Mr Brennan, harassment.'

Phil's face took on a neutral, relaxed aspect. A mask to hide his true feelings about the man before him. Necessary to have a conversation with him. 'In what way and of whom?'

'Darren Richards for one.'

Phil frowned as if puzzled. 'Darren Richards? I don't understand. In what way is he being harassed? And who by?'

'Two of your officers at least. A DC . . . ' He took out a notebook, flipped it open, checked his notes. ' . . . Oliver. DC Oliver.'

Phil found it slightly harder to keep his neutral mask in place. 'DC Oliver is one of my finest officers. Exemplary. I doubt for one minute that she has harassed your client.'

'He says she has. I have to report it.'

'Did Mr Richards go into specifics? Anything in particular you might want to tell me about?'

'Well, not in so many words, no. It was her manner. Threatening. He believes she intends to pursue him for a charge of manslaughter.'

'On what grounds?'

'That he allowed his partner and their child to be murdered

instead of him. Now, Mr Brennan, I'm sure you understand that my client was placed in a very difficult position. There's no telling what any of us would do in the same situation. I dare say—'

'And when did DC Oliver actually tell your client that she intends, or this department intends, to press charges?'

'She hasn't done so as yet. I'm here in a precautionary capacity on behalf of my client. I'm merely the canary in the coal mine.'

Phil struggled to keep a straight face at that remark. 'Is that right?'

'It is, yes.' Looker reddened slightly.

Bet that one sounded better in his own head, thought Phil.

Looker continued. 'I just want to warn you and your colleagues that any action against my client will reflect very badly on you and your department.'

'Consider me warned,' said Phil. 'Was there anything—'

'Detective Sergeant Sperring.'

'What about him?'

'I've just heard that he too paid Mr Richards a visit. Left him in tears.'

Phil didn't know whether to laugh or get angry at having his time wasted. 'And that's why you're here? Because Darren Richards says a big bad police officer made him cry? The state he's in, an episode of *Hollyoaks* would probably make him cry.' Phil shook his head.

Looker shifted uncomfortably in his seat, but pressed on with his attack. 'And that's not all. I received a call from another of my clients, Moses Heap. I'm sure you remember him.'

'Like it was only yesterday,' said Phil.

'I want DS Sperring to stay away from him, too.'

'Seems to have been busy, my detective sergeant. When did he go and see Moses Heap?'

'Well, he hasn't. Not yet.'

Phil frowned. 'So . . . what? You're threatening me, is that it? Threatening me to keep my officers away from your clients, is that it?'

'My clients are innocent. They have done nothing wrong. They are not guilty of any crime.'

'In this instance.'

Looker paused. Phil, for a few seconds, almost expected Looker to agree with him. However, Looker ignored the interruption, kept going. Leaning forward, speaking slowly to make his point. 'As I said, they are not guilty of any crime. If you persist in targeting them in this manner then I will assume you are deliberately harassing them and will have no choice but to take further action.'

Phil leaned forward too. He kept his rising anger down, his voice controlled. 'Mr Looker, let's get something straight. I'm in the middle of a murder inquiry. A very nasty one. And your clients' names have come up in the course of that. If I, or my officers, want to speak to them in connection with this case then we will do so. Without your permission or any compunction to call you. Is that clear?'

Looker sat back, sighed. For a second, Phil saw his professional demeanour come down, his façade crumble. He looked old, tired. Worn out by his words. Then the mask was put firmly back in place and he continued. 'You may question them. Of course you can. That's your job.'

Phil smiled. 'I thank you for your magnanimity.'

Looker, momentarily thrown, paused then continued. 'Yes, your job. And I have no problem with that. But what I do object to, in the strongest possible terms, is harassment. Making Mr Richards and Mr Heap feel like criminals.'

'But they are, aren't they?' Phil knew it was a cheap shot but he just wanted to see Looker's reaction. 'They should be used to it.'

Looker's voice got louder. 'May I remind you that Mr Richards is in no way complicit in what has happened? He is an innocent victim in all of this.'

'Well, if you want to get into semantics,' said Phil, 'he wouldn't have been placed in the position he was and targeted the way he was if he hadn't committed a criminal act in the first place. And if his lawyer hadn't got him off on a technicality.'

Looker looked incredulous. 'Are you condoning what this killer has done? Seriously?'

'No, I'm just pointing out a fact. If he was innocent, wholly innocent, he wouldn't have been there. That's all.'

Looker decided not to pursue that avenue. 'Mr Heap is a respected community figure now. Yes, he may have a criminal past but that's all it is. The past. Surely you believe in redemption? Second chances?'

'Yes,' said Phil, 'I do. Probably more so than some of my colleagues, if I'm honest. But I take each person as I find them. I make my own decisions.'

'Well, I suggest you tread carefully. Or you and your department will find yourselves on the end of a very nasty lawsuit.'

Phil sighed and stood up. He had had enough of this sanctimonious little nobody. 'Just what do you get out of this? Eh? It can't be justice or the sense of justice being done, can it? So what is it? What satisfaction do you derive from what you do?'

Looker opened his mouth to answer but seemingly thought better of it. Instead, he gave what he hoped was a composure-regaining smile. 'There's more than one kind of justice,' he said. He stood up, made for the door. When he reached it, he turned. 'Just stay away from my clients. That's all.'

He let himself out.

Phil watched him go. Slightly puzzled, an idea forming.

More than one kind of justice . . .

43

Sperring sat outside the old Victorian redbrick building, the No Postcode Organisation logo displayed prominently over the doorway. The music being made inside there a world away from the Radio Two easy listening coming out of the car's sound system.

Moses Heap, he thought, I'm on to you.

He had left Darren Richards having his delayed pity party and driven straight to the music studio. Given what he knew and had seen, that was where he figured Moses Heap was most likely to be. So far, he hadn't seen anyone go in or out. Or at least no one he recognised. No one gang-related.

Gang-related. Yes, he knew that Moses Heap had turned over a new leaf. Or said he had. And yes, crime in the area, particularly knife and gun crime, had gone down considerably since the truce was declared. But that didn't mean nothing was happening. There was nothing to stop the two gangs coming together and just carving up the territory, deciding who took which streets and estates to sell drugs on, to traffic women into prostitution, to set up protection rackets . . . Sperring knew that just because they weren't killing each other, didn't mean they weren't doing something wrong.

And then there was this Lawgiver business. Darren Richards was one thing but this banker was a whole different level. His initial thought was that it was too clever for Moses Heap to organise. Too much planning, too many variables. But the more he thought about it, the more it seemed possible. After all, hadn't Heap been head of a gang? Surely that took some organisation, more than just muscle and threat? So it was possible. And if he wasn't actually the Lawgiver himself, then he was certainly connected to him in some way. Sperring didn't know how, couldn't say why. Or at least not yet. But something, his old copper's instinct, told him so. And so he had no choice but to follow it.

He smiled. He could just imagine what Phil would say if he could see him now. The strip he would tear off him. The lecture he would get about how many other avenues he should be exploring instead of carrying out a vendetta against this one person, a person who he had already been warned off. Yeah, well, when he brought Heap in – when he exposed just what he was doing – then we'd see what Phil's reaction would be. What all of them would say.

Sperring jumped. He didn't realise he had been talking aloud. His hands had been going too, gesturing as he mouthed the words. Yes, he thought. Brennan still gets to me.

The song on the radio finished, something equally anodyne took its place. Sperring kept staring at the building across the street.

Something must happen.

Something must happen soon . . .

44

'So what's this place, then?'

DC Nadish Khan looked around the space he had entered. The outside gave no clue to what was inside. The first thing that struck him was how big it was, like a TARDIS. What had been a terraced, redbrick frontage gave way on to what seemed at first glance to be a workshop. It was dark, the only light coming from a doorway through to the rest of the building and what Nadish made out as a set of stairs. He squinted, looked around the room, counted: three large benches positioned at regular intervals, tools hanging up in their correct places on the walls. Everything covered in grime and dust. Cobwebbed. Overhead were old fluorescent strip lights, not turned on. Possibly not even working.

He became aware of Hinchcliffe standing right behind him. Too close, invading his personal space. He turned, found himself face to face. 'What is this place?' he asked again, taking a step back.

'Is that what you wanted to ask me?'

'No.'

'What was it then?'

Nadish looked around. 'Is there somewhere more comfortable we can go?'

Hinchcliffe looked around, seemed to be making his mind up about something. 'Come through,' he said eventually.

He led Khan through the workshop to the stairs and went

up. Khan followed. Once at the top of the stairs, Hinchcliffe turned. 'Will here do? For your questions?'

Khan looked at where he had been led. He was in a corridor, rooms running off it. It looked to have once been industrial or at least a continuation of the workspace down below but there had been attempts to domesticise it. He glimpsed a kitchen at the far end, the corner of a bed in another room.

'This is where you live, then?' he asked.

'Yes.' Hinchcliffe didn't move.

'Anywhere we can sit down? I've been walking all morning.'

Hinchcliffe sighed. Khan caught the flicker of something behind his eyes. Fear, nervousness? He wasn't sure. It brought his eyes more into line with the rest of his body, replacing the earlier fire. Khan still felt an unease about him, like something was off kilter. He still had a good feeling about him. Thought he was on to something.

'Come through,' Hinchcliffe said.

He opened a door at the far end of the corridor from the kitchen, walked through. Khan followed. And stopped, looking round.

'Wow,' he said. 'Someone would pay top dollar for this place.'

The room was stripped, bare brick walls. The furniture was either old or reclaimed industrial. A huge, modern TV stood in one corner. On the walls were models. Planes. Spaceships. A scale model of a huge ship. All in glass cases, carefully preserved.

'Is that,' said Khan, pointing, 'is that the *Titanic*?'

Hinchcliffe nodded, giving nothing else away.

'Okay.' Nadish was feeling slightly uncomfortable. 'So you live here by yourself?'

'My sister. She's with me.'

'Is she here now?'

'Not at the moment.'

'No wife, or anything?'

'No.'

'Kids?'

Hinchcliffe shook his head. 'Are these the questions you wanted to ask me, Detective . . . ?'

'Khan. Detective Constable Khan.'

'Detective Constable Khan. Are they?'

'No, sorry. Just got side-tracked. Amazing stuff.' He was about to sit down but saw something else in the corner. He crossed to it instead. 'Is this authentic?'

'It is.'

'What kind is it?'

'A Rock-ola Princess 435. Quite rare, I believe.'

'Yeah,' said Khan. 'Got a mate who collects them. Does them up, like. Sells them on. Tidy little business. Is it working?'

'It is. Now, these questions . . . '

'What you got on it?' asked Khan, unable to keep the smile from his face. 'If you don't mind me asking.'

'Not at all.' He crossed over to Khan, stood by the machine. 'Sixties soul. That's my passion.'

'You're an old soul boy, yeah? Bit of Aretha, James Brown, all that?'

'Yes.' Hinchcliffe smiled. 'All that. And more.'

'Brilliant. Love a bit of that. Rare groove, they used to call it, didn't they?'

'I believe so.'

Khan was starting to warm to Hinchcliffe. His earlier misgivings pushed to one side. He checked the song listing. 'I've never heard of half of these.'

'Like I said, it's my passion. You know what collectors are like. We enjoy seeking out the most obscure things. They're often the most rewarding. It's the juxtapositioning of a production-line mentality, a factory, and the fact that they produced something truly beautiful. That's what interests me.'

'Yeah,' said Khan, still looking at the listing on the jukebox. 'Brilliant, look at this stuff. Can't beat the old school ...' He straightened up. 'And look at that.' He reached out, touched the wall. 'It's not real.'

The scene behind the jukebox showed a set of French windows leading into a garden in lush, summer bloom.

'Wow. That's almost lifelike. You could step through that.'

'It's a wall,' said Hinchcliffe. 'You'd get a nasty injury. It's tromp-l'oeil.'

'What?'

'*Trompe-l'oeil*. French. Means "to deceive the eye". It's a kind of painting.'

'Right,' said Khan, laughing. 'Nasty injury.' He looked at it again. 'You do it yourself?'

'My ... another family member.'

'Your sister?'

Hinchcliffe said nothing.

Nadish took his silence as agreement. 'You're a talented lot. What about you? What do you do?'

Hinchcliffe made a show of looking at his watch. 'Do you have some questions to ask me, Detective Constable Khan?'

'Oh yeah, sorry. It concerns the building over there.' Khan walked to the window, looked out. 'You've got a pretty decent view of it, haven't you?'

'It takes up the whole of that side of the street. There's nothing to see when you look out but red brick and grey sky.'

'Right,' said Khan. 'I can see why you had that painted.' He gestured to the garden scene.

'Quite.'

'Well, you probably know there's been a murder over there. You'll have seen our presence, the TV news crews, all of that.'

'I have.'

'Well, I'm going door to door round here, seeing if anyone has noticed anything suspicious.'

'You mean did I see a murderer?'

'Something like that.'

'I wouldn't know what a murderer looks like, Detective Constable Khan. I presume they're just like the rest of us.'

'They are. Did you see anyone suspicious going in or out of that building? Perhaps at a time when they shouldn't have?'

'I'm afraid not. I just live here. I don't take part in the comings and goings of the community.'

'So you didn't see anything at all?'

'Nothing. But then I wasn't looking.'

'Even in the days or weeks before?'

'I'm sorry. No.'

'Okay. One last question. Where were you on Sunday night? The seventeenth?'

'Was that when this murder happened?'

'We presume it was. Where were you?'

'Here. At home, I suppose.'

'And you saw nothing? Heard nothing?'

'When I'm in for the night I'm usually listening to music. That would drown out anything else, I presume. Especially anything unpleasant.'

'Right.' Khan looked around once more. 'Well, thank you for your time. Fantastic place you've got here.'

Hinchcliffe smiled. 'Thank you.'

'I'll be off. And if you remember anything else in the meantime, here's my card. Give me a call. Even something little, you never know.'

'I will do.' Hinchcliffe took the card. 'You never know, Detective Constable Khan, you might hear from me again.'

'That would be good. All the best.'

Hinchcliffe led Khan downstairs and outside, closing and locking the door firmly behind him.

Walking up the street, Khan thought about the encounter he had just had.

Odd sort of bloke, he thought. At first. Bit of a loner. Even suspected him. But he warmed up. And what a jukebox . . .

45

The Lawgiver waited for the needle to fall, the snare to hit twice then the horns to come riffing in before dancing round the room, his voice enthusiastic but no match for Curtis Mayfield's beautifully pure and soulful singing. 'Move On Up'. He had that right.

Stupid rozzer . . . stupid thick fucking rozzer . . .

Talk about models, talk about jukeboxes, talk about anything but what he was there for. Easy to fool. Easy to lie to. Stupid. Thick. He had thought at first that the police hadn't questioned him because he had been lucky but meeting that example, witnessing him in action (or inaction) first hand, he knew that luck had very little to do with it. He was cleverer than them. Superior. That was all there was to it.

They hadn't caught him yet and they weren't going to. No stopping him now. Because he was doing the right thing. He knew that. Any doubts he may have had – and there had been doubts, any endeavour worth doing had doubts surrounding it – had been banished by the police officer's appearance. The Lawgiver had been looking for a sign, something to show him that his calling, his chosen profession, was the right one. He had thought that talking to Phil Brennan would have supplied that. But he had been wrong. Brennan was turning out to be just like all the rest of them. And if Khan was indicative of the calibre of people Brennan surrounded himself with, the members of his team, he wasn't surprised. Like attracts like, dull attracts dull.

No. Khan's visit had been just what he needed. He stood still in the middle of the room, let the music flow around him, the beat pound through him. This was it, he thought. This was what he was made for. Put on this planet for. And nothing was going to stop him. No one was going to stop him. No one.

An omen. He didn't normally believe in such things, didn't consider himself to be superstitious. That was for the lesser people, the dullards. The ones who didn't believe in themselves, who needed to blame someone else for the state they were in. Who needed zodiacs and God and crystals and whatever else to get them through life. He was resolutely not like that. His father had drummed it into him. *You work*, he had said. *That's what you do. You work, you get on in life. You make your own chances, you don't wait for anyone else to give them to you. Because if you do, you'll be waiting there a bloody long time.*

He had been right, his father. Even after he lost all his work and soon after that his health then ultimately his life, he never lost sight of what he believed in.

It wasn't his fault that fashions changed. That what he did, what he was skilled at, had devoted his life to, was an *artist* at, wasn't wanted any more. Not his fault at all. And he tried hard not to blame anyone else for it. But in the end he couldn't do that. When his health started to ebb away, when he no longer knew who he was on a day-to-day basis, then he started to say, in his more lucid moments, that it wasn't his fault. He wasn't to blame for this. But watching his father fade away in front of him, seeing him disappear piece by piece and bit by bit, like one of his precious models being made in reverse, the Lawgiver knew that he had to blame somebody. And when his father eventually died, that's when he put his plan into action.

Brian Wildman had been the person that his father did most

of his work for. They made models for films, TV, stage. And his father was very much in demand. But then the work dried up. A slow trickle at first, then eventually down to an arid nothing at all. And Brian Wildman, who had so admired his father's skills, had talked about making him a partner in the company, giving him shares even, the man who had told his father repeatedly when he noticed the work slipping away, not to worry. I'll always see you all right.

But he hadn't. He had sold up, gone to work in-house for a studio. Left his father out in the cold.

His father could have retrained, done something else. But then the Alzheimer's hit. And that was the slow end of that.

But the young Lawgiver couldn't accept that. He knew something had to be done. Some kind of justice. Brian Wildman must be made to pay for what he had done to his father.

So he moved down to where Wildman lived just outside London in Berkshire and followed him. For days and nights. Familiarised himself with his routines, his habits. Where he went, where he avoided. And the most important bit: when he was alone.

That was the easiest bit. Brian Wildman was married with three daughters. He also had a woman he visited in a block of flats just off the North Circular in Finchley. Usually on a Thursday evening. He always drove there alone. Always parked in an unlit street at the side of the building. Always cut through an overgrown pathway round to the front of the building so he couldn't be seen.

Perfect.

The young Lawgiver got there early, crouched down in the bushes, waited for darkness. And Brian Wildman. He had dressed in black, even a black knitted ski mask. And he carried in his hand a huge baking potato in a sock. He had thought long and hard over his choice of weapon before settling on that. If he was caught or questioned afterwards, or even before, he reasoned, he could claim that it wasn't a dangerous weapon. That he was going home to cook it. It was a feeble excuse, even to his own ears, but it was better than a knife or a gun. And easier to use. All he needed was anger.

Eventually, he heard Brian Wildman's car pull up. His heart was pounding, his hands were shaking.

As he heard footsteps approach, his first thought was to do nothing. To stay immobile, go home afterwards. Don't get involved. Because he knew that once he had done what he intended to do, he would have crossed a line. And it was a line there would be no stepping back from.

He tried to stand and for a few seconds thought his feet wouldn't move, his legs wouldn't support him. But they did. He stood quickly. Crossed in front of Brian Wildman, stood there blocking his path. Brian Wildman took in the black clothes, the ski mask and looked instantly terrified.

'Please,' he had said, 'let me through. Let me through or I'll call the police.' The young Lawgiver just stood there.

'Please, I'll . . . I'll scream. I'm going to . . . '

And almost of its own volition, he was aware of his arm lifting up, pulling back, the socked potato making a huge, heavy arc above his head, then coming down hard on Brian Wildman's head, the force knocking his glasses off, pushing him to the ground.

'Oww . . . what did you—did you do that . . . ?'

Without stopping to think, he did it again. And again. There might have been something inherently ridiculous in his choice of weapon but there was nothing remotely humorous in hearing the sound of it hitting Brian Wildman's skull, caving it in, watching it turn to pulp. The potato was as hard and resilient as a rock. By the fifth or sixth time, Brian Wildman was no longer moving and his head was soft and purple, the contents spilling out before him.

The young Lawgiver turned and ran. Never looked back once.

He packed up his rental property, came straight back to Birmingham. Almost numb with shock over what he had done.

It wasn't until a couple of days later when he read about it in the paper that the whole thing sunk in. He had done it. Got revenge for his father. Justice. Or the only kind of justice he was going to get. And how did he feel about it? Well, he had expected to feel terrible. Remorse and pain, guilt. Crying and sorry and insomniac. But he felt none of those things. Quite the opposite. He felt calm, relaxed. Justified. And his sleep was the best it had been for ages.

That was when he knew he had found his calling.

The song finished. There was a pause of a few seconds before the next one dropped. Crackle and hiss, the aural accretion of decades, kicked in first, a prelude to what was to come. Then Ike Hayes at his best. 'Good Love'. Slow to start, but it hit a groove soon and by the end was a huge, stomping, irresistible force. A winner. He laughed. Just like him. A metaphor for what he was doing.

He should wait a few days before the next one. He knew that. Reason told him that. Take some breathing space, savour the last two, plan the next one thoroughly. But the omens said don't listen to reason. Go straight ahead. Do it. And do it now. Because he was unstoppable.

But just in case, he'd better check the calendar . . .

He did so. And laughed out loud. Perfect. *Perfect.* This couldn't be a better day – or night – for what he had planned next. For who he had planned next.

In fact, it was so perfect and he was so sure of himself and his plan, that he might even give Phil Brennan a call. Not just to tell him he was going to strike again, but tell him who was the target and when he was going to be hit.

And there wouldn't be a thing Brennan could do to stop him.

Not a thing.

46

Phil was in his office trying to work through preliminary forensic reports for John Wright's mutilation. See if there was anything, no matter how small, some tiny discrepancy that he could use to crowbar his way into the investigation. So far he had found nothing. Whoever the Lawgiver was, he was meticulous.

That had made Phil think again. Perhaps Glen Looker wasn't in the frame. He was too obvious. And he had no motive. He made enough money from getting his clients off. If he was also murdering and mutilating villains, some that he had successfully defended, then he must be suffering from a severe mental imbalance. No. Phil had been thinking that perhaps the Lawgiver might be an actual police officer. The kind that set up anonymous blogs to moan about aspects of the job that they couldn't otherwise publicly talk about. But surely their blogs and Twitter and Facebook pages were enough for them? Most of them just wanted to get their gripes off their chests and out into the open. Make themselves feel better by stirring up the waters. It was a big jump between moaning and murdering. At least he thought so. He hoped so.

His train of thought was interrupted by his phone. He checked the display. It was an unnecessary act. He knew who it was by the ringtone. 'One Day Like This' by Elbow. Marina.

'Hey you,' he said.

'Hey yourself,' she replied.

He smiled. Never got old, that routine.

'Three times in one day. Must be some sort of record,' he said.

'Modern marriages, and all that,' she said. 'What happens when two career-minded people get together.'

'Still,' said Phil, 'it's worth it.'

'Well,' said Marina, trying to summon up a smile in her voice, 'I've had a couple of nights on the loose with Anni Hepburn ...'

'And now you're not coming back?'

Marina laughed. Her voice lowered, suddenly serious. 'I can't wait to come back.'

'Good. Me neither. When's that going to happen, then?'

'Soon. Very soon.'

He found himself smiling at the handset. 'Good.' He gave a quick look round to see whether anyone was listening in. It was a futile gesture. His office door was shut. Still, he lowered his voice. 'I miss you.'

'Miss you too.' Marina's voice was equally lowered. Talking in a public building.

'How's our mutual friend?'

'Just about to be carted off to Colchester. I've got to hang around with Anni to cross the Ts and dot the Is then I'm out of here.'

'Good.'

'Anyway, what about you? How did the press conference go?'

'About as well as could be expected, I think. We'll have to wait and see what he does next.'

'Unless you catch him first.'

'True,' said Phil. 'But unlikely the way things are going. Hard to get a grip on him. No clues at all. So far.'

'He'll slip up.'

'Yeah, I know. But I'm hoping we might get a break before then, not have to rely on that.'

'Just be careful,' she said.

'Thanks, Mum. Don't worry, I am being.'

'I'm sure you are. But I'm being serious. He's made contact with you already. He'll do it again.'

'I know. As I said, we're waiting.'

'You need me back there. With you on this one.'

'I won't lie. Your presence here would be greatly appreciated. In more ways than one.'

Marina gave a small laugh. 'Seriously, though. Be careful. If you're contacting him. If he's developed some kind of fixation on you. We've got Josephina to think about, remember. We don't want anything to happen to her. To us.'

The unspoken word *again* hung between them.

'I know,' he said. 'And I'm being careful. There's no reason for this nutter to want to get in touch with me personally. No reason. He's solely interested in me as a police officer. And if there's any indication that he wants to go further, I'll make sure she gets protection. And you too, if it comes to it.'

'And you. Promise me you'll stay safe.'

'I will. You're coming home. I want to be there for you.'

'Good.' Her voice dropped once more. 'I miss you.'

'You too.' He found himself smiling again. 'And I can't wait to see you.'

'Likewise. I'll drop Anni off and come straight home.'

'Not tempted to stay for another girlie night out?'

She laughed. 'Definitely not.'

'Good. I'll look forward to it.'

They hung up.

Phil tried to go back to the forensic reports but his mind was still on the phone call, on his wife. Then Imani burst into his office. He looked up, startled out of his reverie.

'Phone call, boss. It's him.'

Phil was out of his chair and straight after her.

217

47

Letisha Watson looked around her flat. Sighed. Jesus, what a dump. What an absolute shit hole.

She was looking at it with outside eyes. Like a visitor would. Not those coppers who had been here yesterday. She didn't care what they thought. No. Moses. How he had looked at the place. What he must have thought of it. She cared about that.

And she was sure it wasn't very positive.

She knew she was still suffering from the appearance of that pig copper, Sperring. Knew she was shaken up by that. But still. She had felt ashamed. That was it. Ashamed at the mess she lived in, the squalor, and ashamed that Moses had witnessed it. What her life had come down to. Seeing it through his eyes made her feel like that. Made her feel like it was the only way *to* feel.

It hadn't always been like that. There had been a time when the life she had wanted – the one she had aspired to, that should have been hers – had been in reach. Or she believed it had been. Back when she was Julian Wilson's girl.

Julian and Letisha. Wilson and Watson. Made for each other, they used to say. Meant to be together. Or at least she used to say that. She used to believe that. Thinking back, maybe she had been the only one saying that.

Her heart became heavy with the memories. She rarely thought about those days. It made getting through these days all the harder. It had been glamorous. Ghetto fabulous, as they used to say back in the day. On the arm of the leader of the Chicken Shack Crew, stepping out to clubs and bars around the city. Being shown deference, even reverence. Knowing that all the boys were lusting after her, their girlfriends and baby-mothers all jealous of her. She loved that. Had thrived on it.

Because she knew what she was, where she was from. She knew how lucky she had been. One of the girls the crew had turned out to make some money. A local girl, Handsworth all the way. School had taught her nothing. Just that she didn't need school. She had started hanging round at the Chicken Shack when she was in her teens. It was exciting. A dangerous, thrilling life that was so different from the one she had at home. All attending her mother's church and straight home from school. The Chicken Shack was full of real gangsters. And players. It was cool. So cool. Like a glimpse into another life. A better life.

There were plenty of wannabes hanging around there but she soon saw through them. The real players always outshone them in every way. She would see the guys, the real guys, come in with their girls on their arms. The guys looked buff. Handsome and rugged, their threads cool, their attitude correct. The girls looked so exotic, with their designer clothes, make-up and expensive hair dos, like they were from somewhere totally alien to her, Hollywood or somewhere like it. They would stand around while the boys did their business, their studied bored looks rendering them untouchable, unapproachable. Occasionally – very occasionally – someone would stumble in there, genuinely not knowing who they were and try to hit on them. They didn't last long. The lessons those fools were taught were short and swift. They were never seen inside the Chicken Shack again. Or anywhere in the area.

That, the teenage Letisha knew, was what she wanted to be. One of the girls.

So she worked towards it, with a passion she never showed for anything at school. She got noticed, got in with the right people. Looked pretty to the boys it mattered looking pretty too. And it worked. Or so she thought. She was invited to parties with the crew. It was only when she got there that she learned what she was expected to do. Letisha had been a virgin until then. And, after the first couple of uncomfortable times, she realised she didn't mind. When the boys realised she was okay she was invited to more parties. And more. And that's when she thought one of them would choose her as a girlfriend. Wrong. That's when they turned her out.

She didn't mind at first. Getting paid for what she had been enjoying seemed fine with her. She didn't tell her God-fearing mother what she was doing, in fact she barely went home, choosing to live at a new friend's flat.

But it wore her down. Being told who to sleep with when she didn't feel like it was exhausting. And sometimes nauseating. She wanted out. But she couldn't see a way.

Then she caught the eye of Julian Wilson. And everything changed.

That's when she became what she had aspired to be all along. Not just one of the girls that everyone was lusting over or jealous of, but the boss's girl who even the other girls were jealous of. She didn't know if she was respected or feared, loved or hated. But it didn't matter. Because she was treated well because of it.

And then she met Moses Heap.

For a while everything got better. Unbelievably so. Happier than she had ever been. And then it changed. From such a great height came the great fall. It was a long fall and when she hit the ground she hit hard. And found herself where she was now.

She looked around the flat once more. Her tiny, squalid flat. Her tiny, squalid life.

And felt nothing but self-loathing.

She didn't often think of the old days because when she did it led her back to this. Depression at who she was now, where she lived. Getting into a fight with that slag Chloe Hannon over Darren Richards. Had she really come down to that? Had she been so desperate not to lose that loser from her life that she fought to keep him? Had he made things any better for her in the short time they had been together? Really? When she thought about how far she'd fallen, what she had had and what she had lost, she seriously doubted it.

Her mother never spoke to her now. She saw her quite regularly, in the street, at the shops. But just looked away. Like her God's love and compassion that she was always preaching no longer extended to her own daughter.

She had nothing. No one. Nothing to look forward to. No future except sitting alone with her memories. And Moses, from last night.

Moses.

She felt that familiar tug at something inside her. He connected with her. Deep and hard. A feeling she had never experienced with anyone before and knew she never would feel for anyone ever again. Only him. And in that moment knew she had to see him again. Not just because of what he had said to her last night, why he had come to call on her, but because it was time to stop playing around. She had had enough of sitting here feeling sorry for what she had done. For what had happened. More than enough. Time to move on.

She got up from her armchair, made her way to the bathroom.

Summon up some of the spirit from the girl she used to be. The one who inspired envy and jealousy. Lust and desire. Hopefully not hatred.

At any rate, the least she could do was make herself presentable.

48

'Look, I was only being polite. That's all . . . '

Anni kept her back to Mickey. She must have heard him, even though he spoke under his breath close up to her, but she gave him no indication that she had. She just kept looking down, her back to him, making notes, waiting for the uniforms to come and talk to her. Tying up loose ends so they could get back to Colchester.

She had been like this ever since he had asked Deepak about Jessie. Nothing had even happened between them on the case they had worked together but Jessie had made it clear – or at least Anni believed Jessie had made it clear – that she wouldn't mind if something had.

She was always like that with him. He didn't know if it was real jealousy or whether she was just play-acting, seeing if she could get a response out of him. Letting him know who was boss. There had never been any long-term damage to their relationship, in fact the make-up sex afterwards had always been phenomenal. Maybe that was why she did it, he thought. If so, he was happy for her to continue. But there was always the feeling he couldn't shake that she would behave like this one time too many and mean it. Then there would be no coming back for him.

A uniformed officer came and spoke to her. She moved away from Mickey, relaying her instructions. He caught sight of

Marina on the phone, her back turned away from him. He knew who she would be calling. He felt a slight pang of envy then. Marina and Phil had such a good relationship. Perfectly matched, complementing each other in every aspect of their lives. But their happiness had been hard won and at some cost to them both. Yet their suffering just seemed to strengthen the bond between them. What he had with Anni was good, the best he had ever had with anyone, but sometimes he wished he didn't have to work so hard for it. That was all.

Anni finished talking to the uniform. Turned to face him.

'Look,' he began, and sighed. 'I didn't—'

'Is everything ready for you to take the suspect back to Southway, Detective Sergeant Phillips?' she said, straight-faced, businesslike.

'Uh, yes, just about. I'll, I'll check—'

'Make sure that you do. We don't want any delays, do we?'

Then Anni moved in close so her mouth was on his ear. 'Just wait till I get you home, tiger . . . ' She pulled away, smiled at him, winked. Then she was off sorting out something else that needed doing.

Mickey broke into a sudden grin. She had done it again. Played him. And he didn't mind. In fact, he felt like his heart was about to burst.

God, he loved that woman. Totally and wholeheartedly. More than love, if he was honest. He firmly believed she had saved his life.

Well, Anni and Phil Brennan. Both in different ways.

He had originally joined the Met. Growing up in Ilford, on the border of East London and Essex, that was all he had wanted to be, a copper. But not some *Dixon of Dock Green*, *Juliet Bravo* type. No, he had grown up watching re-runs of *The Sweeney*. *Thief Takers*. Stuff like that. His favourite film was the old gangster pic *The Long Good Friday*. They had fuelled his fantasies, given him his direction in life. Acted as the best recruitment incentive possible. He had never wanted to wear a uniform, not like some of the others that were attracted to the job, who had been in his class at Hendon; he had just wanted to drive around in a fast car, taking it out on villains, criminals, the scum of society. Giving them what for. Making the streets safer for civilians and if some of them ever wanted to show their gratitude in some way or another, then why not?

And, to his surprise, it had worked out just the way he had wanted. He had ended up on the Drugs Squad and in with a team of guys about the same age as him who all seemed to have been brought up sharing the same collective fantasy. Once they realised that about each other, they lost no time in acting it out.

And it had been fun for a while. Living out his adolescent fantasy in the most untouchable way possible. But it had also been the start of his downfall.

Before long, he and the rest of his team had been taking backhanders, getting freebies from working girls, taking more drugs than the villains and turning more blind eyes than Helen Keller. And while his contemporaries were thriving on it – or appearing to – it was crippling him. Not just physically, with his sickness record starting to attract attention, but it was beginning to damage him, corrupt him, in ways he hadn't imagined. Mickey had never had much truck with those who talked of a soul, happy clappers and the like. But the longer he went on behaving as he was doing, the more he felt he had a soul. And it was being corroded.

Eventually, feeling he had no option, he put in for a transfer. His adolescent dreams and fantasies were, he had discovered, just that. Real life was so much harder. He didn't care where he went. Anywhere, doing anything, so long as it was away from what he had been doing, away from the people he had been doing it with.

Luckily, a vacancy for a DS in the Major Incident Squad based in Colchester, Essex, came up. Mickey jumped at it, grabbing it with both hands. He didn't think he would get it but didn't know what he would do if he didn't. He travelled up the A12 to Colchester to meet with Phil Brennan. At first he thought he had blown his only chance. He had gone into the interview with all the swagger his time at the Met had invested in him. And seeing the man in front of him, wearing jeans, Converse and a plaid western shirt, his hair spiked up and quiffed, Mickey realised he had made a huge mistake. As it turned out, Phil Brennan saw something in him, had managed to look behind all the macho, pseudo-alpha-male posturing to see an intelligent, creative detective struggling to get out.

And that was how, professionally, Phil Brennan had saved his life.

And then there was Anni. Just as Phil had done through the job, Anni did the same for all the other parts of his life. He had never really had a proper relationship with a woman before he met Anni. He'd had sexual relationships, of course. Sometimes taking freebies from working girls or flashing his badge to entice uniform groupies when the mood took him, but never anything long-lasting, meaningful. His worldview was the same as that of his previous colleagues in the Met: women were there to be used, not there as equals. Anni changed all that. She was the first woman that he came to view as an equal. They were colleagues, friends. She just happened to be a woman, too. And gradually, he realised how attracted he was becoming to her. And she, not that he dared admit it to himself, to him.

But he was hesitant to act upon his feelings, to ask her out. If he was honest, he was scared to. He didn't want his attraction to her to get in the way of their working relationship, their friendship. Anni, taking her lead from him, was doing the same. That was why it had taken them so long to get together.

They needn't have worried. He needn't have worried. Anni was perfect. As wonderful a lover and partner as she was a friend and colleague. He had his job, his partner.

Mickey, at that moment, waiting to take Fiona Welch back to Colchester and then meet up with Anni later in the evening, had never been happier in his life.

49

Phil almost ran into the squad room. With its wood-block floor, half panelled walls and painted brick, it looked like an old schoolroom. The way the team were standing around silently, expectantly, only encouraged that impression. He was the teacher, the silence seemed to say. They were all waiting to learn something.

Phil sat down opposite Elli, picked up a handset. Behind her keyboard, she gave him a nod. Phil tried to quell his hammering heart, put the phone to his ear.

'Phil Brennan.' His voice as businesslike as possible.

'Hi, Phil, know who this is?'

The voice was muffled, as usual, but unmistakable. In a short space of time it had become very recognisable.

'Yes, I know who this is.'

A pause. 'Say my name.' Quietly, a shudder running through the words.

'What?'

'Say. My. Name.'

Phil looked up, caught Cotter's eye. She nodded for him to get on with it.

'Lawgiver.'

The Lawgiver laughed. An edge of mania to it. 'That's it, that's it . . . good man.'

Phil tried to ground him, control the conversation. 'We're on to you. We're getting nearer.'

More laughter answered him. 'No you're not, Phil, don't lie. If you were on to me then I'd be surrounded by a whole load of armed police all pointing their weapons at me.' A pause. 'I've just looked around. I don't see anyone.' Another laugh, not as maniac this time. More valedictory. 'You're nowhere near finding me.'

Phil didn't answer. He didn't know what to answer him with.

'So,' said the Lawgiver, continuing, 'I saw your press conference.'

'And what did you think?'

'Not the ringing endorsement I was hoping for, if I'm honest, Phil. I mean, are you with me? On my side? Nothing I heard on the TV made me think you are. Is that the case?'

'Is it as simple as that?' said Phil. 'Either for you or against you?'

'Yes,' replied the Lawgiver, 'it is. Because it sounded like you were against me on the TV. Is that right? That you're out to get me. Would I be correct in thinking that?'

Phil sighed, made his voice sound weary, reasonable. 'Listen, why don't we just talk, eh? You and me. If you don't want to come in, we can go somewhere, somewhere neutral. What d'you think of that?'

The Lawgiver's voice hardened. 'Don't insult me. We've had this conversation before. Clearly one of us is incapable of remembering it. I won't come in to talk to you. I won't meet you somewhere neutral to talk to you. There's no such thing. Your team would be on me within seconds. And then I really would be surrounded by armed coppers. I'm not an idiot so don't treat me like one.' His voice rose on those final words, became filled with menace.

Cotter made a gesture with her hand: *keep him talking.*

228

'Look,' said Phil, trying not to lose control of the conversation, 'I agree with what you're saying. Totally. You've got a right to be angry about the way things are.'

'Oh, have I? Well, that's very kind of you to allow that, Phil, thank you. Thank you very much.'

Phil ignored the outburst, kept on. 'I agree with you. I'm not lying. You've got a right to be angry. We all have, absolutely, at the way things are. I share that anger. Everyone on my team shares that anger. Each and every day.'

'Oh, really? Even when you and your sort are often the cause of that anger? You'll forgive me if I'm not convinced by your words.'

'Why not?'

'Because it seems like the police are on the news on a daily basis for doing something wrong. For falsifying evidence at the scenes of shootings. For covering up for each other when you make a mistake instead of being honest and admitting it. A Brazilian electrician is mistaken for a terrorist and murdered on a tube train. Witnesses gave false evidence to the TV cameras on the police's say-so. A so-called gangster is executed on a Tottenham street. An innocent newspaper seller is attacked and killed by a riot copper with previous for violent behaviour. A discredited doctor even fixed the post-mortem for them. They're all dead. All covered up by the law. Their killers were all coppers. Their killers all walked free. Their killers were all your lot. So you'll forgive me if I don't believe you when you say you share my anger.' His voice was impassioned, rage bleeding through every word.

'You can believe what you want,' said Phil. 'I was just as appalled as you were when I read about those incidents. Police or no police. But you should believe me when I say it.'

'Should I?'

'Yes. You've thrown examples at me, let me throw one at

you. What about this. We get called in to some crime scene. A child's been killed, say. For argument's sake. We go in, talk to the family. Now we know straight away that the father was abusing the child. And threatening the child's mother. Probably abusing her, too. But we've no evidence. We can't prove it. So what do we do? What should we do?'

Silence on the line.

'I'm asking you a question.'

'Oh, sorry,' said the Lawgiver, his voice dripping sarcasm, 'I thought it was rhetorical. You want an answer? Really? Make the father talk.'

'But we have nothing to go on, besides a dead child. The mother won't talk, the father won't crack. So we do what we're trained to do. Gather evidence. Watch. Build up a picture. Then we pull them in for questioning. And we never ask a question that we don't know the answer to, or that we're expecting an answer to. We put aside our personal feelings about these people and what they may or may not have done, and we do our job. Because this is about justice. Not vengeance. About justice being done and being seen to be done.'

'But what if it goes wrong?' said the Lawgiver. 'What d'you do then?'

'You mean get angry?' said Phil, trying to keep his voice calm. 'Anyone can do that. Get all self-righteous and violent. Pick up a weapon and convince themselves that they're doing something positive. But that's still not justice.'

'This case with the dead child. What if it goes to court and the father gets off? Or the mother? Insufficient evidence, the defence tells a better story, what if you or one of your lot follows the wrong procedure? Where's your justice then?'

'That's something we have to live with,' said Phil. 'We don't always get it right. But we try to. It's not perfect, but that's the way it is.'

230

'That isn't justice,' said the Lawgiver, anger again in his voice. 'Not done, not even seen to be done.'

'So what would you do?' asked Phil.

The Lawgiver laughed. It was a harsh, metallic sound. 'I'd make sure he or she could never kill again. Because they would. They've just got off. They've learned nothing. They'd pay for what they did. One way or another.'

'Take the law into your own hands?'

'Why not?' said the Lawgiver. 'You don't seem to have much use for it.'

Phil fell silent. He was aware of Cotter gesturing to him, making him talk on, but he couldn't think of anything to say for the moment.

In the absence of words from Phil, the Lawgiver continued. He sighed. 'Oh, Phil,' he said, 'I had such high hopes for you. Such high hopes.'

'Then I'm sorry to disappoint you,' said Phil, sounding anything but.

'So am I, Phil, so am I. I was led to believe you were someone I could do business with, as that evil old trout Maggie Thatcher used to say.'

Phil was suddenly energised by the Lawgiver's words. He sat forward, grasped the handset harder. 'Who told you? Who led you to believe that?'

There was silence on the line. Phil heard the Lawgiver make a sharp intake of breath. He knew in that silence that even if he hadn't given himself away, the Lawgiver had said too much.

Phil pressed on. 'Who led you to believe that?'

'Just listen,' said the Lawgiver, cutting Phil's question dead. 'I'm going to take the law into my own hands again. Since you've been so comically inept at catching me up until this point, at stopping me, I thought it only fair to give you a head start.'

Phil's heart skipped a beat. 'What d'you mean?'

'Tonight.'

'What d'you mean, tonight?'

'What d'you think I mean? I shall be making someone pay for their crimes tonight.'

Without looking round, Phil could sense the growing unease in the squad room. He tried to keep his voice calm and level. 'Do we get to know where?'

The Lawgiver laughed. 'You get more than that. You get to know who.'

Phil waited. Realised he was supposed to ask the question. 'Who?'

'Someone responsible for keeping most of the criminals of Birmingham on the streets. For making sure they evade justice – both your variety and mine – as much as possible. One of the worst specimens of sub-humanity working in an industry that thrives on it.'

'Who?' Phil tried not to lose control of his voice.

'Glen Looker.'

Phil was aware of the squad room holding its collective breath around him.

'We'll stop you,' said Phil. 'We'll protect him.'

The Lawgiver laughed once more. 'No you won't. Oh, believe me, you won't. Justice may be blind, but you, I'm afraid, are blinder.'

He hung up.

The squad room burst into action.

50

The light was fading, day was coming to an end and Sperring was thinking the same thing about his vigil.

He had sat outside the studios of the No Postcode Organisation waiting for Moses Heap to appear all afternoon. And while he was sure there were things he could have been doing – or that Phil would have preferred him to be doing – before clocking-off time he still felt he was doing something worthwhile. Fair enough, not many people had gone in and out, or at least not many faces that he knew, but that didn't mean it was time wasted. Not in his eyes. He had photographed everyone that went through the doors so at least he would have something to go on when he got back to the station. And even if Phil didn't want him to keep up this line of enquiry, something – some old-time copper's instinct – told him that he would need those snapshots one day. That he was looking at present and future gang members.

He didn't believe that rubbish about Moses Heap seeing the light. Not one word of it. Criminals like him just didn't do that. Not in Sperring's experience, anyway. Fair enough, there were one or two, and they made a big show of it, writing books about their experiences, their poor, awful childhoods, how they were led into a life of crime. How they had seen the error of their ways. Decided to make their living as a writer or an actor or an artist, something like that. Something the world was crying out for more of. Still, Sperring thought, good luck to them. As long as they didn't come back on to his manor he didn't really care.

Circumstances. That was all. And from the look of the place Moses Heap was hanging out in and the people he was mixing with, his circumstances hadn't changed at all. Therefore, he hadn't. Sperring's logic. Never wrong.

Sperring yawned, checked his watch. Jesus, time had started to crawl. Backwards, from the look of it.

He contemplated leaving it for a while, going to clock off, get something to eat, maybe come back later. Follow Heap around in his own time. Heap never used to be much of a one for the daytime. He doubted he had changed that much.

Then his phone rang. Nadish.

'What can I do you for?'

'Get back to the station,' said Khan. He sounded like he was out of breath, like he'd been running the length of Steelhouse Lane.

'Why? Nearly clocking-off time.'

'It's him. The Lawgiver. He's been on the phone again. He's given us a target, location and time. Boss wants everyone on it. Now.'

'Shit.'

Sperring cut the call, started the car.

And that was when he saw her: Letisha Watson making her way up to the entrance of the studio.

'Shit.' Even louder this time.

Now Sperring was torn. Genuinely torn. Her presence at the studio, now, after everything that had happened in the last couple of days, wasn't an accident. Couldn't be. It meant something was happening, or was about to happen. Something major. It also vindicated his decision to sit here all afternoon. Old-time copper's instinct, he thought. Never wrong.

234

And then he thought of the summons, back to the station. The chance to catch the Lawgiver in action. He couldn't ignore it, pretend he didn't receive the call. And he couldn't sit here any longer.

Reluctantly, he turned the car around, headed back to the station.

51

'Right. You got everything?'

Anni looked at Mickey as one professional to another. As if the earlier wink hadn't happened. And he loved her even more for it.

'Yep,' he said. He looked over at Fiona Welch who was standing between two uniforms. 'I'll take her straight back to Colchester. Want to get her there as quickly as possible. Don't want to run down the custody clock, and all that.'

'I should be coming with you,' Anni said.

'Yeah, I know,' he said. 'But you've still got stuff to tie up here. I'll stick her in the back. She's cuffed.' He smiled. 'I think I can handle her.'

'Let's hope so,' said Anni, then smiled. 'Don't want to get any jealous ideas about you and her ... '

'Yeah, right,' he said. He laughed, but there was that slight undertone to her words. He still didn't want to upset her.

She leaned in to him, whispered, 'I'm joking, idiot.'

'Yeah,' he said, mock-affronted. 'I knew that.'

Anni shook her head. 'I'll get Marina to give me a lift back. I'll see you later.'

'Right.' He leaned in to kiss her.

'Not here,' she said. 'Idiot.'

Mickey reddened. 'Sorry,' he said. 'Forgot where I was for a moment.'

Anni smiled, walked off.

Mickey took Fiona Welch by the arm, started to walk her towards the doors.

'Just a minute,' she said.

'What?'

'I want to say goodbye to someone.'

'You haven't been here that long. And I doubt you made any friends.'

She turned to him. Eyes unknowable. 'I want to say goodbye to someone.' She gestured with her shoulder, the only part of her body she could use since her arms were pulled tight behind her. 'Her.'

Mickey followed her gaze. 'Who, Marina Esposito?'

'As one psychologist to another.'

Mickey shook his head. 'Whatever. Make it quick.'

He walked her over to where Marina was. She looked up at their approach.

'Doesn't want to leave without saying her goodbyes,' said Mickey.

Marina looked confused. 'Oh. Right.' She stood there, unmoving, offering Fiona Welch nothing.

Fiona Welch smiled. 'Goodbye,' she said. 'Although it isn't really. I'll be seeing you again very soon.'

Marina looked slightly taken aback at the words. 'I . . . I don't think so.'

'You're wrong, Marina. Very wrong.'

'I doubt it.'

Mickey sighed. He had had enough of her. He grabbed her arm, began to lead her away. 'Come on,' he said. 'You've had your fun.'

Fiona Welch turned, looked over her shoulder at Marina, smiled. 'Give Phil my love.'

Marina didn't reply.

Mickey dragged her away.

'Nutter,' he said, under his breath.

Fiona Welch just smiled.

52

Phil had never been inside Glen Looker's office before. Never even been near it. He hadn't expended much thought in imagining what it might look like, even. However, when he reached it he realised it was exactly the kind of place that he expected Glen Looker to be based in.

Being on the other side of Queensway it wasn't that far from Birmingham Central, the station on Steelhouse Lane he operated from. However, that, he thought, must be only an accident of geography. Concerning everything else, they may as well have been on opposite sides of the city. The country, even.

It was situated near enough to the courts to attract trade but far enough away to keep the rents down. A shabby doorway in a rundown old office block led the way. A handwritten sign on the intercom at the side told interested parties that this was 'Looker Solicitor'. Phil thought of pressing the button but found that the door opened when he pushed it so just went inside.

The stairway was narrow, covered by the kind of loose, worn carpeting that Looker had made many a successful compensation case out of for his clients. It smelled vaguely of cabbage, or something else that had been stewing too long. The walls were all flaking plaster. Phil made his way slowly upwards, breathing through his mouth. At the first-floor landing he found a locked doorway with a buzzer at the side of it.

He pressed it, waited.

Eventually a bored female voice gave the name of the company.

'Detective Inspector Brennan,' he said, 'West Midlands Police. I need to see Mr Looker. Urgently.'

'D'you have an appointment?'

'No I don't. But this is urgent. Can you buzz me in, please?'

There was a pause while Phil was sure she was deciding whether to do so or not. She did and he walked into the reception area.

Sitting round the walls on chairs that looked as if they'd been bought as a job lot from an office surplus store sometime during John Major's time in office were the kind of people Phil dealt with all the time. Some he even recognised and, from the way they became instantly uncomfortable and hands disappeared into jacket pockets and conversation ceased, it was clear that some of them recognised him too.

They were the revolving-door people. In and out of court and prison so many times that it became a home from home for them.

Phil looked at the receptionist, a drab, middle-aged woman who seemed to have lost several battles in her life and had finally accepted who and what she was. Even if that acceptance wasn't wanted or welcome.

'This his office?' said Phil, pointing to another door.

'You can't go in there,' the receptionist said, standing up from behind her desk.

'Police business. Urgent. Matter of life and death.' Phil strode over to the door.

The receptionist, quick for such a large woman, got there before him. Probably used to people trying to barge in on her boss, Phil thought.

'I said you can't go in there,' she announced once more, her arms flung out. 'I don't care who you are.'

'Then tell him I'm here. And he has to see me. Now.'

240

She stared straight into his eyes. It was a gaze that Phil could see usually made people, even the hardest criminals, he would have imagined, back down. But Phil's gaze was steelier than that. Eventually she relented.

'I'll see if he's free.'

'He'd better be.'

She went into the office, making a point of slamming the door behind her. Soon, the door opened again and out came a young black man, angry at having his meeting disturbed, especially when it was for police. He walked past Phil aiming for swagger but ended up just trying not to run to get out of the copper's way. The receptionist followed him out of the room.

'Mr Looker will see you now,' she announced.

'Thank you,' said Phil, managing a smile.

It wasn't returned.

He entered the room, closed the door behind him. Glen Looker sat behind his desk. All the furniture in the room looked like it had come in the same job lot as the chairs in the reception room. It was dark and depressing. The only flash of light and colour was a poster advertising white-beach holidays in the Maldives. The vibrancy in it just made the room seem sadder, more enclosed.

'Detective Inspector Brennan,' said Glen Looker, sitting back, 'welcome to my world.'

'Thank you.'

He sat forward. 'You'd better have a bloody good reason for barging in here like this. You nearly gave poor Janice a heart attack.'

'I think it would take more than that,' said Phil.

Looker shrugged. 'Maybe. So why are you here? It's important, I presume.'

'It is,' said Phil, sitting down in one of the uncomfortable-looking metal chairs. 'Our friend the Lawgiver has been in contact again.'

'Has he now.'

'And he's told us who his next target will be.'

'Oh? And who might that be? One of my clients, I suppose?'

'More than that. You.'

Looker stared at him, jaw open. It took him some time but he eventually regained his composure. 'What?' he asked, voice small and incredulous.

'What I said. He called us, and it was him, definitely, and told us that his next target is you.'

Looker kept staring at Phil. Eventually his face creased up, his shoulders shook. Oh God, thought Phil. He's going to cry. But he didn't. His mouth formed a smile, he threw his head back and began to laugh.

Phil just stared.

The laughter continued for longer than was natural. Eventually it subsided and Looker stared once again at Phil, the smile still on his face.

'Glad you think it's amusing,' said Phil, not knowing whether Looker's reaction was bravado, genuine humour or mania.

'Hilarious,' said Looker. 'And when is this supposed to be happening? Did he tell you that as well?'

'He did, as a matter of fact,' said Phil. 'Tonight.'

Looker stared at Phil once more, then the laughter started again.

Eventually it subsided and Looker sat there, riding the after-shocks, shaking his head. 'Tonight. Oh, that's good. That's really good.'

'Why is it really good?' asked Phil. 'What's so special about tonight?'

Looker kept smiling. 'It's the annual West Midlands Law Society Dinner. Radisson Blu Hotel. Really smart affair. Surprised you don't know about it.'

'Not my kind of thing.'

Looker shrugged. 'Oh. Well. There you go. Black tie, the works. And I'm going to be there.'

'And so will we.'

Looker shook his head. 'You honestly think that he's going to attack me there? In the middle of all those people? Seriously? He wouldn't dare.'

'Apparently he would. So I'm here to talk you out of going.'

Looker laughed once more. 'Piss off. I paid for this months ago. Not losing my money now.'

'Your life is in danger.'

'So you keep saying. What d'you think he's going to do? Poison my gin and tonic? Make me choke on the rubber chicken? That's not a euphemism, by the way. Just a comment on corporate catering.'

'So you're still going to go?'

'Course. Wouldn't miss this. Networking central, that is.'

'I can't persuade you to come into protective custody?'

'Do me a favour. Knowing you lot and what you think of me, I put myself in your hands I'll never get out again.'

Phil shook his head. This wasn't the response he had been expecting.

'Hey,' Looker leaned forward, eyes lit by a manic light, 'maybe it's not me he's after.'

'What makes you say that?'

'Maybe it's a . . . diversion. Yeah, that's it. You know what I mean? Misdirection. Classic ploy. Like they do in the films. You know, you get all of your team, all your forces, concentrating on one area and he fools you, goes off somewhere else. Might be that.'

'It's not like in the films. He's after you. And he's going to get you tonight. That's what we've been told, that's what we're acting on.'

'Right.' Looker put his head down, nodded.

'So what are we going to do, Mr Looker?'

He looked up again. 'Do? What d'you mean? D'you want me to wear a bulletproof vest or something?'

'Would you? Even a stab vest?'

'Course not. Ruin the cut of my suit.'

Phil sighed, stood up. 'Well, I have to say, I thought you'd be more worried than this. It's your life that's in danger, after all.'

Looker spread his arms out in a supplicating gesture. 'Look, Detective Inspector, I deal with these kinds of people every day. I know what they're like. You must do too. They're always saying something or other. They're going to kill me, get my family. Whatever. If I had a quid for every death threat I've had against me, I'd have retired over there long ago.' He pointed to the poster of the Maldives.

'Fine, if that's the way you want to play it. But I have to tell you, we'll be there. My team. We'll have the place surrounded and we'll be watching you all night. Whether you like it or not.'

Looker smiled once more. 'Are you violating my human rights, Detective Inspector?'

Phil sighed once more. 'Have a good evening, Mr Looker.'

He turned, left the room.

Glen Looker watched him go. As he did so, the smile slowly slid from his face. Once he realised Phil had gone he leaned over to his desk intercom.

'Hold all my appointments for the time being, please, Janice,' he said then cut himself off before she could answer.

He reached down into the bottom drawer of his desk, drew out a bottle of Teacher's and a glass. Poured himself a generous slug, drank it almost straight down.

Tried to pretend that while he did it, has hand wasn't really shaking.

53

Letisha Watson had dug out her very best clothes. Or the very best that she could find at short notice and that were clean. She had hoped they would make her feel good, like the kind of woman who had spent a beautiful night of love-making with such a wonderful man. But they didn't. They just reminded her of how far she had slipped from the girl everyone envied. How much confidence she had lost. And the visit from that bastard fed hadn't helped.

But it had increased her need to see Moses. Her desperation to see Moses.

She moved quickly past the reception – some of the old attitude still there – and found her way around the building. The studio. That's where he would be. That's where he always was. His office, he called it. Where he met people, did business, worked and chilled. She envied him that. And loved him for it at the same time.

She walked down the corridors, acting like she belonged there, was meant to be there. Eventually she came to the room she was looking for. The one with the light on above the doorway. Red meant busy, green meant enter. It was red. She put her back to the wall, waited.

Letisha sighed. Heavily. What was she doing? Why was she here? She was making herself look stupid, that was it. Like the kind of girl who's always trailing after a man. Stupid and obsessed. But that wasn't it. Wasn't the whole story. That fed's arrival, twice in two days, had confirmed that to her. She had to see him. Not just for herself, not just for what she wanted to say to him. But for other reasons.

Bigger reasons.

She stood there, waiting, hardly daring to breathe. She wanted a cigarette but knew she would be thrown out if she was found lighting up. So she held that craving inside, joining all the other longings she wanted to act on.

The light went off. Red to green.

Letisha took a deep breath. Another. And walked inside.

The smell of the weed hit her first. And the low lighting. The mixing desk was lit up with a couple of desk lamps but the rest of the room was in shadow. In front of a glass screen was a boy she recognised from the estate. He was just taking off a pair of headphones, looking pleased with himself. The boy behind the mixing desk didn't look much older than the rapper but he clearly knew what he was doing, head down, focused on the switches. Neither had noticed her enter.

She stood by the door, waited while her eyes acclimatised to the gloom. Looked around, tried to pick out the man she was here to see. Couldn't find him. In the furthest section of the room she could see low shadows, figures lying around on bean bags or sofas. The occasional inflamed red dots told her that was where the smell of weed was coming from. Moses must be in one of those.

She didn't know what to do. She had come this far but her courage was beginning to fail her. She could just walk over to the young men, look for Moses. Or she could ask the boy behind the mixing desk.

''Scuse me,' she said, trying to sound confident but fearing her voice would get lost in the room's soundproofing, ''Scuse me. I'm here to see Moses Heap.'

The boy barely glanced at her. He nodded towards the shadowed corner, went back to his work.

Letisha felt her legs tremble as she walked over there. She tried to rationalise it. Why? This was the man she had spent the night with, who had been in her bed, making love to her. Why was she so scared about seeing him again?

She reached the group, stood over them. She recognised Moses straight away.

'Moses?' she said, her voice hushed, almost reverential, like she was in her mother's church, or something.

He turned, smiling. The smile disappeared when he saw who it was. He stood up.

'What you doing here?' he said, grabbing her shoulders.

'I . . . I . . . need to see you . . .'

He looked around quickly, back at the others. Her eyes followed his and she saw a face she recognised. Tiny Wilson, the leader of the Chicken Shack Crew. Julian's little brother. Not so little any more. And he was looking at her. He made her straight away.

Moses pulled her out of the room, past the mixing desk and into the hall. While the door slowly closed, he stared at her. Once it was in place he spoke. His voice was low but there was no mistaking the anger in it.

'What you doing? Why you here?'

'I need to see you. It's . . . that fed was round again today. Askin' me stuff. Stuff about you. We . . . we need—'

'What? We need what?'

'We need to do somethin'.'

'Like what? What would you suggest?'

'I . . . I dunno . . .'

He shook his head.

'Moses, I was scared. I didn't know what to do. I had to come and find you. Had to . . .'

The door opened. Tiny Wilson stood there. Unsmiling. 'You okay?' he said to Moses.

'Yeah, man, everything's cool. Be back in a minute.'

Tiny looked Letisha up and down, shook his head slightly and, still unsmiling, went back inside. Any doubt she might have held that he did not recognise her was now completely gone.

Moses turned back to her. She looked up imploringly at him.

'What are we gonna do?'

'You've done it now,' he said, 'haven't you? Coming here, you've done it.'

'I'm sorry, I—'

'Sorry? Great. You're sorry. Everything's fucked.'

He dropped his hands from her arms, turned and went back inside. The door hissed slowly closed behind him.

Letisha slammed her back against the wall.

He was gone. She had never felt so alone.

54

The Law Society Dinner was about as opulent as gatherings of solicitors got. The main function room of the Radisson Blu Hotel, the huge blue-glass monolith on the Queensway roundabout in the city centre, was a fairly recent addition to Birmingham's skyline but had found favour as an upscale destination for weddings and corporate functions. The function room was huge, leading to two bars, one on the same floor, another on the floor below. The décor veered on the comfortable side of severity, offering corporate hospitality with a self-conscious hipster edge. It gave the intended impression: it was impressive. Being there, guests should feel impressive too.

Phil stood at the back double doors, surveyed the room. He had donned his weddings, funerals and press conferences suit once more and if he wasn't standing out as being neither staff nor guest, he wore it with sufficient unease to avoid being singled out as police either. Everyone else was wearing black tie or evening dress, including Cotter who was already in attendance as a guest along with her partner, a solicitor.

Phil had spread his team all over the room. All in constant communication through in-earpieces, worn as inconspicuously as possible. He had tried to place them in positions of good vantage where there was also little chance of them being seen. It was difficult. Cotter had suggested that they dress as serving staff as a way of blending in but since none of them had any training in that area or any inclination to join in, it had been quickly vetoed. They would just get in the way, stop the staff from doing their jobs, hinder and compromise their ability to do their own. Besides, most of them were known to a lot of the diners. They might find it strange, not to mention worrying, if the Major Incident Squad were to be seen serving their starters.

The diners had finished their meal and were sitting patiently in their seats, drinking post-prandial coffees and liqueurs, listening politely – and laughing politely in all the right places – to the speeches.

Phil, his back to the doors, spoke into his earpiece.

'Imani, where are you?'

'Here, boss,' came the voice in his ear. 'Over by the pillar. Just behind. Moving out now.'

She walked slowly out from behind the pillar. Phil caught sight of her.

'Got you. Can you see him?'

'At his table. Acting like he hasn't got a care in the world. Letching after the woman next to him.'

'Lucky her. Keep on him.'

'I will, boss.'

She moved slowly back again. None of the diners noticed.

'Nadish?'

'At the bar, boss.'

Phil gave a grim smile. 'Why am I not surprised?'

'Just ready for the rush. I—'

'Nadish? Nadish?' Fear began to rise in Phil.

'Here, boss.'

'What happened?'

Nadish laughed. 'Sorry. The barmaid spoke to me. Got distracted. For a second, like.'

'Well, don't. Keep focused. When you get locked on to Looker, don't let him out of your sight.'

'Right, boss. Sorry, boss.' He sounded suitably chastised.

'The speeches'll be wrapping up soon. I'm guessing most of them will hit the bars. Be ready.'

'Right, boss.'

'Good. Ian?'

'At the other bar, chief. Just waiting.'

'You helping yourself, sir?' asked Nadish to Sperring, through Phil's earpiece.

'Far too poncy by half. Give me a decent pint of M and B any day of the week.'

If that's not a contradiction in terms, thought Phil. 'Good,' he said. 'Stay focused.'

'Will do. Very quiet in here at the moment, though.'

Applause came from the diners. It was loud, fuelled by alcohol and relief at the speeches being over. Phil turned.

'Get ready . . . '

The last of the speakers stood down, the host gave a final address and that was the end of the formal part of the evening. Now the rest of the night would be all mingling, gossiping, networking.

The guests began getting to their feet, picking up bags, making their way to the bars and other tables.

'Where's Looker?' said Phil.

'Still on him,' said Imani. 'Chatting to the woman next to him. Hasn't stood up yet. Hold on . . . '

Silence on the line. Phil craned his neck, tried to see what was going on. 'Imani?'

'He's just leaned across to her, put his hand on her arm and whispered something to her.' He heard laughter in his ear. 'Don't know what he's said but she didn't like it. She's got up and left.'

'Sure she ain't gone to get a room?' asked Nadish.

251

'From the look on her face I doubt it very much.' Another pause. 'No, she's off. Picked up her purse and walked.'

'What's he doing now?' asked Phil.

'Watching her go. Looks like he can't believe his chat-up line didn't work. Bet he's the only one.'

Phil tracked the woman he had been talking to as she walked past him, made her way to the bar. The expression on her face said that she had been deeply insulted. Poor Glen, he thought, without feeling much sympathy.

'He's trying to put a brave face on it to the other diners,' said Imani, 'but they've worked out what's happened. He's pointing at the bar now, like he's going to join her. No one's fooled. Not even himself.'

'Get ready, Nadish,' said Phil. 'He's coming your way.'

'On him,' said Nadish.

Phil saw Looker walk towards the bar. Looker saw him, stopped walking. Changed direction and came over to him.

'Having fun, Detective Inspector Brennan?' The smile was back on Looker's face, but Phil noticed it didn't quite reach his eyes.

'Having a great time, thank you, Mr Looker. Yourself?'

'Never better. Never better.' He looked around, back to Phil. 'Rumours of my demise seem to have been somewhat exaggerated, don't you think?'

'I'm keeping an open mind.'

Looker placed his hand on Phil's arm. 'Come and have a drink.'

'Sorry, Mr Looker, I'm working.'

'Oh, come on. One's not going to hurt you. We can call a truce for tonight, eh? What d'you say? Like those soldiers in World War One who got out of the trenches to play football. Come on over to the bar. You and me. Get out of the trenches for one night.'

Phil noticed he was quite drunk. 'Sorry, Mr Looker, I'm working. Another time, maybe.'

'Look, please, I ...' Looker shook his head, sighed, and reluctantly let go of Phil's arm. Resumed his trek to the bar.

There had been something in his eyes, thought Phil. Fear? Was it that? Perhaps he wasn't so laid back as he had appeared to be, he thought.

Phil kept watching.

55

'Mickey,' Fiona Welch said. 'Your first name. Detective Sergeant Phillips. Michael Phillips. Mickey Phillips. Mickey. Mickey. Stupid police. Mickey the thicky.' She giggled. 'Oh, that's good.'

Mickey sighed, stretched out his hand, turned on the radio. Classic FM filled the car. He turned it up, tried to drown her out.

He was driving down the A12 back to Colchester. The sky darkening, the day finished. It had been eventful, one way or another, and he was looking forward to dropping off his charge, wrapping up the paperwork as quickly as possible then getting off home for a long relaxing soak with a couple of bottles of beer and waiting for Anni to return, spending what was left of the evening with her. Really looking forward to it. And the more that Fiona Welch prattled on, the more he concentrated on that bath, those bottles of beer.

'Classical music,' she said above the radio, 'well, I am surprised. Yes, Mickey, you've surprised me. Who'd have thought you'd like classical music?'

He didn't, he preferred something much more modern and abrasive, louder and more fun, but he didn't want to tell her that. Anni had been driving and she had put it on to make for a calming journey north that morning. He had just left it.

'Oh,' said Fiona Welch, 'unless it isn't your choice. I'm guessing you drove up with DC Hepburn this morning, am I right? She might have had it on. Yes, that's it. I'm right. I know I am. As you were, Mickey the thicky.'

He could punch her, he thought. Pull up in to some lay-by off the main road and just lay in to her, stop her mouth with his fists. He shook his head to clear it of those thoughts. That was wrong. The wrong way to think, to want to behave, on so many levels. That was a glimpse of the old Mickey coming through. The one he wanted never to see again. But she did that to him, brought it out in him. Made him emotional, wrong-footed him. He knew, on one level, his professional level, that it was a ploy, something she was doing to get him to open up, drop his guard, respond and become engaged with her. Because if he did that she had him. A way into him. The custody clock would have started to tick and the time at the station would have been limited. If that was the case and she continued those tactics in the interview room then there might even be a way for time to question her to run out and her not to be charged. He couldn't let that happen.

So he said nothing. Soaked it up, let her go on.

'Anyway,' she continued, 'I suppose I should thank you.'

He opened his mouth, ready to respond with a question: Why? But stopped himself in time. Nearly.

Fiona Welch waited for him to reply and when he didn't, she continued. 'Yes, I should thank you, really. I was getting tired in there. Bored. I know I was only there to continue my studies – in situ, you might say – but even so. There's a limit. And most of them had reached it.' She sighed. 'God, but they're so boring. I mean, I had plenty of material, several books' worth, if I'm honest, but really. Drooling idiots, most of them. Just taking up valuable breathing space. Not to mention a drain on the taxpayer.' She sat back, made herself as comfortable as she could with her hands cuffed tightly behind her back. 'But I dare say you know all this. I dare say you agree.'

Mickey's hands gripped the steering wheel tighter. His only response.

'Most police do. And I can't blame you, really. When I think about what you must confront on a daily basis, the kind of people you have to deal with, lock up, well . . . it's a thankless task. The dregs. Aren't they?'

The violins, thought Mickey, were fascinating. Nice tune.

'Yes, they are. It would be a kindness to sterilise them, wouldn't it? I mean, you let them out again they're just going to breed. Then you'll have more of them to deal with. And then they in turn will breed and then you'll have even more. A self-perpetuating cycle. No. Sterilisation. That's the only way. The kindest way, really. Like they do with dogs and cats when they take them into Battersea. The strays, the unwanted. First thing they do is stop them breeding. Makes them a lot happier.' She paused again, waiting for a response. 'You know I'm right.' She leaned forward. 'Don't you?'

Mickey sighed, turned up the volume.

It was going to be a long drive.

56

'Where is he now?' Phil was back by the double doors, watching people enter and leave the main hall. Looking for anyone who didn't look like they belonged there.

Apart from himself.

'He's . . . ' Nadish's voice. 'Yeah, I got him.'

'Where?' Phil, still scanning the area.

'The bar.' There was a pause. 'He made me. Shit. I've been spotted.'

'Don't worry about it,' said Phil. 'He knows we're here.'

'Right,' said Nadish. 'He's queuing for a drink. Bit of a scrum. He's not going anywhere for a while.'

'Good. Stay on him.' Phil hadn't found anyone who looked out of place. But then he didn't really know who he was looking for. He doubted the Lawgiver would turn up in his work clothes.

Nadish seemed to be having similar thoughts, although he was expressing them differently. 'Like that bit in *Batman*, innit, *The Dark Knight*?'

'What d'you mean?' asked Imani.

'When there's that swanky party and the Joker turns up. Starts killing people. Just like that.'

'Just concentrate on what you're doing, Nadish,' said Phil.

'Yeah, boss.' Resignation in Nadish's voice.

Silence in Phil's ear. All he could hear was his own breathing.

257

'He's . . . hold on . . . ' Nadish's voice.

'What?' asked Phil, panic beginning to rise. 'Where is he?'

'He's – he was here, he . . . '

'Nadish?' Phil worked to quell the panic, remember his training.

'Jesus, I just looked away and he's . . . Shit.'

'What?' Phil's panic was rising even sharper. 'Nadish, what?'

'Just saw a glimpse of blue overall. Wait a minute, I'll . . . '

'Nadish . . . Nadish.' Phil heard heavy breathing in his ear.

'I'm – he's moving towards the lifts . . . '

Phil scanned the room once more. Was this it? Was it the Lawgiver? 'Have you got a definite identification? Nadish? Nadish?'

Phil's heart was hammering. One word, that was all. One word and the whole team would be mobilised.

'Nadish . . . '

'Yeah.' He was out of breath. 'Not him, boss. Definitely not him. 'One of the cleaning staff. She's just going off duty.'

'*She?*'

'Yeah. Sorry, boss. Bit jumpy.'

'Don't worry. Where's Looker?' He had almost forgotten about the target for a few seconds.

'I've got him.' Imani's voice.

Phil breathed out a huge sigh of relief. 'Good. Thank you, Imani. Where is he?'

'Just moved away from the bar. Stopped to chat to someone.'

'Man or woman?' asked Phil.

'Woman,' Imani replied. 'IC1 female. At least I think so. Lots of fake tan.'

'Do we know her?'

'Can't see her face, just her back. I can see his face, though. He's smiling.'

'What's she like?' asked Phil.

'Shapely,' said Imani. 'And she seems very interested in him.'

Phil breathed a qualified sigh of relief. 'Well, let's hope she stays with him a while. I doubt our friend would try anything if Looker was with someone else.'

'Right,' said Imani. 'They're moving. Towards you, Nadish. You back in position?'

'Yeah,' said Nadish. 'Got him.'

'Can you get a good look at her?' asked Phil.

'Nah, too many people. And she's walking in front of him. He's got his hand on her arse as well. And he's still smiling. He seems happy.'

Glad someone is, thought Phil.

'Bit of a looker, if her back's anything to go by,' said Nadish. 'Got a good shape. Plenty of curves.' He laughed. 'Hey, maybe she's a 1664.'

Phil frowned. 'Sorry?'

'1664. You know, from behind she looks sixteen, but when she turns round—'

'Shut up, Nadish,' said Imani.

'I get the point,' said Phil. 'Just keep on him. Concentrate on what he's doing.'

'I am,' said Nadish, slightly hurt. 'They've sat down now. Her hair's down, covering her face. Can't get a good look. But they both seem to be laughing. I reckon neither of them are going anywhere any time soon.'

'Hope you're right,' said Phil, and resumed scanning the room.

57

'I suppose you must be curious as to why I allowed myself to be caught?' Fiona Welch said.

Again, Mickey bit back his response.

'No? Well, even if you're not saying anything, I'm sure you are. Those boys in Colchester, the students? Aren't you even curious about them?'

'Save it for the station,' said Mickey.

'He speaks! At last! Oh, if I could clap my hands together, I would. Joy.' She leaned forward once more. 'So you are, then? Curious?'

Mickey mentally chastised himself for even those few words. Technically, he told himself, they didn't constitute a conversation. Technically. He sat silently, trying to listen to the radio, thinking of the warm bath and the cold beer.

'I'll take your silence as a yes. They were easy. Those boys. Testing a theory, nothing more. An empirical experiment. I wanted to be sure that my theories were correct so the best way to do that is to put them into practice. Which I did. I deliberately sought out those boys, worked on them, found out what they liked, and more importantly who they liked. Who their fantasy women were. And then I consciously set out to become their fantasy. Well, they couldn't believe their luck. I mean, who could? There I was, everything they had ever wanted in human form, willing to do everything and anything they had ever wanted. They said the same thing, bless them. It was like someone had opened their heads up and read their minds.' She laughed. 'Simple souls, really. Of course, that was exactly what I had done.'

Mickey, saying nothing, was fascinated despite himself.

'Looked into their minds. It wasn't hard. They were so obvious, really. So typical. Clichéd even. But still, I was testing my hypothesis and it was what I wanted so I went along with them. But that wasn't enough. I had to take it to the next level. Initiate phase two.'

Mickey kept his eyes straight ahead. Darkness was all around him, no overhead lighting, the only illumination from the occasional oncoming car on the other side of the road. It was like he had the radio on, telling a horror story in the most intimate way. He leaned forward, turned the classical music down slightly so he could hear her better.

'Aha,' Fiona Welch said, 'so you are listening. Good. Anyway, where was I? Oh yes. The boys. The second phase. Obvious, really. No point getting them where I wanted them if I wasn't going to do something with them. And I wanted them to do the ultimate. Kill for me.' She laughed. 'You know, you'd be surprised how easy it was. I'd shown them their fantasies, the real them, then I threatened to cut them off from that. No more sex. No more anything. And they did exactly as I wanted. Men always do what you want them to do. Even when they think they aren't doing so.'

Another laugh. Mickey said nothing.

'So they killed their girlfriends. Because I told them to.' She leaned forward again. 'You should writing this down, you know. Or record it, or something. This is the only confession you're going to get from me.'

Again, Mickey bit back his response.

'Oh well, your loss. So yes. The boys killed their girlfriends

261

for me. And had very little remorse about it. In fact, the only remorse they showed was when I wanted nothing to do with them afterwards, when I told them it was over with them. That was the only thing they were bothered about. Don't you think that's strange? Don't you?'

Mickey didn't reply.

'I'll take that as a yes. Because I think so. But it proved my hypothesis. Those boys didn't care about anyone but themselves, ultimately. I showed them their inner fantasies, became their fantasies, manifestly. Became a part of them. And to preserve that part of them they were willing to kill. That was more important to them than their girlfriends, their relationships. Themselves.' She sat back. 'So there you have it. Conclusive proof that people, particularly men, when confronted with their true beings only think about themselves. Only care about themselves. Anyone else is unimportant. My thesis laid bare.'

Mickey fought the urge to talk to her, counter her argument, get her to open up more. But it wasn't his job. She could recant all this at a later date. Instead, he filed it all away, ready to be used in the formal interview room in a couple of hours.

'But I hadn't killed them myself. And of course I'm a dead woman. So no one knew what to do with me. So off to Finnister I went. But that's the end of another chapter. Shall I tell you what happens next?'

Mickey was finding the urge to talk to her stronger and stronger.

He didn't know how long he'd be able to fight it.

58

'**W**hat's he up to now?' Phil was still scanning the room. No one suspicious so far. Or as far as he could tell.

'Still chatting to that bird,' said Nadish, before correcting himself. 'Sorry, woman.'

'Okay, good,' said Phil. 'Keep him in sight. With any luck she'll stay with him all night. Although I use the word *luck* advisedly.'

'Might be a bit of trouble with that,' said Sperring. 'Best we can hope for is they get a hotel room, don't go back to his. Or hers. That way we can keep an eye on them.'

'True,' said Phil. 'But let's not get ahead of ourselves. He hasn't had much success so far tonight.'

'Think his luck's about to change,' said Nadish. 'She's playing with her hair. They're sitting very close.'

'Lucky her,' said Imani.

'Wait,' said Nadish, 'he's stood up. Gone to the bar. Asked the barmaid something. She's pointing to her right. He's thanking her, walking off.'

'Toilets?' said Phil.

'Looks like it.'

'Stay on him,' said Phil. 'Follow him. This could be just the opportunity our friend needs to get to him.'

'On my way.'

'Imani, get over to where they were sitting. Keep an eye on that woman.'

'Will do.'

Silence in Phil's ear.

'She's gone,' said Imani.

'What?' Phil felt panic rise again. 'You sure?'

'Yeah,' said Imani. 'Must have taken my eye off her for a second. Just a second . . . '

'Maybe she's followed him to the toilet or gone to book a room, or something. You know what she looks like. Find her.'

'On it.'

'Nadish, you still got him in sight?'

'Yeah, right in front of me. No wait. He's gone for the stairs.'

'Up or down?'

'Down.'

'Keep on him,' said Phil.

Phil checked the room once more. He had a decision to make: join his team or stay in the room, wait for Looker to return. He made the call. Went to join his team.

'Talk to me, Nadish,' he said, walking towards the exit.

'He's going down the stairs. Coming to you, Ian.'

'Cheers,' said Sperring, 'I'm waiting.'

'You got him?' asked Phil.

'He's here,' said Sperring. 'Just smiled at me. I'm smiling back, little shit, doesn't know what I'm saying . . . He's looking for the toilets on this floor, I think.'

'Stick with him,' said Phil. 'Ian, he doesn't go in there alone. Imani, where's the woman?'

'Lost her. She's disappeared.'

'Shit.' Phil felt panic rising once again. He tamped it down, remained professional. 'Keep looking. What's happening with you, Ian?'

'Be embarrassing if she's in there with him,' said Nadish, out of breath from running down the stairs, 'noshing him off in the cubicle.'

'Keep out of it, Nadish,' said Phil. 'Ian, what's happening?'

No reply.

'Ian? Ian?'

Nothing.

Phil abandoned all pretence of working from the shadows and ran for the stairs.

59

'**I**'m going to be famous,' said Fiona Welch. 'That's what I'm doing it for. Fame and fortune. And to show the world how brilliant I am, of course.'

Fiona Welch was becoming tiresome, Mickey thought. He felt she had told him everything he wanted to hear – or needed to hear – regarding her crimes, and now she was grandstanding. And there was nothing worse than hearing a bore sound off, serial killer or no serial killer.

'And for other reasons. Which will . . . ' She laughed. 'Oh, let's just say, which will become known in the fullness of time. God, I hate clichés.' She shrugged, or tried to. 'But still . . . '

Mickey checked his watch. It seemed like time had stood still for the duration of the trip. She had volunteered some good information but there were gaps that needed filling. Something to work on, though. He just hoped it wouldn't be him. However, since he was the one to bring her in and most conversant with the case, he was sure it probably would be. The bath and the beer were looking more distant the closer he got to home.

The screen of his mobile lit up on the seat next to him. He glanced down at it. Anni. *I'm just leaving. See you soon. Xxx.* He smiled at that.

Fiona Welch was still talking. 'I'm sure I won't have trouble finding a publisher. Not if it's me. And then they'll see for themselves how clever I am. And how valid my theories are. I won't be shunned, if that's what you're thinking. No. There'll be a radical reappraisal of both me and my work. I'll be seen for what I am. A trailblazer. A radical. Someone who didn't just theorise, postulate. No, someone who went out there, saw for themselves. Then came back, wrote it up.' She leaned forward once more. 'Someone who knew the truth.'

Mental, thought Mickey. Completely mental. That was something she had in common with the real Fiona Welch, then.

'I might have to do the talk shows,' she said, laughing. 'Or even *Big Brother*. The celebrity version, of course. I'm sure the great British public would find me fascinating. I mean, they're all narcissists and psychopaths who go on that anyway. I'd just be more honest than most.'

Mickey had to stop himself from speaking once more, this time to agree with her.

'Who won that last one? A comedian whose act is racist and homophobic with a history of alcoholism and wife beating. What have I done in comparison?' Another giggle. 'I should imagine it's very similar to where I've just been, really. Except with better-looking people, of course. Well, slightly better looking.'

Mickey checked his watch again. No time at all had passed.

'I would win, of course. I mean, I would. It's not arrogance saying that. I know I would win. Wouldn't I?'

Mickey felt like agreeing with her just to shut her up.

'You know how I know I would win? Do you?' She leaned forward, her voice dropping to just above a whisper. Mickey had to strain to hear her. 'Because I'm very good at manipulating people. *Very* good. Even when they don't realise they're being manipulated.' She laughed. 'Especially when they don't realise they're being manipulated. Wouldn't you say so, Mickey the thicky?'

She sat back and laughed.

It was one of the most disconcerting sounds Mickey had ever heard.

60

Phil reached the toilets on the floor below just as Nadish was entering. 'Where is he?' he shouted.

'I . . . dunno . . . I just got—'

Phil pushed Nadish aside and ran inside. 'Ian?'

The toilets were gleaming, sparkling. Sperring was lying in the middle of the room, oozing dark red blood spoiling the minimalist décor.

Phil knelt down beside him. 'Ian . . . '

Sperring's eyelids fluttered. He tried to move his mouth.

'Don't speak.' Phil looked up. 'Nadish, get a paramedic here. Now.'

Nadish took out his phone, began to talk in urgent tones. Phil looked down at Sperring once more. He was bleeding through his shirt, pumping out blood in time with his quickening heart rate. He would go into shock soon, thought Phil. But before that he needed to calm down or he would die of blood loss before the paramedics got here.

Phil looked around, trying to find something, anything, that would stop the flow of blood. Towels would be a start but all he saw were hand driers.

'Nadish, get to the kitchen, the laundry, wherever. Get some towels, some linen. We need to wrap him up, stop the blood loss. Cling film, anything. Go. Now.'

Nadish ran from the toilets.

'Come on, Ian,' said Phil, 'don't give up on me, don't let go, come on . . . '

Phil felt so helpless before his bleeding colleague. He had to do something. He took off his suit jacket and tried to pull it tight round Sperring's body. Sperring grimaced with the sudden pain.

'Come on, Ian, don't let go . . . come on . . . '

Imani ran in, saw the sight before her and stopped dead.

'Oh shit, oh no . . . '

Phil turned to her. 'Find him,' he shouted. 'Get out there, get the uniforms, whoever you can. He's got Looker. Find him.'

Imani turned and, recovering composure from what she had just seen, went about her allotted task.

Phil turned back to Sperring. 'Ian . . . Ian . . . can you hear me?'

No response.

'Ian . . . Ian . . . '

Sperring's eyelids no longer fluttered.

The blood kept pumping.

61

'So what's the story with you and DC Hepburn, Mickey? Anni?'

Mickey knew it had been too good to last. After her pronouncement about manipulation Fiona Welch had fallen silent and Mickey had found the drive much more tolerable. But no. She had to start talking again. And about Anni now.

He didn't reply. She carried on regardless.

'How long have you been together? Oh, you didn't have to tell me. I worked it out straight away. Guessed. You don't have to be a psychologist to see that. It's so obvious, the way you look at each other. Especially the way you look at her. Trying to look like the hard copper but you've got these big puppy-dog eyes on her all the time.' She laughed. 'You still act the hard man, though, even when she's there. Is that deliberate? Are you trying to impress her?' Her voice became teasing. 'Does that turn her on? Go on, you can tell me.'

Mickey put his hand down hard on the horn, angry at the driver in the opposite lane who he had narrowly missed while overtaking another car.

'Oh,' said Fiona Welch. 'Think I've hit a nerve there ...'

Mickey didn't reply. Just kept his eyes on the road dead ahead.

Fiona Welch kept probing. 'Is that even allowed? In the force? You know, two people in the same outfit having a relationship? I would have thought you'd have had to get special permission, or something. In case being with your partner in private as well as public life was too much of a distraction. Or if you haven't got permission can they separate you?'

Mickey said nothing.

'No, seriously, I'm interested. Honestly.'

Again, nothing.

Fiona Welch sat back, sighed. 'Well, this is boring.' She looked out of the window. The stretch of road they were on was unlit, hedges either side. She turned back to face front. 'Just put me off here, please.'

Mickey almost laughed.

Fiona Welch didn't. Her face was flat, a death mask. 'I'm serious. Put me off here.'

Mickey shook his head.

'Just stop the car, and let me get out. You don't even need to undo the cuffs.'

No response.

She sighed. 'It'll save a lot of trouble and heartbreak. Really. For you, I mean. And Anni.'

No reply.

She leaned forward, speaking as if he hadn't been able to hear her until now. 'Look, at the risk of repeating myself, put me off here. Please. You'll be saving yourself a lot of trouble and heartache. Trouble for you, heartache for Anni. I'm serious.'

'You're going to Colchester,' Mickey said and was immediately angry with himself for having spoken.

'She sat back, laughed. 'He speaks! He speaks!' The laughter died away. Her face resumed its earlier death-mask quality. 'No, joking aside, I'm not going to Colchester. In fact, it's time I got out.'

'Stay where you are,' said Mickey. 'You're going to Colchester. And you know it.'

Fiona Welch smiled. It wasn't pleasant. 'Mickey, there's a question you haven't asked me. And really, it's one of the most important ones and you should have done it. Before we got into this car. Know what it is?'

He didn't reply.

'Then I shall tell you. It's this: what was I doing in Finnister? Why did I go to all that trouble to be put away in a place like that instead of a prison? And once I was in there, why would I try to make a suggestible patient kill herself? Actually, that's more than one question, that's three, but you get the idea. Three questions you should have asked me. Do you want to ask them now?'

Nothing.

'I really think you should. It's important for what happens next. For you, I mean.'

Again, nothing.

'Fair enough, I'll tell you. I was there to get your attention. Simple as that. You and your team. Especially the psychologist. And I'm sorry about what happens next, but—'

She leaned forward in her seat, the movement too sudden for Mickey to do anything about. She lunged at him, putting all her weight into it. Mickey was too startled to react. Without giving him a chance to move, she opened her mouth as wide as she could and sunk her teeth into the flesh of his neck.

Mickey screamed in pain, his hands coming off the steering wheel and going to her face, trying to push her away.

His actions just made her cling on all the harder, her teeth, unexpectedly sharp, gripping his flesh with the remorselessness of a mantrap, sinking in deeper.

The car began to weave all over the road, Mickey's foot still on the accelerator, his leg stretched out as his body thrashed around trying to shake her off.

But she held on. Harder. He could hear a strangulated

screaming coming from her as she did so, a feral, animal hunting cry.

Mickey tried to grab her face, find her eyes. Push his thumbs into the sockets. He managed to get his thumb in one, pushed as hard as he could. A screaming sound came over the top of his own and he realised that he had drifted over to the other side of the road and a huge articulated lorry was bearing down on him, horn blaring.

With one hand he managed to yank the wheel over to the left, pulling the car back to the right side of the road, trying to regain some semblance of control. As he did so, Fiona Welch renewed her attack.

He could feel her teeth chewing, grinding. Looking for an artery. He knew he couldn't let that happen.

He tried to think logically, work out an order to do things. He took his hand away from her face, put both of them on the steering wheel, tried to control the car, guide it to the side of the road where he could pull over then deal with her properly.

She sensed this and renewed her attack, biting down even harder.

She found the artery she was looking for.

Mickey tried to pull away, taking his hands off the wheel as he did so.

She bit down hard, tugged at it, pulled, like a dog worrying a toy.

Mickey felt his hands, his neck become suddenly wet. The wetness spread down his front. He knew immediately what had happened, tried frantically to get her mouth from his neck.

She just dug in even more, the feral screaming rising from her.

Blood sprayed everywhere, hitting the windscreen, obscuring the view.

Mickey's breathing became short, ragged. His own voice was reduced to a sad whimper. He felt the life pumping out of him.

Unsaid words, unthought thoughts tumbled through his mind. Sadness, panic and fear fought for dominance. The night around him got darker.

He screamed once more. An exhausted, defeated sound. It sounded like 'Anni'. But it could have just been a scream.

His foot slipped off the accelerator.

The encroaching darkness enveloped his vision.

62

The paramedics had taken Sperring away, clinging to life. Phil stood in the hall by the toilet, what remained of his suit covered with blood. He felt unable to speak, almost unable to stand.

Glen Looker had gone. They had searched everywhere and neither he nor the woman who was with him were anywhere.

The Lawgiver had done it. Right in front of them. Taken him.

Phil had never felt such a sense of failure. And with Sperring fighting for his life, that just made it so much worse.

They would keep looking, spend all night doing it if they had to, but Phil knew. Looker was gone.

Cotter appeared in the corridor. Phil couldn't even bring himself to look at her.

'Jesus Christ,' she said, sighing, 'what a fuck-up.'

Phil managed a nod.

'Right under our bloody noses . . . How did . . . ?' She sighed once more, shook her head.

'I failed,' said Phil. 'He was here and . . . ' He sighed. 'I failed.'

Cotter stood directly in front of him. 'Pull yourself together, Phil. You don't have time for that. You've got a job to do. We have to find him. Now.'

Phil nodded absently, not really hearing her words.

Then his phone rang.

He took it out, checked the display: UNKNOWN CALLER. Heart hammering he put it to his ear.

'Phil Brennan.'

He knew immediately who it was. The muffled breathing gave it away.

'What did I tell you, Phil?'

'How did you get this number?'

The Lawgiver laughed. 'Oh come on, Phil. That should be the least of your questions. Amazing what you can get off the internet these days.'

'You stabbed one of my officers. You're not going to get away with that.'

'Really? You think?' The voice hardened. 'I told you. You're either with me or against me. I think we know which side we're all on, don't we?'

'I'll find you. I'll get you.'

A laugh. 'No you won't. Goodbye, Phil. I'm off to have fun with Mr Looker. I'm sure you'll hear about it. One way or another.'

The phone went dead. Phil stared at it and, accompanied by a huge scream of frustration and rage, threw it against the wall.

PART FOUR:

HEROES' END

63

Glen Looker opened his eyes. Saw the masked face staring right into his, jumped.

'What . . . where's the . . . ?'

'Toilet? Light? What are you trying to say?'

Looker didn't understand the jokes, kept talking through his fogged mind. 'Girl. Where's the . . . girl . . . ?'

The Lawgiver straightened up. 'Don't you know?'

Looker stared at his captor. Understood. Shook his head and gave a small, tight smile. 'Yes, yes, I know now.'

'Good. You know who I am?'

'I can guess.' He shook his head slowly, tried to dislodge the fog that was still clinging inside there. 'You look like a refugee from a Slipknot gig.'

The Lawgiver straightened, paused momentarily before speaking again. 'And you know why you're here?'

Looker didn't reply straight away. Instead, he tried to move his arms, which wouldn't budge. Glancing down he realised he had been taped to the chair using heavy-duty duct tape. He looked around at where he was. All he could see was darkness. A light shining on him from behind his host, the halo it cast making the surrounding dark seem even blacker. He tried to pull himself forward. No good. The chair was firmly secured to the floor and something behind him just as he was firmly secured to the chair. He sighed.

'Yes,' he said. 'I know why I'm here. Or at least why you would want me here.'

'And why would that be?'

Looker smiled. 'Oh come on, do I really have to spell it out to you? You're the one that's supposed to have all the answers, you tell me.' His voice came out stronger than he had expected.

The Lawgiver stopped once again, taken aback somewhat by Looker's words, his attitude. He had anticipated fear, apologies. Confession. Instead he was getting . . . this. This attitude.

'Is this bravado, Mr Looker? Trying to make yourself appear brave before me? Thinking that if you appear nonchalant then I might back down before you?'

Glen Looker stared directly at him. Thought of the words he had just heard. He had expected himself to be frightened, tearful even. Start begging for his life before his captor. Pleading for deals like the worst kind of defendant. He thought back to yesterday, the first appearance of Phil Brennan in his office. He had tried to laugh off the threat, not take the detective seriously. Or at least appear to be laughing it off. And even last night – if it was last night, he had lost all track of time – he had been scared but once he had realised what was happening he had actually gone along with it. Willingly.

There had been a chance to escape. The woman at the bar, Diana, had approached him. On first glance he thought that there was nothing wrong her, that his luck was in. Especially after the knock-back he had experienced just after the dinner. Stuck-up cow. But the more Diana talked to him, the more he realised what was happening. Who she was. And when he realised this he should have walked away, or at least raised the alarm to one of the detectives dotted conspicuously around the room. But he didn't. Just allowed her to talk on. And when she suggested that they go on somewhere else, he went willingly, knowing exactly who and what she was by that time.

Part of him even applauded the Lawgiver for doing it that way.

He had walked out of the room and down the stairs on the pretext of looking for a toilet. On the level below one of Brennan's team had accosted him, followed him into the lavatory. Diana had appeared behind them and silently dealt with the police officer. And he had just stood there, watching. Numb. He could have run. Gone back upstairs, told a member of staff what was happening. But he didn't. He just stood there, waiting. Waiting for her to finish.

Then they hurried to the door and the cab rank. And away.

And then . . . this.

He vaguely remembered telling her that she didn't need to do anything, that he would come willingly, but he wasn't sure if he had dreamed that or actually said it. It didn't matter. He had still ended up here. Which was just about where he had expected to be.

He realised the Lawgiver was waiting for an answer. He decided not to give him that, instead offering him another question. 'Where's Diana?'

Wrong-footed again, the Lawgiver paused before answering. 'Don't you know?'

'Yeah,' Looker said, 'I think I do. I just wanted to hear you say it.'

'Diana is . . . gone. For now.'

'Right. And who is she, then? What's her story?'

'You think there's a story to her?'

'Oh yeah. Must be a story.' He tried to shrug. 'I mean, come on . . . '

'There's no story.' The Lawgiver sounded angry behind his mask. 'No story.' He leaned in closer. 'I asked you a question. Are you feeling brave? And do you think your bravery will help you?'

'That's two questions, actually. Which one would you like me to answer and in what order?'

The Lawgiver stepped forward, backhanded Looker across the face. 'Don't play games with me, answer the question.'

Looker's head snapped to one side. He actually saw stars, a little miniature cosmos against the room's darkness. Eventually the blackness swam back into focus. His mouth felt wet. He spat something on the floor. Knew from the taste of old pennies that it was blood.

He laughed. Despite the pain, he actually laughed.

'I'm a lawyer,' he said through his rapidly swelling mouth. 'I deal with words every day. I deal with liars every day. I deal with game players every day. I do all that because I'm one of them. I could wrap you in knots with words tighter than you could tie me to this chair.'

The Lawgiver stepped forward once more. Back in Looker's face. 'But you can't, can you? You're off your home turf. You're on mine. You have to play by my rules here.'

'And what would they be?'

The Lawgiver stood back, walked away from him, turned. The light cast a righteous halo around him. 'You have to pay for what you've done.'

'Oh? And what's that, then?'

'You've allowed criminals to walk free when they should be locked up. You, with your words and your games. You've built a career on it, your reputation's been made on it. Your whole life has been built on the misery and suffering of others.'

Looker stared at him. 'That your opening statement? Nicely presented.'

The Lawgiver paused once again before speaking. Looker saw him breathe deeply. 'This is what I propose,' he said. 'We'll count up all the years that your criminals have had free when they should have been locked up. Then I'll take away something of that number of yours to match.'

'I've got an ex-wife who hates me and a daughter who won't speak to me. Good luck with finding that,' Looker said.

'Oh, I'll find something, don't you worry,' said the Lawgiver, his voice chill behind the mask.

Looker said nothing.

'So what do you say? Have we a deal?'

'On one condition,' said Looker.

'You're in no position to make conditions.'

'You asked me if I have a deal, this is the deal. You can put the accusations to me. I'll counter them. Every one. And if, after that, you still believe you're right, you still think that what I did was wrong and that I need to be punished for it, then go ahead. Do your worst. On the other hand, if you think that I've made a persuasive case then you have to let me go. Fair?'

The Lawgiver didn't answer.

'I said is that fair? Do we have a deal?'

Looker heard a sigh from behind the mask. 'Yes. Fine. We have a deal.'

'Good. But there's one other thing.'

'What?' The voice flat, tired, almost.

'I want to know about Diana too.'

The Lawgiver paused, stared. Looker wondered whether he had gone too far, misread his host. Eventually the Lawgiver gave a curt nod. 'All right.'

'Good.'

Something in him felt that, perversely, he was going to enjoy this. In fact, he actually felt that some redemptive part of him had led him to this moment. Far from being scared by the situation, Glen Looker felt more alive than he had in a long time.

'Are you ready?' asked the Lawgiver. 'Truth or dare time. Do you dare to tell the truth?'

'Sure,' Looker said, as breezily as he could manage. 'Where d'you want to start?'

64

Phil opened his eyes, looked around. At his desk. Still at his desk. He had nodded off again.

He had slept the night at the station. Or tried to: there had been very little sleeping and certainly no rest. The scene at the hotel the night before had devolved into chaos. Looker was gone, Sperring was in a critical condition. And Phil felt he was, in some large way, to blame for both of those things. It had happened on his watch, under his command. Ultimately, the responsibility was his.

Phil rubbed his eyes. He had showered and changed into a spare plaid shirt and a pair of jeans. But the comfort he derived from being in his familiar clothes was limited. There was too much to think about.

Sperring was still in hospital, intensive care. They hadn't heard how he was but knew he had been operated on straight away. He had lost a lot of blood and the knife wound had been deep. But clean, one of the paramedics had said. Easier to stitch up, theoretically. So that was hopeful. That was something.

The hotel had been searched from top to bottom. No sign of Looker. The surrounding streets had also been gone over. Same result. Like they had just vanished into thin air. They had given their descriptions out citywide, but so far there had been no positive responses. The Lawgiver had planned this well.

Phil checked his computer screen once more, scanned his email, read the display on his iPhone. Nothing. No one trying to contact him. No news. He sighed, sat back, rubbing his eyes. Then he ran his hands over his chest. No tightening, no pain. No sign of a panic attack. Yet.

A knock at the door. Not waiting for a reply, it opened.

'Jesus,' said Alison Cotter, 'you look like how I feel.'

'Thank you,' said Phil, sitting forward. 'Always nice to hear.'

She entered, closed the door behind her. 'Sorry,' she said, sitting down, 'probably not what you wanted to hear. Bit tactless of me. My bad.'

Phil hated that expression but he was too tired to make an issue of it. And it had been uttered by his superior. He looked at her. She looked as bad as *he* felt. Back in her usual work clothes, tight, no-nonsense grey suit, flat shoes. The evening dress and accompanying poise of the previous night a world away. She was back to business.

'Have you slept at all?' she asked. 'Been home?'

Phil shook his head. 'Got my head down here for a bit. But I couldn't sleep. So I got up, started monitoring radio chatter. Tried to see if there had been any sightings.'

'And there haven't been.'

He shook his head. 'Nope.'

'I know. I've been checking as well.'

Silence fell between them as neither spoke. They sat like that for a while, not relaxed, just grabbing a brief respite in the trenches before the bombs started falling again.

Eventually Phil spoke. 'Any news on Ian?'

Cotter shook her head. 'Still in intensive care. They'll let us know soon as.' She managed a brief smile. 'Are you concerned for him, Phil?'

'He's my DS,' said Phil, looking away momentarily. 'My second in command.'

'And when you started working together the two of you hated each other.'

'Ah, now, that's not fair.' Phil gestured with both hands, as if surrendering. 'He may have hated me. Thought I got his job. That's all. I never hated him.'

'Really?' A smile played on Cotter's lips. 'You never thought he was a reactionary old dinosaur? Never said he should be pensioned off, that he was the kind of officer that gave the police a bad name and a bad image with the public?'

Phil felt himself reddening. 'Well, I may have said something along those lines . . . not as bad as that, though.'

The smile stayed on Cotter's face. 'Not as bad? I just gave you the edited highlights. The sanitised version.'

'Ah,' said Phil. 'Right.' It was his turn to smile now.

'Right,' said Cotter. 'Exactly.' The smile slid away. 'I'm glad that the two of you have managed to find some kind of accommodation. Some way of working together, of mutual respect.'

'Well, maybe we both have something to learn from the other's approach.'

'Maybe you do.'

Phil flashed a smile once more. 'Or maybe he does. From me.' After the previous night, his words carried only a hollow bravado.

Cotter shook her head. Her smile faded away. 'I'm sure he'll pull through. He's tough. He's a fighter.'

Phil nodded, nothing to add.

Cotter looked directly at him, as if reading him. 'And what about you?'

'What about me?'

'Do you want me to replace you? I could, you know. In fact, I probably should. The morning briefing's coming up. I was going to take it myself. Or bring in someone else from another unit to head this investigation from now on. That's what I should do. Ian's attack may mean that this has become too personal for you and you should step down.'

Phil knew what she was doing. Offering him a way out of his failed operation with his head held reasonably high. A retreat in a dignified manner.

'Unless you can convince me that I should keep faith with you,' she said before he could respond, her voice dropping to a confidential level as if they were being overheard. 'After last night.'

'That what you want to do?' asked Phil. He stood up, began pacing the room. 'I've still got a job to do. A team to lead. A killer to find. You think I can just walk away? Let someone else take over now? Really?'

Cotter looked him squarely in the eye. 'I admire your passion, Phil. But is that going to be applied with professionalism? Or are you going to let your personal feelings cloud what you have to do?'

'I think you know me well enough by now,' he said. 'I won't let my feelings about losing one of my team cloud my professional judgement. I'm fit for this. I know I am. And you know it as well.'

She stared at him.

'Ma'am,' he said.

'You sure?'

'Yes, I'm sure,' he said, as strongly as he could.

Cotter stood up. 'Good,' she said. 'I'm glad. I want you working this case. I want you to succeed.'

'Thank you, ma'am.'

She reached the door, turned. 'But,' she said, with no trace of the earlier comradeship in her voice, 'if this goes south, then on your own head be it.'

'I know,' said Phil.
'Briefing's in thirty.'
She left the room.
Phil was ready.

65

Marina opened her eyes. For a few blissfully empty seconds, she was at peace. Then the full horror of what had happened kicked in and she felt emotionally bereft, physically sick.

She was cold, lying in Anni's living room, back on the sofa, the duvet kicked off during the night and tangled round her ankles. She was wearing a T-shirt and a pair of old jogging bottoms she'd brought with her to sleep in. Despite the cold she was sweating. A cold, shivery, prickly sweat.

She pulled the duvet up over her once more, tried to take comfort from its weight on her. No good. She thought it would be a long time before she found comfort again.

But not as long as it would be for Anni.

She had returned to Colchester the previous night. Mickey was nowhere to be seen back at Southway. Anni had had a few choice things to say about his non-appearance but Marina could tell that she was worried. He was solid, dependable. Not showing up when he was supposed to wasn't like him.

Marina, thinking about those few hours in hindsight, could even claim that Anni was suffering from a premonition that something had happened to him. Or if not a premonition, then at least a sense of dread.

Then Gary Franks appeared, Anni and Mickey's DCI. He

took them into his office, made them sit down. Then he told Marina and Anni about the road accident.

And Anni folded, crumpled, her world collapsing in on her.

'A road accident?' asked Marina, holding tight to Anni who was sobbing her heart out. After speaking she didn't know if she wanted to hear any more. Not now. Not ever.

'A12,' said Gary Franks. Then, searching desperately for something to say, 'Notorious, that stretch, down from Ipswich.' His voice tailed away.

Marina felt her grief threaten to overwhelm her. Anni was still sobbing. Marina almost felt her spirit leave her body and look down on the scene. Like it was something once removed, something that only happened to other people. *Always* only happened to other people. Still life with tragedy.

Franks was still talking, scrabbling to find words to breach the void. 'Apparently there were . . . no other vehicles involved.'

Anni was attempting to control herself, fall back onto her training, ask questions. 'What . . . what happened?'

'We . . . we don't know. His car seems to have gone off the road. Burst— you sure you want to hear this?'

Anni nodded through her tears, eyes closed.

Franks looked unsure but continued. 'Burst into flames. Hit the, hit something at the side of the road and . . . and burst into flames.'

Anni opened her eyes. 'A burnt-out car. On the A12 . . . '

Marina knew what she was going to say next. Dreaded to hear the words.

'A burnt-out car . . . we passed that. Marina, we passed that – we had to slow down.'

Marina said nothing. They had been part of the queue of traffic forced into one lane, Anni complaining that they would be late home. They barely spared it a glance as they drove past, grateful as they were for the traffic to be speeding up again.

'We . . . we passed him,' said Anni. 'My, my Mickey in that car, we passed him . . . And we, we—'

Her sobbing renewed itself.

'He . . . he would have died instantly, if that's any consolation,' said Franks.

Anni looked straight at him. 'No, sir, it's not. It's really, really not . . . '

She trailed off again, Marina gripping her tightly once more.

Marina didn't know how long they stood like that, Anni sobbing, Marina holding her, Franks clenching and unclenching his fists, desperate to be of some use, knowing anything he could do was useless.

Eventually Anni looked up, wiped her eyes, her nose with the back of her hand. Looked at Franks.

'Did you laugh?' she said.

Franks frowned.

'Did I what?'

'Did you laugh? Did you have to practise what you would say to me to not laugh? I've done enough death knocks to know you have to do that.'

Anni had told Marina about that one time. About how officers would sit in their cars before knocking on some soon-to-be-grieving relative's door to give them the news that their loved one was dead. They had to practise, not to say the wrong thing, not to laugh. And they would laugh not because it was funny, but because it was such a serious and solemn moment, sometimes too serious, and the strain would manifest itself in terrible ways.

'No,' said Franks, looking hurt, 'I didn't laugh. What have I got to laugh about?'

And Anni started crying again.

They stood like that for a long time. So long that it felt to Marina that this was all they would do for the rest of their lives.

'What about Fiona Welch?' she asked eventually, breaking the silence.

'What about her?' said Franks.

'She was in the car with Mickey,' said Marina. 'He was bringing her back here.'

Franks looked stunned. 'There was . . . there was no one else in the car, just Mickey. No sign of anyone else.'

'Then where is she?' asked Anni, the words coming out pained.

Where indeed? thought Marina.

Anni had been sent home, given something to help her sleep. She had protested, fought, said she wanted to go out and find Fiona Welch. Find out what had happened to Mickey. Franks had been adamant that she needed rest.

'We'll start looking for her, get onto it right away. But you won't be part of the team, I'm afraid. You know you can't be.'

Anni knew, but she still wasn't going to give in without a fight.

'Look, Anni, if there's anything I can do,' said Franks, 'anything at all . . . ' His words, well-intended, ran out.

Anni nodded. Marina wasn't even sure she had heard him.

Marina had taken her home. Sedated, she had gone straight to sleep. And Marina had sat up, thinking.

She had tried to phone Phil, several times, but got put through to his voicemail. Must be sleeping, she thought. Or working. She hadn't left a message. Thought it wasn't the kind of news that could be imparted like that. Not about one of Phil's close friends and colleagues.

Marina had sat up watching Anni sleep, waiting to hear if there was any news of Fiona Welch. She had had no time to grieve for the loss of her friend. She had to be strong, supportive for her other friend. Grieving could come later for

Marina. She kept half expecting the phone to ring, to pick it up and hear someone tell her it was all a dreadful mistake, that Mickey was alive, the car was someone else's. That it was a case of mistaken identity. But no one phoned. No one told her that.

It had happened. It was real.

She reached for her phone once more. Checked the display. Nothing. From anyone.

She was going to call Phil again but thought better of it. She knew he must be working or sleeping and couldn't be interrupted for either thing. She had given Eileen a call, just to check on Josephina. Her daughter was fine, Phil was working late, she said. Eileen was a godsend.

She put the phone down, threw back the duvet, walked to the bedroom, opened the door. Anni was still sleeping. She looked so peaceful that Marina wanted to her to sleep for ever, spare her the pain that waited for her when she woke up.

But that wasn't how life worked.

She went back to the sofa, back to the duvet. Pulled it up tight.

Tried to keep out the cold, the depressing thoughts.

Then her phone rang.

66

'Hey,' said Phil.

'Hey yourself,' Marina replied.

'Sorry, did I wake you?'

'No, I was . . .' Marina looked around the room. Hoped the noise of the call hadn't woken Anni, although that seemed unlikely, the amount of drugs she'd been given. 'No. I was awake.'

'Right. Josephina got you up.'

'No, I'm . . . still in Colchester.'

Phil's voice became serious. 'Really? Why?'

'Oh, things became— there was something else to do. Went on longer than I expected. You know how these . . . things go.'

'Sure I do. I had to sleep at the office last night. No point in coming home. This case is a bastard.'

Marina was glad that Phil hadn't questioned her further. It wasn't the right time or place to tell him about Mickey. Not when he was in the middle of his own investigation. Not when he was so pumped up about it. He hadn't even asked her about Fiona Welch, for which she was glad.

'What's happened?'

He sighed. 'There's . . . I'll tell you when you get back. But . . .' Another sigh. 'Ian's in hospital.'

Marina sat bolt upright. 'What?'

Phil seemed startled by the pitch of her surprise. 'Yeah, this operation last night went wrong. We tried to catch the Law-giver, that's this vigilante, but instead he got away with his target. And Ian got stabbed in the process.'

Marina felt the news stabbing her also. 'Oh no . . . oh no . . . ' Not after Mickey, she wanted to say, stopped herself from saying, *Not him too . . .*

'It's . . . it's fine,' Phil said. 'Well, as fine as could be expected. Ian's in intensive care. They're looking after him. Everything's hopeful.'

'Oh, thank God,' she said, expelling a breath she hadn't been aware she had been holding.

'Yeah. So not to worry too much. But I need a favour.'

'What?'

'I need a favour.'

'Yes, I heard. What kind of favour?'

'If I send you over everything we've got on this Lawgiver character, could you put together a quick profile?'

'How quick?'

'Twenty minutes?'

Marina laughed through sheer relief. 'I thought you were going to say ten.' She looked around the room once more. The news about Sperring had set everything at an angle, made it all seem even more unreal. This might be just the thing she needed to take her mind off things.

'I've got the morning briefing in half an hour,' said Phil. 'Be good if I had something to present them with.'

'This'll be very basic, you know. Not a magic wand.'

'I know. But at least it's something to go on. If needs be, I'll commission you for a proper one when you get back.'

'Okay.'

'Bit of nepotism never went amiss. I'll get that stuff sent straight across.' Phil paused. 'You sure you're okay?'

Marina's voice was guarded. 'Yeah. Why?'

'Just ... I don't know. You sound ... distracted.'

'It's been a big couple of days. Heavier than I thought they'd be.'

'I know what you mean.' He sighed. 'I miss you. I need you here with me.'

'And I need you too. Right now.' At that moment Marina had never felt a yearning like the one she was experiencing. Phil would make everything better. Just being together would make everything together.

There was silence on the line as the pair of them seemingly communicated without words. Then Phil broke the spell.

'I'll get that stuff sent off.'

'I'll look forward to it.'

Marina took out her MacBook and, glad of the temporary distraction, set to work.

67

Moses hadn't been able to sleep.

Tossing and turning all night, the events of the last few days screening before his eyes, over and over again. And then another set of days were replayed, days from a few years ago. Days involving the Chicken Shack Crew. The Handsworth Boys. Julian Wilson. The days before the peace. The days that led to the peace.

Eventually he had got up. No point in trying to sleep, lying there with his eyes tight shut, willing the dreams to go away, his mind to shut down, peace to come. He knew he was going to get none of that. So he had got up. Showered. Had a coffee. He had wanted to go somewhere, do something, but hadn't known where, what.

His first thought had been Letisha. Go and see her. Talk to her. No. He couldn't do that. Not yet. There were things that needed sorting out before that could happen again. If it could happen again. But that had been his first thought. *She* had been his first thought. He should have been surprised by that. But somehow he wasn't. Somehow it felt right to think of her first. And that, he knew, could be dangerous.

No. He had to do something else. He knew what to do. Wasn't looking forward to it.

He sat on the edge of his bed, looked around the room. This was his. All his. He liked to think he had taste, style. Had decorated his crib in a way that showed he was a successful young man. Not like what was expected, like all the other kids in the gang used to talk about. They would watch that show on MTV, *Cribs*. Watch rappers and sports stars show the cameras around their mansions. Be proud about what they had achieved. Fair enough, Moses had thought watching it, you can't take that away from them. Most of them had started with nothing and made something of themselves. Something positive. Used their talent to further their lives. Good. That was the right thing to do. But some of them seemed to think that money brought them style. It didn't. He could understand coming from the ghetto and wanting to show off, have a whole room panelled in gold and marble, but there were still such things as class, taste. And he liked to think he had both. When he used to watch that with the other gang members, they would all speak with reverence about what they saw. Then talk about their own plans, what they would have in their own cribs, feeding on each other's fantasies, helping them grow.

He thought about where those boys were now. Some of them were still with him, one or two. A few had gone to prison; in and out at first but eventually settling down to life on the inside of the big, metal door. The rest were dead. Didn't ever have the chance to realise their fantasies, tasteful and stylish or not. Street casualties. That was the biggest amount.

He stood up, checked his watch. Tiny would be there by now, at the studio. No point putting it off any longer.

Was the day overcast, dark clouds hanging heavily over the red-brick Victorian building, or was Moses just imagining it? He didn't know, didn't really care. The dark clouds were hanging over him and that was what mattered.

He locked his car, went inside. Walked down the corridor to the studio like he was a death-row prisoner facing his last day on earth. They always asked for ribs or chicken or burgers for their last breakfast. He'd had toast. Hardly seemed fitting.

He reached the studio. The green light was on. He pushed the door open, made to enter. He heard a sound behind him: sucking teeth. He turned. Tiny was already there.

'Thought you'd show up.'

Moses ignored the disrespect, nodded. 'Tiny.'

Tiny came nearer. 'Fuck you playin' at?'

Moses said nothing.

'Eh? Fuck you playin' at? Bringin' that skank here?'

'I didn't bring her,' Moses said, trying to keep his voice calm and reasonable.

'No? Why she here, then?'

'She wanted to see me.'

Tiny got even closer. 'She wanted to see you.' He nodded. 'Nice. Wanted to see you. Good.'

Moses again said nothing. Waited.

Tiny moved in close. His voice dropped low, dangerous. 'You fuckin' her?'

'Tiny . . . '

Tiny nodded. 'You fuckin' her. Jesus Christ. My dead brother's girlfriend. His whore. How long this been goin' on?'

'Tiny, I'm not. She came to see me yesterday on something else entirely.'

Tiny came even closer, got right up in Moses's face. 'Yeah? Like what?'

Moses looked into Tiny's eyes. Really looked. They were black, empty. He had seen that same look in some of the younger kids in the gang, the next generation. Like they had no empathy, no connection. As if they hadn't been wired up properly. As if they could kill and not care.

It scared him, what was happening to the kids. Really scared him.

Tiny was nineteen.

'The cops were talking to her. About her ex-boyfriend. His new girlfriend and kid got killed. You probably heard about it.'

Tiny gave no indication that he had.

'They came to see me, remember? Pulled me in, thought I might have done it.'

'Did you?'

'No, man. Course not. Why would I?'

'So why'd she come back to you?'

'The police have been round to her again. She wanted me to get my brief to help her.' It probably wasn't a lie, if he thought about it. He tried to make it sound like the truth.

'Didn't sound like that when I heard you two talkin' yesterday.'

Moses felt something snap inside. Anger, fear, he didn't know what. But he was sick of being threatened by a teenager. Even one as unnerving as Tiny. 'Then you heard wrong, didn't you?'

Something sparked behind Tiny's eyes. A fire was lit that Moses knew would be hard to put out. 'You dissin' me?'

'No, Tiny, I'm not dissing you.'

'Sounds like it to me.'

Moses didn't reply.

'That whore was with my brother when he got killed. She wouldn't give up the shooter's name. She got no respect round here, not wanted. She whorin' herself out, last I heard. That true?'

'So I hear.'

'She found her level, man. Good. Hope she gets AIDS. Hope she fuckin' dies screamin'. She might have killed my brother. Might have got someone to do it.'

'We couldn't prove anything,' said Moses. 'No one from my side did it. You know that. It was terrible what happened but

303

it got us talking. Got us together. Brokered the peace. Remember?'

'Yeah, I remember.'

'We still got peace, bro.'

Tiny stared at him. 'We had it, till you brought that whore round again.'

'It was nothing to do with anything. You know that.'

Tiny stared right into Moses's eyes. 'You look scared, man. You scared?'

Moses swallowed hard. 'No.'

'Why you scared, man?'

'I'm not scared.'

'You fuckin' her.'

'Not a question this time, a statement.

'I'm not fucking her.'

Tiny nodded slowly. Eventually he spoke. 'Better get out of here, man. Got things to think about. You're not welcome here today.'

Moses opened his mouth, made to argue, but realised there would be no point. Instead he turned, walked away.

Feeling like a target had just been put on his back.

68

Phil stood in front of his team, silently repeating his new-found mantra to himself: *Don't sound like a failure . . . Don't sound like a failure . . .*

'Thank you,' he said to the assembled room. 'Thank you for still being here.' He scanned them, saw bleary, bloodshot eyes, overtired minds and bodies. He had to lead them, inspire them. Encourage them to renew their efforts, put in a proper shift. He couldn't sound like a man who had let their prime suspect escape with his intended target and allowed one of his own to be injured in the process. He had to be the person who would lead the team on from that. Communicate his passion, the intensity he felt for finding the Lawgiver.

He noticed his hand was absently rubbing his chest once more, looking for signs of pain. He quickly took it away. That wasn't helping anyone.

'You all know what happened last night,' he said. 'Most of you were there when it happened. Detective Sergeant Sperring, Ian Sperring, is still in intensive care. The doctors are hopeful. They say he's comfortable, not critical.'

Phil caught Nadish's eye. The younger officer looked like he was distraught but trying to hide it. Or as best he could.

'He's stable,' said Cotter, standing at Phil's side. A show of support. 'In good hands. With luck he'll recover. Hopefully fully.'

'Which is good news,' said Phil. 'But we mustn't let the loss of one of our own deter us from what we have to do. Or cloud our judgement about how we go about it. We have to find the Lawgiver. Find him, bring him in. And find Glen Looker too. Before the Lawgiver can do anything to him.'

A ripple of unease ran round the room. Phil noticed the team weren't totally on his side after those words.

'Yes, I know most of you have had the somewhat dubious pleasure of crossing swords with Mr Looker but this is something different. He's been taken into the hands of a maniac, one we still know next to nothing about but one who is lethal. And we have to do our best to find him, despite what we may think about Glen Looker. And who knows,' added Phil, attempting a smile, 'if we find him alive he might not sue.'

The laughter was polite but it broke the tension.

'Right,' said Phil, ploughing on while he still had the attention of the room, 'we haven't got much to go on, so with that in mind I had a preliminary psychological profile drawn up of our Lawgiver.' He held up a piece of paper. 'Here it is. Any comments, chip in.' He began to read from it.

'Lawgiver seems to be suffering from some kind of psychotic condition.' He looked up. 'Obviously, we'll know more about that when we catch him.' He kept reading. 'This person is extremely focused. Single-minded, even, on a single project.'

'Yeah,' said Nadish, 'we got that.'

'He's educated. Well educated, probably. But here's the interesting thing. He's probably experienced something traumatic in his life. This has caused his perception of the world to become warped. Through doing what he's doing, he's trying to regain his own balance and make sense of the world again.'

'So how would you classify him?' asked Imani. 'Psychopath, sociopath, emotionally numb, what?'

'I don't know,' said Phil. 'That's for us to discover. He wants us to see things his way. And he's willing to do anything, even kill, to do that.'

'So he's a psycho then,' said Nadish.

'Not necessarily,' said Phil.

'So what are his weaknesses?' asked Imani. 'How are we going to catch him?'

'He's a planner,' said Phil. 'Meticulously so. But he's also getting cocky. Think of last night. Had he planned that all along or did something happen to make him feel like he could get away with it? I don't know. But if his plans are upset then he'll start to unravel. And that's how we'll catch him.'

'Let's hope it's sooner rather than later,' said Cotter.

'Exactly,' said Phil. He put the paper down on his desk, mentally thanked Marina for that. 'Right. With all that in mind, what do we have so far?'

He turned to the murder board behind him. Instead of providing the links and clues that it usually would, it looked more like a puzzle that couldn't be completed due to a lack of pieces. Pictures of the victims were up there, arrows linking them when possible. A photo of Moses Heap with a question mark beneath it next to a picture of Letisha Watson, a dotted line linking her to Darren Richards. A solid line linking Richards with Chloe Hannon. Then in another part of the board, a photo of John Wright. No lines linking him with anyone else on the board. And along from that, a photo of Glen Looker. Lines linked him to both Darren Richards and Moses Heap.

'That's it,' said Phil. 'That's what we have. Victims but no perpetrator. Not even a picture, only a description. How does he find his victims? Does he know his victims?'

'Maybe he just picks the ones that are high profile,' said Imani, 'in the case of John Wright, and researches them.'

'That makes sense,' replied Phil. 'But what about the others? They've all got Looker as a connection.'

'Maybe he started looking at Looker,' said Nadish, 'then found out about the others from him. Went after Darren Richards first because . . . ' He tailed off.

'Because he could?' suggested Imani. 'Because he was nearest, because he was easiest, plenty of reasons. Start off with the simplest, build his way up.'

'True,' said Phil. 'Or at least simplest in terms of access.'

'Right,' said Imani. 'Maybe he went after him because Looker would be someone he would have to build up to? Especially the way he carried it out.'

'Yeah,' said Phil. 'That makes sense. So if that's the case, if Darren Richards was easiest and nearest, the opening one of the account, then have we anything on where he was picked up?'

'Nothing,' said Imani. 'He was supposedly on his way to his friend's house in Winson Green. He never turned up. Same with Chloe and Shannon Hannon. No one saw anything, heard anything.'

'That kind of area,' said Nadish.

'Certainly is,' said Phil. 'So bearing in mind we've got nowhere with that line of enquiry, does the location of where he was found matter? That semi-demolished building? Does that mean something to him, the Lawgiver, d'you think? Nadish?'

Nadish checked his notes. 'We've looked into the history of the building. Nothing. Been bought by a development company to knock down and replace with flats or something.'

'Who owned the original building?'

'A holding company. Nothing suspicious as far as we could make out. Got people looking into it but I reckon it's a dead end. SOCOs are still going over it but they haven't found anything. Jo Howe doubts they will.'

'Post-mortems on the two victims?'

'As we first suspected,' said Imani. 'Crossbow bolts. Nothing on them. Could have been bought at any sports or gun shop. Or even off the internet. It's being followed up, but ... ' She shrugged.

'Okay. What about the door-to-door? That give up any-thing?'

Nadish paused before answering, is if weighing something up in his mind. 'Nah, nothing.'

'You sure?'

'Yeah. Nothing out of the ordinary.' He nodded, almost to himself. 'Yeah.'

Phil wasn't wholly convinced by his reply but had no reason to question him further. 'Fine. But if you think of anything or anyone who was acting out of turn, let me know, okay? It might come to you later. Let me know.'

Nadish straightened up. It looked like he was starting to feel victimised. Or at least embarrassed in front of his colleagues. 'Yeah, course. But I know what I'm doing.'

'I know,' said Phil, aware of the effect his questioning was having. Don't look desperate, he thought. Don't grasp for something that isn't there. Alienate the people you rely on. 'I know you do. Right. Moving on. John Wright. What's the state of play with him?'

Matt Trevor, a DS who had been seconded in from another department to help out spoke up. 'Hotel's been gone through. Clean.'

'No sign of the Lawgiver having a room there?' asked Phil. 'Changing?'

'We didn't find one. But to be honest, that would be like looking for the proverbial needle in the proverbial haystack. The rooms are cleaned as soon as the guests have gone.'

'And nothing was left in any one?'

Trevor checked his notes. 'Couldn't find anything.'

'Keep looking,' said Phil. 'Double check. Just in case. What about the victim's injuries? How are they progressing?'

'He lost a lot of blood,' said Imani.

'Not to mention fingers,' said Nadish.

'Thank you, Nadish,' said Phil.

Imani nodded, continued. 'There was talk about whether to attempt to reconnect them. I think they're trying but what with the state the fingers and thumbs were found in, not to mention the overall state he was in, I don't think they're holding out much hope. But I'm sure he'll be getting the best possible treatment that money can buy.'

'If he's got any left after the Lawgiver wiped out his accounts. Where are we with that?'

Another new face, DC Vicki Hazzard, looked up. She had been brought in for the investigation, a specialist in financial crimes. 'He was very thorough,' she said. 'Very thorough. He knew his stuff, knew what he was doing. To take down accounts like he did and in that space of time shows some serious nous. He must have been planning that a while. Real financial hacktivist moves.'

'Is that an avenue to look at?' asked Phil. 'Could he be with, I don't know, Anonymous, a group like that?'

'No,' said Elli, speaking up for the first time. Everyone looked at her. She reddened, but continued. 'I've already checked. I have some hacktivist contacts that I've spoken to. They all claim it's nothing to do with them.'

'Can we trust them?' asked Cotter.

'As much as we can trust anyone,' said Elli. 'The ones I spoke to said that while they might agree with his targets and his aims, they don't agree with his methods.'

'But presumably Anonymous is just that,' said Phil. 'An amorphous organisation. He could be one of them.'

'He could be, yes,' said Elli. 'But given what I've heard from those I've talked to, I'd say it's unlikely.'

Unlikely, thought Phil. But something niggled about that. He filed it away. There were more pressing matters to be dealt with.

69

Letisha Watson walked through her flat like a ghost. She would walk into one room, not remember why she was there, go back to the room she had come from, wonder what she had been doing in there in the first place. On and on, haunting herself all morning.

She hadn't been able to sleep. Her encounter with Moses, and especially Tiny, the day before had left her more shaken that she would have thought possible. Yes, she knew it was going to be difficult to go in there but what was happening now, especially between Moses and her, had to be confronted. She couldn't just ignore what had happened. And it wasn't just sex. It was the connection, the being wanted again for who she was, not just her availability.

She knew what they called her on the estate. Whore. Prostitute. Slag. Slut. She knew all that. And not behind her back, either, right in her face sometimes. In the estate pub, the shop. Whenever someone wanted to have a go, felt like they had the right to. And worse of all, sometimes Letisha agreed with them.

When she had fallen, she had fallen hard. From being Julian's top bitch to nothing. In about the time it took to say it, it felt like. When Julian died Letisha was nothing. Cast out, shunned, only her clothes and jewellery for comfort. And they didn't last long: sold or pawned for ready cash. She had expected Moses to help her, had pleaded with him for help but he had shunned her too. Nicely, saying it was best they never met again, she must understand, it was for the best, even if neither of them wanted it. He had given her what he could moneywise, but that had run out pretty quickly too.

Desperate, she threw herself on her mother's mercy. But all she received was a lecture. Repent of her sins, give herself to God, be healed, cleansed and saved and then she would consider it.

Fuck that.

So she did the only thing she knew how to do. Got by on using her body. Selling it to whoever wanted it, for whatever they were willing to pay. She tried to set herself up as high class at first, visiting transient, lonely businessmen at their hotels, getting what she could out of them, charging top dollar for her services. Wearing what labels and bling she had left in an effort to impress. She didn't last long. The hotels were a closed shop, run by escort agencies she couldn't get a look-in with. There wasn't much demand for a mixed-race ex-gangsta's girl. No matter how many labels she wrapped herself in she still smelled of the street, as one agency boss had delicately put it to her.

So the street was where she went back to. What she knew. Turning tricks on street corners and dark alleys, getting into strangers' cars, wondering if she was ever going to get out of them again. Sometimes the johns wouldn't pay, wanted to smack her around instead, test their car's side windows with her head after she had sucked them off, their lust coalescing into anger at her, self-loathing for themselves. She would be dumped from the cars, battered, bleeding, bruised. Not able to work for a week. And, starving and desperate, would sometimes even get back inside the same cars, knowing what was coming, hoping that she could get away with just a bit of money this time. Any optimism she had was soon forcibly dragged out of her.

And then she met Darren. He wasn't much to look at, wasn't much in bed, had no kind of future that didn't involve getting stuck in prison's revolving door. But he was kind to her. He treated her well. He never beat her up, never hurt her. She had good times with Darren. Getting high as many different ways as they could. On the town, having a laugh. She didn't love him, didn't have time for any shit like that, wouldn't lie to herself. But she was grateful to him for coming along when he did.

She clung to him, like he was her life raft. So when he met that slag Chloe Hannon she was devastated He made her life, her job, bearable. Stopped her getting too hard, too cold. She was scared of what she would become without him.

That was why she fought for him. But it was too late. That slag was pregnant with his kid. And even though he had always said he didn't mind and was happy to be just with her, she knew he wanted kids. Or even just one kid. And she couldn't have them. Too many violent johns had seen to that. So she knew when that happened she had lost him.

And when she lost him, she lost herself again.

She had existed in a kind of limbo for months, not moving forwards, not moving back. Just doing what she did, enduring what she had to. Surviving.

Then the police turned up.

And then Moses.

And she thought her life was about to begin again. Fair enough, that feeling only lasted for the night he was with her. He soon showed her how wrong she was the next morning. And she understood that. She really did. But hadn't enough time gone past now that it shouldn't affect them? That they could move on? Apparently not. As Moses had said and as her trip to the studio had demonstrated. Now, she didn't know what to do, or what the future held for her. But she knew that unless she pulled herself together, thought fast, then it wouldn't be good.

A knock at the door.

She jumped, the noise pulling her back into the present. Was that the police again with their snide insinuations, hoping she would crack and tell them everything? Or worse?

She stayed still, not daring to move. Knowing that if she opened the door and the wrong person was standing there then that would be it. All over.

Another knock.

But would that be such a bad thing? Maybe her mother was right, maybe God was waiting to forgive her, welcome her into heaven. Maybe she would get a long, long rest.

Or maybe not.

Another knock. Accompanied by a voice this time: 'Come on, Letisha, I know you're in there.'

A tsunami of relief washed through her. She rushed to the door, opened it. Moses almost fell inside, so hurried was he to get off the landing.

She grabbed him, arms round him straight away.

'I thought you'd . . . I thought you'd . . . '

Not without gentleness, he took her arms away, moved into the living room. Turned to her.

'Who's been here? Today?'

'No one. Just . . . just you.'

'You haven't been followed, no calls, nothing like that?'

'No. What does—' She stopped speaking, looked at him. There was something in his eyes that she hadn't seen for years. Something that caused them to live apart since then.

Fear.

'We've got to move fast,' he said.

70

'R ight,' said Phil. 'Which brings us back to you again, Elli. CCTV. How you getting on with that?'

'Nowhere, really,' she said. 'Going backwards, I've looked at the footage from last night. We can't get a bearing on the woman at all. It's like she knew there would be cameras on her so she's kept her face shielded as much as possible. Her hair's all down around her face and when she talks she uses her hands a lot, covers her mouth. She also keeps her head down, angled away. Glen Looker has to lean in several times to hear what she's saying.'

Phil nodded. Felt like another brick wall had just been erected in front of him. 'Have we got anything on her? Even some shots that we could put together to try to make up some kind of composite e-fit picture of her?'

Elli smiled. 'I thought you would say that, so I had a go. The software I've got is very limited, still in beta, but without giving it to the specialists, here's what I managed to get.'

She clicked her mouse and an image appeared on her computer screen. A head-and-shoulders shot of a woman. Blurry, like it was taken at high speed and weirdly composed as if – which was exactly what had happened – several images had been stitched together. A Frankensuspect, thought Phil.

Everyone crowded round to look.

'I'll print some off so you can all have one,' said Elli. 'But this is her, as well as I can do.'

Phil studied the image. Beyond the basic physical details, medium height, light build, it wasn't good enough to issue for uniforms to look out for. Or shouldn't have been. Phil had seen a lot worse e-fits handed out.

'Thank you,' he said, 'that's brilliant work. At least we've got something to go on, something to recognise.'

'I'm working on something else, too,' she said, smoothing her heavily ringed hands down her sides. It was a nervous gesture, Phil knew. She hated talking in public, even among her colleagues. As she did it, Phil noted the T-shirt she was wearing today: *Fahrenheit 451*, a reproduction of the Ray Bradbury book cover, with the tagline, 'Read & destroy!' He liked the fact there was someone on the team more individually dressed than he was. It gave him, in only a small way, some kind of hope.

'Here,' Elli said, 'watch this.'

She clicked her mouse once more and the image of the woman disappeared. It was replaced by CCTV footage. Low quality, fixed camera, shot from a distance. The exterior of the Radisson Blu Hotel.

'From last night,' she said. 'I've gone over this a few times. See what you think.'

She started to play the footage. It showed the taxi rank outside of the hotel, rows of black cabs lined up, waiting. Fuller than usual, knowing there was an event going on, touting for business. As they watched, the front door of the hotel was opened and Glen Looker and the woman came hurrying out.

'Right,' said Elli. 'Watch this.'

They did. They saw the two figures walk straight to the first cab. The woman went to the window, spoke to the driver.

'No sound,' said Phil. 'Pity. Would make it so simple for us.'

Instructions given, Glen Looker opened the door for the woman to get in. The cab then drove off.

317

The screen froze as Elli stopped the tape. 'Right,' she said, 'what d'you all make of that?'

'They got into a cab,' said Nadish. 'Drove off.'

'Exactly,' Elli said, 'but didn't you notice anything else?'

'Their body language,' said Imani. 'Glen Looker's especially. He looks, I don't know. Relaxed? Eager. Yeah, eager.'

'Knows what he's gonna get,' said Nadish. 'Or thinks he does.'

'Yeah, but,' said Phil, 'this is coming straight after what just happened to Ian. Looker might have even seen it. And he makes no attempt to escape, to run. Knowing, or even suspecting, what she must have done.'

'We presume,' said Cotter.

'Want to watch it again?' asked Elli.

They did so. At the end, Phil nodded. 'You're right. Looker seems almost eager to get in, to be away. The big question here is, does he know that she's connected to the Lawgiver? Or is he such a knobhead that, even after everything that's happened, he still thinks he's going to get a shag?'

'Well, we have had dealings with Mr Looker before,' said Cotter, 'we do know how his mind works . . . '

Polite laughter.

'True,' said Phil. 'But even so . . . ' He stared at the screen, at the frozen taxi. 'Can we get the number of that cab? Find out where they went. See if any other CCTV camera in the city centre picked them up. Hopefully we can get some idea of the route they took from that. Can we watch it again, please? One last time.'

They watched it again. Phil scrutinised it closely. 'There,' he said. 'Stop.'

Ellis stopped it.

'Look at that. See? What d'you all see there?' He pointed to the two figures on the screen, just about to get into the cab.

'They're both smiling,' said Nadish.

'Look closer,' said Phil. 'She's smiling. You can see that much about her face. But Looker? He looks like he's been told to smile. Like he's posing for a photo he doesn't want to be in.'

Imani moved in closer. 'He looks scared,' she said.

'Do we get a good look at her face there,' asked Phil. 'Or a better one?'

'I'll work on it,' said Elli. 'Try to incorporate it into the e-fit.'

'Thanks.' Something else occurred to him. 'By the way, have we checked the CCTV from the Malmaison to see if this woman's in it?'

'Not yet,' said Elli, 'but it's a damned good idea.'

'Get onto that, too. If she was at the Radisson she might have been at the Mal.'

'Could the Lawgiver be a woman?' asked Nadish. 'This woman?'

'I've heard his voice too many times,' said Phil. 'It's definitely a man. But that doesn't rule out the fact that he might not be acting alone.' He looked around the group once more, straightened up. 'Okay. That's where we are now. Anyone got anything more to add?'

No one did.

'Keep going with what we're doing, then,' he said. 'We'll find him. Remember the profile. He's not invincible. He's going to slip up. He might have already done so and we just need to go over what we already have to find it. Okay?'

Everyone nodded.

'I know you're tired. I'm tired too. But we're a man down and I need you all to step up on this one. Time is against us. We have to find Glen Looker before he succumbs to a similar fate as the previous two victims of the Lawgiver. Work every avenue you can, no matter how many times you've done it before. Check out any hunch or half certainty you had, no matter how ridiculous. Something you might have dismissed. It might just be the thing we need. We have to work as a team. Let's get to it.'

The meeting broke up. Cotter and Phil were left together.

'Well done,' she said. 'You got straight back on that horse.'

'Thank you,' he said. 'I had no choice.'

'D'you think he'll be making him confess?' asked Cotter. 'The Lawgiver. Make him confess his sins before he does something untoward to him?'

'I should imagine so. Try to make him repent, even.'

Cotter nodded. 'Let's just hope, for the sake of us who are trying to track him down, that he has a lot of sins to repent.'

71

Fiona Welch looked at herself in the mirror. She liked what she saw. Not too bad. The clothes were perhaps a little out of date, a few years maybe, and they weren't what she would have chosen for herself but they fitted quite well. Blue jeans, a silk blouse and a jacket. Anonymous, blending in with the crowd. Good. That was exactly the way she wanted it.

She turned sideways, still looking, put her hand over her stomach, flattening it out. The jeans were a good fit. The woman whose clothes these had originally been must have imagined she was going to get herself back in shape. Lose the extra pounds she had been carrying. Fiona Welch smiled. Not any more.

The car had skidded off the road, Mickey Phillips screaming and dying as it did so. She had pulled away from him, braced herself for the impact as much as she could, crouching herself down in the leg space behind the driver's seat. Arms still pulled behind her back, held tight by the cuffs.

As the car hit she tucked her head in as far as it would go, prepared for the crash. It wasn't as bad as she had feared. A hawthorn hedge took most of the impact, its gnarled, twisted limbs and barbed branches acting as surrogate shock absorbers.

The car ended up skewed sideways in a ditch. She knew she didn't have much time. She pulled herself out of the leg space, twisting her body so that her tied hands could reach the door. Tried the handle. The ditch jammed it. Quickly, she turned her body round, hurried over to the left-hand-side door, tried that. It took a few attempts and a shove that seriously hurt her shoulder but she managed to force it open. Crawling and sprawling into the nettle-filled ditch she felt the hawthorn barbs rip at her clothing, her skin. She ignored the pain, boxing it off in her mind as she had done so many times before, leaving it sectioned and dormant, to be dealt with at some later date. She pulled away from the car as swiftly as she could. Her knowledge of engine mechanics based solely on Hollywood films, she didn't know whether it was going to explode or not but she didn't want to take the chance.

She looked up. Headlights were starting to appear at the side of the road they had left. Cars stopping, seeing if they could do anything to help. She didn't intend to stay around and be seen. Crawling as fast as she could, she dragged herself through the hawthorn hedge into the field behind it. Keeping her head down and her eyes closed, feeling the barbs and thorns dragging at her, getting under her skin, sticking and hooking, pulling bloodied slivers away from her as she hauled herself through. She wanted to scream but again kept it all contained. Pain would only slow her down.

She was stumbling away from the scene, her feet negotiating the rutted field, when she was knocked to her knees by an intense heat and what felt like a small bomb.

The car had exploded.

She hurried away, hoping that the blast hadn't illuminated her fleeing self.

She ran, keeping to the edges of the field, staying in the shadows of the edging trees. Hands still cuffed behind her back, her mind working all the time, planning a way to get them free and then herself free.

She kept going until she came to a village. A normal person would have been exhausted by this point, beyond tiredness, even. But the woman calling herself Fiona Welch was fuelled from a different engine entirely.

She kept to the shadows, hiding herself if a car came past, headlights swinging round corners, bouncing over ruts in the road. Keeping herself hidden from the few pedestrians and dog walkers on the main road in the dark. Eventually she saw the lights of the village pub. She smiled to herself. Perfect.

It had gone the way of most country pubs. Original features pointed up, all beams and thatching but tastefully updated. She was sure that it would be more of a restaurant than a pub too. She was right. The windows spilled out a warm, welcoming glow through the darkness and onto the gravel car park. She crept round the perimeter of the parked cars, crouching, sticking to the bushes and hedges. She found a vantage point, waited. Watched customers enter and leave.

And then she saw the ones she was waiting for.

A couple, in their thirties she imagined, well dressed and entering without children. And they didn't look like they were meeting anyone either, just dining on their own. Their car was smart too, a BMW. Perfect. Or she would make it perfect.

The woman calling herself Fiona Welch was nothing if not patient. It was a talent she had developed for herself, at first through necessity but then as a way of life to get what she wanted. Slow burn. Take her time. Plot and plan. She could do it. She had waited so long, a couple more hours while this couple ate was nothing.

She could see them through the window from the car park. She was crouched behind their BMW, waiting for them. They emerged from the restaurant, sated and replete, made their way to the car. That was when the woman calling herself Fiona Welch went into her act.

She curled herself up in a foetal ball behind the tyres, whimpering to herself.

She heard them coming, make to get in the car, stop when they saw her.

'What's—' the woman said, bending down. She saw the pitiful, bloodied wreck of Fiona Welch and stepped backwards, her hand going to her mouth in alarm.

'What the fu—' Her husband joined her, recoiling in fear and surprise also. 'Jesus . . .'

Fiona Welch gathered herself up, tried to run. She made a play of attempting to get to her feet but lost her balance, her cuffed hands supposedly unbalancing her, stumbled and fell down again.

'Hey, no,' said the husband, 'it's all right, we're . . . it's . . . we're not going to hurt you.'

She whimpered, shook. Behaved like a cornered animal, wide-eyed and terrified.

The wife bent slowly down, arms outstretched, like she was trying to gain the trust of a feral cat. 'Hey, it's okay. We're not going to hurt you . . . it's okay . . .'

She extended a cautious hand. Fiona Welch turned, decided to show them the cuffs.

'Jesus,' said the husband. 'Where've you been? What happened to you? Who did this?'

She just whimpered some more.

'Come on,' the husband said to the wife, 'we'll take her to the police.'

'No,' Fiona Welch said, her voice rasping and quavering, 'no police, no . . . they'll, they'll please, no . . . ' She started sobbing.

'But they'll help . . . '

'No, no police . . . '

'Why not?'

She answered with more sobbing.

324

The husband and wife stared at her, at each other.

'We can't leave her here, Graham . . .' Sotto voce, but still audible.

'Well, what can we do? She doesn't want to go to the police.'

The wife looked at the husband, face rosy with wine, eyes slightly glassy. She wanted to help, be the good Samaritan. Do her good deed. 'Well, we can't leave her here, can we? We'll have to take her back to ours. Back home.'

The husband looked as if he couldn't believe what he was hearing. 'We can't do that.'

'Why not?'

'Well, I mean, we don't know anything about her, Lauren. We don't know who's done this to her, or, or why or anything. They might . . . might come after us.'

'Graham, she needs help.'

He leaned in close to his wife, spoke in a voice that she assumed she wasn't meant to hear. 'Can't we let someone else deal with it? There must be loads of people in the pub.'

'That's a disgusting thing to say, Graham. There's no one here but us. Could you have it on your conscience if you just walked away from this woman? Left her here? God knows who might come along next.'

Graham looked at the woman, back to his wife's imploring face. Sighed. 'All right, then. We'll take her back to ours. She can get herself sorted out then we can decided what to do from there.'

Lauren smiled. 'Thank you.' She turned to the wreck of a woman before them, spoke slowly as if to a retarded child. 'We're going to take you back to our house, okay? We aren't going to hurt you. If you'd like me to I'll help you to your feet. If you can do it on your own I won't touch you. Okay?'

Fiona Welch, eyes darting like trapped sparrows, nodded.

She allowed them to escort her to the back of their car, where she made a performance of getting in. Once inside they drove off.

'Don't worry,' said Lauren, turning round. 'We'll take care of you.'

Fiona Welch smiled.

Not half as well as I'm going to take care of you, she thought.

72

'Why do it?' said the Lawgiver.

'Why do what?' asked Glen Looker.

'What you do. Represent scum. Give them a fair hearing.'

Looker stared at his host, tried to make out the man's eyes behind the mask. He couldn't gauge much from the muffled tone of his voice. He had to talk and talk for his life. He had to know what mental state his audience was in. Unfortunately he couldn't see behind the gas mask's round eyeholes. 'And what would you suggest I do? What would you suggest the justice system do instead?'

'They're scum. They're all guilty.'

'Of what, though?' said Looker. 'The people I represent are poor. They've been pissed around by the system. Bad housing, bad schooling, bad family life. Nothing going for them. They may as well be sent straight from school to prison. That's what certain parts of society thinks, if you read the right newspapers. They commit crime and they have no one to speak for them. Apart from me.'

The Lawgiver let out a harsh, distorted sound. At first Looker thought he was having some kind of fit. Then he realised he was laughing.

'Sentimental liberal bullshit,' the Lawgiver said. 'Poor-me politics. They break the law, they should be punished. Simple as that.'

'No it's not,' said Looker. 'It's not simple at all. What do we mean by law? By morality in the law? Is it obeying the letter of the law or the spirit of the law? If you steal a loaf of bread because you're starving and you have to feed your family, is that wrong?'

'Get a job. Feed your family with pride then.'

'What if there are no jobs? Or the jobs you're trained for are too far away and you can't afford to travel or retrain for the ones that are nearby? What if you do have a job but it doesn't pay you enough to live on? That's the reality of life in this country now for millions of people. That's my client base.'

'Like I said, liberal bullshit. I've seen the kind of people you represent. Low-lives. Nothing. You get them off, let them out to do exactly the same things over and over again. They're not the noble poor. They're just scum.'

'That's just your judgement.'

'Yes, it is,' said the Lawgiver. 'And look where we are now. I'm the one whose judgement matters. To you.'

Despite the gravity of the situation, or perhaps because of it, Glen Looker was starting to feel energised by this argument. He had recently been questioning his commitment to the law and to the clients he represented. Every trip to prison was more depressing than the last. Every battle with the police to keep a client out of jail more draining that the previous one. And were they grateful? Did they appreciate the effort he put in on their behalf? Hardly ever. He remembered Darren Richards' face in the hospital bed. All he was concerned about was himself. Not Chloe and Shannon. Himself.

Reluctantly, he had to admit there was something in what the Lawgiver was saying.

'All right then,' said Looker. 'Let's say, for argument's sake, that you don't agree with me.'

'I don't.'

'I know. Let's take that as a given. There's something else that you haven't considered. Something much more important.'

'Such as?'

Looker hid a smile. The Lawgiver was asking questions in response to his statements. That was a good sign, a positive indicator that he wasn't as in control of the situation as he believed himself to be.

'The greater good.'

'There is no greater good,' said the Lawgiver. 'There's only good and evil.'

'And what are you?' asked Looker, genuinely curious.

'Good.' No doubt in his voice at all.

'Even though you kill and mutilate?'

'I don't. I just do what they want me to do. I give them the choice. That's more than their victims ever got.'

'You went after Darren Richards because he accidentally killed a woman and child.'

'Correct.'

'And you went after John Wright because he was a banker who got off with his crimes.'

'He destroyed lives. Ruined families and communities. Deliberately. And he got away with it. Before he met me, that is.'

'So where does this end?'

'All the guilty must pay for their crimes.'

'All the guilty? That's a lot of repayment. Where do you stop? Where do you draw the line?'

'There is no line. There is only good and evil. Innocence and guilt. Justice. That's all.'

'No mitigating circumstances?'

'No such thing.'

Looker smiled. 'Interesting. Because a lot of people would think that you're a criminal, that what you're doing is evil.'

'Then a lot of people would be wrong.'

'You kill and mutilate. Regardless of the context. Is that what the good guys do?'

The Lawgiver walked away from Looker, turning his back on him. He seemed to be thinking. Eventually he turned, stared at Looker.

'I know what you're doing.'

Looker swallowed hard. There was something different about the tone of his voice. Something slightly unhinged. 'And . . . and what's that?'

'You're trying to sow doubt and confusion in my mind. Make me uncertain about my calling. My work. Use your words to get me to stop.' He walked right up to Looker. Looker could smell the sweat coming off him. He bent down, face to mask. 'Well, it won't work.'

'I never said it would.'

'Good. Because it won't.'

'I never said it would,' said Looker, hoping his voice was coming out strong, 'because that wasn't what I was doing. We were talking, weren't we? Having a conversation. I was telling you why I do what I do. You were listening. Isn't that what you wanted?'

The sightless, round spaces stared at Looker. Twin dark pools, he could barely see that there was anything human behind them. Looker didn't realise it but he was holding his breath.

The Lawgiver straightened up, walked away. Turned and stared at Looker once more.

'The greater good,' he said, the light haloed around his head.

'What?'

'The greater good. You were going to tell me about it.'

'Right.'

'I'm getting bored by your *Guardian*-reader lectures. Be

330

specific. Give me an example of how what you do affects the greater good.'

Looker didn't reply, thinking hard. He looked up. 'Okay,' he said, 'how about this. The streets of Birmingham are a safer place now from warring gangs. And I was partly responsible for that.'

'How?'

'By getting people to look the other way when I wanted them to.'

The Lawgiver cocked his head to one side, listening. 'Tell me about it,' he said.

Looker smiled. This was more like it. This was his chance.

73

The couple, Graham and Lauren, were as good as their word. They took Fiona Welch back to their house and helped her inside.

Deciding that the level of hysteria she had started from would be grating and ultimately unsympathetic if she kept it up for any length of time, she decided to drop it a few notches. It would be good for the couple to see that, too, let them know that their ministrations were working. They would feel good about themselves then and, more importantly, drop their guard with her.

Play the victim, she thought, just play the victim and everything will go according to plan.

She sat on the sofa in the living room, a thick blanket wrapped round her shoulders, mug of hot tea on the table before her.

'Let's see what I've got in the garage to get those things off,' Graham said.

'Thank you,' she managed, her voice frail and brittle as spun sugar. 'You're ... you're very kind ...'

As Graham left the room, Lauren smiled at her. Placed her hand on her knee. 'Don't worry. You're going to be all right now. You're in safe hands.'

She nodded, tried to blink back tears.

Graham came back with a pair of gardening secateurs.

'These should do it,' he said. 'Cut the chain, at least. Strong enough to lop off whole branches, these things are.'

The linking chain cut easily. The metal cuffs were harder work. He had to get a hacksaw blade and saw away at them. By the time he had eventually done it, her tea was cold.

'I'll make you another, shall I?'

'Thank ... thank you,' she said, rubbing her wrists. She looked up at Graham. 'And thank you. For this. I thought I was never going to get ... ' She started welling up again.

'Hey,' he said, thinking of slipping his arm round her shoulder, then stopping himself. 'It's okay. Don't worry. You're safe now.'

They gave her space after that. Ran her a bath, found her a spare towelling robe to wear. She luxuriated there for as long as she dared without arousing suspicion. She needed the bath. It washed the blood from her skin, both her own and the police officer's. Soothed her aching muscles. And washed away the stink of that institution.

She looked at her wrists. The red marks looked like she had been branded. She smiled to herself.

This was going to be easy.

Eventually she came downstairs. They were still sitting up. It was well past midnight now and the couple's earlier adrenalin rush was beginning to abate and tiredness starting to creep in. But they wouldn't go to bed. Not until they had learned more about their new house guest.

Lauren smiled as she entered. 'Sit down, love. You must feel so much better after that.'

'Thank you,' she said. 'Yes.'

'So,' said Graham, leaning forward, 'what's your name? We don't even know your name.'

'It's ... ' She hesitated. Not because she hadn't thought of one, but because she wanted to give the impression that it was a big thing, a way of showing that she was coming to trust them. 'Anni. Anni Hepburn.'

'Anni,' said Graham, 'right.' He smiled. 'Hello, Anni.'

She laughed, putting relief into it.

'What happened, then?' asked Lauren then immediately recoiled. 'If, you know, you're ready to tell us. Or can tell us.'

'I'll ... I'll try,' she said, holding yet another mug of tea, clutching it hard as if it were a lucky talisman. 'I was ...' She screwed up her face, dropped her voice, as if reluctantly remembering something particularly unpleasant. 'I was out. With, with my friends one night in Ipswich. We went, went clubbing. And then, then ...' She tailed off, matching the lack of words with a uncomprehending look off into the middle distance.

'Take your time,' said Lauren, reaching across, placing her hand on her knee. 'Take as long as you want.'

She nodded, seemingly grateful for the words. 'Well, I don't know. What happened. I've gone over and over it, but ...' She sighed. 'I was in the club with my friends. Then I felt woozy. And then ...' A shrug. 'I was ... somewhere else. And I didn't know how I'd got there.'

'Where was that?' asked Graham.

'It was ... I don't know where it was. But I wasn't alone. There were other women there too. They'd been there longer than me. I was ...' She closed her eyes, threatened tears again. 'Horrible ... Oh God ...'

Lauren kept her hand on her knee. 'Dear God, Anni ...' She waited for the tears to roll away. 'How did you get out?'

'I ...' Her eyes clouded over again. 'I ... did something horrible ...'

More tears.

Graham shook his head. 'We'd better take you to the police. We've got to do something about this.'

'No!' she suddenly screamed. 'No police. I think . . . I don't know, but I think they might have . . .' Another sigh. 'There were men. Used to visit. Do, do awful things. Some were . . . were police . . .'

Graham and Lauren exchanged a look that they thought she hadn't caught.

'I just . . .' she said, head bowed down, shoulders slumped, 'I just want to sleep . . .'

'Okay, then,' said Lauren. 'I think that's for the best. We'll sort out what to do in the morning.'

The house was small but cosy. The second bedroom had become Lauren's dressing room and the spare room was kept for Graham's study so they fixed up the sofa bed for her. She snuggled under the duvet, found a smile for her hosts. 'Thank you. Thank you so much, I don't know what I'd have done if I hadn't met you, I . . .'

There were the tears again.

They said some more platitudes, told her it was nothing and that she had nothing to worry about, that she was safe now and went up to bed. She could see they were tired, the post-adrenalin come-down having kicked in for both of them. They would be off to sleep soon.

Good.

After that it didn't take long. She lay awake until she was sure they were both off, the sound of light snoring filling the dark, otherwise quiet house. It was easy for her to go into the kitchen, find the biggest knife, ensure the blade was sharp and start slowly up the stairs.

She found their bedroom and entered it, walking so lightly she could have been a ghost. Lauren was the nearest. It was a simple matter of holding one hand over her mouth, pulling the blade quickly across her throat and forcing her down hard, waiting while the blood, and the life, pumped itself out of her.

Graham hadn't stirred. But he soon did. He woke up with her straddling him, the knife tip pushing into his throat, his dead wife's bloodied body next to him.

'Your credit card and debit cards,' she said. 'And their PIN numbers. Don't fuck me about. You can see that I'm serious.'

She saw the conflicting emotions travel swiftly over his features. She pushed the knife in, drew blood to help concentrate his mind.

'Now,' she said.

He told her the PINs. Then he told her where the cards were. She got up from him, crossed to get them. He was lying exactly where he had been when she returned. She smiled at him. 'Good boy,' she said. 'Car keys?'

He told her where they were.

'Thank you.'

'You ... you're going to let me go? Please, please let me go ...'

'You're of no use to me now.'

She plunged the knife into his throat, dragged it side to side. It didn't take long.

And there she was the next morning, showered and changed, in Lauren's dressing room wearing Lauren's old clothes. She packed a few more into one of Lauren's supposed designer bags but was more likely a cheap knock-off bought from a market on a Mediterranean package holiday, looked around the room once more. There was nothing else she wanted.

Picking up the keys, she left the house just as the sun was rising.

Fiona Welch was no more. It was time for a new identity.

And she knew just the one.

She got behind the wheel, drove away.

Bound for Birmingham.

74

'How we doing?' asked Imani. She was staring at the screen alongside Elli, both of them scanning footage from the Malmaison.

'Did you nod off?' asked Elli, eyes affixed to the screen, smile on her face.

'All these hotel corridors look alike,' Imani said. 'It's like watching a twenty-four-hour version of *The Shining*, except that nothing happens.'

'I saw something like that once,' said Elli, eyes never leaving the screen.

'What d'you mean?'

'Well, it wasn't *The Shining* but it was *Psycho*. A twenty-four-hour version of *Psycho*.'

'Jesus . . .'

'It was art. Or meant to be art.'

'How was it art?'

'This guy, this artist, had slowed the film down so that it lasted exactly twenty-four hours. All in slow motion. Incredibly slow motion.'

'Oh.' Imani knew Elli was the resident geek and counter-culturalist on the team, but she looked at her colleague as if there was nothing more she could say that would surprise her. 'And . . . did you enjoy it?'

'Nah, not really. Preferred the original.'

'Good to hear.'

They went back to watching the screen.

More corridors. The lobby. More corridors. Imani yawned again.

'How far back do these go?' Imani asked.

'We've got the day before, too. If that woman came there, checked in, we should be able to catch her.'

Imani took out her notepad.

'What you doing?'

'Just making some notes. Trying to find a timeframe to help us. What time did the call come in to Phil? What time was it logged?'

Elli ran her fingers over the keys, another screen momentarily appeared. 'Six oh three,' she said.

'Right. And he said he was far away by then. That we'd never find him.'

'Yup.'

'So how did he get away? And when did he get away?'

'Before then, presumably.'

'Exactly. Elli, where do these cameras extend to? Just inside the hotel or outside?'

'There are none outside.'

Imani sank back in her seat. She had become momentarily excited by her hypothesis. 'Shit.'

'But I did pick up the ones for the car park underneath.'

Imani turned to her. Elli was smiling.

'Then why aren't we looking at them?'

'Because the boss told us to check the hotel footage. The car park, strictly speaking, isn't part of the hotel. I had to put a separate requisition in for their footage.'

'And you've got it?'

'Yup. Was going to watch it after we'd finished all this.'

'Well, I think the boss will also reward our initiative if we decide to look at this first, don't you think?'

Elli frowned. 'Give me a minute.'

She stabbed more keys and the screen image disappeared. Imani had always liked Elli. She wasn't typical police material, which made her company all the more appealing. Imani could see why Phil wanted her there. They had a lot in common. Or rather, they had more in common than they realised. Both were given a certain amount of leeway in their dress sense but that was because they both got results and claimed their appearance helped them. And neither conformed to the stereo-typical image of a copper yet they were both attracted to the job and had even managed to carve a successful niche for themselves in it.

There were other aspects that weren't so similar. Elli was Indian and from a strict religious background. She was rebel-lious in her outlook with her piercings, skin ink and dress sense, yet she could be quite conservative in her views. Imani found the juxtaposition appealing.

'Here we go,' said Elli. 'Got it. I'll just ...' The screen showed the car park under the Malmaison. Well lit, low ceilinged. Full, as usual. 'What time did you say?'

'He called the boss at six oh three.'

'Six oh three ...' Her fingers played over the keys once more and the screen speeded up, went in reverse, slowed down. 'Right ... Give it an hour or so ... Here we go. Let's start from here.'

'You take those two,' said Imani, pointing to the ones on the left. 'I'll take these.'

They began watching once more. The screen was split into quarters, each one showing a different part of the car park. People came and went. Cars drove in and out. Every time they saw someone pulling a case or carrying a holdall they became interested, jumping forward in their seats. Once they saw it wasn't their target they sank back in watchful torpor.

This pattern continued until Imani jumped forward once more.

'There,' she said, almost shouting. 'Stop it there.'

Elli did so, peered at the screen. It showed a woman, not unlike the one Glen Looker had been talking to the previous night, same height and build, pulling a suitcase behind her.

'That her?' said Imani. Her pulse was racing, heart pounding.

'I think . . . Let's go back.'

Elli's fingers moved and the image moved in reverse. They watched again. The woman came into view once more. Elli paused the tape.

'There,' she said. 'She's about to cross the road. She has to look both ways and we can get a look at her face.'

Elli advances the tape slowly, frame by frame. The woman's head turned slowly. Imani felt another race of excitement through her body.

'Shit.'

The woman stopped short of fully turning, depriving them both of seeing her features.

'She knows where the cameras are,' said Imani. 'She must do.'

'Which means she's been there before. Planned this. Which means there's footage of her.'

'Yes, but we don't know how many days, weeks, months or even years ago she did it,' said Imani. 'Which means we have a lot of watching to do.'

'Let's have a look at her,' said Elli. 'Let's see where she's going.'

'You sure it's her?' asked Imani.

'As sure as you are. You saw her last night, what d'you think?'

'I'd say it's her.'

'Right. Let's watch.'

The woman walked away from the camera, still pulling the case. Something, thought Imani, didn't look right about her. She couldn't say what it was, just a feeling she got.

'She looks ... odd,' said Elli.

'Yeah, I know what you mean.'

'Can't put my finger on it, but ... odd.'

She passed out of range of one camera. The other ones failed to pick her up.

'Where's she gone?' asked Imani.

'She's parked somewhere where there aren't cameras. She planned this.'

'Where's he, then?' asked Imani. 'There's her leaving, but where's he?'

'In that suitcase?' suggested Elli.

'We'll think about that later.' Imani stood up. 'Check the cars as they come out. See if you can spot her.'

'Where you going?'

'Back to my own desk. I want to run the guest names again. Compare Malmaison with the Radisson Blu. See if anything stands out. Keep at it. We're on to something.'

Imani walked away. Elli looked back at the screen. Thinking of *Psycho* again had made her uneasy.

But still, watching that woman walk, she was sure there was something not quite right about her ...

75

'Not there,' said Moses Heap, ending the call before it could go to voicemail. 'I'll text him.' He had been trying to contact Glen Looker all morning. Before he had tried his mobile he tried his office. His secretary said she didn't know where he was, with what sounded like a touch of fear in her voice, and didn't know when he would be back. He didn't want to press her on it, none of his business. Maybe they were having a thing, or something, and he had told her he was going back to his wife. Or girlfriend. Or whoever. He didn't really know much about Glen Looker's private life and didn't much care. He just needed his help professionally now. It was an emergency.

'I'll text him,' he said. 'Tell him what's happening.'

'What . . . what is happening?' asked Letisha.

'You know what, babe,' he said, thumbs working over the screen, 'we've got to get away. Move out. Make ourselves scarce.'

'Look, I know it's dangerous, and all that, you said it was, but . . . can't we just stay here? If we say—'

'No.' Text sent, he put his phone down, took Letisha by the shoulders. Not roughly but firmly. Looked right into her eyes. 'You know what'll happen. You knew what would happen as soon as you came to the studio.'

'I didn't know Tiny would be there.'

'Why not? Think. It's a truce. We're supposed to be on the same side. Whatever suspicions he had about us long gone. Supposedly. Seeing you and me together again, for whatever reason, will start him off again, man. He hasn't forgotten. Never would. And you know what he's like. What he's capable of.'

Letisha shuddered. She had seen, all right. Her head dropped.

'Well, we can't take that chance. We got to get out of the way. At least until things cool down again.' He took his hands from her shoulders, put one gently under her chin, turned her face up to his. 'Yeah?'

She smiled.

'Okay. As long as, you know . . . You're with me.'

'I'll be with you, babe.'

Despite the feeling of apprehension, of danger, Letisha felt more than a little glimmer of hope. 'Then let's go.'

They broke their embrace, Letisha going into the bedroom to pack.

'What shall I take? What have you got?'

'As much as you can carry. I just threw some stuff in a bag. Don't know how long we'll have to be away. Once we're gone I'll get Looker on the case. He can start negotiations for us to come back.'

Letisha stopped what she was doing, put her head round the door. 'What if . . . y'know? What if he can't or they won't let us?'

Moses tried for a brave smile, for Letisha's sake. 'Then we'll just see where we end up.'

She went back into the bedroom smiling. As she packed, putting what she thought of as her good clothes into a cheap, black, frayed holdall, she thought about his words. *See where we end up.* That sounded good. In fact, that sounded even better than them having to come back to Birmingham. Proper romantic. Just the two of them on the road, not knowing where they would go, what would happen. Turning their lives into one big adventure. Together. The more Letisha thought of it, the more she wanted that more than anything else.

She was starting to think that she was glad she had gone to see him, glad that this thing with Darren Richards had put Moses back in her life. Maybe it was fate. Meant to be. Karma. She didn't know what that meant, not really, but she had heard it on telly and thought it sounded good. The way the people on the TV had been talking about it made it sound like for every bad thing that was done to you if you're good you get a good one back. That sounded fine to Letisha. She had had that many bad things done to her over the years, she was owed a whole shitload of karma.

And then there was a knock at the door.

Letisha froze.

Another knock.

Letisha moved as quickly and as silently as she could into the living room. She stared at Moses who was staring at the door, his eyes wide with fear and horror. Neither moved.

Another knock. Accompanied by a voice this time.

'Hey, Moses, know you're in there. Car's down here. Open it.'

Tiny's voice.

Hearing the voice, Moses broke out of the spell the knocks had cast on him. He looked around frantically. He ran to the window, opened the doors. Letisha ran with him. The balcony was small, the distance to the ground huge. He looked along. The next balcony was a couple of metres away. He might make it if he jumped, but he might not. And Letisha might not.

He even thought that they could do a trick he'd seen in films where the hero – James Bond usually – hides from the bad guys by hanging underneath the balcony, only coming back up, pulling himself in when they had gone. Yeah, that was going to happen. That would work. No problems with that.

Another knock. Tiny's voice: 'I'm gettin' impatient out here, man . . . '

Letisha was next to him, looking up into his face, eyes scared but trusting. She would have gone over the balcony if I'd asked her, he thought. She looks like she's ready to follow me to the ends of the earth.

'What do we do?' she asked, her voice a frail whisper.

Moses sighed. 'Let him in, babe.' His voice spoke of resignation. 'What else can we do?'

'But . . . can't we . . . '

'We tried, babe,' said Moses. 'We tried.'

Letisha grabbed his hand. 'I love you, Moses.'

He gave her a sad smile. 'And I love you too, babe.'

Moses dropped her hand, went to answer the door.

76

'So explain, then,' the Lawgiver said, standing directly in front of Glen Looker, blocking out the light, making him Looker's whole focus, whole world. 'Explain. How can tolerating a small evil save us all from a larger one?'

'You've never heard of that principal before?'

'Well, obviously, yes. But I've never believed in it. It's bullshit. There's no such thing.'

'Let me give you a small example,' said Looker, his voice back in lawyer mode, as if he was addressing a room full of people who needed to be impressed by his opinions. 'And, needless to say, this is an example that I was personally involved in.'

The Lawgiver waited, a malevolent shadow eclipsing the light.

'Remember the gang wars?' Looker asked. 'The Birmingham gang wars? Only a few years ago, course you do. You must.'

'Vaguely,' said the Lawgiver. 'Lot of black-on-black killings. The poor wiping each other out. It didn't concern me much. The more of each other they killed, the less of them there would be walking the streets. Win win.'

'Bullshit,' said Looker, getting into his stride. 'You know nothing. The gang wars tore this city apart.'

The Lawgiver bristled at Looker's more dominant, aggressive change in tone but said nothing.

'The Handsworth Boys? The Chicken Shack Crew? No? They tore the city up between them, blew people away. Kids with guns. Scared kids with guns. Don't you remember all the innocent kids who got killed in the crossfire? Shot, knifed? Made all the papers, national news. Remember?'

'Yeah, I remember.'

Looker gave a tight smile. 'Well, I made it all go away. Or at least I helped to. Played a significant part, shall we say. In making this city more peaceful and safe.'

'How?' The Lawgiver's voice was flat, emotionless.

'There was this gang leader. Let's call him Julian.'

'Wilson,' said the Lawgiver.

Looker smiled widely. 'So you do know what I'm talking about.'

'Just keep going.'

'Okay. It was like this. He had a girlfriend. The number-one bitch in his stable of bitches. His words, incidentally, not mine. Well, this girlfriend was only with him because of what he could offer her. If we're being honest. I'm sure she liked him, probably, but she liked what he gave her more.'

'Jewellery,' said the Lawgiver. 'Material things.' A sneer of contempt behind the mask.

'Yes,' said Looker, 'to an extent. But more substantial things, too. A better life. A way out of the dead-end drudgery she'd been born into.'

The Lawgiver said nothing.

'But there was a problem. While this girl was with Julian for what she could get, she fell in love with someone else. Really fell in love. Properly head over heels. And that was with the rival gang leader.'

The Lawgiver let out a harsh, grating sound. A laugh. 'The Montagues and the Capulets.'

'If you like. Now she wanted to leave him for this other leader. Let's call him—'

'Moses Heap.'

Looker laughed. 'You know, you pretend you don't know what I'm talking about . . . '

'Someone from the Handsworth Boys killed Julian Wilson. We know that. Is this story going anywhere?'

'If that's what you think then you don't know as much as you think you do. That is the official version of events. I know the real one. Listen up and I'll tell you. Now, as I said, this girl wanted to leave. But she couldn't. The trouble was, Julian found out about this. Now, I'm not saying this girl was the love of his life. He probably felt about her the way she felt about him. Good arm candy, willing in bed, that sort of thing. But he didn't want to lose face, didn't want her to go over to the enemy. He'd be a laughing stock. Severely weakened. So he tried to kill her.'

'Tried?'

'Tried. He should have got someone else to do it, one of his soldiers, but no. He wanted to do it himself. Except it went wrong. He tried to shoot her. There was a struggle. She got the gun off him. Shot him.'

'And this is all true?'

'All true. Now, not knowing what to, she called Moses over. They had a choice. Play it straight, throw themselves on the mercy of the police, tell them what happened, that it was self-defence and he was trying to kill her, then stick to the truth and take their chances with that through the legal system. A system that hadn't been skewed in their favour up till now, I hasten to add. In fact, it had been actively biased against them.'

'That's what all the liberals say.'

'Yeah, they do,' said Looker. 'Especially the ones who work

in it every day. As I said, one way of doing it. The other way was to try to get out of it. That's when they called me in.'

'To do what?'

'To stage Julian's death, make it look like he was killed somewhere else, by someone else.'

The Lawgiver leaned forward, peering at Looker through the eye holes of his mask. 'Why are you telling me all this? What do you hope to gain?'

'What d'you think?' said Looker, louder than he had intended. 'You're going to kill me, I've worked that one out. No matter what I say, what arguments I come up with, you're going to kill me. I know that.'

'You don't know that.'

'I do.' Looker laughed. 'I know you better than you know yourself. So maybe I'm just getting it off my chest. One last confession.'

The Lawgiver stood back, blocking the light once more. 'Keep going then.'

'Fine. We staged Julian's death. There are people I know, friends of friends really, who can do that kind of thing. I don't call on them often, but, needs must . . . ' He attempted a shrug. Continued. 'But while we're getting this sorted, Moses decides he wants to use it for something else. Not just for him and Letisha – oh dear, I said her name.'

'Keep going.'

'Okay. Him and Letisha to get away with murder. He wants to make something of it. Use it as a springboard to bring peace between the two gangs. I told him it was risky, but he wanted to do it. So this is what he did. He approached Julian's younger brother, Tiny, knowing he'd be the one to take over. Now Tiny's a bit mental, bit unstable, so he has to tread carefully. He does. He tells Tiny that he's sick of all the bloodshed between the two gangs, the violence. He wants peace. Tiny's not interested. He wants blood. Moses tells him that if he can find out who was responsible for Julian's death – because the order hadn't come from him – find out and deal with it, will Tiny sit down and talk? He says he will.'

'So he killed one of his own men.'

'No. He found one of his gang who was willing to take the rap for it. But he didn't kill him. This is where I came in again. Again, friend of a friend ... So this gang member gets a new identity. And money. He's not dead, just living in Runcorn. Which, admittedly, some would say is the same thing.'

The Lawgiver said nothing.

'Now obviously, Tiny must never know. That it was Letisha who killed his brother and that the person he thought responsible isn't dead. And that Moses lied to him. If he found out, the peace would be over. If Moses and Letisha even see each other again then Tiny would suspect. He's never fully believed Moses but he's gone along with it.'

'Why?'

'Because he can see how beneficial peace is as well. For everyone.'

Looker sat back. Or attempted to. 'So there you go. A small evil covered up for the sake of a much larger good. Not really evil, in fact, just a messy accident that couldn't be reported. So what d'you think, Lawgiver?' Looker seemed to relish saying the name. 'Where does that fit in with your philosophy?'

The Lawgiver said nothing. Just stared at him.

Looker smiled. 'Right. That's me done. Do with that what you like, it's in your hands now. So fair's fair. I've shown you mine, you show me yours. I want you to tell me about Diana.'

The Lawgiver stared at him. The staring went on so long that Looker began to tremble, feeling he had gone too far. Then

350

the Lawgiver did something Looker hadn't expected. He ripped off his mask.

Looker had no idea who he was. Although his eyes looked smaller, his face more nondescript, he kept staring.

And that was when Looker realised. *I've seen his face.*

I'm not going to walk out of here alive.

77

Phil was just replacing the handset into the cradle on his desk, smiling slightly, when there was a knock on the door.

'Yeah?'

Nadish poked his head round. Looked from side to side as if he was in danger of being overheard. 'Can I . . . can I have a quick word, please, boss?'

Phil put the phone down, sat back. 'Course you can. Come in, Nadish. What's up?'

Nadish took the chair in front of the table, looked slightly sheepish. 'Well, it's . . . I don't know. I was thinking about what you said before, in the briefing. The psychological profile and all that.'

'What about it?'

'Well . . . you said think about anyone you'd come across who stuck in your mind, that kind of thing. There was this guy . . . '

Phil leaned forward, interested. 'He kinda ticked a few of the boxes.'

'What's his name?'

'Stuart Hinchcliffe. Lives just opposite where the first crime scene was.'

'I'm interested. Go on.'

'Well, he seemed like a bit of a loner, bit odd. Said he collected old Sixties soul, something about it being the last great manufactured thing, or something like that. Had a vintage jukebox. That's what we got talking about. Got a mate who does them up, an' that. We chatted about them.' Nadish sighed. 'Well, I think I may have been, you know, blindsided a bit by that.'

Phil studied his young officer. Despite his flaws, Nadish had good instincts. 'Anything else?'

'Well, it was just a vibe, really. I got the feeling, when I think back, you know, I got the feeling that he was ... laughing at me. Taking the piss a bit. Thinking here was this thick copper he was getting one over on. You know what I mean?'

'I know what you mean. I've been there.'

'Yeah?'

'We all have. Carry on.'

'Right.' Nadish put his head back, thinking. 'Well, he seemed well-educated but a bit odd. Said he lived with his sister but I never saw her.'

Phil felt that familiar tingle when he knew he was on to something. It wasn't infallible but it was a good indicator. 'Grounds for being the Lawgiver, you think?'

'I don't know. Sounds a bit ... thin when I say it aloud. But it was just something I felt.'

Phil thought for a moment. 'When did you talk to him?'

'Yesterday. Afternoon.'

'What time?'

Nadish puffed out his cheeks, thinking. 'Around ... threeish, something like that?'

Threeish. Phil checked through a file on his desk. The call from the Lawgiver had come in at just before three thirty. 'I got a call from the Lawgiver yesterday. Just after you'd finished with Stuart Hinchcliffe. He sounded jubilant. Like he'd ... won something. Maybe he thought he'd fooled you. Maybe that gave him the impetus to target Looker last night.'

'Shit, d'you think I let him get away?'

'You couldn't have known, Nadish. We'd have all done the same thing. But thanks for letting me know.'

'What d'you want me to do?'

Phil thought. 'Well, we don't want to go tearing over there with a full armed response unit, not just yet. We've got no evidence. No probable cause. Just your gut instinct, which may well be right. However, if you're wrong the media'll crucify us. Especially after last night's cock-up. We'll all be moved to Traffic. So let's tread lightly. Take Imani with you. Go and interview him again. If your suspicions are still intact, bring him in for questioning. I'll get Elli to look into his background while you're on your way. Call me if you think you need back-up. I'll sort it.'

Phil stood up, grabbed his jacket from the back of his chair.

'Where you going, boss? D'you not want to come as well?'

'Can't. That was the hospital on the phone. Ian's awake. And he wants to talk to me. Urgently.'

78

Moses and Letisha sat opposite each other in her living room. Moses on the couch, Letisha in the armchair. A henchman stood each side of them. Moses knew them. Would have called them friends, even, until yesterday. Today, even. Knew their names, had shared jokes, good times. But not now. Something seemed to have happened to their faces. All traces of warmth had been removed, just blankness instead. A dangerous – murderous – blankness.

Tiny seemed to be enjoying his moment, Moses thought. It was like something in him that had been long-suppressed had been given free reign once more. Like he had reverted to what he believed was his natural state of being. Or at least the one he enjoyed the most. He strode around the flat, picking up items, examining them, making judgements. None of the judgements, Moses could see, were complimentary.

He found Letisha's bag, upended it, spilling out clothes and toiletries. He left them in a small heap on the floor, threw the bag in the corner. Looked at her.

'Goin' somewhere, were you?'

She just stared at him, didn't answer.

Good girl, thought Moses. He could see she was terrified but she wasn't going to give in to him. She knew as well as he did that if they engaged him in conversation, it wouldn't be long before the whole story came out. One way or another. It was best to wait, thought Moses. Let Tiny talk first, see how much he knew. Then take it from there.

If they could. *If* Tiny was going to be reasonable. Two big *if*s.

'Asked you a question, girl.' Tiny stood in front of her. He wasn't tall but his lack of height didn't stop him being intimidating. Letisha swallowed hard. Didn't look at him.

He reached down, grabbed her face in his hand. She gasped, squirmed. Moses saw the look of immediate pain on her face, the skin whiten where he grabbed her, where his fingers dug in.

'Asked you a question . . . '

Gasping, she tried to pull away. Tiny just tightened his grip.

'Were you planning on going somewhere?'

'Leave her alone, Tiny.' Moses could see how this was going to go. He didn't want to see Letisha hurt.

Tiny dropped her, turned. 'What? You don't get to make the rules here. You just answer the questions. Yeah?'

Moses raised his hands in a shrug. 'Yeah, Tiny. What you say.'

Tiny nodded. 'That's better. Show some respect.' He crossed the room, kicking Letisha's few clothes as he went. 'Now. What's goin' on? What should I know about?'

Moses hoped his face was hard, stone. Like it used to be back in his gangster days. Back when he was a different person. But that person, he remembered, had been stone on the front, terrified underneath. Looking up at Tiny, he didn't feel like that much had changed.

'I told her to go away for a while. Was helping her to get started.' Still stone. Or so he hoped.

Tiny gave an exaggerated frown. 'Why would that be? Got somethin' to hide? To run from? Or someone?'

'Yeah,' said Moses. 'The police.'

'The police.'

'Yeah,' said Moses, hopefully warming to his theme. 'Darren

Richards' girlfriend and kid got killed. Letisha was seeing Darren. They thought she might have had something to do with it.'

'Did they now?' Clear from Tiny's voice that he didn't believe what he was hearing.

'Yeah. You know that. They came to question me. Dragged me out of the studio. Remember?'

'I remember. I was there.' Tiny's face stone now.

'Yeah. Well, that's it. They kept going, kept harassing her. She came to me. Desperate. I told her she should go away for a while. I was helping her sort it.'

'Right.' Tiny smiled. It wasn't pleasant. 'I remember the police coming to call. They wanted to know whether you'd done the murders yourself.'

'Yeah, but—'

'Or arranged them yourself. That's more your style, innit? Gettin' someone else to do it for you?'

'Tiny, I don't know what—'

Tiny got right down in Moses's face. The henchman behind him grabbed him by the shoulders. It was like being stuck in a tightening vice.

'Do a lot of that, do you? Arrangin' people's deaths for them? For friends?'

'Tiny, I—'

'Lovers?'

Moses said nothing.

Tiny straightened up. Smiled like he had just won his argument.

'No,' said Moses. 'I don't do that. Wouldn't do that. Never.'

Tiny smiled again. Again, it wasn't pleasant. 'Liar,' he said.

'I'm not lying—'

'I don't believe you. And I want to hear the truth.'

He turned, gestured to the other henchman. At the signal he

came forward, grabbed Letisha, hard. She screamed. He clamped his hand round her mouth. Tiny turned back to Moses.

'I want the truth, Moses. The truth. So far, all you've given me is bullshit. I've had my doubts about you for years, my suspicions. You've always managed to talk your way out of them, make me see somethin' else.'

'I haven't given you bullshit, Tiny. I've just—'

'Shut it. Now I was prepared to let it all go. Sake of peace, an' all that. We were gettin' on well together. I was even startin' to believe you. But then she comes back. An' the way she looked at you, an' the way you looked at her . . . I didn't need to be told. I knew as soon as I saw that. An' it all became clear.'

He stood in the centre of the room, looked between the two of them.

'Now. There's no point hurtin' you, Moses. You're a soldier. Or you used to be. Might still have some of that about you. And you might try to bullshit your way out of it.' He turned to face Letisha. 'But her . . .'

'No, Tiny . . .'

Letisha began to struggle. The henchman increased his grip on her.

Tiny turned back to face Moses. Smiling. 'Bet you don't want to see her hurt . . .'

Moses tried to get up. The henchman kept him pinned down. 'Please Tiny, no . . .'

He turned back to the man holding Letisha.

'Hurt her,' he said.

79

Marina heard a scream, then a sob. She dropped the teabag back in the mug and ran to the bedroom. Anni was awake.

'Anni?'

Her friend looked up, disorientated, struggling to focus. She saw Marina, her shoulders slumped.

'I dreamed he was still here, still with me ... I dreamed ... then I, I woke up ... ' Anni started to sob once more.

Marina knelt down beside her, put her arms round her shoulders, pulled her close. Said nothing just gave her closeness, let her ride the tears out.

'Oh God ... Oh God ... '

Marina nodded, said nothing.

'I wished I hadn't woken up. I wished I could have just ... stayed asleep until the pain went away. If it ever does ... '

'I know,' Marina said, stroking her hair, 'I know.'

Anni pulled back, looked at her. 'Do you?'

'Yes, Anni, I do.' Marina's voice was polite, unobtrusive.

Anni frowned. 'How?'

'Tony. The man I was with when I met Phil, remember?'

'Oh,' said Anni. 'Yeah. Sorry.'

'I know it was a bit different, not anything like this, in fact ... '

'Yeah, I remember,' said Anni. 'He was killed. By someone we were hunting.'

Marina nodded. It was the first time she had thought about Tony in years. Really thought about him. 'Yeah,' she said. 'But he was still alive. Or some of him was. It was up to me to turn off the machine. One of the hardest decisions I've ever had to make.'

'Do you regret it?' Anni's voice shivering and small.

Marina thought before answering. 'No. It was the right thing to do. On reflection. But it hurt. So, so much. I . . . couldn't cope for a while. I was just glad I had Phil to help me through.'

Marina stopped talking, realising what she had just said.

'Sorry.' A whisper.

'No,' said Anni. 'You . . . don't be.' She sighed.

Marina nodded. 'I still think of Tony. He still comes into my head from time to time. And that's how it should be. I shouldn't forget him, no matter what happens I'll never forget him.'

Anni said nothing.

They stayed like that for a while. Neither moving, neither speaking. A still-life tableau of grief.

Eventually, Anni spoke. 'I've done this loads of times. And you never know, never think . . . '

Marina said nothing, her silence a prompt for Anni to keep going.

'What they must be going through. The victims. The ones we deal with. I mean, really what they must be going through. You walk up to someone's house, knock on the door. You've rehearsed it in the car beforehand, but even that rehearsal can't prepare you for actually doing it. And no matter how many times you've done it, it never gets any easier. But you can still walk away at the end of it. Still go home. You might feel shit, you will feel shit, but you're not sitting there, in that house you've just been to, dealing with what's been lost.' She gave a sigh that threatened tears again. 'And now I'm in that house, I've had that call. And I can't just get up and go home, I am home . . . '

The tears started again. Marina kept hugging her.

Eventually they subsided. 'Shall I make you a cup of tea?' asked Marina.

Anni gave a sad little laugh. 'That's what we always say. When we've done the death knock. Have some tea, make it strong, sweet, even if you don't like sugar, it'll be good for you . . . ' She sighed. 'Load of shit.'

'Sometimes it's better to just keep talking. To just say something.'

Another sigh from Anni. 'Yeah. Talking. Keeps the light on. Stops the dark from getting in.'

'So is that a yes or a no, then?'

Anni smiled. 'A yes. But no sugar. Bloody hate it.'

Marina made two mugs of tea, came back into the bedroom. Anni was sitting up. She had been to the bathroom, wiped her tears away. She gave a small, indebted smile as Marina entered, handed her the tea.

'Thanks.'

She put it at the side of the bed. Marina was sure she would just leave it there. She held hers in her hands.

'Look,' said Marina, 'I'll stay with you. As long as you need me. As long as necessary.'

Anni shook her head. 'No. I can't have you doing that.'

'Why not?'

'You've got your own family in Birmingham to look after. They need you.'

'Anni,' said Marina, putting her mug down and taking her hand, 'you need me.'

Anni nodded. 'Yeah. But so does Phil. So does Josephina.' She sighed. 'I'll call my sister. Get her to come down.'

361

'When?'

'I'll do it today.'

'I'm not leaving you on your own, Anni. Give me the number, I'll do it now.'

'In a while.'

Anni settled back in her bed. She closed her eyes, looked suddenly tired again. Marina could imagine what horror shows were unspooling behind her eyelids.

Marina sat by her until she was asleep once more.

80

'My father was a modelmaker,' said the Lawgiver. 'A craftsman.'

Looker tried to listen but found it more difficult to focus on the words when there was another human face in front of him rather than just a mask. He knew what he was about to hear was important, so important that his reaction to the words would determine whether he lived or died. Since the Lawgiver was now unmasked, he guessed that his chances weren't good.

'Your father?' said Looker, playing for time while he adjusted to the new situation.

'Yes,' said the Lawgiver, 'my father. I'll tell you about Diana but first you have to understand. My father. The family. Philosophy.'

There was near pleading in his eyes as he spoke, thought Looker. Near pleading to be understood, or near madness. He wasn't sure which.

'Right. Okay. I'm listening.'

'Good. My father. The craftsman.' Pride in his voice as he spoke. 'And an Objectivist.' More pride.

'A what?'

The Lawgiver looked at his prisoner as if he had committed a disgusting social faux pas. 'Typical. Typical . . .'

Looker sensed he was about to lose him, tried to bring him back. 'What is it? I've never heard of it.'

'It's a philosophy,' said the Lawgiver, as if explaining to an inferior. 'An honest day's pay for an honest day's work. Ayn Rand. *The Fountainhead.* The opposite of liberalism.' He sneered round the word. 'Freedom through work. Strength through work. You work or you don't exist. There is no such thing as society.'

'Right,' said Looker. 'I've heard all that before.' Cobbled together from the Nazis to Thatcher, he thought.

'He was like a god in our house,' the Lawgiver continued. 'A god. The strongest man I ever met.' His eyes misted over, a wistful smile appeared on his face.

Keep him talking, thought Looker. He's on a nostalgic track. It might soften him. 'What about your mother?'

The smile disappeared. 'A ghost,' he said. 'Nothing. She served our father. That was her role in life. All she had to do.'

'Right. Sounds . . . like an interesting set-up.'

'It worked. Worked perfectly. The way it should have done. Until . . . ' He sighed.

'Until what?'

'Until he was no longer required. Times changed. Craftsmanship became a thing not to be prized any more. No longer recognised and praised.' He stepped back into the shadows, his features darkening too. 'He . . . drank.' The word released from his lips reluctantly, like it was enveloped in shame. 'A lot. Declined.'

'Couldn't he have got another job?'

'No.' Fire in his voice, his eyes once more. 'He had a code to live by. What is a man if he has no code to live by? No morality? No ethics? Nothing. *Nothing.*'

'Right. I see.'

'But he couldn't do it. Couldn't.' His voice was heavy with grief, reliving it all once more. 'He . . . died. Took his own life.'

'I'm sorry,' said Looker.

The Lawgiver looked directly at him, as if seeing him properly for the first time, as if he had forgotten he was there. 'Are you. You never even knew him.'

Looker fell silent. Knew that anything he said now would be wrong. Dangerously so.

'I grew up with hatred inside me,' the Lawgiver continued. 'Hatred at what the world – the system – had done to a proud and gifted man.'

Looker remained silent. Waited.

'My mother brought us up after that.'

'Us? That would be . . . '

'Diana and I. My sister.'

'Ah. Right.' Looker waited again.

'And my mother . . . ' The Lawgiver's face twisted once more, anger to the fore. 'My mother was wealthy. Came from a rich family. But my father was too proud to take her money. Too proud. It wasn't the woman's role. It was the man's to provide for his family. To make his way in the world. The way it should be.' He sighed. 'But she secretly gave him money for us to live on. And he took it. He had to. It was that or we starved. The shame of doing that contributed to his suicide.' Another sigh, angrier this time. 'My mother, and her money, helped to drive him to his death.'

'What happened to your mother?' asked Looker, wondering when he was going to get to Diana.

'She died. When I was in my late teens. Just . . . faded away, it seemed. And I inherited everything. *We* inherited everything. Diana and I. And that's when the trouble started.'

Looker said nothing. This was the part he had been waiting for.

81

Sperring opened his eyes. 'You should see the other fella ...'
Phil smiled weakly at the weak joke. Sperring looked awful. Almost flat on his back, only his head propped up slightly, tubes and wires coming from his body. His already bulky torso was enlarged by the heavy dressing on his side that extended round his stomach and chest. His face looked grey, lined, like he had aged ten years overnight. From the grimaces that twisted his face when he tried to speak or make the most infinitesimal movement, it was clear he was in considerable pain. There would have been a time, Phil thought guiltily, that he might have enjoyed his junior officer's extreme discomfort. But not any more.

Sperring was in a private room. Phil didn't know whether the man liked the seclusion or whether his solitary existence would start to irritate him. He imagined it was the former. Probably.

Phil sat down on the bedside chair, pulled it close to the bed. 'How you feeling?'

'Like I've just been stabbed by psycho.'

Phil returned the smile to his face. 'Well ... that's to be expected, I suppose.'

'Yeah. Occupational hazard, and all that.' He started to cough and tried to stop himself. Phil could see how much the action hurt him. But Sperring had only prolonged and exacerbated it by trying to stop it. He allowed himself to cough properly. Rode the wave of pain.

'Jesus,' he gasped, pressing a hand-held button with his thumb. 'Morphine. Or something like it. Brilliant stuff, though. See why the junkies get hooked.'

Phil waited for his equilibrium to be restored to a semblance of normality, continued.

'So apart from the pain and the permanent discomfort,' said Phil, aiming for lightness, 'how you feeling?'

'Never mind all that,' said Sperring. 'I've got to talk to you. It's important.'

'What about?'

'There's something I have to tell you.' Grimacing and gasping through the pain, the drugs not yet fully hitting their target.

'Tell me.'

'It's ... important.'

'You said. Is it about the Lawgiver? Something from last night?'

Sperring frowned. 'What? No. I don't know. Last night's a bit of a blur. I can't remember what happened. I was in the toilets, I turned ...' He attempted a shrug. 'Nothing. I've tried to think, tried to remember, but it just won't come.' He sighed. The drugs seemed to be kicking in now. 'You know, I used to think that when people said that they were talking bollocks. Something as important as that, as traumatic as that, course they would remember. But they're right.'

'So what did you want to talk to me about?'

'I think I'm on to something. I need something chasing up.' He managed a feeble smile. 'I don't seem to be in any fit state to do any chasing.'

'Okay, then. Tell me.'

'Moses Heap.'

Phil sighed. 'Ian—'

'Just listen to me. Hear me out.' He tried to move forward, impress upon Phil the urgency and importance of his words. The move only resulted in pain. He lay back again, gasping.

'I can't deal with anything that doesn't involve the Lawgiver at the moment,' said Phil. 'I haven't got time for this.'

'Please,' said Sperring, 'just hear me out. Letisha Watson went to see him yesterday. At the studio.'

Phil shrugged. 'So?'

'So, it's important. I've been ...' Sperring looked slightly shame-faced. 'I've been trailing them. Her. Him.'

'What?' Phil's voice rose. 'You were supposed to be working on the Lawgiver investigation, not carrying out your own vendetta.'

'It wasn't a vendetta.' Steel had entered Sperring's voice. Despite his pain, his situation, he was still a forceful personality. 'It was work. I had ... an intuition. I thought there was more to them than they were letting on. The fact that when we brought Heap in he just hid behind that fucking bent mouthpiece Looker confirmed it, in my book. So I went digging.'

'When you were supposed to be doing something else.'

Sperring sighed. 'Yeah, all right. You've got me bang to rights. It's an honest cop, guv. Now can we get over that and can you listen to what I've got to say?'

Phil held up his hands. 'Go ahead.'

'I was following them because I suspected something more was happening. I don't know when or what but I knew it. I could feel it. I was sitting outside the studio. Waiting for ... I don't know. Something to happen.'

'And did it?' It was clear from Phil's tone of voice that he expected a negative answer.

'Well,' said Sperring, 'that's the thing. I'd just got the call to come back to base. But before that, I saw Letisha Watson going

368

into the building. She didn't look in a good way. She looked round, all anxious and nervous. Then she went in.'

'Then what?'

'Don't know. Got the call to come home.'

Phil shook his head. 'Moses Heap isn't the Lawgiver. I think we've established that.'

Sperring gripped Phil's arm. Despite his pained and precarious state, there was real force behind the clasp. Eyes imploring, he continued. 'Boss, listen to me. I've been doing this job long enough to know when my copper's instinct is on to something. And I was on to something. I know I was.'

The grip lessened, fell away.

'Okay,' said Phil finally. 'I'll check it out. I'll pay them a visit when I've got time.'

'Go now.'

Phil stared at him.

'Sir.'

Usually, Sperring would have given a smile when he said that. Or even a sneer. But there was nothing in his eyes now except honesty. 'Now. Please. We'll miss something if you don't. I feel sure of it. Whatever's happening there is happening right now. We leave it, it'll be too late.'

'Right,' said Phil. 'I'll pay Letisha Watson a visit.'

Sperring relaxed. 'Thank you, boss. If I'm wrong, feel free to take it out of my wages.'

Phil smiled. 'Oh, I will. One way or another.' He stood up. 'I'd best be off. But look after yourself.'

'Like I have a choice.'

'I'll come back and see you. And I'll bring grapes next time.'

Sperring smiled. 'Fuck the grapes. Just bring me a bottle of Bell's.'

82

The Lawgiver was just getting into his story.

'Diana started . . . living it up, you could say. Enjoying herself. She said she had hated being cooped up with me and my oppressive father. That's what she said. Her words exactly. And her doormat mother.' His voice shook as he continued. 'She said she hated the way I was trying to suck up to my father, be like him. *Be* him. She said she could see the damage it was doing to me, twisting me out of shape . . . ' He shook his head. 'She had no idea. No idea. Yes, I wanted to be him. But that was because he was a great man. I *loved* him.'

The words echoed round the dark space. Died away.

'Diana said she hated her childhood,' he continued, his voice lowered now. 'Wanted to get away. Just . . . get away. I wanted to keep the place as it was. Honour my father's memory. Keep the house and the workshop as it was. Make sure his work, his life wasn't forgotten. Keep his memory alive.' Another shake of the head. His voice dropped even lower, like he was only talking to himself. 'Diana and I argued. Some . . . awful things were said. Hurtful things. Deliberately so.' He sighed. 'I told her she was just some . . . slag. Some drunken, pill-popping slut who went round town fucking anyone who would have her. She said horrible things to me.' His voice trailed away.

Looker sensed he was getting to it, the heart of the

Lawgiver's story. He knew he had to proceed carefully. 'Such as?' he said, voice low, like a priest in confessional.

The Lawgiver sighed. He kept talking in the same small voice, as if accepting his role as confessor. 'I was a . . . weirdo. A freak. I . . . that my obsession with my father had twisted my mind. That my father and the things he used to do to me had twisted my mind. That's what she said.'

Looker remained silent, knowing there was more to come.

'That I used to spy on her in the bathroom. And in her bedroom.' His voice even smaller now, like he was no longer confessing to someone else, but only to himself. 'That I used to . . . to try on her underwear when she was out.'

Gotcha, thought Looker. This is it. 'And did you?' he asked.

The Lawgiver nodded. 'Yes. And she knew, of course she knew. Because of the . . . way I used to leave her, her knickers . . .'

Silence in the dark space as the whispered words echoed away.

The Lawgiver sat down on a nearby chair, shoulders slumped, head in hands, body forward.

'Well . . . I hit her for that,' he said. 'I had to. I couldn't have her . . .' A sigh. 'I had to.' He looked up. 'I didn't mean to, not as hard as I did, but . . . I was angry . . .'

His shoulders began to shake as the sobbing started, reliving the moment once again.

'She fell backwards, down the stairs . . . into the workshop.'

'Was . . . was she dead?'

The Lawgiver nodded. 'Her neck was broken. She . . . she was . . . she didn't get up again.'

Looker waited. The air felt suddenly cold.

'I was terrified, didn't know what to do. I went to pieces . . .' He sighed. Looked up. Eyes red-rimmed, wet. 'But I knew I had to do something. So I . . . I imagined what my father, what he would have done. Tried to be like him. Used his strength to guide me.'

'So what did you do?' Looker was dreading the next part. He had a good idea what was coming.

'I used his tools.' There was pride in his voice now. Self-congratulation at his resourcefulness. His eyes were shining. 'Dismembered her. Right here, right in this workshop. It seemed fitting, somehow. I mean, she'd gone, my sister, she was just meat now. Components. To be disassembled or reassembled. Then I wrapped her up neatly in parts and took those parts to the incinerator. And that was that.' He gave a little smile.

'And nobody questioned you?' asked Looker. 'Nobody called, came to see where she was? None of her friends were interested or suspected anything? Surely she was missed.'

'Not really,' said the Lawgiver dismissively. 'A few people called – on the phone. No one came round here. I just told them she'd taken her inheritance. Gone round the world. World tour. No idea when she'd be back. Eventually they just … forgot all about her. Moved on to leech off someone else.'

'So you got away with murder.'

The Lawgiver stood up. 'No,' he said, finger pointing at Looker. 'No. That's where you're wrong. Dead wrong. Here's the thing.' He put his hand over his chest, his heart. 'I can still feel her. In here. Inside me. Always. With me all the time.' Eyes shining with a twisted kind of joy. 'After she left, after I got rid of her meat, I fell apart. Like when my father had died, bad as that. But she came to me. Told me what to do. What my calling was. It was Diana who told me to become the Lawgiver. To get justice for those who've been denied it. Like my father. Like Diana. That's what she told me to do. And that's what I did.'

The Lawgiver smiled at Looker, like his logic was irrefutable.

'Bollocks,' said Looker.

83

Tiny's henchman grabbed Letisha by the wrist, twisted it hard. She gasped, screamed. With his other hand he applied the pair of pliers he was holding to her little finger. Tiny bent down, picked up something from the pile of clothes he had shed on the floor. A T-shirt. He crossed to Letisha, stuffed it in her mouth. Roughly and hard. She nearly choked, nearly gagged.

'Don't want you wakin' the neighbours,' Tiny said, then gave the nod to his henchman.

The henchman nodded in response, squeezed the pliers, twisted her finger back at an unnatural angle. Letisha screamed, the T-shirt in her mouth acting as a partial silencer. There was a snapping sound, then he removed the pliers, looked down at his handiwork. Her little finger was hanging uselessly off her hand.

Tiny had been watching the whole thing. He turned to Moses, raised his eyebrows. 'Enough? Or you want more?'

Moses, chest and shoulders heaving with ill-suppressed rage, was being held in place on the sofa by the other henchman. He stared at Tiny, eyes burning into him, wishing him death. And a painful one at that.

But there was something else in his eyes also. Compassion for Letisha. And fear of what would happen to both of them if he spoke. Or even if he didn't speak.

Tiny shrugged. 'No? Oh well.' He turned back to his hench-man who, after being given the nod once more, moved the pliers to the next finger along. He grasped her wrist, twisted once more. Squeezed the handles.

'Wait,' shouted Moses. 'Stop. Please . . . stop.'

Tiny gave the henchman another nod. He removed the pliers from Letisha's finger. His face betrayed no emotion, no pleas-ure, no pain. Like he didn't care one way or the other whether he hurt her or he didn't. A flesh-and-bone automaton, doing his master's bidding.

'You got something to tell me, Moses?' asked Tiny, crossing the room, walking slowly towards him. 'If you don't . . .' He gestured to the henchman once more.

'Yes,' gasped Moses. 'All right. I'll tell you. I'll tell you what you want to know. Everything that happened.'

Tiny smiled. 'Good. Now we're gettin' somewhere.'

'But you let her go, Tiny. You got to let her go.'

Tiny laughed. 'Look around, bro. Does it look like you're in any position to be issuin', like . . .' He couldn't think of the word. It irritated him, he let that irritation show. 'Just look around you, bro.'

'Let her go, Tiny,' Moses said again. 'She had nothing to do with what happened to your brother. She's innocent.'

Tiny stared at Letisha as if she was some inferior sub-species. 'Her? Innocent? She ain't never been innocent, bro. Not since she was born. She's a slag. Takes it for money, or, like, the worst kind. Just takes it for fun.'

Moses struggled to keep his anger controlled, his voice calm and even. 'She's innocent. Stop hurting her. Let her go.'

Moses was aware of Letisha staring at him, trying to catch his eye, shaking her head at what he was about to say. He looked away from her, at anything in the room but her. He knew what he was about to do. So did she. And she was trying to stop him.

374

'I'll let her go when I've heard what you've got to say.'

'Okay then,' said Moses. 'I'll tell you. But it's not going to be pretty.'

Tiny frowned, suspecting a trick. 'What you mean?'

'About Julian. Your brother.'

'What about him?'

Moses stared at Tiny. Wanting to be listened to, understood. 'He was a bad man, Tiny. A very bad man. I know you idolised him, grew up thinking he was your hero, but he wasn't.'

Moses could see that Tiny was getting angry but he continued.

'He was a monster. Especially to women. Especially to this woman.' He pointed to Letisha. 'The things he made her do, the way he used to make her behave . . . you wouldn't believe it, man.'

Tiny smiled. 'I might. Tell me.'

Moses could see from the sick, prurient gleam in Tiny's eyes that his approach wasn't going to work. That Tiny seemed to be as bad as his brother had been. But he persisted. 'A monster, Tiny. A real monster. And she,' again he gestured to Letisha, 'didn't deserve it. She was too good.'

Tiny's grin persisted. 'Sounds like you got the hots for her.'

'I fell in love with her, Tiny.'

Tiny laughed out loud. 'Oh, bad move, bro. Really bad move.'

'We don't plan what we do,' said Moses. 'The heart wants what the heart wants.'

Tiny laughed again. Moses knew this wasn't going the way he wanted it to. Again, he persisted.

'I fell in love with her, Tiny. That's not something your brother could ever say about her.'

'My bro didn't have to,' said Tiny, rage building behind his words. 'He didn't need to. She was his woman, his property. Man could do with her what he wanted. His right.'

'No, Tiny, she wasn't his property. She wasn't his to do with as he wanted. She's a woman. A human being. She's no one's property. All right, she was his girlfriend when we fell in love, and that was wrong, getting into another man's territory.'

'Wrong? You don't know the half of it, man. Gonna suffer now 'cause of it.'

'Is that it?' asked Moses. 'Can we only be men, can we only be strong, if we're punishing someone else? Inflicting pain? Trying to hurt someone, own them? Can we?'

Tiny didn't answer. From his blank expression, Moses' line of enquiry wasn't one he had ever considered, nor ever wanted to.

'Just tell me what you did, Moses. Tell me how you killed him.'

Moses just stared at him, stalling. Trying to formulate a story that Tiny could believe. That would make him let Letisha and him go.

'Tell me,' said Tiny, the rage there again in his voice.

'Hurting someone, owning them, doesn't make you strong, Tiny. Not really. It makes you weak.'

'Yeah?' said Tiny. 'What makes you strong, then?'

'Love,' said Moses simply.

Tiny laughed like it was the funniest thing he had ever heard, howling and guffawing, bending double with his hands on his thighs. 'Love . . . ' He shook his head, laughing again.

Eventually, he straightened up, stared at Moses, still laughing. He pointed a finger at him. 'Man, that bitch got you pussy-whipped good. Real good. Love don't make you strong, Moses. Look where you are now.'

376

'No?'

'No,' said Tiny with finality. 'Just makes you weak.'

Before Moses could reply, Tiny looked at the henchman holding Letisha, gave him a command. 'Get in the kitchen. Put the gas on.' He turned to Moses, smiled. 'Boy's gonna tell us a story.'

84

The Lawgiver stared at Looker.

'That wasn't your sister talking to you,' said Looker, voice as steady and plain as he could make it. 'That was your guilt talking.'

'Bullshit.' His voice vehement again.

'It's not bullshit.' Looker knew he shouldn't have continued, should have just agreed with him, but he couldn't let it go. Had to challenge him. 'You couldn't cope with what you'd done to her. To your own sister. So you externalised it. You needed to punish someone and it couldn't be you. So you came up with the idea of the Lawgiver.'

'Shut up ... shut up ...' The Lawgiver started pacing. Looker was suddenly struck by how small the space was, how near he was to him. 'Guilt ... guilt ...' He turned back to Looker. Eyes wild, mouth white at the edges, spittle-flecked. 'You think guilt could do everything I've done? Everything I've achieved? Could guilt choose victims as well as I've done? Contact online hacktivists and learn how to hack bank accounts? Plan everything as meticulously as I've done? Leave no trace, no sightings, no forensics?' The Lawgiver shook his head, leaned in close to Looker's face. 'That's not the sign of a guilty mind. A guilty conscience. That's the sign of revenge. Retribution. Justice.'

'Or the sign of a sick mind with too much time on its hands,' said Looker, again unable to stop himself. 'This isn't an origin story. You're not Batman.'

The lawgiver stared at him, breathing hard through his nostrils, eyes unblinking red-hot coals. 'Shut up,' he said, and slapped him across the face. Hard.

The force of the blow, unexpected, stung. Looker reeled from it, tasted old pennies in his mouth. He smiled. This was more like it, he thought. Now we're getting to it.

'Couldn't be you,' said Looker through a mouthful of blood. 'Just couldn't be yourself you punished. Had to be everyone else . . . '

'Shut up . . . ' Another slap, even harder this time.

The Lawgiver stood over him. Stared down at him, breathing heavily, teeth gritted. 'You met Diana last night. Talked to her. Came here with her.' Then, screaming in his face: 'Didn't you?'

'I met you wearing a dress,' said Looker.

The Lawgiver straightened up, a stunned expression on his face. 'You . . . knew?'

'Of course I knew. How could I not know? I mean, you were convincing from a distance, you've got the figure for it. But close up . . . Jesus . . . ' Looker shook his head.

'No,' shouted the Lawgiver. 'It was Diana! Diana! She was helping me again . . . '

'You were a bloke in a dress. Admit it. You honestly think you fooled me? Really? If he'd been sitting as close as I was, even Stevie bloody Wonder could have seen that you were a man.'

The Lawgiver's rage was increasing. He walked backwards and forwards in front of Looker, fists clenching and unclenching all the while. 'So . . . so why did you come with me? Hmm? Why did you leave with me if you knew who I was? You knew what would happen.'

Looker sighed. 'Yeah, I knew. I suppose I knew all along. I was bored. I didn't come with you because of your great master plan; you got lucky. I was bored.'

'Bored? How?'

Looker sighed again. 'Because maybe you're right. Maybe I do hate what I do. The clients I have to work with. Maybe I wanted to change my life and couldn't. Maybe I've got too much baggage. An ex-wife who hates me, a career that's going nowhere. I have to keep working just to stand still. Whatever idealism I had has long since gone.' He fell silent, choosing his next words carefully. 'Maybe I'm just tired. Sick of my life. Can't see a way out and I'm too much of a coward to do anything about it.'

The Lawgiver stood there, stared at him, unsure what to say, how to react.

'So go on,' said Looker, voice rising, 'what are you waiting for? Do it.'

No response.

'You're going to do it anyway, going to kill me for what you think I've done. You've already judged me and nothing I can say will change that. I know that now. So do it. Come on, do it now.'

The Lawgiver looked around, trying to find something familiar to settle on, confused at what was happening.

Looker sensed him wavering, kept at him. 'Come on then, what you waiting for? You've got all that guilt swilling around inside you, just ready to take it out on the world. Come on . . . you killed your sister.'

'No . . .'

'Yes you did. You killed your sister and you want to take your guilt out on me.'

'No. That's not true.'

'Bullshit. You know it is. You're guilty as fuck. You're the one who's been judged. That's the verdict. You're guilty.'

'No . . .' Confusion was giving way to anger.

'Yes you are. That's exactly what you are. That's all you are.'

'No . . .' His anger welling now, gathering force within him. Waiting to spill out. 'I'm not guilty. I'm the Lawgiver.'

'No you're not,' said Looker, letting go with all the force he had bottled up so far. 'You're not. You're just a murdering little fuck-up. But hey, a good lawyer could have got it down to manslaughter for you. You could have afforded that. But no. You decided to go the fuck-up route. The poor-me fuck-up route. How predictable.'

'Shut up . . .' Another slap. Even harder.

The slap was so fierce, the pain so intense that Looker saw stars burst before him. He twisted his head straight, stared at the Lawgiver, smiled. 'That the best you can do?'

The Lawgiver stared back at him. Unsure whether to give in to his rage or to examine these new feelings further.

'Well, come on then, what are you waiting for?' Looker laughed. 'You guilt-ridden, useless, cross-dressing fucking weirdo . . .'

That was the trigger. The Lawgiver picked up a wrench from a nearby bench and began bringing it down on Looker with more ferocity than he knew was within him. Screaming all the time.

The blows hurt, the pain beyond anything Glen Looker had experienced before. But with each one that fell, the pain receded. The world around him began to disappear, blackness took over.

Glen Looker closed his eyes. And then he saw something else. The blackness itself gave way. And there before him was the island paradise he had only ever seen in holiday brochures. It looked so welcoming, so reachable.

Happy to be on his way, Glen Looker smiled. Gladly went there.

For ever.

85

Jessica Elton née Hepburn stood on the tiny balcony of her sister Anni's flat, sucking down smoke from her cigarette, blowing it out over Colchester. Marina came to join her, mugs of coffee in hand.

'There you go.'

Jessica nodded her thanks, took the mug. She shook her head slowly, as if to dislodge unpleasant events from it, looked out over the town.

'You just ... ' She drew on her cigarette, let the smoke go, started again. 'Awful, really. What an awful state of affairs.'

Marina nodded in agreement. Said nothing.

Jessica continued. 'We knew something like this would happen.'

Marina frowned. 'Knew?'

Jessica turned to her. 'Well, you know. Maybe not knew. Suspected. Thought. Feared, I suppose. Frightened. With our mother, when Anni had just joined the police, every time she watched the news and saw something about a police officer having been killed or injured, she would always think it was going to be Anni.'

'I suppose you do,' said Marina. 'It's natural. My husband's her boss. Was her boss. I know exactly what you mean.'

'But you still go on letting him do it.'

'What choice do I have? It's what he does, who he is. He's

been in some . . . tight situations, shall we say. I've been with him. And we've managed to get out of them.'

Jessica nodded. 'But Mickey wasn't so lucky.' She turned, looked out over the town once more.

'No,' said Marina, sighing. 'He wasn't.' She joined Jessica in looking out over the town. 'I think that all the time. Every time something happens to Phil, or to me. Or Anni . . . any of the team. We get through. We get lucky. I always think, we dodged a bullet that time. Next time we might not be so lucky.'

'He wasn't.'

'No.' There was nothing more for her to say.

They stood in silence, looking out, watching the traffic come and go.

'When I got the call, you know what I first thought?' said Jessica. She continued, not waiting for Marina to reply. 'I thought, Oh God. It's Anni. Something's happened to Anni. *The worst* has happened to Anni. And then it was Mickey. And you know? You know the awful thing? I thought, Thank God it's him and not her. Just for a second, a short moment, but I thought it.' She turned, looked at Marina. Guilt in her eyes. 'Isn't that awful?'

'Don't worry about it,' said Marina. 'She's your sister. It's a perfectly natural reaction.'

Jessica turned away once more. Not answering.

More silence.

'How d'you do it?' Jessica, still staring outwards. 'Go through it all, every day? Thinking he might not come home, wondering where he is all the time.'

'It's not every day,' said Marina. 'I always think that if you can imagine all the things that could go wrong in a day they won't. That's not, strictly speaking, a psychologist's most professional advice, but it's what I do. It's just the days you're not expecting to hear it, when you can't imagine it. They're the ones to watch out for.'

'Hey.'

A voice from behind them. They both turned. Anni had come to join them.

'Didn't hear you get up,' said Jessica, turning, flicking her cigarette butt over the edge and embracing her sister. 'How you feeling?'

Anni just shrugged.

'D'you want some coffee?' said Marina. 'I've just made some.'

Anni shook her head.

'Okay,' said Marina. 'Well, if you change your mind—'

'Please, Marina. Just . . . I'm . . . I need space. That's all.' She looked at Jessica. 'That's all. I've got to come to terms with . . . process . . . ' She sighed, on the verge of breaking down once more.

Marina and Jessica exchanged looks. Marina nodded.

'I'll go,' she said.

Anni looked up. 'I didn't mean it like—'

'I know,' said Marina. 'I'll give you some space. Jessica'll look after you.'

Anni hugged Marina. 'Thanks. You've—' Tears were threatening once more.

'Don't worry. I'll call you later.'

Marina turned away from the two sisters, made to gather up her belongings and go back to Birmingham. Back to her husband and daughter.

Hoping, following her conversation with Jessica, that it wasn't going to turn out to be one of those days she couldn't imagine.

86

'I mani Oliver.' She put her phone to her ear, turned down the music that was playing in the car. Nadish, driving them to Hinchcliffe's house and knowing the call was probably work, looked across at her.

'Hi, Imani, Elli here.'

'Just putting you on speaker so Nadish can hear.'

She did so, turning off the radio.

'Okay. Are you there yet?'

'Still on the way,' said Nadish. 'Run into traffic.'

'There's a surprise. Well, I did some digging around, some checking on Stuart Hinchcliffe. Think you should hear this before you get there. I've been through the guest registers for both the Malmaison and Radisson Blu for the nights in question. And they both had a guest registered by the name of Diana Hinchcliffe.'

'Any relation?' asked Imani.

'Well, that rang some alarm bells so I did some more digging. Apparently Stuart Hinchcliffe had a sister called Diana. Same address. Mother and father both deceased.'

'He said he had a sister who lived with him,' Nadish said. 'But I didn't see her. She was out.'

'And she's been out for a long time,' said Elli. 'The brother and sister came into an inheritance four or five years ago and she was never heard of again.'

'Never?' said Imani.

'Stuart Hinchcliffe told everyone that she had taken off, gone on a world trip. No one seems to have paid much attention to her after that.'

'You think she's back now?' asked Nadish. 'Was that her last night with Glen Looker?'

'Seems odd to actually use her real name to book in to the hotel. Would lead us straight to her,' said Imani.

'Maybe he thought we'd be looking for a bloke,' said Nadish.

'What about credit card details?' asked Imani.

'I was just coming to that,' said Elli. 'The credit card is in the name of Diana Hinchcliffe. And registered to the Legge Lane address.'

Nadish and Imani exchanged glances. 'Would he really be that stupid?' asked Nadish.

'If he thought he wasn't going to get caught, he might be,' said Imani.

'There's something else,' said Elli, 'something I just thought of.'

They waited for her to speak.

'I've been watching the footage from last night again. And that woman, Diana, if it's her, doesn't look right.'

'In what way?' asked Imani.

'She's convincing, but I think she may be a man. Stuart Hinchcliffe in drag, perhaps?'

Nadish laughed in surprise. 'Jesus, man . . .'

'Seriously?' asked Imani.

'Well, I'm fairly convinced. And it would make sense: putting the room in her name, using her credit card.'

'So where's Diana?' asked Imani.

'We'll have to ask Stuart Hinchcliffe that,' said Nadish.

'Should I tell Cotter?' asked Ell. 'Get you back-up?'

'Cotter?' asked Imani. 'Where's Phil?'

'Still visiting Sperring in hospital. Apparently Sperring had something for him. I've tried to reach him, can't get a signal. Goes straight to voicemail.'

Another glance between the pair of them. Nadish shrugged. 'Boss just said questions. Said it a few times. Made sure I got it.'

'But does this change anything?' asked Imani.

'What d'you want me to do?' asked Elli.

Imani thought. 'Leave things as they are for now,' she said. 'We'll be straight on the radio if things change.'

Elli rang off. Nadish and Imani shared another glance.

Nadish pushed down on the accelerator.

87

'You shouldn't have made me angry ... shouldn't have made me feel weak ...'

The Lawgiver, still maskless, stood over the ruined body of Glen Looker. He stretched out a hand, moved what was left of Looker's head from side to side. He was still attached to the chair, which had been attached to a workbench so the majority of his body was still in place.

'You shouldn't have done that ...'

Looker's head made wet, squelching noises as it was moved.

The Lawgiver was fizzing with energy. Beating Glen Looker to death had been the wrong thing to do. He knew that now. But once he had started a kind of righteous anger had enveloped him and he hadn't been able to stop.

Or at least he told himself it was righteous. And kept telling himself that.

'It's your own fault,' he said to what was left of the head, ignoring the blood and other liquid matter that was seeping into his cuffs. 'All your own fault. You made me do it. Made me tell you about Diana. About everything. Made me feel weak. Laughed at me ...'

He felt that anger rising again and slapped the head sideways, where it stayed, hanging twisted from the body.

The Lawgiver stood up. Looked around the workshop, took in the history of the place, tried to imagine, not for the first time, what it must have meant to his father. The pride the man must have felt at spending his working days in here. The sense of accomplishment on completion of a project, the way he must have held his head high when he took payment for it. The way he must have embarked on the next one with a renewed sense of optimism.

It was an alien world to him. He had never had a real job, just lived off his mother's money. Never known any of that, only tried to touch it through his imagination.

Being the Lawgiver was supposed to be recompense for that. A way to balance the books, make his father posthumously proud in the process. That was why he had brought Looker here. It had seemed important for him to do that.

Now, he wasn't sure. Wasn't sure about anything any more.

He stared down at the body. Sighed. This was the end. He could feel it. He had gone wrong, seriously wrong. Instead of sticking to the plan that he had carefully mapped out, he had let his temper get the better of him when he should have remained in charge. Been able to see the bigger picture.

He had done exactly what Glen Looker had wanted him to do. Kill him. The man was too much of a coward to do it himself so he had forced the Lawgiver to do it. He felt angry at being used. And something else. The other feeling that was curling and curdling inside him. He had been denied his righteous kill. Yes, he knew that, if he was being honest with himself. His anger hadn't been righteous. Nothing about what he had done, shared, with Looker had been righteous. He had been tricked, taken advantage of.

Played.

And the feeling that was now coiling in his guts was one he couldn't put into words. But it itched away at his insides, spoke to him in a loud, urgent voice. Something had to be done. The scales had to be balanced.

389

He closed his eyes, waited. Nothing. He had expected Diana to be there, to talk to him, tell him what to do, or advise him, even. But there was nothing. Even Diana had abandoned him now.

He looked down at the body of Glen Looker once again, saw his phone sticking out of his inside jacket pocket. The blows must have dislodged it. The Lawgiver took it out, looked at the screen. A text from Moses Heap. He opened the phone. Read the text.

At Letishas. Need to get away NOW. Need your help. Come ASAP.

The Lawgiver threw the phone on the bench, smiled. Nodded his head. Oh yes. This was a sign. This was divine intervention. Here, in the place that had been so important to his father, he had found the means of his salvation. A new path for the Lawgiver to tread.

If it was all to come to an end, this could be his final, glorious act. They had got away with murder. Or thought they had. He could correct that assumption for them. There was still time.

He looked around the workshop one more time. He just had to hope that no one came in while he was out. No one found the body. He could salvage everything. Be ready to start again. Just this one act of justice and then the future beckoned.

He turned, walked away.

Went to visit his armoury. Prepare himself for battle.

88

'It's not locked . . .'

Nadish pushed the door to Hinchcliffe's house. It swung slowly open. He looked at Imani.

'What d'you think?' he said. 'Should we go in?'

'The boss said just to talk,' said Imani. 'That's all. If the door's open and there are bars on the windows then I think we have probable cause to enter.'

Nadish gave a grim smile. 'Was hoping you'd say that.'

He pushed the door gently again. It swung right back on its hinges. Nadish stepped inside, looking round as he went. Imani followed him.

'Mr Hinchcliffe,' he called into the gloom, waiting for a response, getting none. 'It's Detective Constable Khan. We met the other day.' Nothing. 'Just wanted to ask you a few more questions.' Silence. 'Mr Hinchcliffe?'

He was now firmly in the room that he remembered as the workshop. His eyes were becoming accustomed to the dark.

'Light switch?' asked Imani.

'On the wall, probably,' said Nadish. 'I was only here once. Can't remember where everything is.'

'Tetchy,' said Imani.

'Well, where d'you think it is? Stupid question.'

Imani thought Nadish was probably just nervous and

trying to cover that by being angry with her. She let it go, thinking that if it was any other reason he would have said something.

She moved over towards the wall, ran her hand along it. She found objects hanging there, felt them. Tools. Kept going. Eventually she found the switch, turned it on.

The overhead strip lights flickered into life. When she saw what was there, she wished they hadn't.

'Oh, Christ on a bike . . . '

She stared at what was before her, horrified yet unable to draw her eyes away. She turned round. Nadish had run for the door. She heard retching sounds from the street outside.

She put her hands in her pockets, took out latex gloves, slipped them on. Moved closer to the body once more.

'I think we've found Glen Looker,' she called. 'I think we've gone beyond the chatting stage with Hinchcliffe as well.'

Moving slowly so as to preserve the crime scene, she began to back out of the workshop. Then noticed something. A mobile phone, smeared with blood, was on the bench that Looker had been tied to. She bent down to look at it. Pressed the button to turn it on. Immediately the screen lit up with a text message, the last thing that had been read. Imani read it.

A shudder ran through her. Why was the phone left here? With that message open in particular? She checked the screen again, saw the time the message had been sent. Today. This morning. She doubted very much that Looker had read the message. So that only left one other person.

Quickly, she made her way back out into the street, her phone already at her ear. Once outside, Nadish stared at her, shamefacedly. He was about to make an apology, or at least an excuse, but she didn't allow him the time. She held up her hand to silence him. The call was answered.

'Elli? Imani. I need an address for Letisha Watson. Quick.

392

And get a message to the boss. Tell him to get over there as quickly as possible. With back-up this time.'

'Okay. Anything else?'

'Yeah,' she said, looking at Nadish, 'we've found out who the Lawgiver is. And where he's going.'

89

Letisha couldn't bear it any more. And if Letisha couldn't bear it, she had no idea what Moses was going through.

Tiny's henchmen had pulled him into the kitchen. It took two of them to hold him, stop his trying to escape. Moses had started screaming and shouting, trying to raise help, attract attention, his face a mask of terror. Tiny's henchman had punched him in the stomach with such force that Letisha half-expected his fist to go straight through his body and emerge from the back.

Moses doubled over, nearly vomiting in pain.

'Shut it,' said Tiny. Then found a dishrag and stuffed it into his mouth. All the way down, so far it nearly choked him.

Tiny went to the living room, dragged Letisha into the kitchen, holding her by her hair. She offered little resistance, by now almost completely broken.

'Look,' he said, 'watch what your lover's going to do for you now. See how I, like, avenge my brother. His murder.'

The gas was lit, all four rings. Bottom left, nearest the front, nearest Moses, was the largest. One of the henchmen turned it up full.

'Ready?' asked Tiny, a sick smile on his face.

Moses looked like he was about to faint. He stared at the flames, eyes round with horror, terrified about what they were about to do, which part of his anatomy they were going to push into the heat. One of the henchmen grabbed his wrist. Moses tried to pull away, aware of the whimpers that were coming out of his mouth, filtering around the stuffed dishrag. He shook his head. Tiny nodded in response.

'Oh, yeah . . .'

The henchman pushed Moses's hand into the flame. Moses screamed. Sobbed, bleated.

The smell of burning flesh, skin and hair filled the kitchen. The tiny flat was now awash with pain and suffering.

Moses watched as his left hand was consumed by flame. As the skin cracked and burst, the blood and flesh blackened. He had his hand clenched into a fist, a futile attempt to protect it as much as possible.

Tiny held up his hand. The henchman pulled Moses's hand from the flame. Moses stared at Tiny, almost too pain-wracked to stand, almost unable to not faint.

'So you killed my brother, yeah? You did it. For that skank there.' Tiny pointed at Letisha.

Letisha shook her head at Moses, eyes imploring him not to go any further, not to take the blame for her. At that second, Moses knew if she had the gag removed from her mouth she would tell Tiny all about it. What had happened, who was really to blame for his death. Moses knew he couldn't allow that to happen.

Through the pain and the suffering, Moses nodded.

'Hope she was worth it, bro,' Tiny said. 'Hope she was a good fuck.'

Moses just closed his eyes.

Tiny nodded at the henchman again. 'Do his face now.'

Letisha started screaming behind the gag, tried to wriggle free from Tiny's grip. He just held on to her harder.

The henchman behind Moses grabbed his head, started to push it towards the flame. Moses tried to pull back, push away, do anything that he could to avoid what was about to happen. Everything was futile. The two men were both stronger than him, bigger than him. He had no chance.

His face was pushed into the flame. He felt his left cheek start to sear, the pain coursing instantly through his body. He smelled his own hair burning. Felt his ear take fire. He closed his eyes as hard as he could but the flames just burned through his eyelid. He was trying to scream, to pull away, but the amount of pain he was in, another part of him just wanted to let go, embrace it. The sooner he gave in, the sooner he would be dead.

His face burned until he could no longer feel the pain. Then he was abruptly yanked away from the flame.

He opened his eyes. Only the right one remained. The henchmen loosened their grip on him, left the kitchen and hurried into the living room. Tiny had already gone there.

Moses moved slowly forward. What he saw stopped him in his tracks. The front door had been broken open. In the centre of the living room stood a man dressed in overalls and a tight-fitting gas mask with darkened eyeholes. In his hand he held a fierce-looking crossbow. One of the henchmen was already on his back on the floor, a crossbow bolt sticking out of his forehead. The intruder had quickly reloaded from the quill he kept on the front of the bow and in the process of taking advantage of the stunned silence that greeted him, put another bolt into the forehead of the other henchman.

Tiny was staring at the man, immobile.

Moses looked behind him. The gas was still on. He tried to turn it off, but he was in so much pain and disorientated that he only succeeded blowing out the flame. The gas supply was left on. He was in the process of trying to switch that off when the masked figure entered the kitchen.

'Jesus Christ, what happened to you?' he said.

Moses didn't – couldn't – answer.

'In here, now.'

Moses did as he was told, shambling forward.

In the living room Letisha was pulling the gag from her mouth with her good hand.

'Please,' she said, her voice near hysteria, 'he needs a doctor, an ambulance. Please . . .'

Tiny took that moment to make his move. He tried to get to the door but the Lawgiver was too quick for him. The crossbow bolt didn't land fatally, just went through his left shoulder. The force of the bolt smacked him against the wall. He slid down to the floor, clutching at the wound, which was spilling blood already.

'I didn't give you permission to leave,' said the Lawgiver. 'Stay where you are.'

No one moved. He turned back into the room. 'Moses Heap. Letisha Watson.' He raised the crossbow. 'I can't let you both get away with murder, can I?'

Letisha and Moses clung together, neither knowing what had just happened, only sure of what was about to. Their rescuer had turned out to be even worse than Tiny.

Moses closed his one good eye. Prayed that it would be swift and painless for both of them.

But the shot never came.

He was aware of a knock at the door. The door was then opened.

Moses opened his eye once more.

In walked Detective Inspector Phil Brennan.

90

'Jesus Christ . . . ' Phil stared at the scene that greeted him, rooted to the spot, heart in his mouth.

Two dead men, both large and black; another wounded man, as small as the other two were large. Then there were a mutilated couple. Phil recognised them immediately as Moses Heap and Letisha Watson.

And there, standing right in the centre of the room, was the Lawgiver.

The Lawgiver turned, stared at him. Behind the mask, Phil knew that he was smiling.

'Detective Inspector Phil Brennan,' said the Lawgiver. 'What a pleasant surprise.' He raised the crossbow, pointed his last remaining bolt, the one intended for Moses and Letisha, at him.

'The Lawgiver, I presume,' said Phil. 'Should I say, we meet at last, something like that?'

'Say what you like,' said the Lawgiver. 'It'll be one of the final things you ever say.'

Phil tried to focus, concentrate on the here and now. He had only been coming here as a favour to Sperring, checking out something for him and then back to the real investigation. But things hadn't turned out quite the way he had expected them to. Sperring said he had a good copper's instinct, thought Phil. I must tell him he's absolutely right.

Assuming I manage to walk out of here.

'So,' said Phil, finding his voice, hoping his professional training would kick in when he started talking, 'what brings you here?'

The Lawgiver pointed his crossbow at Letisha and Moses. Briefly; then back to Phil again. 'I'm making house calls now. Dispensing justice to murderers along the way.'

'Where's Glen Looker? What have you done with him?'

'Mr Looker is no more,' said the Lawgiver. 'He had to answer for his crimes.'

'You killed him.' Less a question, more a statement of fact.

The Lawgiver didn't answer immediately. Like he couldn't admit to what he had done. Phil found his restraint slightly puzzling. But he didn't have to dwell on that now.

'Look,' said Phil, voice calm and steady, 'we can resolve this. Amicably. It's not too late, we can do it. Just . . . put the crossbow down.'

The Lawgiver laughed. 'I think we've gone beyond that now, don't you?'

Phil remembered Marina's profile: they'll catch him when he starts improvising. That's when he'll begin to unravel. Looking at the sight before him, seeing how much the Lawgiver was shaking while holding the crossbow, he believed that time had come now.

If he handled it the right away.

'Has it?' said Phil. 'It's over. Finished. Look where you are, look around you. All over.'

'No it isn't, no it isn't . . .' Voice becoming louder, more cracked.

Unstable, thought Phil. Definitely unstable. Have to be careful.

'It's over,' he said again.

The Lawgiver said nothing. Just stood there, breathing heavily.

Phil continued. 'I haven't come here alone. Back-up is on its way.' He edged closer to the Lawgiver, hoped he wouldn't notice. 'Any minute.'

'Liar . . . ' said the Lawgiver, his voice rasping from more than just being behind the gas mask.

'Any minute,' said Phil. 'What are you going to do then? How do you propose to get out then? To walk away?'

'Liar,' said the Lawgiver. 'You're bluffing.'

'Wait and see.'

'Oh, I will.'

'One question, though,' said Phil. 'Serious question. Why me?'

'What?'

'Why me? What made you choose me instead of all the other police officers out there?' Still edging forward towards the Lawgiver while he was talking.

The Lawgiver laughed. 'Why not you?'

'That it? Nothing better than that?' Phil was still moving forward, still listening when he noticed something else. Could he smell gas?

'Yes,' said the Lawgiver. I saw you on TV. You'd just made some high-profile arrest, had the whole of Digbeth closed, helicopters in the sky, the lot. I wondered what kind of copper had done that, been in charge of that kind of operation. And then I saw you. Scruffy, no suit, leather jacket and check shirt. And I thought, He looks different. He might be a man I can do business with. Not like all the others.'

'And am I?' asked Phil. 'Different to all the others?'

'No,' said the Lawgiver flatly. 'You're exactly the same as them. Exactly the same.'

'You mean because I catch criminals and protect the public? Whether I wear a suit or not? I suppose I am.'

'No,' said the Lawgiver, 'that's not what I meant. I thought you might be different, able to think for yourself, see things differently. Realise that what I'm doing is not a criminal thing but merely a campaign to correct criminal acts. I thought we could work together, be on the same side.'

Phil moved forwards slightly. He noticed that the Lawgiver was also moving, but backwards. He also noticed that Moses, in pain and mutilated, was trying to get behind him.

'We can never be on the same side,' said Phil, 'so long as you take it upon yourself to kill who you feel like.'

'I'm not a criminal. I'm a . . . lawgiver.'

'If that's the case, then why don't you put down the crossbow and we can talk about it?'

The Lawgiver looked down at his hands, as if he had forgotten he was holding the crossbow. Phil's words reminded him. He raised it up, pointing it once more at Phil.

'I don't think so,' he said.

Phil saw his finger tighten on the trigger. Felt his heart hammer in his chest. Knew this wasn't one of the things he had expected, planned for, happening today.

He looked left to right, tried to work out where he could dive to avoid the bolt. Felt like a goalkeeper facing a penalty. Whichever way he dived would be the wrong one.

But he had reckoned without Moses.

The destroyed man put himself behind the Lawgiver, forcing his damaged arm round his neck, pulling as hard as he could, the pain giving him strength, pushing the crossbow down towards the floor with the other. Screaming in agony as he did so.

The Lawgiver fired. The bolt went harmlessly into the carpet.

The Lawgiver pulled hard against Moses's grip, tried to wriggle free from Moses's embrace, but he had him too tight. The Lawgiver tried to squirm around, find pressure points to hurt Moses with. It was no good. Moses was beyond pain now.

As they fought, Moses lost his balance and pulled the Lawgiver over onto the ground, never once letting go. Moses held the Lawgiver tightly round the throat, the other man had his hands at his neck, fighting for air through his mask.

Phil ran forward to help Moses, but he held up something in his hand. Phil stopped moving.

Letisha's lighter. Moses brandished it like a weapon.

'Go,' roared Moses through his ruined mouth. 'Just go . . . '

'No, Moses,' shouted Phil, I'm not leaving you . . . '

Moses moved his thumb to the wheel. 'Go . . . '

The Lawgiver was still squirming in his grip, trying to kick against his captor, hit him. Moses ignored him, pulled tighter.

'No, Moses,' said Phil. 'There's another way . . . '

Moses shook his head. 'Too late . . . too late for that . . . '

Phil knew from the look in Moses's one remaining eye that he wasn't going to be dissuaded. Phil put his arm around Letisha and ran towards the door.

'No,' she called, 'no, Moses . . . I love you . . . '

Moses looked up. Tears in his one good eye. 'I love you too . . . '

Tiny had already managed to escape from the scene. The two henchmen were dead. Phil kept his arm tight round the sobbing, protesting Letisha and dragged her out of the flat.

They reached the landing and he kept going, kept running. Not letting her go.

As he ran, Phil became aware of figures appearing from the stairwell in front of him. Imani and Nadish.

'Get back,' he shouted. 'Down the stairs. The flat, it's going to—'

The explosion knocked them all to the ground.

91

Phil was exhausted.

He had made it back to his home in Moseley hours later. His clothes, skin, hair all stank of smoke from the explosion. He had spent hours following up what had happened, giving statements, writing statements, briefing and debriefing until he couldn't talk any more. All he wanted was to grab a quick shower then crawl into bed and wait for Marina to get home.

She had texted him a couple of hours ago to say she was on the way from Colchester. He could tell just from her words that she sounded about as tired as he was.

There was no sound in the house, no lights on in any room. She wasn't back yet. Josephina was still with Eileen. She would stay there for the night. Phil toyed with doing his usual post-work ritual, a beer from the fridge, sitting down and listening to music to reorient himself, but decided against it. A shower then bed.

He went into the bedroom to take off his clothes, grab his bathrobe. And saw a lump in the bed. A Marina-shaped lump in the bed.

'Hey, gorgeous,' he said, as quietly as he could, 'you awake?'

He stretched an arm across to touch her shoulder. Responding to his touch, she turned to face him. Then put the light on. Phil recoiled, pulling his arm back quickly.

'You're not Marina . . .'

'Not yet,' said a woman he had never seen before. 'But I will be. Soon.'

She sat up. Her hair was almost like Marina's and she was wearing make-up that was an approximation of Marina's. But it wasn't her.

Phil's stomach flipped over.

'What have you done to my wife? Where's Marina?'

The woman got out of bed, stood naked before him. Smiled. She began to move towards him. Slowly, languorously, swinging her hips to a lazy, sensuous beat he couldn't hear.

He backed away.

'Where's Marina?' Fear in his voice now.

'You won't be needing her,' she said, her voice low. Phil realised it was an approximation of Marina's. 'Not any more. Not with me here.'

Phil stared at her. He genuinely didn't know what to do. Whether to use force against her, restrain her, or get out of the house as quickly as possible.

He looked around, desperately trying to find some trace of Marina. There were none. No bags, no suitcases. It seemed like she wasn't back home yet. That was something. That was a relief.

'Who are you?'

The woman laughed. 'Don't you know? Really?'

'You're not Marina. Don't even pretend. So who are you?'

'I'm younger than Marina. Better than her. In every way . . .' She moved closer to him.

Something struck a chord in her words. Younger. What was that Marina had said on the phone? *Am I too old for you? Fiona Welch said it* . . . And Phil immediately knew who this woman was now. But he found that impossible to believe. That woman was in custody.

'Better than her? You're pathetic. I don't know who you are, but just stop where you are right now. Don't come any closer or I'll have to use force to restrain you.'

The woman laughed. 'That might be fun . . . '

'I can assure you it won't be.'

She laughed once more. 'I've come a long way to be here. A very, very long way. I'm not going to let you stop me now . . . '

She lunged at him, arms stretched outwards. Phil was ready. He grabbed her arms, twisted them down to the side of her body. Immediately she managed to get one free. Phil was surprised by her speed and strength.

She punched him in the side of his head. He saw stars, felt pain slice through his jaw and cheek. She hit him again. Same place, more force. He loosened his grip on her.

She slithered from his grasp, her naked body moving as if it were oiled.

Phil made another grab for her, made to twist her arm behind her back. She dodged out of the way, a smile on her face, her eyes lit by an intense, almost erotic light.

'Want to play?' she said. 'I'm warning you, I'll win.'

Phil looked around the room, all thoughts of making a clean arrest gone, now desperately trying to find a weapon to subdue her with. His eyes settled on the bedside lamp. It wasn't very tall, with a thin neck and small shade, but it had a sturdy, heavy brass base. Phil grabbed it, ripping the plug from the wall as he did so, and swung it at her head.

She ducked down, her body jack-knifing, almost bending in two. The lamp arced past her, connected only with air.

Phil responded quickly, swung the lamp low. It hit this time, catching her shoulder. The woman's hand went to it. She looked up, fire in her eyes, lips curled back, hissing at him.

He swung the lamp again but she was ready. She managed to twist her body out of the way, roll over on the floor and come up by his other side.

Before Phil could react, she pulled back her hand, flattening it out, bending her fingers down to make a hard ridge of knuckle and punched him hard in his kidney.

Phil screamed, his body giving way on one side, crumpling down to the floor.

She bent over him, did the same to the other side. Agony punched its way through Phil's body, like his torso had been wrapped in razorwire and she was pulling it tight.

She stood over him, looking down. Then took her fingers and moved around for a spot on his neck. Squeezed. Hard. It felt like Phil's bones had been instantly removed and he lay there, a useless sack of skin and blood, still gasping in pain. He was paralysed.

'This is a taste,' said the woman, getting right down beside him, whispering in his ear in Marina's voice. Her fingers still digging in to him. 'Just a taste. Of things to come.'

Phil tried to speak, respond. Couldn't.

'You're mine, Phil. Mine. From now on, I own you.'

Phil just stared up at her. Questions hammered through his brain. Nothing came out of his stupefied mouth.

'I just wanted to see you. Again.' She smiled. 'And I'm not disappointed. But I'm not quite ready for you. Yet.' She bent down to him, tenderly kissed his forehead. Straightened up again. 'Don't worry, my darling. I'll be seeing you again. Soon.'

She took her hand from his shoulder, stood up. Crossed to the wardrobe and took out a full-length coat of Marina's, put it on. Then she swept across the room, coat pulled round her, fluttering her fingers at him in goodbye, blowing him a kiss. She left, closing the door behind her.

He heard her walking down the stairs, then the front door opening and closing. Sighed.

He didn't know how long he lay there, his heart hammering. Gradually, feeling began to return to his body, the pain of pins and needles taking over from the earlier pain, and he managed to sit up. As he did so, he heard the front door opening once more.

Panic swept through him. The woman was back.

He tried to pull himself to his feet, grabbed the door handle for support.

He heard footsteps on the stairs, managed to open the door. He was ready for her. Or as ready as he could be.

He saw a figure walking towards him.

Marina.

He sighed.

'Hey,' she said.

'Hey yourself,' he just about managed to reply.

She smiled. 'I'm home.'

He collapsed onto the floor.

PART FIVE:

EPITAPH

92

The Colchester crematorium was a mid-century redbrick building edging a Victorian cemetery. The mourners had filed in, taken their seats. Gary Franks and his team, Mickey's most recent work colleagues, were occupying a space in the centre. Phil and Marina sat away from them near the back. Franks saw them, beckoned for them to join the team. Phil shook his head. It didn't feel right somehow.

Anni was at the front with her sister next to her, among Mickey's family. She stared into the middle distance, eyes studiously avoiding the coffin that lay before them all.

The room was bright and airy, verging on sterile. Music was playing as everyone entered, some old Queen tracks. Phil almost smiled. He hated Queen. And Mickey had hated his taste in music. It was one of the biggest causes of arguments when they drove together. Then what felt like a shadow passed over Phil as he realised he would never have those arguments again and he felt a gaping hollowness inside him. Mickey had been a good friend.

The service started. To Phil and Marina's surprise it was a humanist service. They had both felt sure that Mickey would have had some kind of religion lurking in his background, something he would have fallen back on out of childhood sentimentality or superstition, but apparently not. It made Phil think that there was even more to his old DS than he knew.

The woman hosting the service began to speak. She talked of Mickey's childhood, some of the scrapes he got into, his schooling, his friendships. She talked of his work in the police force and how proud he was of that. She mentioned Phil by name as the person in a professional capacity who had shown him what he was capable of. Then she went on to talk about Anni and how happy she had made him. The lectern was then given over to friends and relatives of Mickey's who came and talked about what he had meant to them. The first one, his cousin, couldn't finish what he was saying. Shaking so much he broke down in tears and had to be led away. The second speaker, a friend from his schooldays, fared better. He told some jokes about what he and Mickey had got up to, eliciting laughter from the audience. Then paused, as if realising that he would never be able to share them again. The rest of the room sensed what he was thinking. They were feeling the same thing.

Phil felt his hand being squeezed. He turned. Marina was smiling at him. He returned her smile. Then he realised why she was holding him. He was crying.

It had been over a week since Phil had narrowly escaped from the burning flat. Not to mention the woman in his house. And he still didn't feel he had fully recovered from either experience.

Stuart Hinchcliffe's place had been examined by the SOCOs with their usual attention to detail. Apart from the body of Glen Looker in the workshop it had yielded up an arsenal of weapons, enough, said Phil, 'to equip a small army of Omaha tax dodgers.' Tasers, crossbows, rifles, automatics. Also stun grenades and gas. 'Explains how he managed to capture Darren Richards, then,' Imani had said.

'I think it's clear,' said Phil, back at the office, 'that Hinch-cliffe murdered his sister.'

'Where's the body?' asked Cotter.

Phil shrugged. 'No idea. And we can't ask him now.'

Nadish had put in a bid for the jukebox if nobody came forward from the family.

'What about his father?' Phil had asked Cotter.

'Well, there's a story. Committed suicide. Was under investigation for abusing neighbourhood children. Lost his job as a result of it.'

'You think he abused his son?'

'The way he turned out?' said Cotter. 'I'd put money on it.'

The media had gone into overdrive. Hinchcliffe's story was manna from heaven for the tabloids. Books were rushed into production and there was even talk of a film being made.

'Who d'you want to play you in the film?' Marina asked, not entirely seriously.

'Not sure,' said Phil. 'Well, George Clooney, obviously. But knowing my luck I'll probably get one of the Chuckle Brothers.'

Marina laughed. 'As long as it's the good-looking one.'

Phil just stared at her.

Sperring was on the mend. He was out of intensive care and into an ordinary ward. Being amongst other people was starting to get to him.

'I keep telling them I'm well enough to go home,' he said when Phil and Cotter went to visit him. 'But they don't bloody listen.'

'Then you should listen to them,' said Cotter.

'But don't you want me back? How's the place surviving without me?'

'Surprisingly well,' said Phil, smiling.

Sperring bit back his retort since Cotter was there but Phil could guess what it was.

They talked some more, brought him up to speed with what

413

had happened. He had already gleaned most of it from other colleagues and the media.

'What did I tell you?' Sperring said. 'Have I got good copper's instincts or what?'

'Yeah, all right,' said Phil. 'You were lucky. Don't let it go to your head.'

'Go to my head? I'm going to make sure you listen to everything I say from now on.'

'We'll see.'

They left him while he was shouting at their backs, 'Where's my bloody Bell's, then?'

Outside the hospital, Cotter turned to Phil. 'Well done, Phil. Seriously. You and your team did a great job. You came back from the fiasco at the Radisson and really came through.'

Phil shrugged, looked around. The wind was getting up so he pulled his collar in close. 'Thanks, ma'am, but it was luck. That's all. We got lucky.'

'You ever watch football?' she said.

Phil frowned. 'You can watch some God-awful game that seems to be trudging along to a soulless goalless draw, and then suddenly one of the players scores. Usually by accident. And your team wins.'

'Yeah,' said Phil.

'Lucky or not, it's a goal. It's a win.'

'Thanks, ma'am.'

She walked off. He watched her go.

I got lucky, thought Phil. I dodged a bullet. But next time it might be different.

Next time.

It felt like Letisha hadn't stopped crying for days. She had lost everything. Everything. Not just her possessions, which weren't much to start with, but most of all Moses. She couldn't believe it, would still wake up crying about it. She would dream that he was with her, that they were starting the new life together he had promised. They'd be driving away in his car, having adventures, laughing and happy. Then she would wake up. See the temporary room in the bed and breakfast the council had put her into. And start crying again.

She tried to make do, to get on with life, but it was so hard. Just getting up in the morning was hard. And she hated all the other people in the bed and breakfast. Well, not hated. Just feared. She would lie in bed at night in her run-down room, smelling the mildew, seeing the breeze from the broken window lift the curling, damp paper in the corner of the room, and hear noises from the rest of the house. Crying. Laughing. Sobbing. Screaming in foreign languages. Then more sobbing. This was her life. What it had come to. She couldn't see a way forward. Couldn't see a point.

Tiny, when he had recovered and been questioned by police, told them he had gone to Letisha's flat to talk about his brother's death. He blamed Moses for it. The police had asked Letisha to corroborate his story. She had no choice. It was either that or face jail for manslaughter. So she agreed. Told them Moses had done it. She felt like she was pissing on his grave and hated herself even more for doing it. She tried to put it behind her, get rid of the pain inside her. Eventually it just dulled down to an ache. Then a hollow, empty feeling. Numbness.

Then she received a phone call. A publisher wanted her to tell her story. Gangsta girl. Serialised in the newspapers, on the chat-show circuit. Famous. At first she said no, retreated into her shell. But then, after another couple of nights in the bed and breakfast, she thought about it. And said yes.

Now she had a publicist working for her. A ghost writer listening to her, writing her life story. Newspapers lined up ready to give her money. This was it, she thought. Her big chance. Her only chance.

She would become a celebrity. Turn this into a career. *Big Brother*, whatever. They might even want her to get her kit off in the lads' mags. Fine. As long as it paid.

She could still feel the same hollowness inside her but now it was starting to crust over, a hardness form around it. And deep down, some part of her hated that. But she had no choice. It was this or nothing.

And she had had too much of nothing.

The coffin moved along on its conveyer belt, the curtains closed behind it. Mickey Phillips went to his second cremation.

The mourners filed out of the funeral service, into the cold, hard daylight.

The wake was at a nearby pub. Phil and Marina had intended to attend but after he found himself crying, Phil wasn't feeling up to it. The service had upset him more than he had thought it would.

Anni came over to them, hugged them both.

'You coming to the pub?'

'I think we'll head off,' said Marina. 'Phil's . . . ' She didn't finish. Didn't need to finish.

Anni nodded, understood.

'What about you?' asked Marina. 'How are you coping? Sorry. I bet everyone's asked you that.'

'They've got a right to,' she said. 'I'm . . . ' She sighed. 'I don't know. I've got people around me. You. My family. It's going to be difficult going back to work, though. Expecting those doors to open and see him walking through every day. That's going to be hard.' She nodded. Thinking about it. 'Very hard.'

'You could put in for a transfer,' said Phil. 'I could always make space on my team for you.'

She managed a smile. 'Thanks, but ...' She shrugged. 'I don't know if that might just be the same thing. You both there.' She shook her head. 'I don't know. I'll see.'

'The offer's there,' said Phil. 'Whenever.'

'Thank you.'

There were tears in the corners of Anni's eyes.

'Right,' she said, trying to sound brave. 'I'd better go to the pub.'

She left them.

Phil and Marina said their goodbyes, walked away from everyone else through the garden of remembrance.

'Garden of remembrance,' said Marina. 'Colchester's got an Avenue of Remembrance as well.'

'That it has,' said Phil.

'That's what this town's all about. Not forgetting. For us anyway.' She took his arm in hers.

There was still something else, something they barely addressed but nevertheless hung over them, a sword of Damocles.

'That woman,' said Marina. 'Fiona Welch. Whoever she was. Have you ...?'

'Have I heard anything from her?' said Phil, finishing her sentence. 'No. I haven't. I would tell you if I did.'

They fell into silence once more. Phil's attack had become the elephant in the room for both of them. Any room. They no longer felt safe in their own home and were thinking of moving. There had been a full search for her that night but it was as if she had just vanished without a trace. No one knew who she was, where she came from. They knew she wasn't Fiona Welch and she certainly wasn't Marina. Phil had been questioned repeatedly about old enemies he had put away, anyone bearing a grudge against him, someone out to settle scores. Every investigation drew a blank. She seemed to not exist.

Cotter had sent plain-clothes officers to guard the house and to escort, from a distance, Josephina when she went to nursery. But both Phil and Marina knew that wouldn't last for ever. Funds were tight and if she hadn't appeared by a certain point, no threat would be adjudged and the officers reassigned.

'And what did she say to you again?'

Phil sighed, about to tell her.

'Sorry, I know. I know. You've told me enough times. I've memorised it. Not yet. But soon.' Marina sighed. 'Should we move house?'

They had had this conversation many times. Phil knew that Marina was talking because she was scared and he didn't blame her. He was too. 'Would it make any difference? Is that the answer?'

'What about security?'

'Private security? Costs a lot.'

'Those officers won't be able to sit outside ours for ever.'

'I know,' said Phil. The conversation was a circuitous one. This was just the latest iteration. 'I'm a police officer. I'll call in favours. Make sure you and Josephina are protected.'

'What about you?'

'I should be able to take care of myself. I'm ready for her now.'

'So we just have to, what? Be vigilant?'

'Yeah. Be vigilant.'

Phil sensed it was still on Marina's mind. He knew it was never far from Marina's mind. Ever. He pressed himself close to her, tried to make light of it. 'Come on. She's not the first nutter who's come after me.'

Marina responded, sketched a smile. 'No. That description fits most of your ex-girlfriends. Before me, of course.'

Phil smiled. 'Of course.'

They walked on in silence.

'It'll be one of those days when we're not prepared for it,' said Marina, 'when we can't imagine everything that could go wrong. That's when she'll be back.'

'Then let's make sure we imagine everything that could go wrong every day. Let's be prepared,' said Phil. 'And face it together.'

'Yes,' said Marina, pressing herself close to him. 'Let's.'

THE SURROGATE

Tania Carver

A sickening killer is on the loose – a killer like no other.
This murderer targets heavily pregnant women, drugging them
and brutally removing their unborn babies.

When DI Phil Brennan is called to the latest murder scene,
he knows that he has entered the world of the most depraved killer
he has ever encountered. After a loveless, abused childhood,
Phil knows evil well, but nothing in his life
has prepared him for this.

And when criminal profiler Marina Esposito is brought in to
help solve the case, she delivers a bombshell: she believes there is a
woman involved in the killing – a woman desperate for children . . .

'With a plotline that snares from the off, and a comprehensive cast
of characters, Carver's debut novel sets the crime thriller bar high.
A hard act to follow' *Irish Examiner*

CHOKED

Tania Carver

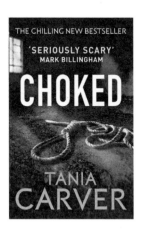

'I have something you've lost,' the voice said. 'Your daughter.'

The honeymoon is over for newlywed criminologist Marina Esposito. Her house is in flames. Her husband is in a coma. Her baby daughter is missing. And then her phone rings . . .

The voice on the other end wants to play a game. If Marina completes a series of bizarre tasks within three days, she wins her daughter's life. If she fails, her little girl dies. The clock starts now.

In a desperate race against time, Marina begins to suspect that the madman is someone she knows – someone with a past as troubled as her own. But the truth is far darker than she imagines . . .

'The best in the series so far. Gruesome and fast-paced, with Carver's trademark staccato sentences and plenty of suspense, this is definitely a white-knuckle read' *Guardian*

THE CREEPER

Tania Carver

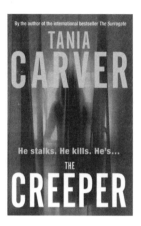

Suzanne Perry is having a vivid nightmare. Someone is in her
bedroom, touching her, and she can't move a muscle. She wakes,
relieved to put the nightmare behind her, but when she opens the
curtains, she sees a polaroid stuck to the window. A photo of her
sleeping self, taken during the night. And underneath, the words:
I'm watching over you. Her nightmare isn't over.
In fact, it's just beginning.

Detective Inspector Phil Brennan of the Major Incident Squad has
a killer to hunt. A killer who stalks young women, insinuates himself
into their lives, and ultimately tortures and murders them in the most
shocking way possible. But the more Phil investigates, the more he
delves into the twisted psychology of his quarry, Phil realises
that it isn't just a serial killer he's hunting but something – or
someone – infinitely more calculating and horrific.
And much closer to home than he realised . . .

'Tania Carver [is] a bright new talent when it comes
to edge-of-your-seat suspense' *Bella*

CRIME AND THRILLER FAN?

CHECK OUT THECRIMEVAULT.COM

The online home of
exceptional crime fiction

KEEP YOURSELF
IN SUSPENSE

Sign up to our newsletter for regular recommendations,
competitions and exclusives at www.thecrimevault.com/connect

Follow us the latest news @TheCrimeVault